CW00548552

Lady Ti
and the
Demon Warrior of Hanoi

Mark W Sasse

Copyright © 2023 Mark W Sasse.
All Rights Reserved.
ISBN: 979-8-8689-3576-3

Contact the Author

www.mwsasse.com
Email: Mark@mwsasse.com
Facebook: www.facebook.com/markwsasse

Cover by Moonpixel Creative. Thanks, Steve!

Map and Hanoi drawings by Julieann Babcock.

A Word from the Author

I moved to Vietnam in 1994 just a few months after the U.S. lifted its trade embargo, which had been in place since the end of the Vietnam War in the '70s. I lived in Haiphong for three years, Hanoi for a year and a half, and Thai Nguyen for five years. I left Vietnam in December 2003. Though the first couple years were challenging for a young man from the Pennsylvania countryside, I slowly fell in love with Vietnam; the people, the food, the culture, and the history.

In the story you're about to read, I talk about the protagonist's teacher, who was a contemporary of Vietnamese revolutionary leader Ho Chi Minh in 1945. I called the man Mr. Khoi. The fact is, Mr. Khoi was my Vietnamese teacher in 1998 as I was learning the Vietnamese language and culture. However, Khoi's father, was in fact, Ho Chi Minh's contemporary, and his father did indeed sign the Vietnamese Declaration of Independence in the summer of 1945. In a way, learning under Thay Khoi seemed the same as if I was learning American history from Thomas Jefferson's son. It was an experience I'll never forget.

I learned a lot from Thay (teacher) Khoi, and I even, with his help, translated the introduction to Keith Taylor's lauded book about the origins of Vietnam entitled *The Birth of Vietnam.* That article was subsequently published in the Vietnamese journal *Ngay Xua* shortly thereafter. I used Mr. Khoi's name in the book as a way to honor him as a teacher and thank him for everything I learned. He's the one who taught me about the significance of the bronze drum and the long-tailed bird and the Hung Kings and the turtle of the lake and, of course, Ba Trieu—Lady Trieu. You'll be meeting all of these and many more in the pages that follow. Some things, however, are my own invention. The marble tablets, for instance.

This fictitious story weaves a lot of Vietnamese history and culture into the plot. It is my hope that this novel will show my admiration for these resilient people. They have lived for millenniums scratching out their desire to be free and independent from outside forces, which found them too wonderful to resist.

I want to thank Thay Khoi, Co Hien, Ong Tao, my former Vietnamese students, and the people of Vietnam, who treated me, an American outsider, like one of their own.

Tôi rất nhớ các bạn! Until we meet again, may this novel show you my true feelings.

Mark

A Note about Names

Vietnamese has been written in Romanized script for centuries. But that fact still doesn't make the pronunciation obvious to the average English speaker. As you come across names in this story, you may, of course, use whatever pronunciation naturally comes to you. If this is the case, you can ignore what's below.

However, if you would like an approximation in English for some of the names in the book, this short and simple guide will help. I apologize for the linguists reading this. I will forgo phonetics for a more blunt approach. But it works.

Also, this is based on the northern Vietnamese dialect, which I studied full-time at a foreign language center under the authority of the Hanoi Foreign Language University. I studied there from January 1998 to June of 1999.

Character Names:
Lady Trieu - "Chee-ooo"
Mr. Tho - "Mr. Taw"
Minh - "Ming"
Lien - "Lee-en"
Lieu - "Lee-oooh"
Sun Quan - "Sun Kwan"
Nhan - "N-yun"
Cuong - "Koo-ong"
Tuan - "Twan"
Hung - "Hoom"

Places Names:
Hung Temple - "Hoom"
Co Loa Citadel - "Koe-Lwa"
Ba Dinh Square - "Baa-Ding"
Hoa Lu - "Hwa-Lou"
Van Mieu - "Vun Mee-oooh"
Ngoc Son - don't bother

The Battleground

The Real Places

Each of the following play important roles in the story. Here are some brief descriptions of these real places.

Ho Chi Minh Mausoleum

Granite edifice constructed in Hanoi's Ba Dinh Square to commemorate the revolutionary leader. To this day, his body is preserved in a glass casket, which is displayed in the dark interior of the mausoleum.

Ngoc Son Temple

The revered temple situated on a small islet inside Hoan Kiem Lake. It can only be visited by walking across the iconic red wooden bridge, which connects it to the eastern shore. Or, you could take a boat.

Hung Temple

This temple complex, located outside the city of Viet Tri northwest of Hanoi, commemorates the origins of the Vietnamese people. The Hung kings (Hung=hero) were the first Vietnamese kings, originating in the bronze era. The pre-Chinese link to this time period is proven by the bronze drums, whose discovery shows a vibrant Vietnamese nation prior to any Chinese invasion. The bronze drums can be seen at the temple's museum. On the drum, you'll notice the *chim lac,* the mysterious bird lost to history. History comes alive in this book.

Co Loa Citadel

This citadel north of Hanoi dates back to the 3rd century B.C. It is an important archeological site commemorating one of the earliest Vietnamese kingdoms.

Hoa Lu

Located amidst the beautiful granite cliffs and outcroppings of Ninh Binh Province south of Hanoi, this former capital of Vietnam was moved to present day Hanoi in the 10th century A.D.

Turtle Tower

This tower on a small islet inside Hoan Kiem Lake commemorates the legend of the turtle of the lake, which retrieved the magic sword from warrior Le Loi. Consequently, the warrior named the lake Hoan Kiem Lake – the lake of the returned sword.

Van Mieu – Temple of Literature

This thousand-year-old site was Vietnam's first university. Pupils would come to master Confucian studies, then return to their villages as venerated scholars. Its importance for Vietnam, or for this story, can't be overstated.

Saint Joseph's Cathedral

In Vietnamese, it's simply called 'the big church.' It's the largest Roman Catholic church in Hanoi, built by the French in the 19th century. It's a short walk from Hoan Kiem Lake. The demon warrior will use this church more than once in the story.

Long Bien Bridge

The first steel bridge over the Red River – this cantilever bridge was built by the French in 1899. It is still used today for pedestrians, bicycles, and motorbikes. In the story, a certain boy learns a lesson here.

for Thầy Khôi, and Cô Hiên, my teachers

Table of Contents

Preface

Ba Trieu or Lady Trieu was a 3rd century Vietnamese heroine. She led a revolt against the Chinese and became a folk heroine for the Vietnamese people.

Now in the 21st century, as modern Vietnam perilously slips away by the iron grip of the Chinese invaders, she is needed once more. But who can awaken her?

Only those who can bring history alive.

Chapter 1

History. Again

Saturday morning—unlike any other in recent history. A stillness hung in the air alongside the wisps of smoke from the recently ceased fighting. Mr. Tho fidgeted on a plastic stool at the edge of the traffic-less street. A fly was being particularly bothersome.

"Mr. Tho? You're outside?"

"What are they going to do to me? I'm already ninety-five. Or is it ninety-four?"

"Mr. Tho?"

"I knew the day would come. History returns. This fly keeps returning too."

"Mr. Tho?"

"History repeats itself so often that we never predict it. Even though it's written on our calendar."

He clapped his hands together attempting to trap the insect.

"Mr. Tho?"

"We shall have to find the strength within us once more to repel the Hans." He swatted again and watched the pest escape past him. "They never learn, nor do we."

"Mr. Tho? The electricity is coming back on. Now. There's supposed to be an announcement. That's what everyone's saying." The young teen seemed eager, if not agitated, but old Mr. Tho barely paid attention. "Mr. Tho, come. My mother wants you to see the announcement."

Tho didn't acknowledge the invitation. He just stood up with great difficulty. His knees ached from another poor night's sleep. "Though I wish I had passed on from this life before I saw another occupation. This body will do no one any good in the struggle. Good thing my mind is razor sharp." He let out a belly laugh, which converted to a cough.

"What, Mr. Tho?"

"Did you have to live on the second floor? The puffiness on the backs of my knees …"

The boy helped the old man through a metal gate and up two flights of stairs into a modest two room apartment. The mint green walls were pocked by the constant attack of oppressive humidity. A middle-aged woman lit the tips of red joss sticks of incense on a shelf clasped to the wall, holding several photographs of loved ones who had passed.

"Mr. Tho," the woman greeted him. "Come. Sit. The power is supposed to come back on at 8 o'clock. Then we can have tea and watch the announcement together."

"Oh, we are being civilized again? Since when does anyone in this country follow the clock?"

As the clock struck eight, the surge of electricity could be heard all around them. The fan started and the dimly hung bulbs glared every wattage they could afford. They each looked around the room as if they were seeing something new, a magical power they hadn't ever experienced.

"This is a sure way to know our own compatriots didn't flip the switch," quipped Tho. "We'd still be in the dark if it was our Vietnamese engineers at the helm. There never was a hash mark on a clock they didn't enjoy ignoring."

"Behave yourself," said Lien, the mother of the teen. She switched on the television and turned to channel four. A live feed of Ba Dinh Square caught everyone's attention.

"My glasses," said Tho. "I didn't bring them."

"Here, use mine," said Lien.

"I can't see far. I can't see near. I can't see at all without them."

"Then why don't you keep them with you at all times?"

"What is it about Hanoi on a day like this that I would like to see? Actually, I would like to see the Auntie Linh selling *pho* again. I would like to taste it too. And I don't need my glasses to eat *pho.*"

Lien smiled. "Well I see you're as ornery as ever. I hope you never lose that."

"When I do, I pray my nieces and nephews will be placing incense next to my photo on the family altar."

"Tho, you don't have nieces and nephews. You were an only child."

"At my age, everyone is my niece or nephew."

"Look!" Minh, the young teen boy, pointed as the camera panned to the backdrop of the Ho Chi Minh Mausoleum, the granite structure towering over the square, which honored the legacy of the patron saint of modern-day Vietnam. In front of it stood the most disconcerting, incongruent image only meant to instill fear in the masses—if the last thirty days of raids hadn't done that enough—a contingent of Chinese soldiers.

A wooden rostrum had been constructed in the foreground of the soldiers. Several Chinese officials, mostly in uniform, stood in a row behind a narrow lectern with one microphone.

"Oh, these Chinese have a flare for the dramatics, don't they?"

"Why do you say that?" asked the teen.

"Mimicking the day Uncle Ho stood right there and declared independence in 1945. Mark my words, the Chinese will do the same. I guarantee you they use the word independence."

The mother gripped a towel in her hand and squeezed it. "Tho, what do you think will happen?"

"Look to the past."

"Mr. Tho," asked Minh, with a passionate plea in his eyes. "Do you think the rumors are true?"

"Which rumors? I can't keep them straight."

"The rumor of the demon warrior. That's what everyone calls him. The demon warrior who penetrates the most guarded fortress in the middle of the night. Nothing can stop him."

"Rumors are always true, but always half false at the same time."

"They call him the black demon," said the mother.

"Nonsense," said the old man.

"Tho, you of all people should believe in magic."

"Only when I need to make a living. But what's a man of my age need? A bowl of *pho* and a place to squat and do my business. Preferably not at the same time. Though that's not always controllable."

Lien slapped him in a playful way. "Look."

A figure stepped to the microphone. He wore a Chinese Communist insignia on his hat and a Chinese-Vietnamese unification pin on his lapel. He spoke flawless Vietnamese, not missing a tone or inflection. The words eased off his lips like the methodical and smooth-flowing Red River during the dry season.

"Residents of Hanoi. The electricity was returned at exactly the moment we promised. Because we keep our promises, unlike the filthy liars who have poisoned your government for years. We are here to confirm that Hanoi has been liberated by the traitors …"

"Oh yes, a great start. Wait for it," interrupted Tho.

"… to ensure the people's independence …"

Tho burst out laughing.

"… and to re-establish the ancient ties which have always linked our two great peoples."

Tho hit his knee with another howl. "Oh, I was not aware you invited me to a comedy show."

"Shhhh—"

"As of this moment, the lock-down within the city limits of Hanoi has been lifted. You may, and are encouraged to go about your normal lives."

"Normal lives?" Lien burst out, mimicking Tho's best mocking tone.

"Oh, you're seeing the humor, too?"

The broadcast continued: "The markets will be filled with meat and vegetables; indeed, they currently are as we speak. The traitors have made the countryside too unstable at the moment, so you will need a special pass in order to leave the city. This is for your own protection. We are on the cusp of great peace and stability, which will end the bitter regional feuds which have plagued our existence."

"What a fictional tale!" screamed Tho in delight.

"Shhhh—"

"Community, solidarity, peace, prosperity. This is what we strive for …"

"Says the man who overthrew our government and slaughtered an untold number of our people," complained Tho.

"Shhhh—"

"Oh, you are so enamored with them … yes, yes, I shall be quiet."

"Look at this," said Minh. As the Chinese official continued his monologue, a startling figure with broad shoulders a foot higher than the speaker moved incrementally into view. "Who is that?"

"He's like a monster."

"Who?" said Tho. "I can't see."

He had a neatly manicured black beard and mustache with slicked-backed hair in a ponytail.

"He must be seven feet tall."

"Could that be the demon everyone is talking about?"

The camera zoomed in, almost as if they intended to show a closeup of the giant. He was in uniform, but different from the soldiers to the rear or the officials to his left and right. His arms hung off his shoulders like a bodybuilder, and he wore large half-oval sunglasses across his eyes, almost as if it was a mask fused to his face.

"Let me see him?" asked Tho and moved closer. "Oh, I still can't see anything."

"His head is twice as big as the man in front of him."

"Give me your reading glasses." Tho inched his plastic chair closer to the television with help from Minh.

The man continued speaking. "Disruptions, unwieldy speech, whispers and rumors will not be tolerated. We are at a new beginning, one which will …"

Tho moved as close to the television as the chair would allow him. He put on Lien's reading glasses and leaned in to inspect the screen.

"Look," he said. "That insignia on his left chest. That's from the Wu Dynasty."

As he was about to say something additional, a shot rang out on the television. The speaker turned in terror and soldiers roared into action but unsure of what to do. The giant man had been struck dead-center chest with a high-capacity rifle. It ripped a hole right through him, a visible hole which didn't disappear. In fact, the wound didn't bleed. The camera zoomed in on the chaos and the giant man removed the glasses from his eyes and staggered backwards for a moment, but then he let out a roar, almost beast-like, and the hole in his chest fused together as if it never happened. He gazed directly at the camera, and that's when Mr. Tho saw all he needed to see. The giant man's eyes were red, not bloodshot, but solid red as if bing cherries had been deposited in his eye sockets. They glowed as he seethed and hissed once more before putting the glasses back over his eyes.

The Chinese man, who had given the speech, stepped back in front of the microphone. "Do not be foolish in your attempts to overthrow us. We will cut off your heads, all of them, if necessary. That is all."

The feed fell to static, and Tho sat back in his chair.

"Did you see that?" asked Lien. "He was shot and …"

"A Vietnamese sniper must have tried to take him out, but he didn't bleed."

The mother and son bantered back and forth excitedly as the old man pondered the scene.

"Wu Dynasty. I've seen that before. I know that. I know him. I …"

The mother and son stopped when they noticed the look on Tho's face. A terrified look.

"What is it?"

"It can't be."

"What did you see, Mr. Tho?"

"That man, the beast, that giant …"

"What, Mr. Tho? Who is it?"

"That was Sun Quan."

"Who?" asked the teen.

"Mr. Tho," said Lien. "Sun Quan? The Chinese emperor who lived …"

She trailed off as Tho finished her sentence. "… eighteen hundred years ago."

Chapter 2

The Warrior's Face

Tho, Lien, and Minh spent the next two hours in a heated conversation as they discussed with wild abandon every dizzying aspect of the broadcast. Every tangent of every angle always ended with Tho insisting: "I must examine the warrior up close." Lien asked the "whys" and Minh asked the "hows." Those elusive questions didn't worry Tho. There was little the near-centenarian hadn't seen in his lifetime, and as mid-morning passed, he felt bold enough to instruct his neighbors to allow the deep magic of the universe to do its bidding because "… it has already happened. Did you see him?"

The month-long lock-down had taken its toll on the battered residents of Hanoi. They scrapped for food and feared through the daily rumors of brutal oppression for those who defied the orders. So when they stepped into the streets the morning of the broadcast, they did so with caution. All motor vehicles, including motorbikes, had been banned, so people walked and rode bicycles as if the air had been transported forty years into the past. Neighbors passed each other, nodded, but said little. Men were scarce, unless they had a long white beard like Mr. Tho. Nobody needed to explain the scarcity.

"Mr. Tho, are we going to keep fighting the Chinese?"

"Shhhh—" Lien cut off her son quickly. "We don't talk about such things. Not out in the open like this."

"That's true," said Tho. "We know. No need for words. All we need is our history. And patience."

They turned a corner on the near empty street of shuttered shops only to discover a massive line of people, mostly women, standing in a three-person wide scrum leading far into the distance.

"What are they all doing here?" asked Minh.

"Getting in line for the market," said a woman at the back of the queue.

"But the market's three blocks away."

"Yes, and by the time we get there, there won't be anything left."

Tho chuckled. "Chinese efficiency is starting to remind me of *thoi bao cap*."

Lien shuttered at the thought, but Minh with a pensive glare followed-up. "What is that, Mr. Tho?"

"Your mother would have been a child then. She knows. When the government provided all of our needs, but never seemed to know what our needs were. I haven't seen lines like this since 1983. I used to bring a brick and write my name on it and put it in line and come back two hours later."

"Mr. Tho, wouldn't you be afraid that you'd lose your place in line?"

"Oh, Minh. The brick moved faster than the people." He laughed and settled into the back of the line.

"Are we really gonna wait?" asked Minh.

"Well, what else are we going to do?" asked Lien.

The woman at the end of the line glanced at Minh and sized him up. "How old is the boy?"

"He's thirteen."

"What are you going to do when the Chinese conscript him?"

"What do you mean?" Lien looked at her in a queer way.

"That's what I've heard. Young boys who are big enough will be taken in by the Chinese for education and training. They will be the new Vietnamese leaders of the future, of course."

"I'll never go with the Chinese," Minh flared.

"Minh, stop." Lien turned to the woman. "Where did you hear such a thing?"

"Put your ear to the ground and you'll hear many things."

Tho laughed. "You'll also be prone to ear infections."

The woman rolled her eyes. A rumble of motors roared from behind. Several open-topped armored vehicles approached filled with Chinese soldiers holding rifles. It wasn't uncommon to have patrols pulse through the city, flexing their muscle and cowering the populace into the dark alleyways. As the first patrol was about one hundred feet from the back of the market line, a rocket shot out of a side street and split the armored car in two in a fiery crash. Voices screamed from all angles and the weary-headed shoppers cowered their backs against the nearest cement wall. The soldiers in the second vehicle jumped off and pursued two men in black shirts on foot. Shots rang out in the chaos. As the two men were overcome by the soldiers, five more in black emerged from different directions. They overpowered the patrol with a steady crossfire of bullets. The resistance had overwhelmed two contingents of Chinese soldiers.

Lien pushed Minh behind her and the old man crept in front of them both, willing to give whatever was left of his life in case a stray bullet was destined to cross the boy and his mother. Tho was ready to tell them all to run when a sound became a presence, like a deep pulsing spirit had descended upon them. Everyone felt it. Everyone heard it. The Vietnamese rebels in black stopped shooting and looked upward. A blackness sped across the sky. It wasn't in human form. More like a visible pulse of energy, gripping one black rebel fighter after the other with a deadly vice grip across their necks. They couldn't move, and the Chinese soldiers and the terrified market goers watched as they expired without warning like falling sacks of bricks onto the ground. The vehicle burnt in the background like an altar sacrifice. Even the Chinese displayed apprehension in their eyes. They didn't welcome the darkness but didn't fight against it and slowly slithered backward as a black mist coalesced into human shape and the giant warrior landed in front of them. He towered over the soldiers and pointed at the bodies of the rebels. The soldiers obeyed without delay and dragged each rebel corpse to the fire and threw them in.

Tho stood up.

"What are you doing?" whispered Lien.

"I need to see him up close. This is my chance."

"You can't go over there."

"I'm ninety-five years old. No one will tell me what I can and can't do. Only my body does that."

He walked toward the seven-foot-tall warrior still facing away from him. The warrior had two swords strapped across his back. He had a long ponytail bound tightly at the neck and a sheath on his right hip holding a dagger. His dark uniform had a metallic quality to it. Tho was determined to see the warrior's face up close. He didn't trust the grainy shot of the television broadcast. He had to know for sure. When he was no more than twenty feet from him, Tho tripped on purpose, making a noise which shattered the eerie quietness of the moment. He cried in false pain as the giant turned and walked towards him.

Tho focused on his eyes, but they were covered by the half-glass shield. The warrior towered over the old man, but Tho wasn't afraid. He marveled at the size before he spoke.

"I know who you are." The warrior said nothing. "Would you remove your glasses to allow an old man to see you face to face?"

The warrior smiled slightly, and he reached up and removed the glass shield from his burnt red eyes, which glowed like a raging pit of fire.

"Your eyes. Like a fading sunset."

"You're wrong, old man. They burn as the new dawn sun."

Tho laughed as he often did. "You aren't going to hurt me, are you?"

"Longevity is to be revered in all its forms."

Tho stood up and looked like a boy gawking at a towering beast in the zoo. "Then you are to be revered more than most, Sun Quan, because your longevity is truly without equal."

The warrior smirked. "It is good to see wisdom still emerging from the masses. It's futile to resist. I hope you will use your wisdom to pass along the message."

Tho cleared his throat. "But …" He started, then stopped.

"What is your message, old man?"

"Sun Quan, do you not think that your unexpected return might cause a certain counterbalance? Surely you know this." A pause passed between them. Lien and Minh, mostly breathless, watched the standoff in the middle of the street: the arched-back, aging man and the powerful warrior from the past. "There is only one way in which you could have returned, and if you have accomplished the impossible, is it not possible that someone else could do it as well?

Perhaps ..." Tho paused again. He was almost afraid to say it. "Could it be possible for her as well?"

The word 'her' caught Sun Quan's attention in a surprisingly pleasant way, as if he welcomed the threat. He took one more step closer to Tho and reached down to grab his hand. "You think your hands are talented enough?"

Tho knew what he meant.

"I don't know. If they were, would you feel threatened?"

"Did she send you?" Tho was taken aback by the question and didn't answer. "Did she send you?"

"You are expecting her?"

"Why else would I come?"

"And me?"

Sun Quan leaned down over him and whispered a thought Tho had been thinking himself. "Why else would you still be alive?"

Chapter 3

The Marble Tablets

The open market faded to an afterthought of their consciousnesses. The two peppered the old man with questions as they returned home to Hang Bac Street. Tho had been a silversmith, who retired thirty years ago. He still lived in his old workshop, across the street from Lien, who had spent countless hours in his shop when she was a little girl.

"You spoke to him?"

"Yes, yes."

"What did he say?" asked an excited Minh.

"No, what did you say to him?" clarified Lien.

"It's not important."

"Of course, it's important."

"I have to get home, that's all. None of us should be on the street, not with that beast on the loose. Who can be safe from that?"

"And yet, you were not afraid to talk with him." Lien grabbed Tho's shoulder, and he pivoted towards her. "Mr. Tho, what are you not telling us?"

"Everything you needn't worry about."

"What are you going to do?"

"I just need to get home."

He waited for them to ascend to their second-story apartment before he unlocked the door to his place, stepped down into the cramped quarters and looked for the long-forgotten items.

"Where did I put them?"

He searched behind a stack of books. Half of them fell onto the floor, but he didn't notice. He opened a wooden chest and leafed through folded cloth and trinkets, which had been stowed away for decades. But he couldn't find them. "Where, where, where?" A blue silk cloth with embroidered dragons caught his eye. "Ah-ha." It was wrapped around an object on the top shelf of a bamboo book stand. "Who put it up there?" He dragged a small red plastic stool to the edge of the shelf and stepped up, wobbling the entire time. "People would scold me." His first attempt fell a few inches short. He grunted and move closer to the edge of the stool. "Come, now." His foot slid off the side, and he hollered an unintelligible sound as his body careened downward and he landed back-first on the floor. The pain settled in as he found himself unable to move. He waited, but for what, he wasn't sure. Then the door flung open. Lien and Minh rushed in with all the questions and exclamations they could muster.

"Mr. Tho, what happened?"

"We knew something wasn't right with you. What are you doing?"

"Can an old man take a nap in peace?"

"Mr. Tho, here." Lien put her arm under his shoulder while Minh helped from the other side and brought the old, fragile soul into the closest chair.

"My back has seen better days. But that could also be said for all of my body parts."

"What were you doing? Were you standing on this stool?"

"I haven't heard that kind of scolding since my dear wife passed twenty years ago."

"Mr. Tho, you were never married."

"Well, that explains a lot."

Lien slapped him softly on the arm. "What were you doing?"

He glanced upward and pointed at the silk cloth.

"The dragon cloth. It's wrapped around some items. Can you reach it for me?"

"I can," volunteered Minh as he righted the stool and reached up with ease to bring the cloth and its contents down. "What is it?"

"Let me see, let me see."

Minh placed the silk wrap in Tho's lap, and the old man peeled back the layers of silk one at a time as if he too was expecting to find something unexpected.

"Mr. Tho, what is this all about?" asked Lien.

"I spoke to Sun Quan."

"It's him? For sure?"

"Yes."

"But how? How is that possible?"

"There's only one way," he said as he unwrapped four black marble tablets. Each one fit comfortably in the palm of his hand. They had been hewn smooth as silk, and he rubbed his fingers against them.

Lien moved in closer to inspect. "Mr. Tho, is this what you used to use when …" She didn't finish.

"They are one of a kind. Given to me many years ago. Originally from Marble Mountain in Danang. I used them for …" He paused. "Many things."

"Oh, Mr. Tho, you don't mean?"

"What? What?" pleaded Minh.

"I understand now what must be done to defeat the Hans. Someone has summoned forth the dead, and the only chance we have is to do the same. No amount of rebel spirit will be enough, not against this foe. We need a spirit of independence forged many centuries ago, which links our present with the past. That's the only way. We must summon her."

"Her?" asked Minh and Lien at the same time.

"He's waiting for her. He wants to finish it once and for all, and he's all too happy to use our modern-day misfortunes for his advantage."

"Mr. Tho, who are you talking about?"

He hesitated. It seemed absurd to say the name sitting on the tip of his tongue.

"Mr. Tho?"

"Ba Trieu."

"Ba Trieu? That's the name of a street on the other side of Hoan Kiem Lake," said Minh.

"And why do we put Lady Trieu on a street sign?" he asked the boy.

"I don't know."

"To remember how she raised an army and crushed the northern invaders. We need her once more."

Lien and Minh looked at each other in disbelief. Tho had the same look.

"Mr. Tho, do you think you should ..." Lien paused for a moment and looked around. She scooted closer to Mr. Tho's ear then whispered. "Do you think you should get word to the resistance? Shouldn't they know they're fighting against a spirit king of the past?"

"He's no king. Not anymore. He's a demon. An impostor. Always remember that."

"Well, shouldn't the resistance know what they're up against? Something not from this world?"

"No. We must tell nobody."

"Then what?"

"We ... I must summon her myself. You two have helped me a lot these many years, but I can't have you involved. It's too dangerous."

"What about you? You can't do this alone," pleaded Lien.

"Why do you think I've lived to be this old? I have one final task. I cannot fail."

"Mr. Tho, we can help you," said an eager Minh.

"Yes, you could have killed yourself stepping on that stool. Then what good would you have done?" scolded Lien.

A rumbling in the street wrested their attention away from their disagreement. Minh peeked through the window as a Chinese patrol with four soldiers stopped right in front of their house across the street. They yelled something, then snapped the lock off the metal gate and charged upstairs.

"Ma! Why are they going in our house?"

Lien looked over Minh's shoulders. "Mr. Tho, what's going on?"

"It's what I feared. Sun Quan already knows who's involved and has sent a squad to take you."

"How? Why?" Lien shook her hands, grabbed her son by the neck, and pulled him to herself. "What are we going to do? I thought you said Sun Quan wanted Lady Trieu to return? Why would he go after you and your neighbors? That doesn't make any sense."

"Possibly to test me."

"Test? What kind of test?"

"He doesn't yet believe in me."

"Ma, they're leaving the apartment, and they're coming this

way."

"Quickly, out into the back courtyard," instructed Tho.

"But there's no way to escape."

"Go."

"What about you?"

"This is my test."

"We're not leaving you," protested Lien.

Tho motioned them toward the back. "I know what I'm doing."

"Tho—"

"Go."

Lien sighed, grabbed Minh's hand and ran through the small kitchen and out the back door to an enclosed courtyard. They held each other and huddled in the corner behind a large flower pot, which would provide little cover if the soldiers emerged looking for them.

Tho sat in his chair facing the unlocked door. He held the four marble tablets in his palms and rubbed them back and forth, keeping enough pressure on them so none would slip out. He closed his eyes. He heard the Chinese soldiers approaching, yelling for him. Neighbors from all sides cowered in fear and curiosity as their eyes peered out at the humble former silver shop they all knew so well. Tho hummed a wordless chant, like the sound of a steady deep vibration, and he concentrated on the marble stones. He imagined their smooth surface sliding over top each other. Then he shifted the stones into a circular motion. The first soldier ripped open the door and stepped inside. Tho didn't look at him. He kept his eyes closed and thought only of the movement of the stones. Then a word came to him, and he said it out loud.

"Chain."

The soldier stepped fully inside the small house.

"Nguyen Van Tho, where are you? We know you're here?"

He was plainly in view, three feet in front of the soldiers.

"Mr. Tho. Show yourself."

He couldn't have shown himself in a more ostentatious way if he had stood up and smacked the soldier in the face. But they didn't see the man massaging the stones in front of them.

"Check the courtyard."

Two soldiers ran through the house and scoured the enclosed courtyard. The soldier in front of Tho stood mere inches from the smooth stones rotating in Tho's hands. His breath glided over the objects and dissipated into the blank air. Tho never opened his eyes, but he could hear the breathing over top of him, and the backs of his eyelids outlined the attacker against the light of the noonday sun coming through the window. The soldiers who had checked the courtyard returned after a few moments to report all was clear.

"They couldn't have gone far. They were together at the market this morning. Let's check the neighborhood. Someone has to know where they are."

"Why are we searching for them?"

The patrol commander paused and let out a sigh before filling in the blank. "The beast wants them."

The beast, thought Tho. Even they don't know who he is.

The other soldier nodded, needing no other explanation.

"Keep a patrol on the street. They have to come back sometime."

The door slammed behind them, and the rumble of the patrol vehicle tore off down the street. Tho opened his eyes and the four marble stones fell from his hands and into his lap. He admired them and smiled in a giddy, childish way.

Lien and Minh peeked through the back door and rushed toward Tho when they saw him sitting alone.

"Tho. Are you alright?"

"Never better. Indeed, I haven't been this right in many decades."

"What happened? What did they say to you?"

"To me? Nothing. They didn't see me."

"Didn't see you?"

"Their eyes decided not to see what was glaringly evident."

Minh couldn't contain his excitement. "They didn't see us either. The soldier walked right up to the potted plant, but it was like we were invisible."

"Mr. Tho, what does it mean?"

"It means I passed the test."

"Now what do we do?"

Tho thought for a moment and the word came to him. "Chain.

We need a new link in the chain."

"What chain?"

"The chain that binds Vietnamese history together. From Lac Long Quan, to the Trung Sisters, to Lady Trieu, to Quang Trung and right up to our beloved Uncle Ho. Our people are bonded to this land. Remember what Uncle Ho said?"

Every good Vietnamese student knew the answer to that question. "There's nothing more precious than independence and freedom."

"That's right. And for as long as we have breath, we have to strive as our forebears did to preserve what's most precious to us."

"So what do we do now?" asked Minh.

"We ..." Tho emphasized the word. There was now a we, an unlikely threesome chosen for some unknown reason to search for an impossible path to freedom once again.

"Minh, do you know where Ho Chi Minh delivered Vietnam's Declaration of Independence?"

"Ba Dinh Square. Where they built his mausoleum."

"That's right."

"We can't go there. That place is a fortress of Chinese soldiers," said Lien.

"No, we can't," confirmed Tho. "But where did Uncle Ho write the declaration?"

"I don't know."

"I do," said Lien. "Hang Ngang Street."

"Yes, 48 Hang Ngang Street. It's where we will look for the link in the chain."

"What are we looking for?"

"I don't know."

"How will we get in there? There will be a patrol there. I'm sure of it," said Lien.

"Then we will need help. Lien, you said you have a contact with the resistance?"

"Yes, my nephew," said Lien. "I know how to get word to him. He's still within the city limits."

"Set up a meeting with him at midnight tonight at the closest safe house to Hang Ngang Street."

"I'll try," said Lien. "What do we do in the meantime?"

"Feed the boy some sticky rice. And pack some extra in a plastic bag. We might need it."

Chapter 4

The Firecrackers

Mr. Tho donned a conical hat, Lien a scarf, and Minh a cap as they blended into the late afternoon foot traffic and slipped past the patrol through the still-eerie streets of Hanoi. Lien had managed a meeting with her cousin off the back side of the Bach Ma Temple, a few blocks from Tho's house and just around the corner from Hang Ngang Street and the historical site Tho insisted on accessing. The meeting wasn't until midnight, but Tho didn't want to chance staying in his house or having to navigate the streets after dark. The lock-down had technically been lifted, but the same oppression hung in the air, especially with a darkness-loving demon warrior patrolling the city. Tho arranged for Lien and Minh to stay in the back room of a family friend's house near the temple, no questions asked. Tho helped his friend, the pho seller, on the edge of the street all evening. He hid in plain sight and maintained the broth with his conical hat cutting off sight lines of whoever walked past. He figured if he was supposed to be seen, he would be. He had the marble tablets safely hidden in a woven pouch hanging from his neck.

Minutes before midnight, Tho loitered in a narrow alley off the back of the temple. He continued wearing the hat, pajama bottoms, and rubber sandals.

"Over here."

A young man emerged from the shadows. Tho followed halfway down a narrow walkway and into a small room with a single dim light bulb. Lien, Minh, and two other young men were already in the room.

"We shouldn't be doing this," said the young man.

"Tho, this is my nephew, Cuong."

"I don't like this at all," said Cuong. "It's extremely dangerous here and …"

"You don't know how dangerous," interrupted Tho. He looked at Lien. "Have you told him?"

"No, I haven't said anything, just that it's urgent."

"Good."

"What's this all about?" Cuong pressed.

"I need a way into 48 Hang Ngang Street."

Cuong didn't respond at first and glanced over to his aunt. "What? Why?"

"The why is extremely important, but I shouldn't tell you. It's the Ho Chi Minh historical site."

"I can't get you in there."

"Then this has been a mistake." Tho turned to walk out. Minh stood up and grabbed the arm of the old man, pleading for him to be patient.

"The Chinese warrior," Lien blurted out, directing the question at her nephew. "What do you know about him?"

"We're still gathering intel on him and—"

"He's not of this world, or at least not of this time."

"What?"

Tho sighed. "You shouldn't be telling him this."

"What do you mean?" asked Cuong.

"Because you're going to think we're crazy."

"I already think that."

"So can you get us into that house?" asked Tho.

"Look, even if I could, it would take a couple days of planning, and I would have to get approval from my—"

"We need it done now," said Tho flatly. "As in now."

"That's impossible."

Minh turned to the old man. "Mr. Tho, could you show him something? So he'd understand. You know."

Tho hesitated.

"There's nothing you could show me that would change my mind. I shouldn't even be talking to you, so there's no way I'm going to help you with a suicide mission."

Tho untied the pouch around his neck and retrieved the four marble tablets. He placed them flat on a small table and told everyone to gather around. The stones touched each other along their lengths, and he reached into his pocket to remove a handful of silver shavings. He held them in the palm of his hand over the marble and began a chant: "From the dawn of this country to the way forward, link the chain." He released the silver shavings, and they exploded with tiny bursts of light on the surface of the marble. The light spread and wove layers upon layers of light over top of each other until the textured colors created a depth rising off the surface of the marble, outlining a face with sunken red eyes, a broad forehead, and tightly carved beard—Sun Quan. The face hovered over the marble until the tip of a sword ascended in the light and mist and pierced its skull. A hand reached upwards holding the sword, and it disappeared as the light and shadows shifted to form the image of a young woman, a warrior in her own right, with a tightly-wound ponytail and intense eyes, making everyone in the room gasp. She tried to speak, but the words muffled into an unintelligible gibberish as the image disappeared, and the silver shavings laid half melted on top of the marble.

The other two young men had bounded to their feet and circled around Cuong as the magic show commenced. Complete silence fell on the room as everyone, including Tho, tried to grasp what they had witnessed. The speechless three stumbled over their words. Minh felt as confident as any to speak up.

"That was Lady Trieu arriving to defeat Sun Quan. It's the only way."

"No," said Tho. "That was not a vision of the future. No one path is so set in stone that we can predict with a certainty what will happen. That was a vision of the past, when Ba Trieu defeated the Hans—Sun Quan, to be precise—to establish an independent nation for the Viet people of the south."

Cuong allowed a confused look to greet everyone in the room. "Are you saying that the Chinese soldier is a resurrected Chinese emperor?"

"The demon spirit of the same. They have unleashed the other world on us to ensure victory. How else was it so easy for them? We must try to summon Lady Trieu to help us once again."

"And you think you'll be able to do that once you access the house on Hang Ngang Street?"

"It's my theory."

"I've never known Mr. Tho to be wrong," said Lien.

"Well, that's quite a burden to bear. The belief in one's eternal rightness," quipped the old man.

"Well, I've seen Mr. Tho do many amazing feats over the years, and if he says he needs to access the house, then we must help him."

One of the rebels tapped Cuong on the shoulder, and they conferred with each other in the corner of the room while the threesome held their breath. The other two nodded at Cuong and exited. Cuong turned back to the group.

"This must be completely unattached from the rebel plans, do you understand?"

"Yes."

"If this is traced back to the resistance, who knows what kind of kickback this could encourage."

"Yes, I understand."

"What is it that you need from the house?"

"I don't know."

"So we're going to break into a well-guarded house without a plan to look for something that may or may not be there?"

"Yes, correct."

Cuong paused for a moment, slid the door open, and peeked out. "We don't know what's out there."

"Yes we do," replied Tho. "Which is why we need to do this."

"An old man, a woman, and a young teen," said Cuong, looking over at them.

"Mr. Tho taught me something when I was much younger," said Lien, with defiance in her demeanor. "Resistance has no gender or age. When our very livelihood is at stake, we are all soldiers. That's what the Chinese don't understand about us. It will be their downfall."

Cuong seemed unconvinced. "I'm wondering if our resistance leadership has remembered that lesson. I have my doubts. Now, here's what we need to do. We have an hour."

Every historical site related to Vietnam's past struggle for independence had at least one Chinese guard posted at it. Forty-eight Hang Ngang had two soldiers guarding the padlocked door. At precisely 1 AM, Minh started running down the deserted street yelling at the top of his lungs.

"I've been robbed. We've been robbed. Help! Help!"

Minh stopped about a hundred feet from the guards, who had raised their weapons and shouted for him to halt. But he didn't.

"Help! Someone got into my house. It's right up there. Aren't you going to do anything?"

It was unclear how much the two Chinese guards understood what he was saying, but it served its purpose. One of the guards started walking towards Minh, telling him to raise his arms. Minh didn't understand the command, nor was he inclined to listen.

Precisely at 1:02, a case of firecrackers erupted from behind a house opposite the historical site. The hundreds of shrill explosions all at once, from the mass of firecrackers measuring two feet high by several feet wide, pierced the stillness of the night. Such a firecracker display was once popular with wedding parties and holiday celebrations but had been long since banned by the government. The intense sound burned on. Every shop-front lit up with nosy neighbors. The two young Chinese soldiers seemed unsure of themselves. One of them phoned a superior but couldn't be heard over the noise. The house where it had been lit was empty, and one of the guards opened the door and moved inside to investigate. One of Cuong's collaborators shut the metal gate behind the soldier and snapped a lock and chain around the gate, trapping the guard inside the house.

The other guard, who had been chasing Minh, found himself caught between the cacophony of firecrackers and the yelling boy, who was now surrounded by neighbors. The guard threatened everyone with the barrel of the rifle, but Cuong's second collaborator accosted him from behind with a brick to the head. The Chinese guard fell to the ground. The resistance fighter zip-tied his hands and gagged him with a cloth. He picked up the rifle and ran down the street.

As the chaos continued, Cuong escorted Tho and Lien into the middle of the street. Lien snagged Minh's attention, and he joined them as they approached the entrance to the site. Cuong carried a pair of bolt cutters and lopped off the chain around the door handles. Then he inserted a bump-key into the lock allowing him to turn the knob. He opened the door, but the Chinese soldier locked in the house across the street aimed his rifle and fired several shots which pierced the door and frame.

"Get in," yelled Cuong, as he pushed the three into the darkened historical site. "You have no more than five minutes until we're swarmed with soldiers or worse."

"Then we mustn't waste any time, should we?" Tho had his chance.

Chapter 5

The Picture Frame

Cuong provided reconnaissance from the cracked-open door of the Ho Chi Minh historical site. The Chinese soldier locked in the house across the street yelled and fired sporadically as the firecrackers continued exploding in the background. It was 1:04.

Lien switched on the light and badgered Tho to pick up his moribund pace, while yelling specific instructions for Minh to stay away from the door. She also asked Cuong if he had a plan for their escape. He didn't reply.

Tho methodically scanned his way through the fore room with photos and historical placards describing the building's significance. He walked into the second room. The table used by Ho Chi Minh to write the Declaration of Independence in August of 1945 sat off to the left. Tho imagined the leaders of Hanoi greeting the mysterious Ho Chin Minh around the table for the first time as he prepared to deliver the declaration in Ba Dinh Square on September 2nd of that year. Tho remembered himself as the young teen, experiencing the whisks of excitement in the air as they prepared to cast off the yoke of French colonialism. Now he stood as a messenger, searching for a link in the chain. As he swatted away the memories of that innocent young teen caught up in the revelry, Lien wrested his attention back to their current predicament.

"Tho, do you see anything?"

"No. Nothing."

1:05

"Mr. Tho, we have to go. Minh, stay away from the door."

"I need more time," said Tho.

"We don't have more time," yelled Cuong. "The patrols are going to be here any moment, and we're all dead if we're caught."

"Think Mr. Tho. Why here? Why you?"

Lien's question struck a nerve. Why indeed? His mind suggested this house to him, but why? Historically significant places litter Hanoi. Many of them related to the Vietnamese existential struggle for independence. But his brain set upon this one. He walked into the front room again and glanced at the walls.

"Mr. Tho."

"Patience."

Another bullet pierced the outside of the wooden door.

1:06. The firecrackers died out. People on the street had scattered for shelter as the Chinese guard yelled like a chained-up tiger, occasionally firing a warning round. Then the guard went silent. Cuong poked his head out the door. The soldier had slumped over in the locked doorway. Cuong's compatriot stood behind him, holding a rifle, and he signaled to Cuong with two fingers.

"Mr. Tho. Aunt Lien. We have two minutes."

"Why did the Chinese guard stop shooting?" asked Minh.

"He's dead."

Lien took her son's hand and walked over to Tho, who wandered an aimless route in the middle of the room.

"Mr. Tho. We don't have any time left. If you don't know what you're looking for, then let's leave. We'll figure out a different way."

"Mr. Khoi."

"What?"

"In 1946, Mr. Khoi was my professor for a year at Hanoi University."

"Mr. Tho, why are you saying this?"

"He was a signer of the Declaration of Independence. A contemporary of Uncle Ho. And my teacher."

"So, what does that mean?"

1:07. Cuong stepped outside the door and listened. Rumbling. He went inside.

"They're coming."

"Who?" asked Minh.

"The Chinese soldiers. I hear the vehicles. We have to go. Now!"

"He wasn't a communist. And that was the key. Uncle Ho wanted a broad cross-section of ideas because he knew victory required a total effort. One ideology was insufficient. We were Vietnamese foremost and forever."

"Mr. Tho," Lien pleaded.

They heard a motor scooter pull up alongside the front of the house.

"Is that them?" asked Minh with terror in his voice.

"No," said Cuong, standing in the doorway. "But they're on the next street over. You have to go now!"

"Mr. Tho!"

"He's the only link I have to this place."

"Mr. Tho!"

"Lien and Minh, just leave. If the old man wants to stay, let him." Cuong waved them onward.

"We can't leave him."

"You're going to die in one minute."

Tho had moved closer to the wall to observe a photograph in a wooden frame. Ho Chi Minh stood in the middle flanked by his first cabinet, chosen in 1945 in exile as they fought the French for independence.

"Mr. Tho!"

"That's him, right there. Second one from the left. Nguyen Van Khoi."

Lien grabbed Tho's hand and pulled him in the direction of the door. He resisted for a split second and reached for the photograph and snatched it off the wall. He slid it under his arm for safe keeping and allowed Lien's insistent tugging to win the day. They exited the house to find an idling Honda scooter.

"All of you, on the bike. Minh, you can drive?"

"Yes."

"Cuong—"

He cut off his aunt's questions. "This is the only way. Now!"

A Chinese patrol pulled onto the street with a megaphone pulsing out instructions. "Stay in your houses. Clear the streets. This illegal action will be punished severely."

"What are you going to do?" Lien's hands shook as she reached for Cuong.

"Make this worth it, Aunt Lien. Go."

Minh, Lien, and Tho crammed together on the seat of the scooter. Tho still had the photograph tucked under his shoulder. Before Minh could leave, Cuong started running across the street to the now unlocked house when a deafening shriek rose throughout the neighborhood. Tho could feel its presence, and it appeared in bodily form, knocking Cuong to the ground.

"Go," he yelled.

The patrol approached from the rear. Several shots fired from the house, striking Sun Quan in the back. He writhed as if in pain, but turned his back on Cuong towards the other young man standing over the dead Chinese guard. Sun Quan removed a dagger from his side sheath and threw it at Cuong's compatriot. It struck him dead-center chest, but instead of leaving a deep incisive thud, it exploded in a force of light that vaporized the young man.

"Go!" Cuong yelled.

The young motorbike driver had been frozen in the chaos, but suddenly turned his wrist on the accelerator, and the bike jerked forward, jolting the photograph from Tho's grasp, sending it to the pavement and shattering the glass frame.

"Stop!" yelled Tho. Minh hit the brakes, causing the momentum of Lien and Tho to push Minh against the steering column.

"Go!" yelled Cuong, who had reclaimed his footing when the patrol skidded to a stop behind him.

Sun Quan had turned when the frame fell on the ground. Tho lifted his leg over the seat and was ready to pick up the frame when the towering beast, twenty feet away, moved towards him.

The Chinese soldiers captured Cuong from behind while several more ran towards the three, telling them to put their hands up.

Sun Quan stopped them with one command. "Let them go."

The Chinese commander stepped out from the approaching soldiers. "We have to investigate. We can't let them go."

Tho had frozen directly in front of Sun Quan. As the commander spoke, Tho scooped up the photograph, allowing the errant pieces of glass to fall to the pavement, and he backed up toward Minh and Lien waiting breathlessly on the scooter.

"Go!" yelled Cuong, hands bound behind him, leaning up against the patrol vehicle.

"Cuong!"

Sun Quan swung his massive left arm and smacked the Chinese commander on the side of the face, knocking him to the ground. "I said let them go."

Minh didn't hesitate any longer. He sped off down Hang Ngang Street and disappeared into the dark through the winding Hanoi alleyways.

The Chinese commander, unfazed by the knockdown, rose to his feet. "We'll dispose of this rebel trash."

"No, I need him alive."

"But—" The commander censored himself and covered his face with a reflexive, protective response.

While still in the building, Cuong had slipped Lien a small piece of paper with an address written on it. Lien pointed Minh down the winding alleys until she told him to stop. He turned off the bike. More patrols could be heard rumbling on the main street in close proximity. Minh pushed the motorbike behind a large tree on the side of a cement wall which hid a small courtyard. The rusty metal door swung open, and Cuong's second accomplice waved them in.

Tho clutched the broken frame, and Lien clung onto her son's arm with tears not far from falling.

"Where's Cuong?" the young man asked.

"They caught him," said Tho flatly.

"And Doan?"

"Dead," said Lien. "Sun Quan killed him."

The young man took a moment and rubbed his forehead. "How did you get away from Sun Quan?"

"He let us go."

"He let you go?"

"Yes."

"Is Cuong dead?"

The talking paused. "We don't know," said Lien.

"Well, did you find it? Did you get what you needed?" The young man reeked of impatience with a raw-simmering anger tucked underneath the tone of his voice.

"What's your name?" asked Tho.

The young man laughed. The kind of uncaring laugh you might

expect from a wily teenager.

"Tuan."

"Tuan, we can't help them now. One's fate has been sealed. The other's we will one day know. But for now, we have to do our best to understand the task we've been given."

"Why did Sun Quan or whoever it is let you go?"

"I suspect he saw the broken frame on the ground."

"You went there for a photograph?"

"No, no. This is what I saw when I went. A photograph of my old teacher."

"And this is the magical photo that has killed at least one and threatened the survival of the resistance in this district. Do you understand what you've done?" Tuan flared in anger but kept his voice low.

"This isn't his fault," Lien said. "We're trying to help the resistance."

"There's a reason the Chinese left the women, children, and old men alone."

Tuan turned to walk away.

"Where are you going?" asked Lien.

"I have to get word to the underground. I'm finished with this. You're on your own."

"What are we supposed to do here?" asked Minh.

"This place will be compromised by morning, so that's up to you."

Tuan exited the courtyard and disappeared into the cadence of the night. Patrols sifted through the streets with higher frequency. The Chinese soldiers picked up their dead comrade and several others inspected the inside of the historical house, discussing the reason for the evening's events. Sun Quan lowered his head at the door frame of the house and entered. He knew where to look. A row of photographs had one frame missing. The commander instructed the soldiers to scour the insides of the house to see if anything else had been taken or disturbed.

"Don't bother," said Sun Quan in his low steady voice. "They got what they came for."

"Then why did you let them go?"

"Because I want them to have it."

Sun Quan walked out into the street. The neighboring doors could barely contain the peering eyes, bulging from the cracks to catch a terrifying glimpse of the strange warrior. He could have terrorized them with one glance from his red eyes, but he allowed himself to float into the air, formless, and disappeared into the night. Several residents stepped out onto the street wondering what had happened to him, but the gloomy hours of early morning and the blood spatters on the pavement soon sent them back into their illusory safety chambers.

Chapter 6

The Saying from the Past

The old man, the woman, and the teen conversed in quick, hushed tones in the darkness of the courtyard. They couldn't return home, and they now had no connection to the underground resistance.

"Ma, do you think Cuong is dead?"

She hesitated. Tho replied.

"It's useless to focus on things we can't control and don't yet know. What we do know is when they apprehended him, he was alive."

"Why did Sun Quan allow us to escape? He could have crushed us."

"His intentions and actions tell two different stories. I believe we have something he needs."

"What's that?"

"I'm not quite sure."

"Tho," asked Lien. "Why did you take the photograph?"

Tho handed Minh a flashlight and instructed him to focus it on a cement table. He reached into his pouch and removed one of the black marble tablets, placing it on the rough tabletop.

"Mr. Tho! You're bleeding."

He had cut his hand on the broken glass of the frame, and a droplet of blood smeared the surface of the black tablet. It began to sizzle and a mist rose into the air, accompanied by a voice echoing in the thick, humid evening with a simple plea: "Follow me."

The voice triggered a backwards step from all of them, and they conferred in silence with shocked looks under the deep shadows of the night. Minh's voice sprang with excitement.

"Did you hear that?" All of them had, even though difficult to admit. "What does it mean?"

No one had an answer. "Keep linking the chain, that's all," said Tho.

Lien wrapped a tissue around Tho's hand as he placed the rest of the marble tablets on the table.

"Why this photograph?" Tho asked himself under his breath.

"You mean even you don't know?" asked Minh.

"I chose it because it contains an image of my former teacher. But beyond that, its significance eludes me."

They placed the frame over the stones and inspected the image of the photo with the flashlight. Nothing.

"We need to remove it from the frame."

"Careful of the glass," said Lien, and brushed away crushed pieces with her sleeve. The frame had a thin wood backing held in by four flush turnkeys. Tho moved each and lifted the backing by the metal wire used to hang it on the wall. The back of the photo had no identifying marks.

"I don't see anything," said Minh.

"Always look more than once. Our eyes are not always accustomed to seeing the truth upon first glance."

"That's what mom says."

"I got it from him," she smiled.

"Well, upon second glance, I still don't see anything."

"Perhaps we're looking in the wrong place." Minh had his head so close to the photo it nearly touched.

"Where else can we look?"

Lien turned over the backing of the frame. A small, flat reed the size of a bookmark had been placed on the wooden backing with a sticky substance. Tho removed it and held it under the flashlight. Faint characters were etched lightly into the reed.

"I need my glasses," said Tho.

"It's in Chinese characters," exclaimed Minh.

"No, that's Han-Viet. Old Vietnamese script."

"Well, I can't read it," said Lien.

"No, but perhaps if we …"

He lowered the reed until it lay flat across the marble tablets with both ends barely touching the first and fourth stones. The characters lit up as if on fire, illuminating all its meaning like the sun had back-lit it from underneath.

"Mr. Tho, can you understand it?"

"Oh, yes."

"What does it say?"

Tho studied each graceful stroke delicately inlaid on the reed.

"Remarkable."

"What?"

Tho paused for one further study of the characters. "A passion to be free. Bound together, each link. Generations of ancestors. A bronze drum. A dragon. A sword. United. The past revealed in the present."

He read it a second time and a third until Minh asked the obvious question.

"What does it mean?"

The light began to fade from the characters. Tho read it repeatedly, admonishing the others to commit it to memory before the strokes completely disappeared.

It was nearly 2 AM. They recited it together in the shadows of the courtyard. A private chant for a task yet to be defined.

"Mr. Tho. What does it mean?"

"The chain."

"What? Mr. Tho?"

The man stumbled and nearly fell on top of the table. "Sorry, I … I—"

"Mr. Tho, you're tired," said Lien, clutching his arm to stabilize him.

"We're all tired," he replied.

"We must sleep. Remember that Tuan said this place will not be safe for long. Tho, come. I think I know where we can go. Miss Huong lives near here."

"Your dear friend? I haven't seen her in years."

"Come. It's the only idea I have."

Miss Huong had a hot serving of *chao* rice porridge as the three woke up on top of red reed mats in her living room. Tho noticed the dragon imprinted on the mat flanked on each side with the ironic Chinese characters for 'Double Happiness.' It had been a long while since that phrase had held meaning in Hanoi. Minh stood up and remembered the saying sitting on the tip of his tongue. He recited it word for word with an intrigued Miss Huong listening most intently. She had spent many afternoons with Lien in Mr. Tho's silver shop, learning myriad wonders about the universe, so she wasn't surprised to find the ragged three knocking at her door in desperation in the middle of the night.

"Thank you for taking us in," said Tho.

"No questions need to be asked in times like these. Just react to the beat of the moment. That's what you always taught me."

Tho smiled.

"My husband and son are both somewhere in the resistance, if they are still alive."

It wasn't a somber statement. Just a fact. One each person in the room understood as a great truth.

When the *chao* had been eaten and the necessary words of reunion spoken, they all sat under the ticking of the ceiling fan regaling Miss Huong with the events of the previous evening and reciting the words from the reed. Even Miss Huong committed them to memory.

"Such a beautiful saying."

"And we're trying to link it to Lady Trieu."

"Which makes sense because she defeated Sun Quan in the third century if I remember my history."

"You do," confirmed Tho with a smile. "And what of the bronze drum …?"

"I know," said Minh. "It represents the origins of our people."

"That's right. The stately drums from the bronze age which prove a different lineage from our northern neighbors. Then we come to the dragon …"

"*Thang Long*. The ascending dragon. The emperor saw a dragon ascend from the Red River, which encouraged him to establish a new capital city eventually renamed as Hanoi," said Miss Huong.

"Yes, the establishment of our people. Bronze Age. A civilization being built. A new capital. And the sword?"

"The only one I can think of is *Ho Hoan Kiem*, Returned Sword Lake."

"The turtle," said Minh.

"The turtle brought the sword back from the depths of the lake and …"

"Is there a turtle still in the lake?" asked Minh.

"People say there are sightings," said Lien.

Sightings. Tho remembered something. From when he was just a boy. He hadn't thought about that for decades. He brushed it away. "But can we base our actions on what people say and the lore we were taught?" asked Tho.

"Don't question the past until it proves itself wrong," said Huong. "A wise man once said that."

"Old decrepit man, that is," Tho chuckled.

"So what are we saying? Is the turtle the key to the sword?" asked Lien.

"Why don't we ask the marble tablets? Will they know?" Minh asked in an excited tone.

Tho shook his head. "The tablets are not a source of knowledge. They are a conduit to the past." As he spoke, he removed the marble tablets from his pouch and placed them on the floor.

"Where did you get them?" asked Huong.

"They were gifted to me by my grandfather, and he said they were gifted to him by a mysterious stranger with instructions to 'Keep the Legacy Alive.'"

"What does that mean?"

"I never knew … until today. I had used the stones many times over the years, mostly trying to understand a way forward in a dilemma, but …"

He trailed off as the three hung on the edge of his words. "The stones, the reed, the silver shavings, the drop of blood, the bronze drum, the dragon, the sword …"

He retrieved a small cloth pouch from within the larger pouch. He opened the string and turned it over. Silver dust floated downward.

"The turtle."

The dust sprinkled randomly on the surface of the marble creating small puffs of smoke which whirled upward in a glowing cloud. He repeated it again.

"The turtle."

And the same voice they had heard previously echoed once again through smoke. "Return the sword once more." The smoke morphed into a rounded dome.

"A turtle shell!" yelled Minh.

Then the smoke dissipated into the air.

They all breathed in the moment of silence.

"Mr. Tho, what does it mean? We don't have a sword."

"You were right, Minh. The marble tablets are telling us what to do."

"Which is what?"

Tho took a moment to reflect over his life. There were many things he couldn't remember, but an image of his grandfather came to mind. He sat with his grandfather on the arched bridge, which led from the shore of Hoan Kiem Lake at the center of old Hanoi to the small islet holding the sacred Ngoc Son Temple. He could picture the sun beating down on his grandfather's head, and he waved the boy into the shade across the bridge. As they sat under a tree, his grandfather pointed at the surface of the water. A turtle stuck its head out from the surface and glared at them for a moment, then it dove out of sight into the belly of the lake. His grandfather stood to his feet and had instructed Tho to stand up. He patted the boy's head and said it was right. It was good. It would be so. Tho never understood what he meant until today. As he pushed away the memories, he knew exactly what they would do. "It means that at midnight, we shall be a boat on Hoan Kiem Lake, believing the universe will gift us a turtle."

"Where are we going to get a boat?"

Huong raised her arm excitedly. "I might be able to help. My father-in-law is the caretaker of Ngoc Son Temple. I'll contact him. I'm confident he can arrange something."

"I knew there was a reason we came here," said Lien. "Now, how are we going to sneak past the patrols? And once we're in the boat, how will we remain undetected? We'll be exposed on the lake."

"And what do we do if we see the turtle?" asked Minh.

Tho raised his arms to temper the questions. "Listen, we don't need to know the answers to know the way forward. Let our steps show us our path. Each one reveals the subsequent. Perhaps the universe knows not to overwhelm us with knowledge. Maybe we wouldn't be keen to continue if we knew what awaits." He turned to Miss Huong. "We would be much obliged if you could contact your father-in-law. If it's all right with you, we'll rest here until dark. My body is in a frightful shape."

Several Chinese soldiers had beaten Cuong to a semi-conscious state and thrown him into a windowless pitch-black room. When his senses began to revive, he had no recollection of time, and it puzzled him why they allowed him to live in the first place. He rested against a smooth black wall and willed his mind to tranquility. He believed agitation and anger would yield no tangible results. He would keep his mind fresh, even if his body pulsed with pain.

The wall opposite him opened. The black facade drew upward and smoke appeared around the edges like theatrical fog determined to heighten tension. The corners of the ceiling lit up with a line of red lights, and Sun Quan parted the fog with his glowing eyes. The dominating figure towered over the beaten young man.

"Do you know why you're alive?" His voice rumbled low with only small variation in tone.

"No."

"As long as you answer my questions, you will remain so."

"I'm not afraid of death. I knew what I signed up for—to vanquish the filthy Chinese scum."

"A young man not afraid of death can be a useful pawn." The giant beast took a step forward. "What do you know of the old man?"

"I know nothing of him."

"Yet you willingly helped him."

"I regret it. It's all foolishness. For nothing."

A presence encircled Cuong, and a weight fell across his chest, pausing his breathing. The force pressed him against the back wall and pressured his wounds on all sides, like the damage had drawn inward and gutted the will to live right out of him. He writhed in pain, and as the grip released him, he collapsed to his side.

"The woman. What do you know?" Sun Quan knelt over top the victim.

"What woman?"

"The one they are summoning?"

"The woman I was with? She's a nobody."

"Not that woman." Sun Quan lashed out and smacked the cowered soldier across the face.

"What woman? I don't know what you're talking about?"

"Ba Trieu."

Cuong lunged at Sun Quan and tried to hit him, but Cuong's arms felt tired, like stone weights drooped over his wrists. He hit the giant man in the arm, but the warrior smirked as if flicking off a pesky gnat. Cuong looked down at his hands, but they looked different— like they belonged to another person.

"What do you know of the woman?"

"It's all nonsense. The old man showed us some magic trick and … if you think …" Cuong laughed. "It's all nonsense."

"Your face tells a different story."

"What do you mean?"

"Look in the mirror behind you to see the nonsense."

Cuong turned and a section of the wall became a clear piece of glass reflecting his image back at him. Cuong reached out to touch the mirror and screamed. The image wasn't his. Wrinkles and weathered lines had bored a different age into his skin. He screamed again. "What's happened to me?" He had become an old man.

Sun Quan turned his back to the blathering Cuong. "Your age reflects your way of thinking. Your transformation has proven to me how little your rebel army knows. It's just the old man, the woman, and the boy where your hope lies. And also mine. I'll leave the lights on for you, so you can become well acquainted with your new self."

Sun Quan exited the cell. The walls closed down behind him. Cuong remained on his knees, looking at this new reflection. "No!"

Chapter 7

To the Temple

Ngoc Son Temple sits on an island in the middle of the northern tip of Hoan Kiem Lake in the center of Hanoi's old town. The former bustling tourist area now consisted of tepid residents searching for their next meal under the watchful eye of strict patrols circling the lake on a consistent basis. The temple could only be reached by a red wooden walking bridge spanning the water from the eastern shore of the lake.

Tho had tried his best to dissuade Lien and Minh from accompanying him on such a foolhardy quest, but as Lien reminded him, she had no home to go to and would not abandon the important national work right as it got interesting. Minh gave a passionate plea about being a man and being big enough and clever enough to help the resistance. They would traverse into the unknown and allow fate to have its way. All three together.

Miss Huong left the house during the day to contact her father-in-law. By late afternoon, the best assurance she could offer was that her father-in-law would attempt to fulfill the request. If they could find a way into the temple before sunset, he would try.

Tho's logic encouraged them to split up in their pilgrimage to the temple, but Lien wouldn't part from her son, and since Tho's body didn't feel particularly adept at making the trek to the lake on its own, they decided to chance it together. Miss Huong also wanted to go, but Tho reminded her that a fourth person would add to the likelihood of being spotted. They thanked her for the help, and she wished them luck in their endeavor. Before they parted, the four recited the phrase verbatim once more: "A passion to be free. Bound together, each link. Generations of ancestors. A bronze drum. A dragon. A sword. United. The past revealed in the present."

Huong had one final gesture of help. Disguises. Tho would wear his conical hat, light pajamas, and sandals. He looked like a thousand other retired grandfathers on any Hanoi street corner. She outfitted Lien with a bamboo shoulder pole, which balanced two baskets—one in front and one behind—and put a heaping of greens on each side as if she were a countryside hawker bringing her vegetables to market. Minh wore a cap and carried a knapsack. Tho walked slowly, requiring Lien to slow down and squat sometimes so she wouldn't get too far ahead of him. She had a few Hanoians ask her about her greens, but she asked for an exorbitant price that sent the shoppers off in disgust.

They turned a corner and saw the lake straight ahead, with the bridge leading to the temple on the other side of the street, which wrapped around the entire body of water. Two Chinese soldiers stood at the entrance, rifles in hand. The main street was empty. Abandoned cars had been parked on the opposite side. Tho had hoped for some traffic to help them blend in, but the good old crowded days were long gone. The only way to approach the temple was to walk directly toward the soldiers.

"What are we going to do?" asked Lien.

Tho paused and glanced both directions.

"Isn't there any other way to the temple?" asked Minh.

"No. This is the only path. We must face the danger directly."

"What if they stop us?"

"Then they stop us."

"What if …"

Tho raised his arm. "One thing I've learned in my long life is to not question the what-ifs. Plan as much as circumstance allows. If there is nothing more to prepare, then move forward and allow your best laid plans to take you as far as they may. This is bigger than us. Let us hope the universe recognizes it."

Lien nodded and patted her son's back. "How do we approach? Together, or one at a time?"

Tho continued to peer toward the soldiers. "You're my daughter. Minh is my grandson. This is the day of my wife's death, and we have come to the temple to light incense for her soul."

Minh reached into his knapsack and pulled out a handful of red joss sticks. "Look what Miss Huong put in the bag."

"Of course she did," said Tho with a determined eye staring at the soldiers. "Let's go."

Tho ignored his aches and pains and the better-than-average chance the soldiers would stop them in their tracks to question them. He kept his mind clear—thinking of the smooth black tablets in the pouch around his neck. The three were on the offensive, not with weapons that could hurt the soldiers, but with a courage buoyed by the stories of the past. The black tablets had come alive after many years as proof the courage was warranted. He led the way, with the two at his rear. He rubbed his hands in a circular motion as he crossed the street as if he held the tablets between his palms. His eyes remained intent on the soldiers, and as they approached, one of the soldiers raised his rifle and motioned with the barrel's tip for them to move along.

"The temple is closed today."

"But today is my wife's death anniversary. We must visit the temple to—"

A tremendous sound ripped through the end of the sentence. All of them jumped backwards and cowered to the ground, turning to look back across the street. A parked car had exploded, sending debris fifty feet into the air. Screams. Yelling. A pulsing silence across their ears, loud and chaotic on one hand and slow-motion silence on the other. The soldiers ran from their post towards the explosion. It was unclear if anyone was hurt, but the street quickly filled with people and sirens from other patrols approached from both sides of the lake.

"Come on," whispered Minh. "This is our chance."

The boy sprinted across the grass and onto the red bridge spanning the water. Lien grabbed Tho's arm and helped him to his feet. She pointed in the same direction as Minh and moved as swiftly as the aged man would allow. Lien looked back, but the Chinese soldiers had disappeared into the mayhem of the car bomb. A few gun shots sounded behind them, but Lien and Tho moved on. By the time they crossed the bridge and approached the entrance of the temple, Minh greeted them with another older man standing beside him.

"This is Miss Huong's father-in-law."

"Come, come," he said. "Quickly. I have a place for you."

Lien stopped to bow her head to the altar of the past Vietnamese kings, but the old man wouldn't let her.

"No, they will understand. We don't have time. Please hurry."

He pushed a wooden panel behind a large display of Buddha and motioned for them to go inside a small room.

"You'll need to wait in here until dark. Just keep still and quiet."

"What about the boat?" asked Minh.

"Later. Just remain still and quiet."

It was more like a compartment and less like a room. It spanned only four feet wide by six feet long. Three plastic stools had been arranged in a row—one for each. The wooden walls had patterned carvings on them, which allowed in enough light to see each other's faces.

"How long will we have to sit here?" asked Minh.

"Until dark," whispered Tho.

"Shhh—"

Voices rose from the main section of the temple. The voices didn't whisper and had a harsh tone to them, but no one could understand what was said. Then without warning, someone slid open the wooden panel and in the secluded opening of the compartment stood a man, but it was not Huong's father-in-law. It was a young man. They had been discovered. Tho's mind flashed a warning of arrest as he expected the Chinese soldier to speak.

"It's me. Tuan."

Cuong's compatriot stood in front of them. Tho stood up. "The bombing. It was you?"

"You needed a distraction."

"But how?" Lien asked.

"I reported back to the rebel leaders, and I told them about you, about all of you, and …" He paused for a moment. "They assigned me to you."

"To us?" asked Lien.

"Commander Lieu. He knows you, Mr. Tho."

"I know of the Mr. Lieu you speak. What did you tell them?"

"All I said was that you believed you knew the origin of the giant man, and you had a plan to defeat him. He didn't want to know any more. He only instructed me to follow you and help in any way I can."

"Well, we need a—"

"I know. A boat. You shall have it. Stay here until dark, and I'll return. You'll have your boat. But what you do with it …"

Tho raised his hands. "We cannot speculate on what we will find on the waters. We will wait for you."

Tuan pushed the wooden panel closed, and they sat in the dimly lit room waiting for night to descend.

"Tho, is that Commander Lieu? *The* Commander Lieu?" asked Lien.

"Yes, his father was an old friend of mine, but I haven't spoken with the son in years."

"Why would he send Tuan to us after what happened last night?"

"Well," Tho pondered. "It may be because I saved his life."

Chapter 8

On Its Back

Sun Quan entered the black cell, still illuminated with glowing red lights in the corners of the ceiling. Cuong's head remained lowered as the commanding figure approached. He had been staring at his wrinkled hands for hours. Age was a curse far greater than death to the young man.

"Come with me," commanded Sun Quan.

Cuong obeyed. His back twinged as he stood to his feet, short of breath. He followed.

Nobody handcuffed him. He walked down a corridor and through the sliding doors of the slick stone building, which had been built on the corner of Ba Dinh Square. He thought it strange he had never seen the building before. An open-air armored vehicle waited for them. Cuong climbed into a back seat and Sun Quan sat behind him on the deck, like a vulture or a gargoyle studying the prey below before the attack. The vehicle whipped through the streets. Myriad people gawked at the domineering figure in the backseat, swords strapped to his back, glass shield across his eyes. On one turn in the street, someone threw a bottle at the beast and it smashed into glass shards against his back without any acknowledgment from Sun Quan.

The Chinese soldier driving the vehicle came to a stop in front of the *Nha Tho Lon*, St. Joseph's Cathedral, a block away from Hoan Kiem Lake. The soldier told Cuong to enter the church. Cuong looked behind him at Sun Quan, but the warrior ignored him. Cuong stepped out of the vehicle with a fair amount of difficulty and walked up the steps and into the cathedral. The soldier walked to the rear holding a rifle and pointed to the narrow, winding stairs leading to the front spire of the cathedral. Young Cuong could have run up the stairs without much difficulty, but the present Cuong, the one with aged lungs and creaky knees, paced himself step-by-step, frequently looking behind him to see the soldier urging him from the barrel of a rifle.

"Why am I going up here?" Cuong finally asked, to no reply.

Out of breath, he pushed open a metal door and stepped out onto the top of the cathedral's north tower, across from the twin south tower and several meters above the tip of the cross which centered the cathedral between the two towers. Sun Quan appeared, seemingly out of nowhere. He stood on the ledge of the tower, and he motioned to Cuong.

"Stand on the ledge."

Cuong did. He wasn't afraid to die, but he still couldn't help but feel the fear in his chest as he stood one hundred and three feet above the pavement below. Sun Quan pointed in the distance, down Church Street to the water of the lake shimmering in the evening sun.

"Hoan Kiem Lake. What will your friends do at the lake?"

"They are not my friends."

"Isn't Miss Lien your aunt?" Cuong looked over at Sun Quan with a surprised glare. "You can tell me or not tell me. It doesn't matter," added the giant.

"Why did you bring me here?"

"There was a car bomb on the other side of the lake today."

"I didn't do it."

Sun Quan smirked. "They will attempt it. Tonight on the lake. I won't prevent it."

"I don't know what you're talking about." Cuong's voice almost sounded like a plea. Asking the warrior to end it. Mercifully.

"No, you evidently don't. You are so bound by your own self-rightness that you can't grasp the reach of the past and how it lingers over every part of this city, especially over this lake. You're a stubborn people. Foolish, but of one mind. That is to be commended."

"What do you want from me?" asked Cuong.

"Nothing you can give me."

"Then why am I here?" His breath was airy and weak.

"I wanted you to see the lake one more time."

"Why?"

"Cause it will either swallow your friends like a vicious beast or …" His voiced trailed off and he continued looking off toward the lake.

"Or what? What?"

"The past shall be opened, and we shall both feel pain in all of its glory."

"I don't understand what you want."

"Don't look down."

Unable to resist, the young man in the old body did look down, and exactly at that moment, wind rushed behind him and lifted him off the edge into the open air. He fell head-first off the tower, screaming and flailing and calling out for help. He didn't care about age or rebellion or the lake or anything else. He pleaded for his life against the sure death waiting him on the pavement below. He closed his eyes and screamed once more. When he opened them, Sun Quan stood below him on the stone steps. His arm stretched out to stop Cuong's fall. His body didn't touch the outstretched arm. It hovered for a moment before falling the final few meters into a frail ball of emotions at Sun Quan's feet.

"Take him away."

Two Chinese soldiers seized Old Man Cuong by each arm, returned him to the vehicle, and sped off into the dying evening. He had fallen off a church tower but was still alive and couldn't understand why.

The long, quiet hours passed in a slumping stupor. Tho leaned against the wall and snored much more loudly than Lien would have liked. She watched through the cracks and only noticed a scant few visitors to the temple, coming to light incense and say a prayer. She figured they had bribed the guards to allow them on the islet, and so was confident the prayers were for the resistance. Minh bit his lip and stared intensely at his mother. His leg pulsed up and down like an impatient toddler. She patted it and whispered, "Rebellions are usually boring. Be grateful for these moments."

The dark hours commenced as night fell upon Hanoi. They had short respites from the boredom. Huong's father-in-law escorted them to the bathroom one at a time and passed them loaves of crunchy French bread to satisfy their appetites.

"I always wondered if we should be thankful for the French bread," whispered Tho. "A vestige of colonialism." He took a bite. "On a day like this, I bless the colonial bastards."

Lien cuffed the old man quiet.

The weary souls wondered if they would ever be permitted to leave their compartment, but as midnight approached, the panel slid open and Tuan stood in the doorway, back-lit by the candles on the altars to his rear.

"Come. All of you."

They slipped out the back of the temple under the canopy of several large trees surrounding it on all sides. Tuan led them to the southern end of the islet and stopped under the cover of one of the branches.

"Mr. Lieu, what did he say about me?" asked Tho before Tuan could speak.

"He reveres you. He trusts your judgment. His only warning was we couldn't make any guarantees."

"What does that mean?" asked Minh.

"Your safety is out of our control. I can help you, but I can't save you. No one can."

Tho chuckled. "We don't need saving. We need a boat."

Tuan pointed towards the water with his forehead. "A small rowboat. Big enough for three."

"That's all we need," said Lien.

"What is it you're hoping to do?"

Tho turned away and patted the young man on the shoulder. "It would be better not to know the foolishness we will attempt."

"But I saw what you did with the silver shavings on the marble tablets. I know there's something more at work here. I want to know what it is."

"If we're successful, then everyone will know, including you. And if we're not, we'll sleep quietly in the water tonight."

Lien turned harshly towards the old man. "Tho, don't say that. I don't want Minh to think—"

"Ma, I'm not a little boy. I know what we're doing."

"Minh, your mother loves you. That is all. She also knows you're ready. We've been led here—all three of us—to ride the smooth waters of Returned Sword Lake at the stroke of midnight in hopes of finding a generous turtle."

Tuan looked at Tho. "That's what you're doing? Looking for the turtle?"

"Why else would we be here?" laughed Tho. "Do you think Mr. Lieu would approve of such a mission?"

"This is crazy," Tuan said, shaking his head.

"Of course it is. Why do you think we were chosen?" Tho reached out his hands and Lien grabbed one side and Minh the other. They walked toward the edge of the lake and stood a solemn trio at the tip of the row boat. "Minh will row. He has the strength. Lien will sit in the front and scout. She has the eyes."

"And what will you do, Mr. Tho?" asked Minh.

"I have my marble tablets to keep me company."

They all climbed in, each giving a helping hand to Mr. Tho. Tuan put his hands on the side of the boat and pushed it gently into the water.

"Where did you get the boat?" asked Tho.

"During the explosion. Someone brought it over. We were lucky."

"It's funny how truth and luck are closely related," said Tho. "Minh, let's go."

"Where to?"

"Toward Turtle Temple." The turtle temple had been built on a small island on the southern part of the lake to commemorate the legend of the turtle. It seemed to Tho as good a place as any to begin the search.

"Be careful, Tuan," said Lien. "And thank you. Any news from Cuong?"

"No, ma'am."

The boat pulled away from shore when they heard a voice from behind Tuan.

"Wait! Wait!"

Minh pulled the oars straight. Huong's father-in-law descended the bank to the edge of the water carrying something with both hands.

"Wait. You may need this." A sword. He held it out with open palms as if paying tribute to an ancient king. "Perhaps the turtle will be more accommodating to your request if you don't come empty handed."

The legend of the returned sword wasn't lost on anyone. As the legend goes, a fisherman found a magical sword in his net. The sword was used to defeat the Chinese aggressors in the 15th century, only to be returned to the golden turtle when the battle ceased.

"Where did you get that sword?"

"It has been hidden in Ngoc Son Temple since its construction. Look what is engraved on it: *thuan thien*."

Minh had rowed the boat back to the edge of the shore. "The Will of Heaven," said Tho. "Thank you. We will take it as a tribute."

He handed the sword to Lien, who laid it flat in the hull of the boat.

"Good luck," wished the old man on the shore, along with the young rebel.

Minh turned the boat around, and it drifted into open water. The moon shone overhead and the eerie quietness of the lake's surroundings caught all of their attention. Alone on the lake, in a small boat, searching for a mythical turtle. They tried not to think about the absurdness of it all.

Minh sat between the two adults and rowed in a methodical but slow manner. Lien scoured the water but it lay perfectly still with a sheen of lights reflecting off its surface.

"Tho, tell us when it's time," said Lien without looking back at him.

He had removed the tablets from the pouch and placed them in his hands. He began with the familiar circular motion, and the other two could hear the faint friction from the marble.

"A passion to be free. Bound together, each link. Generations of ancestors. A bronze drum. A dragon. A sword. United. The past revealed in the present."

Tho spoke it first then the other two joined in to create a low monotone chorus. They were exposed on the lake. Anyone from shore could easily have spotted them, so they didn't think much of the noise they created. If they were caught, then so be it.

It took ten minutes for them to cross the open water and approach Turtle Tower. They continued the chant without ceasing as Tho manipulated the tablets in his hand.

"Stop," yelled Tho.

Minh held the ends of the oars upright and the boat slowly glided to a peaceful stop on the tranquil water. The chant ended, as did the rubbing of the tablets.

"Here. Lien, try the sword. Dip the tip of the sword into the water. The will of heaven."

Lien lifted the sword with both hands and pierced the surface of the water with its tip. She held it for a moment as Tho commenced the saying and the other two joined.

"A passion to be free. Bound together, each link. Generations of ancestors. A bronze drum. A dragon. A sword. United. The past revealed in the present."

After they spoke the word 'present,' the boat jolted upwards. All three screamed and expected to plunge into the deep. But the boat didn't capsize, and the force underneath kept lifting them out of the water. Then the head of a giant turtle emerged from the deep and snatched the sword with its mouth. The water dripped down from the sides of the boat and Minh peeked over the edge.

"Ma, Tho! The boat's on the shell of a giant turtle!"

Chapter 9

Into the Depths

Sun Quan peered from the edge of Turtle Tower, sitting on a small islet in Hoan Kiem Lake. He stood in plain sight, filling the tower's arched opening, but the threesome on the boat, tottering on the top of a giant turtle shell, were not in a position to care about onlookers. The turtle held the sword firmly across its mouth and raised his head once before splashing downward into the depths. The surface of the water parted as if a large drain underneath had been unplugged. The shell of the turtle dipped with the boat still balanced on its center. Each of the three intrepid riders screamed for mercy, like the thrill of descending over the peak of a roller coaster, headed to sure death. The turtle and boat disappeared under the surface. Sun Quan sprang forward—part-running, part-gliding, part-flying across the water—and dove into the spot where the turtle had sank. The harsh water closed in and repelled the ancient emperor so that he slid on his back across the expanse of the water and curled into a ball against the eastern shore of the lake. Sun Quan sat up and gazed at the water as it returned to its peaceful setting against the moonlight. The water had rejected him. He would have to wait.

Minh frantically held the ends of the oars; Lien and Tho clung to the sides of the boat. No one spoke or screamed further. The moment suspended them from all human action, until Minh pointed out the water. "Look!" It stood in luminous walls, radiating a fluorescent glow clearly painting awe on each of their faces. A giant air bubble encompassed the top of the turtle shell as the animal swam at a slow, steady pace.

"Ma?" Worry sat on the forefront of the question.

Lien's tense arms gripped the wooden sides with such force that she didn't hear the first call.

"Ma?"

"Ya…Yes?"

Minh had nothing more to add. He just wanted to hear her voice as he extended his gaze into the dark depths of the water. Tho reached forward and touched the teen on the shoulder.

"Minh, you don't have to row anymore." He had been futilely rowing still air. Tho's words broke him out of the trance, and he relaxed his hands and dropped them to his side. "Enjoy."

"Enjoy?"

"Yes. How often do we live through a dream?"

"Mr. Tho, where are we going?"

"I would guess the past, but—"

A face of a bearded warrior appeared on the outer rim of the air bubble watching them curiously as if the three were in a snow globe. He swam down to the head of the turtle. The turtle looked back and stopped swimming. The warrior pulled the sword from the turtle's mouth and ascended to the top of the snow globe. Releasing a ferocious call, he pierced through the air bubble with both hands clenching the sword, but the walls of water didn't burst. It accepted the sword without surrendering the integrity of the seal. The tip of the sword expanded several times its actual length and descended straight down towards Minh. He screamed, leaned back as far as he could, and opened his thighs wide as the tip of the sword poked into the wooden hull and stood straight up with the warrior holding its handle on the other side of the pressed in bubble.

"Who do you think you are? Why have you returned the sword in the middle of a rebellion?"

All three stared upward, fumbling over incomprehensible words. But it didn't matter, as the turtle stretched his neck up and around the edge of the bubble and pushed the warrior away. He held onto the sword and pulled it out of the bubble, but lost his grip as it popped from the seal. Now the sword floated freely through the open water. The turtle jolted forward. All three of the passengers lost hold of the boat and tossed and tumbled into the side of the bubble which repelled them all with firm elasticity. They flew from one side to the other like in a child's bouncy house before bounding head first back into the boat. The turtle had reclaimed the sword with its powerful jaw and continued swimming deeper.

"That was … horrifying," Lien panted. "Are you both alright? Who was that—?"

The answer would have to wait. Small bubbles erupted around the perimeter of their personal snow globe like it had been placed inside a boiling pot. Thousands of bubbles spread in all directions around the circumference of the turtle. But the bubbles gave way to two amber glowing lights charging at them. The lights formed eyes— piercing ovals which lit up the face of a monster with giant nostrils, ears, and jaw covered by a leathery green-black skin. The beast breathed once and hurled a thousand more bubbles to engulf the turtle and the snow globe on its back. The beast hissed and confronted the tortoise.

"Is that a dragon?" asked Minh.

No one had ever seen one before. Tho muttered something unheard under his breath and pointed. He mumbled again and jabbed Minh's back to look beyond the eyes of the dragon to a figure behind it. A rider, gripping one hand on the back of the beast's neck, pointed directly at the three.

"Ly Thai To," Tho whispered.

"What?" said Minh.

"The Ascending Dragon," said Lien, now with a clear view of the ancient Vietnamese king.

"You are not welcome here," said the king with an echoing voice booming off the sides of the air bubble. He reached for the sword, but the turtle swerved to the left. The three passengers clung to the sides of the boat. None of them had any intention of bouncing off the walls of the globe again.

"Give me the sword!" yelled the king.

The dragon turned its head toward the turtle and let out a deafening screech. Its massive jaw opened and its sharp teeth pierced through the wall of the bubble and closed in on the three—now lying flat on their backs in the boat, screaming for the nightmare to end— but the air bubble flung back with great force, sending the dragon and its rider flipping backwards out of sight. The turtle glanced back and caught the eyes of the three red-faced passengers, peeking over the edge of the boat. The turtle nodded and continued its descent into the depths.

Before they could gather their bearings and begin to decipher their dragon experience, two women appeared above them—floating apparitions. They looked identical, with long flowing black hair and simple peasant outfits with cloth belts tied around their waists. They held long bamboo poles in their hands and poked the sides of the air bubble.

"Pace yourself. Question yourself. Know the ending before it begins." They uttered these words in perfect unison. "Answer us."

They uttered no question but demanded the answer nonetheless.

"What do you want?" asked Tho.

"We want to know one thing?"

"What?"

"Are you willing to die?" No one responded. "Are you willing to die for what you believe?"

Minh reached back for Tho's hand, and the old man reassured him. Lien noticed the fierce stare from Tho.

"You know them, don't you?" she asked.

"Yes."

"Who are they?"

The apparitions asked once more. "Are you willing to die?"

"The Trung sisters."

"Hai Ba Trung?"

"Yes."

"What do they want, Mr. Tho?"

"They want to know if we are willing to go the distance like they did."

"What did they do?" asked Minh.

"They jumped into a river and drowned themselves."

"Pace yourself. Question yourself. Know the ending before it begins. Answer us." They repeated the mantra in unison once again.

Minh stood up and pointed directly at the pair of women floating freely in the water. "We are not afraid. We'll do anything for our country. Can't you see us? We went into the lake on the back of a turtle!"

"Minh!" Lien yelled, but said nothing else. She smiled. After all, he had learned it from her. And she from Tho.

The turtle had stopped swimming but seemed disinterested in the two female ghosts. They both looked closely at the boy standing on the boat, and without saying a word, they floated in front of the turtle. One held her bamboo pole on a high horizontal plane and the other on a low horizontal plane. The poles flashed white and lit up with fire, creating a burning square portal. The turtle resumed swimming and passed through the portal to the dark water on the other side. The turtle stopped, and all three in the boat stood up and glanced toward the horizon. A faint light from the surface of the water hovered above them. They watched as a dark apparition slid across the water.

"Sun Quan," said Tho.

The light spread outward from the location of the turtle and illuminated an army of Chinese terracotta soldiers, standing at attention, waiting to be deployed by their commander. The soldiers had animation without breath. They were a revelation at the disposal of history. As Sun Quan slid across the lake, his foot dipped mere inches below the surface, bringing the soldiers to life in a deafening chant. They drew their swords and attacked the turtle. The turtle shifted the handle of the sword into the tip of its mouth and held it *en garde*. The turtle flung its head back and forth, slicing the terracotta warriors one at a time, but their numbers overwhelmed it, swarming over the turtle's body and stabbing it several times. Undeterred, the turtle fought on. Other soldiers pierced their swords through the air bubble, causing the three to prostrate themselves in the hull of the boat.

"What are we going to do?" yelled Minh.

"What can we do?" asked his mother.

Tho shuffled around for the pouch. He opened the drawstrings and reached for the marble tablets. As he pulled them out, the turtle shifted its body in a great struggle to survive against overwhelming odds. Tho lost his grip on one of the tablets and it fell downward. Minh lurched forward with outstretched arms and snared it with his fingertips before it hit the boat. He reached over and handed it to Tho, who placed all four in his palms and started chanting:

"A passion to be free. Bound together, each link. Generations of ancestors. A bronze drum. A dragon. A sword. United. The past revealed in the present."

Lien and Minh joined him. They repeated it again and again as the turtle continued to fend off the warriors while taking repeated blows from the swarming army.

In the middle of the fourth incantation, Tho stopped, stood up, and looked at the battle on the other side of the bubble: "We need you Ba Trieu. We need you."

A voice rose from the depths and echoed off the bubble, like a whisper, as if a breeze lifted the words and sailed them out smoothly in all directions. The soldiers ceased fighting and fell still, remaining alive but not active. They listened as a deer hears the broken twig of an approaching hunter. The words dazed them, like they suddenly remembered a past defeat and its gripping horror entered their chests. They heard a voice—not of words, but of sound; almost melodic, and in a second, the sound split the warriors next to the turtle in two. A sword came hurling from the deep. The turtle reached its head upward, still holding the sword in its mouth as the two swords collided in an array of white light that blinded all of them for a moment. The three lowered their hands from their eyes and stood face-to-face with a large-breasted young woman, hair tied back, leather strapped across her legs leading to a mid-thigh length skirt and a thick leather belt strapped around her midsection. Her arms and shoulders were exposed, and she had a tight warrior's chest plate across her torso. Her eyes sunk into her skull, almost invisible, but a beauty shone from her skin, a radiance that attracted the attention of all.

Tho, eyes lit, shook with excitement. He reached for her and smiled through the fuzzy, iridescent shards of light spreading in the water and said the two words on everyone's mind: "Lady Trieu."

Chapter 10

The Lady

Sun Quan had returned to the islet and waited against Turtle Tower—a centurion with authority, pacing back and forth at the gate of the palace. He guarded Occupied Hanoi in his own way, not concerned if the Chinese leadership understood his actions. Several patrols called to him—technology not needed—and asked for his assistance with rebel outbreaks. He brushed them off and remained in isolation, staring at the surface of the water. He desired to be there—needed to be there—when the turtle re-emerged from its adventures below, if indeed the strange magic permitted their survival. He doubted it. He would try to slide into the deep. He would never stop trying; unless, he thought, she did return.

Another patrol stopped on the western shore and waved to the giant figure leaning against the moonlit tower. One antagonized glance from Sun Quan sent them on their way without further inquiry.

"Come, my friend. Return. I'm here."

The terracotta warriors backed away. Lady Trieu yelled once into the abyss and swung the mighty sword over her head, causing the water to whirl in a vicious torrent, sweeping away the warriors and disintegrating them to ancient dust particles. History reasserted itself and revealed its lessons once more to the three sojourners. As the dust settled into the depths of the water, the image of Lady Trieu emerged once again. She held the sword by its handle with the tip straight down into the water. She floated with ease as if perfectly in harmony with the ebbs and flows of the lower currents.

"Why have you come here?"

No one replied. Young Minh glanced at Tho for leadership. Lien cowed her neck into her shoulders just a pinch and too yielded authority to the wise and elderly Tho. Age was to be revered, was it not? And Lady Trieu, from a different millennium, earned even more reverence. Too wonderful to speak to. Too marvelous to look upon, yet they couldn't help themselves. Her beauty entranced them. But Tho knew his role—the messenger—the one expected to put it all together—the one who would need ninety years of experience and research to muster the courage to speak into the face of the afterlife. He marveled at her vibrancy, her free spirit, like the power of freedom in the human soul confronting the oppressor, never yielding, always hopeful for the day of deliverance to usher in peace. Tho stood, balancing his weight on the boat resting on the floating turtle, and decided to answer.

"Ba Trieu, we have come to—"

"I'm not talking to you," she cut him off mid-thought, and stroked the top of the giant turtle's head.

The turtle lifted its neck and spoke in a dark voice. "The sword needs to be released once again."

All three of the sojourners jumped back at the audible, intelligible sound coming from the animal's mouth. Minh's eyes flamed in dismay.

"Ma, it spoke."

"Shhh—"

"While the sword remains with us, it is safe, is it not?" Lady Trieu still hadn't glanced back at the three humans yet.

"We all know what safety will bring us," said the turtle. "In a world of danger, a safe course of action may be the most dangerous of all."

"Tell me." Lady Trieu rubbed her hands up and down the blade of the sword.

"They unlocked it."

"These on your back?"

"They may not look like much …"

"They are not even worth looking at yet."

Tho had witnessed many miraculous moments in a life which

had spanned more than nine decades, but the scene in front of him, a turtle (the turtle!) presenting the sword to the great Vietnamese heroine as they talked about the three ordinary people surviving in a bubble on the back of the turtle was something he never could have predicted or seen with his marble tablets. The most remarkable part rang in his ears—an audible conversation between the turtle and the heroine about them. He had wondered if he had died already and had been granted a water burial in the sacred depths of history. But death couldn't have explained the presence of Minh and Lien, so he accepted the miraculous at face value. This value could not have been purchased or bought. It could only have been prayed into fruition.

"They may not look like warriors, but they are the ones who uncovered the truth. He has returned."

Lady Trieu snapped her gaze away from the sword and looked directly into the turtle's eyes. "He is here?"

"Yes."

"Sun Quan?"

"Yes. He is waiting for you above the surface."

Lady Trieu turned her back toward them. She had the form of a young woman of great beauty. Minh watched wide-eyed at her, but her youth was not inexperience or weakness. Her youth sat upon her as a renewal, an eager hope that the present never tells the whole tale, that the future and the past always collide no matter what bargain the next aggressor makes with the demons of the deep. A rightness sat upon her. Almost a righteousness. Earned within the historical record and now free to decide for itself how to proceed because of the foolish action of a long-lost Chinese king and three over-matched Vietnamese idealists.

Tho watched as she floated upward, looking for the one lurking above the surface. She let out a gentle melancholy sigh—like a lover missing her soul mate. She turned again and swam back to the turtle.

"If he has come, it is to settle the score."

"Yes," confirmed the turtle. "Or … maybe even something more."

"And the outcome?"

"The Hans have complete control."

"It's not the first time."

"No, but you must admit, it's the first time they have reached into the past and …"

"Yes. I know," pondered Lady Trieu.

"That's why I brought the sword to you. You're the one they seek. Wisely, I might add."

For the first time, Lady Trieu lifted her gaze from the turtle's eyes and looked through the transparent bubble at the three faces: one of a fit-middle-aged woman, one of a boy transitioning to manhood, and one of the elder sage.

"The turtle trusts you," she spoke to them. "Why have you come?"

"Venerable Lady Trieu." Tho had taken a tiny step forward in the rowboat. "The sacred trust of our nation has been broken. She weeps for her children, bloody and bruised, strewn about like waste with no regard for life or the sacred bond of history."

The eyes of Lady Trieu became glossy, as if she knew the tale he told.

"… and they have not done it with strength or cunning. They have cheated history from us by selling their very souls to the demons who were once under our feet, under our command because of the heroic deeds of the heroes and heroines like yourself who came before us."

"Don't flatter me!" she yelled with spite, sending Minh into a seated position, eyes bulging, lips mum, yet quivering.

"Flattery doesn't erode the truth, and the truth never speaks in flattery. It simply lives," replied Tho, with a sternness in his voice.

"What do you want from me?"

"I saw him, Lady Trieu. Sun Quan. He and he alone holds the grip of fear over our people. We need a warrior who can stand against the arms of history, where all our modern weapons fail. There is a limit to our knowledge. Modern man sees the possibilities in front of him and builds the evilest machines to cause the maximum destruction. It's for our protection, we say. It's for our defense, yet we all know it's only a half-truth. It's also for our aggression, and for our lusty desires. Yet all of the murderous destruction that we show to each other is nothing compared with the arm of history. It is the only way to defeat this tyranny upon our land. In our hour of greatest need, Lady Trieu, we need you once more. Take the sword in your hands and help us fight for the very survival of our nation. We have but one hope, and it is you."

"You said it was Sun Quan? He alone has done this?"

"Yes."

"You're wrong," replied Lady Trieu. "There must be another."

"But who?"

Without warning, arms reached from the depths and grabbed the legs of Lady Trieu. She screamed, unaware of the source, and soon the turtle remained alone in the water with the three still on its back. No one spoke. Everyone froze in a moment of terror. If she could be whisked away without a split-second warning, then what could become of them in the next moment?

They found out. More arms, dotted, like long tunnels of dirt lifted the underbelly of the turtle, flipping it over on its side. The travelers were tossed against the side of the bubble, which shifted back and forth, breaking their fall but not relieving their fears. They screamed in terror as the arms swallowed them on all sides and squeezed the bubble with great pressure. The turtle reached its' neck out and tried to nip the demon arms, but his reach had little effect. The arms continued to crush the bubble, pushing the three humans into a smaller and smaller space over the turtle's shell. They tossed and turned with each push until the feeble walls, thin and worn in the struggle, gave way. Water collapsed upon them, and the three were engulfed by the cold depths, choking them with fear and expunging the remaining oxygen from their lungs. The turtle let out a great yell as the three floated helplessly away from the destroyed haven. Tho looked at Lien. His eyes apologized, but she wouldn't accept it. They had come together, and live or die, they would do so with honor. She reached out for his hand and Tho reached out for Minh, in their last breath, closed their eyes, knowing they had done all they could.

Another arm reached from the deep, but this one held a sword, the sword, and the arm of Lady Trieu rose between them, cutting through the grotesque arms of time and obliterating them. As Tho lifted his gaze for one last look, Lady Trieu stood below them and blew with a torrent of force like an exploding volcano. The underwater current lifted the three through the depths of the lake as if they were rising on top of an ascending pillar. The current pulsed through the surface of the water and spewed the three on the western shore of Hoan Kiem Lake. Each of them felt the force of the shoreline push the water from their lungs. They coughed and sputtered like fish out of water, trying to acclimate to a new environment. Minh breathed first and jumped over to his mother's side.

"Ma, are you alright?"

She opened her eyes and smiled as she placed her hands on his cheeks. She glanced over at Tho, still unresponsive on the ground. Minh pounced first and helped to turn him over. Lien was right behind him, and they lifted his head slightly while saying his name. He coughed several times and opened his eyes. He saw the two faces, alive and happy, over him.

"Mr. Tho, you're all right!"

"Tho, we were worried about you."

"Did you see what Lady Trieu did?" asked Minh. "She saved us. Do you think she's going to help us?"

Tho's face turned quickly from one of contentment to distress as a dark shadow appeared above the two faces. Minh and Lien turned around, gasping loudly as the dark one towered over them.

"You know what to do. Take them," he ordered.

Swarms of Chinese patrolmen grabbed the three and bound, gagged, and blindfolded them. They had no time to scream or express their fear. They were all alone, each in the dark, separated into three different patrol vehicles. Captive.

Chapter 11

The Rooms

Mr. Tho had blacked out. He remembered the undercurrent of water pushing him upward, but nothing more. His eyes opened upon four black walls—shiny, with what seemed to him like light pulses of energy passing through them. But he leaned against one anyway and nothing happened. He noticed he was dry, yet in his own clothes. A black metal table sat a few feet out of his reach. Three of Tho's black marble tablets sat parallel to each other on top of the table. He pondered briefly about the location of the fourth and patted down his clothing to see if he still had it. But his attention turned as a wall opposite him opened straight up into the ceiling creating a rectangular entrance. Sun Quan stepped inside and walked to the middle of the room, towering over the table like an adult would with a doll's tea set.

"Where's the fourth tablet?"

Tho paused and itched the side of his face. "I suppose the same place you found these three."

"Produce it, old man."

"I haven't produced much of anything in the last twenty years."

Sun Quan stepped over the top of the table. His massive feet pinned Tho against the wall.

"Did you see her?" Sun Quan asked. A whisper he tried to hide from the prying walls.

Tho smiled. He remembered her, as unbelieving as his heart felt. Her image rolled over in his mind like a soothing waterfall. "Yes. Yes, I did. I hardly know how to explain it; not that I would to you." The giant didn't reply, nor leave. "I can see it's gotten in your head, such human emotions still eating you alive, knowing she might have a role in this. I find that fascinating."

"You're not afraid of me."

"Why should I be? At my age, what have I to fear? I will say, however, I'm still not fond of pain if that is your inclination."

"I suppose I should thank you," replied Sun Quan.

"Thank me? I would prefer that to chopping off my head. You're welcome."

"Perhaps you're weaker than I thought."

"When you're 94—or is it 95—strength is not a strong suit. I suppose that sounds rather funny."

Sun Quan scoffed—almost a laugh. He turned to leave but added, "You don't know where the fourth tablet is, do you?"

"I haven't the faintest idea. I thought I had them all. Perhaps in the lake."

"You tell the truth."

"Only youth have motive enough for lies. Why would I waste these cracked lips on falsehoods? So tell me the truth; are my friends all right?"

"For now."

Sun Quan exited and the wall closed behind him. Tho pushed himself to his feet with a harsh sigh and took feeble steps to the table. He sat on the edge and lifted the three marble tablets into his palm. "Wherever you went, fourth one, I'm glad you're there. I would not like to see all four in that beast's hands." He lifted his head towards the wall. "Did you hear that? I suppose you did."

After Sun Quan exited the room, he peered at Tho through the transparent walls. A Chinese gentleman stood beside him. He wore a burgundy-colored Mao collared shirt with black trousers. He had a sophisticated air about him, and even though he stood beside Sun Quan, who dwarfed him, the man looked comfortable in the relationship, like he wasn't afraid of getting slapped.

"Why don't you get rid of them? All of them?" he asked the giant without looking upward.

"She will come for them."

"Let's lessen our worry. Get rid of them. She'll come for them either way, but at least we'll have less to worry about."

"Why empower her more?"

"Don't forget how you got here."

A pause drifted between them as they watched Tho leaning against the edge of the table.

"Don't threaten me."

The Chinese man smiled. "Oh, my friend, you know very well we threaten each other."

"Never kill the wise. It makes you unwise."

The Chinese man tapped the glass and laughed. "It seems like the old man's foolish sayings have rubbed off on you. So where is the fourth tablet?"

"Unknown."

The Chinese man removed his glasses and rubbed the lenses against his shirt. "At least there's nothing he can do with only three. Why do you let him keep them?"

"Because it gives him hope. Hope will tell us much more than despair ever would."

The Chinese man shook his head and retrieved an electronic device from his pocket. It had a shiny black touchscreen, which matched the walls.

"Sun Quan, you have an intriguing sentimentality about you. It worries me a little, if I am to be completely honest. You can tempt him with hope if you like, but I'll use this facility the way I had it built. You have to get into their heads and keep them distracted, wondering, fearing the worst."

He pressed out a code and the wall behind Tho became as transparent as a windshield. Tho jerked upward and peered upon another old man, seated in an identical room, palms flat against the floor, exchanging stares with Tho from the other side.

"Who's head are you trying to get into? Tho or the other?"

"Why do I have to choose?"

Tho placed his face against the glass wall and looked carefully. "Can you hear me?"

The other old man nodded his head.

"What's your name?" asked Tho.

"Mr. Tho. It's me. It's Cuong."

Lien had bruised the bottom of her left fist by repeatedly pounding on the sheen sides of the walls. She, too, had found herself alone and dry inside a shiny black-walled room. She yelled for her son and for Tho, but the hollow echoes bounced harmlessly around her.

Lien remembered everything. She replayed in her mind the strange happenings in the depths of Hoan Kiem Lake and being thrown onto shore by the torrent of water blown from the lungs of Lady Trieu. She remembered Sun Quan standing over them until they blindfolded her and drove her around the city to this location. She had never been taken outside. The vehicle had already been inside the building when she exited, and they whisked her into a small compartment and strapped her on a table while hot air surrounded her on all sides, drying her clothes. Then she was thrown into this room where a young Chinese officer removed her blindfold and restraints. She had been alone for hours without food, water, or a place to relieve herself. But she drowned out all physical worries because of her son, whom she yelled for hour after hour. Eventually, the wall opened.

Sun Quan entered, dipping his head beneath the frame of the opening, and Lien backed herself into a corner on the other side of the room. She wasn't afraid, she told herself. Her thoughts often returned to the stories she had heard of her grandmother, who helped Ho Chi Minh's troops drag artillery up the formidable mountains surrounding Dien Bien Phu in early 1954. Her grandmother never complained, spoke only of duty, of freedom for the nation, of sacrifice for the common good as the greatest human deed. She spoke of having little food, open sores, swarms of mosquitoes, walking in torn sandals in the saturated mud, and taking hours to drag a wheel or a lever up a fraction of the mountain, one heroic increment at a time. She imagined the torture, the strained muscles, the desperate cry of a human beast of burden doing what an animal couldn't have done, what the French didn't think possible.

Her grandmother never thought she would survive, but she was ready to give her all to help the Viet Minh position the artillery in impossible places and rain shells down on the French redoubt below. Her grandmother was there. She was part of it. And she witnessed the day of the French surrender, the day that shook the world and ushered in an era of freedom once again for the Vietnamese people. Lien had nothing to complain about. No physical worry could ever rival those of her grandmother, so as Sun Quan entered the room, she felt an excitement; a thrill, actually. Her turn had finally arrived.

"You've been calling for your son."

"Yes, he's a strong boy. But you should know. I won't betray the cause for anyone. Even my son."

"Oh, I know the nature of your patriotism. I admire conviction. The world has an inadequate supply of it."

"What do you want?"

"I want to give you your son back."

"In exchange for what?"

"The answer to a simple question."

"Which is?"

"Did you see her?"

Lien understood of whom he spoke, but she wondered how to respond; not that answering him would have betrayed anything. Would a simple answer bring her son back to her? For what purpose?

"So if I answer that question, I'll have my son back?"

"That question and one more."

"What is the second question?"

"You must answer the first one before you hear the second."

"Are we playing a game? I'm not afraid to die if that's what it takes. By all means necessary to drive you filthy Chinese from our land, you butcherous animals."

Sun Quan patiently smiled. "Did you see her?"

"Yes. What's the second question?"

Sun Quan moved in closer. His eyes intense. "Is she beautiful?"

Lien paused. She had not expected this question. She recalled the countenance of the lady from the lake and gave the description which flowed freely from her lips. "Like a goddess emerging from a lily pond, painted on the wall of a pagoda. Young, beautiful, innocent, true. She spoke like the sound of bells heralding the beginning of time itself. A bosom like no other. Skin as tough as a snake, yet as fragile as the smoothest silk." Lien watched Sun Quan's face fade into the unconscious. He looked far away. "Does that answer your question?"

Sun Quan rubbed his massive right palm in front of his face, his eyes staring at the movement of his hands.

"Where's my son? You said I could have my son."

Sun Quan turned and exited in haste, allowing Lien's hollow words to bounce off his high, broad shoulders. The wall slammed behind him, and Lien ran to it and pounded her fists once again against the wall, blotting out the pain in her mind.

Without warning, the wall to her right retracted into the ceiling, and Minh fell face first into his mother's room.

"Minh!" She ran over and hugged him. "Are you alright, Minh?"

"Ma!"

"Oh, Minh. Did they hurt you? Did—"

"Ma, I have to tell you something."

"Oh, Minh—"

"Ma, when I was in the boat, I reached up and—"

Lien placed her hand over his mouth and glanced around the room nervously. "Minh, don't say anything." She leaned in next to her son's ear. "We have to expect they can understand everything we say, even the faintest whisper. Keep it inside you. Okay? Keep it inside. Tell me when we're out of here. Okay?"

Minh nodded and rested his head against his mother's shoulder.

"You're alright?" she asked him.

"Yes, no one even came to see me. And you, Ma?"

"Don't worry about me. We have my grandmother on our side."

"And Mr. Tho? Have you heard from him?"

"No, nothing."

"I hope he's safe. They wouldn't hurt an old man, would they, Ma?"

"They would hurt anyone for their cause. But we should never worry about Mr. Tho. If there is one thing he hates, it's people worrying about him, especially in the middle of a rebellion."

A whooshing sound wrested their attention. Minh stood up and Lien turned around to see the opposite wall retract into the ceiling, and then one more beyond that. Two old men stared back at them with blank looks as if they indeed had not seen it all. Lien and Minh yelled Tho's name. Lien led the charge through the open space. Minh moved slower, as if his leg had been injured, but he caught up with his mother who had taken Tho by the arm with a hearty welcome. Tho urged them onward into the other man's room and circled around him.

The man on the floor had watery eyes, and he barely looked up at them. Bruises covered the sides of his face.

"What have they done to you? They're animals, beating an elderly man like this," Lien snapped, crouching down beside him.

"No, Auntie Lien," said the old man.

Lien jerked her head back and looked closer at the man's face.

"Yes," said Tho. "This is Cuong."

"Cuong!" exclaimed Minh. "How … ?"

"I don't know how," Cuong breathed heavily. "I became old without warning."

"It's all right. We won't leave you here," said Lien.

"There's nothing we can do," he replied.

"There's always something," added Tho.

"Yes, the tablets. Mr. Tho," said Minh, "Do you still have the marble tablets?"

"I only have three. I must have lost the other."

"Where are they?"

"Over there. On the table." He pointed back to where he had been sitting.

Minh moved quickly toward the tablets with his strange cautious walk. His mother noticed.

"Minh, why are you walking like that?"

"We only have three of the tablets," reminded Tho. "There's nothing we can do."

"Mr. Tho, there's something I have to tell you." He reached for the marble tablets, but before his hand touched them, a jarring alarm pulsed through the rooms, and every retracted wall crashed to the ground, sealing Minh off from the others in a split second. Lien ran to the wall and pounded her already bruised fists once more against the solid black barrier. But to no avail.

The Chinese man surveyed a massive open warehouse with dozens of damaged vehicles. He called to Sun Quan, not with any device, but simply a whispered command through the air. The alarms continued their surround sound, and frantic soldiers ran back and forth contending with competing instructions. Sun Quan appeared out of nowhere at the Chinese man's side to view the cause of the frenetic energy. A dozen armored carriers had been split in two, a clean cut, like a giant laser had melted its way through a stack of butter. The remnants of the vehicles smoldered and radiated intense heat. Chaos encompassed the scene, except for Sun Quan and the Chinese man. They looked on without movement or emotion.

Sun Quan broke the silence and said the unnecessary: "So it begins."

Chapter 12

The Lady of the Night

In the dark of the night, a woman in a black, hooded robe walked along the southern end of Ho Chi Minh's mausoleum. Every other lamp post illuminated the desolate strip in a dim trance. The half-darkness of the re-instated night curfews allowed the quietness of the scene to seep into the idle thoughts of the Chinese patrols. One such young soldier yelled at the woman approaching him.

"Stop. Put your hands up."

The woman, head down, approached the uniform at an unaltered pace. The man called out a second warning and raised his rifle. She didn't flinch. He threatened to shoot, and while still ten feet away, she pounced on the soldier with a tiger fury, knocking him to the ground with a precision strike to the throat. She kicked him in the groin. The rifle fell onto the pavement. She ignored it. He lay a curled-up ball, writhing back and forth. She stepped past him and continued around the edge of the mausoleum's fence, pushing open the door to the courtyard of the One Pillar Pagoda. The thousand-year-old pagoda stood still and austere in the humid night air with high-winged roof tips like that of an ancient ship. A lily pond surrounded it, with slanted wooden support beams hanging over the water's edge.

The woman walked up the stone staircase and removed her slippers. She bowed once and reached into her pocket for several sticks of red incense. She removed a match from her pocket. Water dripped from it. She rubbed it in her fingertips until the match flared, and she lit the five joss sticks and threw the match over the edge into the lily pond. She inserted the sticks vertically into the incense holders on top of an ornate red carved table. She bowed several times to each of the individual altars, then turned to put on her slippers and descend the steps.

As she emerged onto the desolate walkway, the wounded soldier writhed in pain with two other patrolmen attending him. They caught her eye and yelled in the woman's direction. She bolted forward like a burst of wind unleashed from an approaching storm and used each of her arms outright to pummel the chests of the two men, sending them to the ground gasping for air. One reached for his pistol and aimed, but she unsheathed the knife on his belt and stabbed him through the chest before he could pull the trigger. She leaned over the other one still on the ground. He panted in fear and pushed off with his hands trying to escape her. She whispered a low threat.

"Tell Sun Quan I'm here."

She straightened upright and walked behind the edge of the mausoleum. She leaped over the fence with ease and approached the locked entrance. She ripped the handle off the door and entered the dimly lit hall. The remains of Ho Chi Minh—Uncle Ho—embalmed and preserved from his 1969 death, were illuminated inside a glass coffin. She walked to its base, reached into her cloak, and removed a small wooden plaque. She placed the plaque on the coffin and backed away. A round knob had been carved into the shape of a bronze drum. On one side were names written in *Chu Nom*—the ancient Vietnamese script. The flip side had the same names written in *Quoc Ngu*—the Romanized national language from the 17th century. There were many names: Hung Kings, Le Loi, Le Thai To, Trung Sisters, Quang Trung. All the names were written in gold lettering except one. It alone had been written and underlined in blood red: Ba Trieu.

Lady Trieu removed her hood and bowed in respect. Footsteps

approached. Soldiers filled the hall from both entrances, rifles aimed and cocked upon the single lady, who didn't flinch.

"Hands up."

She complied. She raised both hands over her head and stated in a low tone: "There's nothing more precious than independence and freedom."

She swung her arms to the side and a blinding flash of light engulfed the hall and backed the soldiers into a step-tied frantic retreat. When the light evaporated, they pulsed forward to arrest her but found themselves aiming their rifles at each other. She had vanished.

When the lights went out and the siren released the vertical collapsing walls separating Minh from the others, a strip of emergency light illuminated the base of the wall just enough for Minh to see the three marble tablets sitting on the table where Tho had left them. Minh concentrated and tried not to feel the anxiety of separation from his mother. Something more immediate pressed on his mind. He closed his eyes and slid his hand inside the back of his pants. It ran down along his buttocks, and with his index finger and thumb, spread his cheeks apart to reach inside. He breathed with caution in the squeamish moment, but he had resolved to do whatever was necessary. He thought of his great-grandmother, whom he had never met. But he knew the stories and the sacrifice. He thought of her pain and the daily struggle she endured as he reached further inside his resolve and felt for the piece. He felt the hard edge and pulled it out slowly—its edges rubbing harshly along his insides. With one final tense yell, he retrieved the marble tablet from his buttocks and held it up in front of him. During the frantic moments in the lake, when the water tossed them from the turtle and Lady Trieu blew them upwards in a whirlpool onto the shore, he had seen the tablet slip away from Tho, and with great concentration had grabbed it in his hands before being cast upward. When he arrived on the shore with Sun Quan towering over him, he inserted it without thinking into the only place he thought it might be safe. Where the Sun couldn't see it. An instinctive reaction to the way he had been raised. No sacrifice too great and no action too small for the cause of freedom. For the cause of country. It had been stuck inside him for hours, but now he clasped it between his fingers, and the smell didn't bother him.

The siren continued. He didn't have much time, so he concentrated only on what was in front of him. "Why worry about things you can't see?" his mother would often say, no doubt some iteration of what she had learned from Tho.

He placed the tablet parallel to the other three and shifted them in order so the scrolled line across the middle of them matched perfectly.

"What do I do with them?"

Silver shavings. That's what Tho used. But he had no silver. Then he remembered the time Tho simply chanted without the silver. But what? What should he say? He barely noticed the pulsing siren around him.

"Come, spirit." He shook his head. "From the bronze drum to the …" He yelled out in disgust. "Le Thai To. The two Trung sisters … ah …" He couldn't remember anything.

He placed all four tablets in his palms on top of each other. He lifted them straight up above his head, as if presenting them as a sacrifice.

"Lady Trieu. The maiden of the lake. Take up the sword returned to you. Help us once more."

A rumble shattered his concentration. A cold gasp of air sent chills through his body as he looked for something that wasn't there. The walls shook slightly and a shadow appeared over him. Tall and foreboding. His thoughts went to Sun Quan. He was sure of it. He turned, but the darkness shifted and disappeared in the blackness of the wall. He moved toward the wall beside him, but another shadow whirled him around in circles until he stood face to face with an image of a woman, translucent on the surface of the polished black stone wall. The woman appeared young and wore leather straps along her tender shoulders. Her hair fluttered freely like it blew in the wind.

"Minh," said the apparition. "Am I beautiful?"

Her chest drew his eyes and paralyzed him. He couldn't answer as his intoxication wrested his body away from reality.

"Are you so easily swayed by beauty? Then how will you fight the ugliness, Minh?"

He gazed on her face as one who gazes at the marvels of a statute coming to life. It was her, from the water.

"Don't let them have the tablets. Run, Minh. Run."

He looked around, still locked inside the four walls.

"Where do I run?"

"Run, Minh. Be the man you think you are."

"But—"

The wall behind him lifted, and he ran without thinking into the next room. The wall closed behind him as the next one opened in front of him. He held the four tablets as tightly as he could. He wanted to run faster, but her beauty haunted him, and he longed to gaze on her again, hoping her reflection would be in every ascending wall. He searched for her and leaned his back against one of the walls, calling, "Lady Trieu. I need to see you again." The wall gave way into the ceiling, and he fell backwards, losing his balance; all four marble tablets slipped from his hand. They scattered on the floor, and he sprawled out on his chest reaching for them, but the wall smashed downwards, nipping the tip of his middle finger. He jolted backwards into the seated position. Once again, he only had one of the tablets." He stood up and pounded on the wall. "Open, you damn wall! Lady Trieu!" The wall didn't listen, but he heard a voice. "Run." "But I only have one." "Run!" He turned and sprinted the other way. Another wall opened and he ran through. Then one more. He could feel the soreness inside his buttocks. He thought of the three isolated marble tablets but he controlled what he could. "Endure." "Be the man." "Be the man you think you are."

He stopped waiting for the walls to open. He simply ran at full speed with faith the walls would open in time. At last, the final wall revealed a wide-open space as part of a massive warehouse. He paused to witness the unsettling scene—smoldering armored vehicles on one side with a towering figure standing beside a Chinese man on the other side. Their eyes locked, and Minh let out a cry—not that of a man or warrior—but of a scared child. Sun Quan moved toward him at great speed and would have overtaken him in a second, but a shadow clipped the back of his shoulders and sent him sprawling to the floor.

"Run!" he heard himself yell internally. He took off in the other direction and slipped out a side door into the night air. He dove through a row of thick hedges and slipped through a narrow metal wall. If he had been a full-grown man, he wouldn't have fit through the wrought iron. He panted and looked both ways, finally recognizing the street. The old French houses gave it away. He was northwest of the old city, not far from Ba Dinh Square and the Ho Chi Minh Mausoleum. He fled down the street, hiding behind massive trees and parked cars whenever a vehicle passed by. The only place he knew to go was the Old Quarter.

A few dogs barked as Minh rapped against the door behind locked metal gates. He knocked again, looking around with an air of guilt. The small side street afforded him some protection from prying eyes. He had just been there the day before. Was it the day before? He had trouble remembering the date or the day or the last time he had slept. He rapped again, this time louder.

A light flickered and a middle-aged woman opened the wooden door.

"Auntie Huong."

"Minh? Where did you come from?" She opened the padlock on the metal gate and whisked him inside, locking everything behind her. "Where's your mother and Tho?"

"He still has them?"

"Who?"

"The Chinese giant. Sun Quan."

"He has them?"

"I escaped. I need to know how to get to the resistance."

"Shhhh—" She motioned him back further into the house, and they retreated to an internal room without any windows to the outside.

"What's going on?"

"I remembered you saying your husband was in the resistance. How can I contact them?"

"Minh, I have no way to contact him. I haven't heard from him in months."

"Do you know any way? Anyone? I'm desperate. I—"

"You look exhausted."

"Your father-in-law. We saw him. We got a boat from him. We— You won't believe the things I've seen. I have to get word to the underground. To the resistance. Do you have any way?"

She paused for a moment. "All right. First, sleep. Lie on this sofa. Here."

"Auntie Huong!"

"Now, Minh. The best thing you can do is preserve your energy. You're gonna need it. I'll get word to my father-in-law. I'll see what we can do. Are your mother and Tho all right?"

"I can't think about such things right now. That's out of my control. I have to do what I can only."

Huong smiled. "You don't seem like the little boy I saw just yesterday."

"I'm all grown up now."

"Almost," said Huong, pushing him into the sofa. "But even grown-ups need sleep. Do it!"

Chapter 13

A Skirmish and an Escape

Tho, Lien, and Cuong each rested against their respective black walls.

"How long have we been here?" asked Lien.

Cuong coughed. "For me, about seventy years."

"I'm sorry, Cuong."

"We all are," added Tho.

Lien hated the tears in her eyes. Frivolous. Meaningless emotion, but even her will couldn't stop a few from escaping, and as they did, she thought it better to grieve the butchery than to accept it.

"Lien, Minh is resourceful. You taught him well."

She nodded, wiped her cheek, and fanned her face with her palm, pretending she felt hot.

"I still don't know why they haven't killed me," said Cuong. "But now that you're both here, I suppose the reasons are even fewer to keep me alive."

"Cuong, don't—"

"No, it's all right. I can't live in this body."

Tho laughed and peeked down at his saggy skin on frail bones. "I understand that sentiment well. But don't lose hope, son. Your age is only on the outside. Mine, however, is soul-deep."

Lien closed her eyes and put her head back against the wall. "He's just a boy."

"He's a brave boy," said Cuong. "I saw what he did on the street when we were looking for …" He stopped and glanced at Tho. "I forgot what we were actually looking for. Did you succeed?"

"We will soon find out," replied Tho. "But the stories we could tell you."

"Tell me, please."

"Not yet. The less you know, the better. Besides, you may not believe us. They're too fantastical to even ponder."

As they talked, the shadow of the woman who had clipped Sun Quan and instructed Minh to run appeared in their midst, like a theatrical cue had come to turn. There was no mystical fog or grand entrance, just being. Just there. In between them all, more radiant than real. Their eyes simply adjusted to her like they would to a darkened room after walking in from the piercing sunlight. Lien jumped to her feet. Tho pushed back with his palms and sat at attention. Cuong shook his head a couple times, afraid he hallucinated. The woman played every bit the part of a warrior. Her hair knotted behind her neck. Sword strapped to her back. Dagger on her leather belt.

"Ong Tho." She revered him with her language, and she bowed her head in reverence. "You do not understand your lineage, do you?"

Tho rubbed his chin under the white strands of his beard, which pointed downward from his face. "I … I'm afraid to speak. These walls have ears."

"Do not worry. Do you know your lineage?"

"I … I do not understand your question."

"What do you know of your family?"

"My grandmother was a farmer. She married my grandfather at age sixteen and two decades later moved to Hanoi to open a small silver shop."

"And who was your great-grandmother on your mother's side?"

"My great-grandmother?"

"Do you know?" the warrior asked.

"She came from a farming community. Her family grew rice. That is all."

"So a simple man with a farming heritage grows into a sage of the mystical arts?"

"No…I—"

"Have you ever wondered why the heavens gifted your hands with such deeds?"

"I never considered anything I did as special. I simply …" He paused.

"You simply what?"

"Whatever I was given by my ancestors, I have tried to use

honestly, without any favor for myself or family. If I—"

"Yes, I can see that."

"What do you want, Lady Trieu? I'm an old man. My time here is over. I know that."

"Lady Trieu?" Cuong responded, his eyes unwavering from her visage.

"Your time is not yet over, Ong Tho. Your great-grandmother never married."

Tho looked astonished. "No. That's not true."

"She had a child, who grew up to be an ordinary farmer, yet from an extraordinary background."

"I don't understand."

"Your mother was a mistress. But not as you think. She was sent into hiding, and her story was lost to the past, even from those who lived it."

"What story?" Tho had pushed himself up, and he pleaded with her with his arms stretched in her direction.

"Your great-grandfather was Tu Duc."

Tho's thoughts wandered far off. The words Tu Duc flipped through his mind as if he fingered through the pages of history.

"Tu Duc?"

Lady Trieu didn't answer.

"Emperor Tu Duc?"

"The final Vietnamese emperor before the French corrupted the lineage. You alone remain from that line. Your blood traces back through time."

Tho breathed heavily. "That's impossible. My grandmother grew rice."

"You know this to be true. You can feel it, can't you? This is why you're still alive; your ancestors have been hoping for this day when we would find each other."

"I—" The old man, who always had a wise comeback or pithy saying, was speechless.

"You are the chosen overseer of the line. Fate's choice to help us through this one great challenge. Without you, honorable Tho, I wouldn't be here. And for us to achieve our goal, you must leave this place."

"How can we leave?" asked Lien. "We're stuck here. And my son ..."

"Minh. He is free."

"He's free? Can we get to him?"

"Not now. It's far too dangerous."

"How can we leave?" asked Lien. "We're inside this prison."

"Walls always have two sides. You just need a little help to get to the other."

"But—"

Tho barely heard their conversation. He sifted through the years and wondered of its veracity. His mother had never spoken a word of it. Not even a hint. But how could he doubt the words of the resurrected Lady Trieu standing in front of him?

"If my time isn't yet over, then where do we go?"

"Take the marble tablets back to the beginning."

"But I don't have the tablets anymore."

She reached into a sachet on her belt, and handed the three marble tablets to Tho.

"Take these back to the beginning."

"Where did you find them?"

"Minh used them to summon me. But he lost them again as he escaped."

"Is he alright?" asked Lien with vigor.

"He still has one. Take these to the beginning."

"The beginning?"

"You will know."

"How will only three help me? I've always had four and—"

"Those on the cusp of survival will find a way."

"And how ...?"

Before he could raise the question of their method of escape, all of the walls lifted into the ceiling. They were alone in a cavernous hall. Fifty yards in front of them was the warehouse and Sun Quan. The warrior turned directly towards them. Lady Trieu squared in his direction and reached behind her to retrieve the sword. She held it downward with its tip resting on the floor. Lien scooted to the other side of Lady Trieu.

"Exit behind me."

"But we can't leave Cuong here," said Lien.

"Go," Cuong said. "I can't help anyone now."

"Do what he says," said Lady Trieu, without looking back. "Leave Cuong here."

"But—"

"Leave him. His time hasn't come yet."

"What?" asked Lien.

"Lien," said Tho. "Everything has a purpose. Even a young man's lame legs. The spirit doesn't need legs to walk."

"Leave now!" Lady Trieu yelled. It became apparent why. Sun Quan had moved steadily towards her and was now only ten yards away.

Lien grabbed Tho's hand, and they retreated as quickly as the old man could move. Cuong watched them and then turned his head back to the mysterious figures facing each other.

"You are even bolder than I imagined."

Lady Trieu didn't respond.

"The sword … you have the sword. I expected that."

"The fools have no idea what they've done by releasing you, do they?" Lady Trieu stood firm.

"My dear Trieu, that is not true. They know precisely what they have done. That, my dear, should make you very frightened."

"I know there is more. There has to be."

"We all have parlor tricks."

"I have never been afraid of you."

"So you help them escape, but do you not think I can find them again? The old man? The boy? What vain games you play! But if we shall play games, let's play them together."

He pulsed forward, and she swung her sword past his head as his arms grabbed her around the waist and pushed her downward, almost crushing Cuong at the rear. The old man rolled over as much as he could, while the two wrestled. She still gripped the sword and loosened her grip long enough to gash Sun Quan across the back. He released her and reached around to touch the wound. He yelled as the sword passed by his head, but this time he stopped it in his bare hand—not without pain—but his hand had swollen into a writhing ball of light, which threw the sword out of her grip. It glided along the floor several yards away. The physical blows coming from both of them only affected the other in minimal ways, like an irritation, not a mortal wound. She lunged toward the sword as he unlatched a sharp dagger from his belt. He sliced her three times on the leg, but she moved without flinching and took the sword into her hands, stood to her feet and pointed it at him. She didn't say anything.

"You're weak," he said.

"The weak will be made strong by time and energy."

"Two things you have very little of."

He moved towards her. "Cuong," she said. "Do not give in to your thoughts of despair."

"Always the encourager," Sun Quan smiled. "She thinks you still have a purpose."

"We all have a purpose," she said. "To vanquish you for good."

She turned and ran the opposite direction of Tho and Lien. She ran directly toward the Chinese man, her sword out and focused on him. Sun Quan shifted forward and tried to stop her, but her sword slashed him across the chest, giving her just enough time to bring the sword around and impale the Chinese man through the stomach, splattering blood and entrails all over the floor. The man fell to the ground and convulsed as she turned back toward him.

"This is what you can expect, Sun Quan."

"Oh, my dear Trieu. It is exactly what I hoped for."

The Chinese man screamed, but as Sun Quan's shadow covered the dying man, the blood reversed, and crawled back inside him. He put his arms out to stabilize himself, then lifted himself to his feet and stood beside Sun Quan, unharmed, as if nothing had happened. He peered at the lady from the lake with great curiosity, and he lit a cigarette as if he relaxed at home in his living room.

"So this is the one you have spoken of?" he asked without any regard to the stabbing he had just experienced. "She's spectacular."

"What are you?" Trieu asked the Chinese man.

The Chinese man laughed. "Do you doubt my humanity? All humanity is to be very much doubted these days. Ask my friend here to see if he agrees."

"Friend is too generous a word," said Sun Quan.

"Indeed. Shall we say beneficiary. So now what do we do? A

beautiful standoff. I do love it."

Lady Trieu backed away a step. Lien and Tho had disappeared from sight as had all of the Chinese soldiers. The three of them remained with only a lonely Cuong sitting immobilized at the center of a grand hall as company.

Sun Quan reached his right arm out sideways and opened his palm. A dagger-axe on a wooden pole flew toward him out of the darkness of the walls, and he grasped it firmly in his hand. The axehead had a sharp blade with the image of a dragon on its reverse side. He raised it over his head.

"I'm almost disappointed this has been so easy. I didn't expect you to be so weak. But I guess that's what centuries in the water will do to you."

He swung the dagger-axe at her. It caught the leather strapping around her chest, but she turned in time. It missed her stomach. Her sword crossed in front of her, knocking the dagger-axe away. She lunged forward toward the Chinese man, who this time moved and pulled a pistol from his pocket. He shot twice and ripped two holes into her right shoulder, before it started to close up and heal itself. But it had slowed her down. The dagger-axe swung at her again and dug into her left side before she pulled away, ripping a side of her flesh open. It remained that way as she screamed once, lurched backwards, and twirled away from her attacker towards the destroyed armored carriers.

"Close them," said Sun Quan to the Chinese man, who punched out a code on his device.

The walls crashed down in front of Lady Trieu, and she would have run head first into the solid wall, but the structure transformed to a wall of moving water. It shifted fluidly and Lady Trieu dove head first into the water and disappeared. Sun Quan pulsed forward and attempted to pass through the water wall, but as Sun Quan touched it, it repelled him backwards, not unlike the water of Hoan Kiem Lake. The Chinese man emptied the rest of his rounds into the water over Sun Quan's left shoulder. Then he laughed. The water turned back to the smooth, glossy black walls, and as Sun Quan approached it, it opened on command into the next empty cell.

Lady Trieu drifted downward in the center of Hoan Kiem Lake.

Her bullet wounds had disappeared completely, but she held her side, still ripped open by the dagger-axe. The head of the turtle emerged from the deep.

"They've escaped," she said.

Her side didn't bleed; there was just an emptiness. An openness that upset her. The turtle reached his head out, opened its mouth, and licked the wound with its tongue. Lady Trieu closed her eyes as the turtle attended to her in the quietness of the lake.

Chapter 14

Separate Journeys

L ien and Tho exited the massive hall and burst onto a street only two blocks from Ho Chi Minh's Mausoleum—still very much behind enemy lines. They dove into the first alley they crossed and rested against a house's cement wall behind a garbage dumpster.

"How are you feeling, Mr. Tho?"

"I wish my legs were as sharp as my mind. And I wish my mind were as sharp as my wit."

"What should we do?"

"I feel tired," he said, slumping down farther on the wall.

"What did she mean, go back to the beginning? The beginning of our journey? To the lake?"

"No. I think not. Farther still. I believe she means back to the original Vietnamese kings."

"The Hung kings?"

"Yes. They predated everything. Before one single Han ever stepped into our land, the Hung kings ruled in the bronze age. The bronze drum proves everything."

"Well, how can we find the Hung kings? They're long dead as far as I know," said Lien, throwing her arms in the air. "But hey, I thought Lady Trieu was dead too. And the turtle. And don't get me started on the terracotta warriors. This has been quite the experience."

Tho chuckled through a raw cough. "We'll go to Den Hung, the Hung Temple."

"In Viet Tri? That's northwest of here. Almost fifty miles. How would we get there? And what about Minh? How are we going to find him?"

Tho smacked his lips and yawned. "The little I used to know has been dwarfed by the greater amount I don't know."

"And Tho. Is it true what she said? You come from a royal line?"

He simply shook his head slightly out of exasperation and

chuckled in silence. He leaned his head against the side of the cement wall and fell fast asleep. Lien leaned against him and placed her head on his shoulder. They would take every respite given to them.

The deep sleep came to an abrupt halt when the beeping sound of a truck backing up awakened them. It reversed to the edge of the alley and stopped two feet short of the dumpster. The stench made them both stand up and cover their noses. They had nowhere to run, so they waited for fate to decide who would step out of the cab to confront them.

"Mr. Tho, look!" The license plate on the back of the truck had the words Phu Tho. "That's where Viet Tri is! Do you suppose?"

The cab door opened and out popped a middle-aged Vietnamese woman. "That's a strange place to be standing," she said to them.

"I see you're from Phu Tho. Are you going there?"

"I make a run every day. I took over my husband's job when he, well … he's gone. And with the Chinese bringing services back to order, I come down here every day and remove all of this crap."

Tho and Lien looked at each other and smiled.

"Can we ride with you to Viet Tri?"

"There's no way. They'll arrest me if I take anyone else. I took a young man with me one day and they ripped him out of the truck at a checkpoint and accused him of being a spy and beat him within an inch of his life. Of course, he was a spy. But anyway, no. You can't ride with me. Although you sure don't look like spies. But I suppose that's what spies look like. Not like spies. Oh, you know what I mean."

"How about in the back?" said Lien, pointing to the garbage compacter.

The woman cocked her head and looked at them queerly. "You want to ride in there? With all that shit?"

"Please?"

"You're begging me to ride in garbage?"

"It would mean so much," added Lien.

"This war has done some screwy things, but desperate times I guess. I got like three more stops."

"We don't care," said Tho.

"I'll be dumping garbage on top of you."

"That's fine," said Lien.

"It's your grave. If they discover you back there, it's not on me. I never saw you."

"We agree."

"Hop in!"

Minh slept solid the rest of the night and woke up in Ms. Huong's modest home with two other gentlemen waiting for him—Huong's father-in-law, whom he had met at the temple before their adventure in the lake, and a short man in his mid-thirties. Minh's backside still bothered him, but he felt refreshed, except for the nagging, persistent worry for his mother and Tho.

The small man introduced himself as Mr. Hung—meaning hero. He had a simple confidence about him, bordering on cockiness. Minh told them the story—not all of it, lest they think him a lunatic—but enough about the Chinese and the mysterious warrior to make it believable. Minh never mentioned the giant's name, again so they didn't balk at the story.

"That's quite a tale. Quite a tale. Very difficult for a young teen like you to get anywhere near the rebel HQ. A story won't do as an entrance ticket. You must have proof. Something to convince them to let you through."

Minh thought for a moment then reached into his right pocket and pulled out the marble tablet. "I'll show them this. One of the tablets which helped us."

Hung's eyes lit up and reached for the tablet, but Minh recoiled his arm.

"I've heard of Mr. Tho's tablets. Who hasn't in the Old Quarter?"

"Would this help me get through? To find the resistance?"

"Perhaps."

"So you can help me? You can take me there?"

"I know where the resistance is," bragged Hung. Huong's father-in-law admonished him to speak softer. "I've been there, you know. If you want to go, I can take you. It won't be easy. We will need a great many resources. But, let's not talk of that. This is an important matter. I'll do it. I'll take you this evening."

Minh didn't know what to think of the man. "Are you part of their network," he asked Mr. Hung.

"No, no. I'm a school teacher."

"Why aren't you fighting with the resistance? There aren't many men your age left in the city."

Hung smiled and rubbed his hands in front of him as if he just finished a big, satisfying meal. "I fight my own way. The Chinese think I help them, but I'm always one step ahead of them. Whatever you do in life, keep a quick foot about you, and stay one footstep ahead, I always say."

"So you'll take me? I must speak to the Vietnamese resistance leaders as soon as possible."

"Yes, yes, my boy. I can take you there."

Huong's father-in-law spoke up. "I've known Mr. Hung for many years. You can trust him."

Minh nodded. "How would we get there?"

Hung put both hands on his forehead and rubbed it in circular massaging motion. "Let me see. Meet me at the pylon of the Long Bien Bridge at dusk. Once across the river, your ride will await you."

"Aren't you going with me?"

"That's what I mean. Our ride will await us."

Tho and Lien nestled themselves in the middle of the stack of garbage under the covered truck. Lien gagged as the driver used the hydraulics to pick up the dumpster's contents and fling it right behind them. Lien thought of her grandmother once again. Was this how bad it was? Enduring rotting stench? Overcoming the human desires for a bigger goal? She gagged again and almost threw up. Tho laughed.

"Oh, I've been complaining of my diminished olfactory system for decades, but I've finally come to realize there are advantages." Lien gagged again. "Close your eyes, Lien. Breathe slowly. Focus on the darkness. Focus on your peace."

Her peace erupted three times as she hurled all the contents of her stomach, and some she didn't even know she had, into the midst of the rest of the garbage piled around her.

The truck pulled out. It had no trouble passing the check point at the Thang Long Bridge leading out of the city to the north. No guard even bothered investigate the back of the truck because the stench kept everyone at a distance.

Tho and Lien rattled and shook in the back for well over an hour. Lien had nothing more to vomit, but it didn't prevent her from gagging. The truck came to a stop along a stretch of trees a couple miles outside the town of Viet Tri. The woman pounded on the back of her cab and yelled for them to exit. Lien didn't have to be told twice. She sloshed her way to the back and jumped down onto the pavement. She fell and scraped open her pant leg on the right knee. But she didn't care. She could breathe fully again, and she took in the open air as if a cleansing shower.

"Lien?"

She had nearly forgotten about her companion. "Sorry, Mr. Tho. Let me help you." She reached up to help the old man down out of the filth and onto the ground. They walked around the back corner of the truck and onto the sides of the road filled with overgrown grasses. Brown sludge and soaking wet filth covered from head to toe. The woman opened the cab door and stepped down.

"You can't go any farther," she said, holding her nose. "You'll have to go on foot from here."

Tho nodded. "Thank you."

The woman rolled her eyes as if the guilt of staring at the disheveled man had started to eat away at her harsh exterior. "Where do you need to go?"

"Hung Temple."

She let out a sigh. "Pilgrimage? At a time like this?"

"It's not a pilgrimage, it's …" Lien didn't finish her sentence. "Thank you for your help."

The woman turned to climb back in the cab but stopped. "Why would you two endure a ride to Viet Tri in the back of a garbage truck?"

"Perhaps it was always a dream of ours?" Tho laughed and coughed at the same time.

The woman let out another befuddled cry. "What's up with you two?"

"It's important that we get to the Hung Temple."

"Temples are a great place to find peace," the woman said. "… and feel free."

"And there's nothing more precious than independence …" Lien stopped and looked at the woman. Almost daring her to finish the sentence. It had become a common plea, using Ho Chi Minh's words as a battle cry of sorts to link people together. To remind each other of their common cause.

"And freedom," said the woman. "All right." Her gruff agreement was followed by a what-in-the-world sigh. "Hide down over the bank there. I'll be back with some new clothes for you. And I'll find you a ride to the temple. Wait here. Out of sight."

"Thank you."

"No," the woman cut them off. "No thanks needed when we're playing on the same team."

Minh left Huong's house an hour before sunset. She had fed him well and forced him to rest while eking out every bit of the story from the previous day. It all seemed too amazing to believe, but it convinced Huong to support such a perilous trip into the countryside to find the rebel base—even for a thirteen-year-old.

Minh edged his way through the Old Quarter, using every type of hiding spot available to avoid the Chinese patrols. Fortunately, the Old Quarter has an endless supply of trees to hide behind, convoluted alleyways to slip into, and myriad houses, which would gladly hide a boy without question.

He eventually walked onto the railroad tracks which take the Long Bien Bridge out of the city. He knew the bridge itself would be blocked, so he slipped through an alley a few blocks from the bridge and climbed along the edge of a bank below the tracks, making his way to the first pylon still on dry ground under the bridge. When Minh arrived, no one was there, and he rested against the pylon facing the river, out of sight of anyone who might happen to look down. He held the fourth marble tablet securely in his right pants pocket and thought of his mother and Tho, wondering their whereabouts. He knew they were alive. It was the only option his mind allowed him. A noise startled him out of his thoughts, and he stood up. Mr. Hung walked around the edge of the pylon with a smile on his face, as if meeting a long-lost friend without there being a war to complicate life.

"The boy made it."

"So how do we cross the river?"

"It's all arranged. Don't worry."

"Well, let's go."

Hung stood two inches shorter than the thirteen-year-old. "There's just one thing we have to discuss."

"What's that?" Minh felt an uneasiness in his chest.

"The money."

"What money?"

"You didn't think I'd take you on a dangerous journey without compensation, did you?"

"You didn't mention anything about money before. You just said you'd be happy to take me."

"And I am happy to take you. As long as you have the money."

"I don't have any money."

"That's unfortunate." Mr. Hung circled Minh and looked him over. "What do you have?"

"I don't have anything. I just need to get to …" He stopped. He realized he had raised his voice, and he looked upward at the underside of the trestles and steel beams which crisscrossed every which way.

"All right. Mr. Hung is a man of his word. I'll take you. For sure. In exchange, you can give me the marble tablet you spoke of earlier."

"No, I'll never give you that tablet. It doesn't belong to me."

"Well, you have to give me something."

"I promise. At some point, I'll give you what you want, but I don't have anything now."

"You have the tablet, and that's enough."

Hung came a step closer.

"How are we crossing the river?"

"First payment."

"How do I know there's even a way across the river?"

"Fair enough. Here. See!" Hung climbed to the top of a small sand bar and pointed to the right. Minh goose-necked out and saw a small rowboat, flapping in the current of the Red River. "It's right here. There's a motorbike waiting for you on the other side of the bridge. He'll take you there."

"I promise I'll pay you," said Minh. "Just get me across."

"Promises mean nothing when Hanoi is occupied by the Chinese. I want the tablet."

Hung became more aggressive and moved towards Minh.

"Get away from me."

"Give me the tablet."

Minh backed away further.

"Leave me alone."

"Don't be a fool, boy."

Hung grabbed the boy by the arm and started patting him down. Minh pulled away and slapped Hung on the arm. Hung made a fist and punched the boy in the stomach, sending him to the sand.

"Give me the tablet."

Hung came at him but Minh sideswiped him with his right leg, knocking the attacker off balance. Hung screamed and turned over like a wild beast. He punched Minh in the eye and sat on top of him hitting him repeatedly. He patted down his right pocket and reached in to pull out the tablet. Hung climbed off the boy and laughed, holding the tablet up in front of him. Before he could begin to walk away, a large dead branch whacked the small man across the side of the head. Minh stood behind him holding the limb and breathing heavily. Hung lay on the ground dazed and semi-unconscious. The tablet had slid free and lay to the rear of the man. Minh picked it up.

"Boy, you don't know what you're doing."

"Yes, I do."

He hit Hung again with the branch before throwing it off to the side. He ran down the sand bar and climbed into the rowboat; after all, he had experience with such vessels. He pushed off into the slow-moving current of the Red River.

Chapter 15

Into the Nest

Minh struggled against the current and landed on the east side of the Red River, a hundred yards south of the Long Bien Bridge. As he climbed out of the boat, a gunshot pierced the wooden hull. Minh flipped backwards onto the ground and backpedaled with his body like a slithering crab. Another shot hit the dirt near him. The rifleman sat on the bridge between the metal trusses. He fired again. Minh ran towards the bridge, jumping down behind scraggly bushes and any available rock outcropping. He had to get to the north side of the bridge. He considered climbing the bank and making his way from there, but before he could make a decision, a motorbike sped at him from under the bridge. He couldn't tell who was driving it. Two more shots followed after the speeding bike, which skidded to a stop on the banks of the river. "Get on." Minh didn't hesitate. He straddled the bike and the driver accelerated towards the bridge, weaving and swerving as much as possible. Minh tucked his head behind the back of the man or boy or teen—he still hadn't gotten a good look. It could even have been a Chinese patrol being shot at by the rebels for all he knew. The motorbike sped under the bridge and ascended a steep trail on the other side. It crested over the top of the bank and flew into a back-alley residential area. The driver didn't stop, swerving past chickens and parked cars and roadside hawker stalls still shuttered from the lock down.

After a few moments of hanging on for his life, the bike flew across an empty main road, clamped down by a Chinese checkpoint only fifty yards away. The bike continued unabated and drove onto another small feeder road at the highest possible speed. A rumbling followed them. Minh looked back. A stripped-down armored carrier bounded after them. It was light and quick. A soldier stood behind the driver and braced himself with his hands on a mounted rifle. He fired several wide shots. Minh cringed and ducked his head farther with each sound. He clung to the driver like a parachute strapped to a skydiver. He wanted to pull the cord and have the parachute coast him to safety, but his back was exposed to the gravest threat at the highest speed after the craziest day. Mother and Tho seemed light years away. Even the marble tablet paled in significance, but he prayed it remained in his pocket. The driver tilted his head back towards Minh, "Hold on tight," as if tighter were an actual option. But he tried sinking his fingers farther into the driver's ribs. The bike charged up an embankment and soared off the edge—floating in the air for a moment—before crashing to the ground with a thud and landing on a narrow walking path on top of a rice paddy ridge. The bike roared with precision along the edge. Minh glanced back to see the Chinese vehicle careening over the embankment and landing vertically in a small waterway. The men climbed out of the vehicle and aimed their rifles from the edge of the paddy. The shots reverberated into the distance, but the motorbike had disappeared into the wild of a Vietnamese rice field.

After another thirty minutes of knuckle-clenched fast driving— the motorbike driver didn't slow any after losing its tail—the bike came to an abrupt stop at the base of two hills with banana trees fanning out on both sides.

"Wait here."

Minh dismounted the bike.

"Here?"

"Yes."

The bike took off in the same direction it had come from. Minh wondered what the prudent action was. Few options revealed themselves in the midst of banana trees. He tucked himself up under one of the curved leaves to wait. For what? He didn't know. There weren't even ripe bananas. That would have been too convenient. He breathed heavily for a moment, just long enough for reality to sink in. He sat in isolation once again. The smooth black walls had disappeared, but others loomed over him. Walls of uncertainty. Fear of the unknown. Fear of what had happened to Tho and his mother. He remembered the bullets whizzing past him. He could very easily be dead at this moment. A tear formed in the corner of his eye, but he didn't welcome it. It angered him.

"Stop. You're not a baby."

He stood up and flung his arms wide in a warrior's stance.

"You're a man now. Act like it."

He released an angry growl and proceeded to kick his leg into the air in a fierce, martial arts move, but the tip of his toe caught the side of the banana tree, and he fell face-first into the matted grass. As he opened his eyes, two feet stood right in front of him. Small feet in rubber sandals. Then a voice.

"You're a boy."

He looked up and quickly rose to his feet.

"You're a girl."

She was about his height. She wore a green cap and camouflage jacket and pants.

"I'm just going to leave you here." She turned around and began walking up the hill.

"Wait."

"This is a waste of time."

"Wait, I need to see the rebel leaders."

She turned and threw an angry look in his direction. "Why don't you just send off fireworks and give up our location?"

"Sorry. Who are you? Am I supposed to go with you?"

"I was supposed to meet up with an important informant. Not some snotty-nosed boy."

"I'm more than that." Minh gathered himself and ran towards her. "You can't leave me in a banana tree grove. Who are you, anyways?"

"I can leave you wherever I want." She kept walking. "Don't

follow me."

"But I have important information."

"Well, tell it to the bananas, if you think it's that appealing."

"I'm serious."

"So am I!"

She crested over the top of the hill and jumped onto a parked motorbike and kick-started it. "Go back home."

"I can't. Listen to me. It's Lady Trieu. Lady Trieu!"

The young woman sped off without looking back and disappeared around the corner of a small bend in the dirt path. The lone boy watched the dust lingering in the air. He had no idea where he was. He kicked the dirt and concentrated on holding back that single tear trying to reassert itself. A buzzing motor sounded behind him. The young woman sped at him and skidded to a stop, forcing him to back away. She turned off the bike.

"What did you say?"

"What?"

"When I was driving off, what did you say?"

"Listen to me."

"No. After that. What did you say?"

"Oh." Minh hesitated. "Lady Trieu."

"Ba Trieu."

"Yes."

"Why did you say that?"

He hesitated again. "I'm afraid you won't believe me."

"I'm sure I won't. But tell me."

"I met Lady Trieu." He paused before completing the farce. "In Hoan Kiem Lake."

Craziness hung in the air, and if the sound of the absurdities hadn't made him realize its insanity, the look on the young woman's face cemented it. She threw her hands, surrendering to the lunacy, questioning why she decided to circle back.

"The demon warrior. I know who he is. And I know what must be done to defeat him."

"The demon warrior? Boy, what fantasy world are you living in?"

"It's the truth."

She started the bike. "You've wasted enough of my time."

"Wait!" As she started to twist the accelerator, Minh pulled the marble tablet from his pocket and lifted it into the air towards her. "Look!" She stopped and leaned towards Minh to examine. She turned off the bike. "This is the stone tablet of Ong Tho from Hang Bac Street. He—"

"I know who he is."

"Well, I—"

"You know Ong Tho?"

"Of course, I was arrested with him along with my mother."

"Oh God. Nguyen Thi Lien is your mother? You're one of those three. The ones …"

"Yes."

She released a disgruntled breath and motioned him on the bike. "We've got a long way to go."

"You want me to go with you?"

"I'll leave you with the bananas if you aren't on my bike in the next two seconds!" she yelled in frustration. Minh climbed on without further question, and the bike disappeared down the same path it had taken a moment before.

They rode non-stop for another hour through a dizzying array of small paths amidst rice fields and steep hills. Occasionally they had to cross a main road. The young woman would crawl up the bank of the road, lying flat on the berm, and look both ways for patrols or checkpoints. Then she would speed across and into the most impractical paths a motorized scooter could take, but they accepted it anyways. Minh focused on his grip until she pulled to a stop behind a row of thick bushes at the foot of a large hill. Before he could even dismount, five heavily armed soldiers in camouflage surrounded the bike, yelling for both of them to put their hands up.

"It's me!" she shouted.

"Who's that?" said a soldier, pointing his rifle at Minh.

"The one I was sent to fetch."

"Who is he?" He poked the rifle into Minh's rib. "Who are you?"

"Minh. I'm thirteen. I have to meet the commander."

"Shut up!" yelled the man, who turned back to the woman. "We're pulling out soon. Maybe tomorrow. Too much activity in

Hanoi. We don't trust this place any longer. Especially with someone like him coming here today."

"I think the commander should meet him," she said, pointing at Minh. "He was one of the ones in Hanoi."

Minh stepped off the bike and pushed the rifle away. "Just a few hours ago, I escaped from the facility, the one the Chinese built. I was there with the demon warrior."

"Shut-up."

"But I was."

"Let me bring him up," she said.

"It's too late. It's all a commotion up there."

"You want to know what I know," inserted Minh with authority. "…what I've seen. You won't believe it, but they must hear it."

"I'm gonna take him up."

"It's going to be a waste of time."

"I've already wasted my time with him, but he might have some useful insight."

The man motioned them on with a quick snap of his neck. Minh and the young woman began an uphill walk on a muddy path. Minh quickly found himself out of breath, but she swore at him to continue. She was fleet of foot and skimmed over the rocks and around the slippery mud without breathing heavily. Minh tried to keep up, but by the time he arrived at a rock outcropping near the top of the mountain, she had already disappeared and Minh stood alone, panting vigorously, leaning against a large boulder. Someone accosted him with a sack and shoved it over his head. He felt someone tying a rope around his mid-section. He yelled, but with each word, he felt a hard thud on his back, which forced him to go silent in the dark. They led him into the unknown. At one point two or three people—he wasn't sure how many—lifted him into the air and then threw him onto the hard ground. Someone untied him and ripped the sack off. He sat in a cloistered section of a cave, back against a rock wall. Three bright flashlights blinded his eyes, and he winced and turned away from the piercing beams. A middle-aged man wearing a Vietnamese army jacket stepped forward. He lowered his flashlight. Minh could see the silhouette of his face and body.

"You've cost us dearly," he said.

"What do you mean?"

"Two dead soldiers because we listened to the whims of that old fool of Hang Bac Street."

"Sir, please—"

"But she said I should see you, and out of respect of the old man I'll give you a second. Plus, I do know your father."

"You know my father? Is he still alive?"

"Oh, he's alive."

"Can I see him?"

"That would be impossible."

"Where is he?"

"What is so urgent that cost the lives of two good soldiers in a very critical place for us?"

Minh sat up a little straighter. "No, you're mistaken. Cuong is alive."

"What do you mean?"

"I saw him. He's alive in the Chinese facility. But, now he's an old man."

The man shone the light back into Minh's face. "What nonsense are you speaking?"

Then, without any filter, Minh released all the information at the mysterious man in front of him. He spoke of the lake and the turtle, the encounter with Lady Trieu, the capture and the black-walled facility, the meeting with Cuong, and finally the escape that brought him there. The man stood in front of him for a moment without saying anything. He turned and started walking away.

"Where are you going?" shouted Minh. "Everything I said is true. Lady Trieu is real, and she's the only way to defeat Sun Quan. And Cuong is alive. He's alive. Where are you going?" He sat alone in the darkness with only a faint light in the distance.

The Vietnamese man in the military jacket walked into a large cavern with dozens of soldiers and myriad equipment and tables spread out like a messy grand hall. Two soldiers dragged Minh behind him.

"Where is she?" the man yelled.

"I'm here." The young woman stepped in front of him. She displayed none of the cocky confidence she had previously shown to

Minh.

"You've wasted so much time."

"You said to follow every lead."

"Not every fantasy notion of some deranged boy."

"I believe there's some truth to what the boy—"

"You really think Ba Trieu ascended from Hoan Kiem Lake and helped him escape the demon warrior, who just happens to be Sun Quan, the ancient Chinese emperor? And you believe Cuong is still alive, though now an old man?"

She gulped without reply.

"Get rid of him."

The young woman motioned her head at Minh, and they released him towards the entrance of the cave. He walked out into the fresh air and another soldier pushed him forward. He slipped off the edge of the landing onto the muddy path. He picked himself up and started his descent on his own, unsure of his next move.

A young soldier in camouflage ran towards the others still in a huddle and stopped a few feet away to salute the older man. "Sir, word of a massive explosion in Hanoi. At the facility."

"We don't have any activity around there."

"No, sir. We don't."

"Any idea what—"

"Sir," interrupted the young woman. "Could it be as the boy said?"

Each officer gathered around had a dumbfounded look. No one was willing to speak up. The commander glanced out toward the opening of the cave.

"Get him in here!" he yelled at two other men standing behind the messenger. They sprinted off. "Do we have any other details?"

"No, sir. We received a few images from one of our drones. It showed a row of armored vehicles sawed completely in half."

The commander looked at the woman and then glanced up at the men approaching. "Where's the boy?"

"He's gone."

"Find him!"

"I'll find him, sir," said the young woman.

"You better."

She ran out of the cavern area and up through the rock outcroppings. Soldiers scurried back and forth carrying supplies and bags, unaware of her task to find Minh. She peered down from the top of the ridge. Minh was halfway down the incline, sliding on one of the muddy sections as if it were a ride at a carnival. She called after him, but quickly pulled back, afraid to make too much noise. She slid down the first steep incline and descended after him. When she reached the bottom, the group of soldiers came around her.

"Where's the boy?"

"He left on the motorbike."

"Why didn't you stop him?"

"I don't know. It … he just left … and we couldn't stop him."

"What do you mean you couldn't stop him? He's a boy!"

"It's all kind of blurry."

"What happened?"

"A woman. She—"

"What? Who?"

"A woman with large breasts pushed us all to the ground, and he took off."

"A woman with large breasts?" The men raised their shoulders in unison in a boyish way without replying. "And where is this woman?"

"She disappeared."

The young girl looked around. "It can't be. It can't … Do you have another motorbike? I have to go after the boy."

Chapter 16

A Long-Tailed Bird

Tho and Lien rested out of sight in the stench of their own clothing.

"I'm too old for this."

Lien glanced at the old man half-panting in the weeds on the side of the hill. "Where do you think Minh is?"

"Leave your thoughts alone. Worrying doesn't change a ripple in the water."

"Yes, but worrying makes me feel better."

"Really?"

She chastised him with a harsh sigh. "No. Tho, you've always been so grounded and focused."

"It's easy to be focused when one has no family of his own. I'm sure if I had a son, I wouldn't be spouting benign mantras about ripples in the water."

"What do you think of this? The royal line? You're the last one."

"Hmmm," he hummed a sigh of his own.

Lien smiled and reached over to grab his hand. "You've always been like a grandfather to me."

"I've been a grandfather to everyone I've met for the past fifty years. I can hardly remember a time I wasn't a grandfather. Minh will be fine. You've raised a smart boy."

"I didn't raise him alone."

"I hope you're not blaming me for any of his behavior."

A vehicle stopped just out of sight a short distance away. The woman from the garbage truck trudged over the top of the hill and called out for them. "I'm surprised I don't smell you. Where are you two?"

"Over here," shouted Lien.

The woman ransacked through a cloth bag as she approached. "Here, I brought you both some clothes. Grandpa, I hope a pair of pajamas will work for you. I took them from my father."

"You're a good soul. I rarely leave the house without loose-fitting, thin cotton pajamas. I shall feel at home."

"And I brought you some of my clothes," she said, handing Lien a shirt and pants set.

"Thank you so much."

"Now, change quickly. Two motorbikes will be arriving shortly. They'll take you the back way to the temple. I figured you didn't want to go through any checkpoints in Viet Tri City."

"That's perfect, thank you."

"And what are you going to do when you get to the temple?" Lien and Tho looked at each other. "Well, I see even you don't know what's about to happen next. Good luck on your journey. May the spirits show their favor."

"Thank you, but … I don't mean to be rude. However, could both of you turn around so an old man can change in peace?"

"Gladly," said Lien. "And don't look back my way."

"Don't worry, Lien. I wouldn't know what to do anyway if I stared at a beautiful girl. Actually, I might just die."

"Then don't look! I need you alive."

After twenty minutes of enjoying clean clothing, two young teens arrived on motorbikes and drove them through a maze of small roads and paths until they emerged below one of the temples of the Hung King complex. A small set of steps with a metal railing hung onto the side of the hill.

"Grandpa, take this path up the hill and then you'll see the main temple."

"Steps," Tho commented, pondering the incline with a doubtful glance. "Lien, you wonder why I rarely went to your apartment? Those steps of yours. My knees can't take it."

"I'll help you." She turned to the boys. "We owe you a debt."

They both nodded and scooted out of sight, leaving the pair the daunting task of step-climbing. They plodded up one at a time. Lien felt the complaint of every one of Tho's breaths on the back of her neck, until the final step led them into the courtyard of the main Hung King temple, nestled in the trees on top of a small mountain. The walkways were desolate, but they could smell the wafting of incense drifting out of the darkened hall.

"Tho, I don't mean to be skeptical, but what are we doing here?"

He chuckled as he continued to catch his breath, hunched over with his palms on his knees. "Searching and waiting. And hoping. Let's not forget hoping."

"Hoping?"

"Hoping that our ride in the garbage truck was not in vain."

"Shall we go in?"

"Yes, we must pay our respects."

Lien helped Tho up the few steps leading into the hall when she came to an abrupt halt. "Look." An intricate chalk drawing of an ancient Vietnamese bronze drum had been etched into the outside wall of the temple with the caption underneath: Long live Vietnam!

"Do you think it's true what's been rumored about the Hung Temple Museum, that the Chinese confiscated all the ancient bronze drums?"

Tho reached over and touched the chalk drawing. He rubbed the chalk residue between his fingertips. "That's what I would have done if I were the conquering Chinese. Try to eliminate anything that reminds our people of its true independence." He inspected the chalk. "This has been drawn recently. The images of the boats and birds on the drum are quite accurate."

"What do you think it means?"

"I hope it means we're at the right place."

They stepped over the raised wooden door frame directly

toward the main altar in line with the entrance. Large figures of bearded men overshadowed the table holding a plethora of incense holders, bowls of fresh fruit, and small figurines of Vietnamese lore. They both bowed in reverence, lit a joss stick, and placed it in one of the holders. As Lien mumbled a special prayer over the safety of her son, Tho removed the three marble tablets from his pajama top pocket and placed them flat on the altar. He shifted them around in order but left an empty slot for the missing one.

"Tho, I've never seen you without all four tablets."

Tho paused for moment. "Well, four is terribly bad luck. Perhaps that's why I never found a wife."

Lien smiled. "What are you going to do?"

"Seek guidance."

He placed the three middle fingers of his right hand in the empty slot of the missing tablet and closed his eyes. He whispered a phrase even Lien couldn't understand. She watched his intense expression until his mouth opened wide and he spoke a short supplication: "The great Hung Kings from the bronze era—our roots that prove our cause is just—may the spirit of our ancestors live once more in our time of need. Lady Trieu has been awakened, may we all do the same. May all of our spirits rise to the occasion."

He ran his hands over the three marble tablets before picking them up and placing them back in his pocket. He stared at a figurine behind the table. "I haven't been here in many years."

"What's that noise?" Lien looked back into the bright sunlight. A steady croaking sound in a precise cadence grew louder and louder. "What does that sound like to you?"

"Toads."

"Toads? On the mountain?"

"Come, quickly. Outside." Tho grabbed Lien's hand, and they moved out of the darkened sanctuary into the bright light. The sound of the toads became deafening like being surrounded by thousands of locusts spread out in the tree tops.

"Look!" Lien pointed at a miniature long-tailed bird, standing under the chalk drawing of the bronze drum.

"I can't believe it," he said.

"What?"

"That's the long-tailed bird, from the drum. Look at it."

"*Chim lac*. Lost bird."

"Indeed, the lost bird," confirmed Tho.

A spitting image of the mysterious bird had walked out of the chalk drawing. Lien reached down and scooped the bird into her hands. It had a long, pointed beak and a long, striking tail with full-feathered wings on both sides. Its front and rear seemed to teeter-totter back and forth on its mid-section. It sat comfortably in her hands without making a sound as the croaking of the toads surrounded them.

"Everything is waking up." Tho smiled in amazement into the air. A patch of blue sky could be seen through the tree canopy. "We thought the lost bird was indeed lost to history. But here it is. Stepping out of the bronze drum."

"What do you think it wants?" asked Lien. "This is a monumental discovery."

"Indeed," said Tho. "Every ornithologist in the world will want to examine this beauty." Tho tapped the bird's beak lightly. "What's that?" An object hovered overhead the courtyard. It was metallic and ten feet wide. "Is that a drone?"

A projectile shot from the hovering object and hit the back side of the temple. A massive explosion knocked Lien and Tho off the front steps and onto the ground.

"Missile. We're under attack!"

The drone hovered above them, slowly descending. The long-tailed bird had jumped away a few feet and looked up into the sky. The bird grew larger. Lien and Tho witnessed the transformation in front of them. It expanded out ten-fold, then twenty, and its long tail grew outward and shot back right between them. Its beak protruded like a massive needle. They instinctively knew what to do. They grabbed onto the plumage, and the bird let out a giant call like a mighty eagle ready for battle. It lifted into the sky with Tho and Lien holding on with all the strength their grip could muster. The massive bird careened toward the drone and clamped onto its propellers with its mighty jaw. Its beak sliced down like a pair of scissors, splitting the drone in half and sending splinters to the ground in a fiery crash. The bird continued its ascent with two flabbergasted hitchhikers watching the flames below. It released another mighty call into the sky, and the toads echoed in reply.

The two travelers glanced earthward. The temple for the ancient kings had a gaping hole at its rear, and the burning embers from the drone engulfed the entry way. Tho thought it was fitting, though. The struggle for independence reached back to its genesis, and the Hung Kings and the mighty roar of the toads and the lost long-tailed bird of lore all played their parts, coaxed on, no doubt, by a mighty female warrior awakened from the deep of the sacred lake. If the Vietnamese experience indeed stood at the brink of extinction, it would not end quietly without every spirit of the living past bursting forth to counter the strange and terrible whims which had awakened Sun Quan. The tongue-tied journeyers realized they didn't need to hold on anymore. The mighty feathers on the long-tail of the majestic bird had formed a ridge on both sides—like a carriage holding them in place. They gawked at each other like youngsters in an amusement park, equally in awe about riding the turtle in the lake and riding the great bird on the edges of the clouds. The vibrant green fields spread out in all directions, signaling a country still growing and a people still working to fulfill history's promise. They swooped over the edges of the Red River, snaking along toward the city in the middle of the river, the beautiful city of Thang Long, the modern city of Hanoi, the thousand-year-old citadel, which had warded off floods, natural disasters, foreign invaders, and modern bombers—now standing at the foot of a crossroads, which would determine its future. The bird turned north from the city and within minutes descended with ease and landed in an ancient temple complex. The bird lowered its tail, allowing Tho and Lien to slide gently off onto the ground.

Lien helped Tho to his feet, and they both remained silent as the bird turned around and glared at them as if it wanted to say something. Then it sat on the ground as if protecting an egg ready to hatch.

"Tho, we're at a citadel. This is … this is Co Loa."

"Yes. The Au Lac Kingdom. The first established Vietnamese kingdom."

"Why are we here?"

A sharp voice from behind startled them.

"I wanted us to meet."

They turned to the presence of the lady warrior standing over them.

"Lady Trieu."

"A drone attacked the Hung Temple and—"

"Yes."

"And the long-tailed bird—"

"Yes, Mr. Tho. You have brought her to life."

"Me?"

"You'll be safe here for the time being."

"Do you know if Minh is all right?"

"I'm afraid he will have a difficult time convincing the rebellion about the true nature of our fight."

"What do you mean?"

"It takes belief to truly understand that which is right in front of us. The rational mind doubts anything it can't explain away. It wants to deny it until the proof is unmistakable."

"But Minh is all right?"

"Don't worry about your son. He has a role to play, and you've taught him well."

"But—"

Tho reached over to stop Lien from saying any more. "Lien, release him to his task and allow fate to bring us all back together when this terrible war is finished." She nodded and gripped Tho's hand tightly. "Lady Trieu, what is it you want us to do?"

"Protect the tablets until you hear word."

They nodded. The female warrior walked past them toward the bird. She stroked its head and climbed onto its back. "Stay out of sight." The bird flexed its wings and stood to its feet. The majestic span of feathers fanned out as it leaped into the sky, roaring as Lady Trieu clung to its back.

"She wants us to stay out of sight, yet she rides a giant ancient bird into the sky?"

Lien playfully slapped Tho as the long-tailed bird disappeared like a speck into the blue. But their gaze didn't shift, even after they could no longer see the winged beast. They stood between the dark and gloom of Hanoi and the piercing brightness of an unknown world, which had opened its doors to untold possibilities—all of which seemed too preposterous to believe.

"Tho. I'm at a loss for words. How can we believe what we've seen?"

Tho nodded in agreement. "Yes, indeed. Her breasts are supposed to be much larger."

Lien twirled around in half-cocked shock. "Tho? What?"

"In all the ancient stories of Lady Trieu, she always had massively big breasts."

Lien burst out laughing and slapped the old man on his arm. "Probably because men told the story."

"No, no. That's not it. Next time I'll ask her."

"You will not ask her about her breasts."

"Lien, you are not my mother."

"You're lucky I'm not."

The Chinese man and Sun Quan entered into the once-again walled-off cell of the newly old man named Cuong.

"Your friends left you here," said the Chinese man.

"I told them to leave me."

"They were eager to save themselves."

"What do you want?" he asked with an uncaring attitude.

Sun Quan turned his back to Cuong but didn't say anything at first.

Finally, he asked, "Would you like to be young again?" Cuong looked up quickly. "Wouldn't it be nice to have young legs once more? Ones that worked?"

"What do you want?"

"I want the location of the rebel headquarters. That's all."

"I'll never tell you."

Sun Quan turned back toward Cuong. He hovered over him and smashed Cuong's leg with his foot. Cuong buckled over in pain, but as he opened his eyes, his limp leg grew firm and strong. Cuong reached down and felt the muscles restoring themselves to complete mobility. It felt like he could jump to his feet and run. He glanced up at the two.

"I'm … I'm …"

"You're turning younger if you want it. A small taste of the good days. Tell us. We'll restore you and let you go."

"I—"

His mind wandered. The only headquarters he knew might have been abandoned by now. They changed often, he thought. I would be of greater help to the resistance if I were younger. Just a word and I could be free, if I can trust them. Of course I can't trust them. But my leg is better, and I'm feeling … His thoughts betrayed every one of his instincts. He would tell. It made sense to tell. It felt good to tell. He desired to inform them of everything they wanted to know just to be complete—just to feel himself alive again.

"I—"

The smooth black wall behind them opened and a uniformed soldier ran in.

"Sir, a giant bird has been spotted in the sky."

"A bird?"

"It destroyed the drone in Viet Tri."

Cuong burst out. "I'll tell you. I'll tell you where the headquarters is."

The Chinese man kicked him in the leg. "You fool. It's too late for that."

"What do you mean? I'll tell you. I'll tell you everything, just let me be young again."

"The rebel base means nothing now that the bird is here."

"The bird? What bird? I don't know anything about a bird. I'll tell you everything. Everything!"

The Chinese man turned without a sound and exited beyond the walls. Sun Quan stayed for a moment and leaned over Cuong. "You're weak. All of you. You'll die here an old man, because no one would come for a weak old fool like yourself."

Sun Quan left, and as Cuong reached down to rub his leg, his body once again atrophied. He lay prostrate on the floor and cried alone in the reflective, black-walled cell.

Chapter 17

Toward Hanoi

Within the first minute of the next great motorbike chase—there had been many during this young rebellion—she witnessed a cloud of dust in front of her rolling off the back of Minh's motorbike. It felt too easy. The young woman maxed the throttle and bounced fluidly over the pock-ridden country path until she ate his dust between her teeth. He puttered like a thirteen-year-old, she thought as she punched out to the right and pulled alongside.

"Stop," she yelled into the wind. "Stop."

The young fool didn't, and he would pay. She would make sure of it. She swerved quickly to the left in front of him. He braked—the back tire locked onto the dirt and skidded sideways, knocking the bike off its tires and sprawling Minh to the side in a ball of hurt. The young woman screeched to a stop and ran over to the boy.

Minh backed away, mostly unscathed from the accident.

"I'm not going back. I'm going to prove to you everything I said is true."

"Do you know how much trouble you're in?"

"I'm not going back there. They don't want to know the truth."

"Like you know everything?"

"Yes. Yes, I do know everything."

"What are you going to do?"

"I don't know."

"What a great plan."

"I'll think of something. I'll get into the facility, and I'll free Cuong. You'll see."

"You'll get into the facility? You don't even know how to get into Hanoi. The patrols will eat you alive."

"I've made it this far."

"Yeah." She approached him. "How do you explain that? How did you get this far? A woman with large breasts?"

"What?"

"The guards said a woman with large breasts accosted them. This makes no sense. What happened back there?"

"I don't know."

"Was it …?" She didn't finish it.

He saw the wondering in her eyes. "You do believe me."

"What happened back there with the guards?"

"It's all a blur. When I got to the bottom of the hill, the guards overwhelmed me, and then suddenly this woman cracks them all upside the head with a series of kicks, and …"

"Who was it?"

"I didn't get a good look at her."

"Liar."

"All right, maybe it was Lady Trieu. I don't know."

The young woman turned her back to him in frustration. "What's going on?" she repeated several times to herself.

"What's your name?"

"Nhan." She faced him.

"What are you, twenty?"

"I'm sixteen."

"Sixteen?"

"You thought I was older?"

"How's a sixteen-year-old girl get to whiz in and out of rebel headquarters anytime she pleases?"

"None of your business. And how's a thirteen-year-old barely in puberty able to escape from the facility. Nobody does that."

"Maybe I know the right people. And I'm not in puberty. I'm a man."

"You're a childish boy."

"I could whip you any day."

"Oh, I wish you'd try."

Minh lunged and tackled her into the tall weeds. She twirled her right elbow around and smacked the boy in the side of the face. He grunted once and escalated the issue with another assault which landed his body on top of hers. She flung him to the side and kneed him in the gut. He coughed for air and flailed his arms back and forth until he panicked and yelled "stop" repeatedly.

"What is it? You afraid a girl will beat you up?"

"Stop, stop. The marble tablet. Careful. I can't break it."

Nhan stood up immediately and looked around. "Where is it? Did you lose it?"

Minh scrambled for it in the grass for a moment before clasping it high as a trophy over his head. "Here. It's here. It looks okay. Wait. Why do you care so much about it?"

"Cause I'm familiar with it."

"Why didn't you tell the commander about it?"

"He doesn't believe in those things. My mother told me about Ong Tho and his tablets. I even went to his house once when I was very little."

"Then you were right across from my house. I'm his neighbor. Why did you mother visit him?" She didn't respond. Minh pressed. "What did she find out?"

"Nothing. Only that … it doesn't matter. She died."

Minh remained silent. He slid the marble tablet back into this pocket. "How did you get into the rebellion?"

She hesitated. "The rebel commander is my father."

"Commander Lieu? He's your father?"

"I don't want to talk about it." She walked towards Minh with aggressive resolve. "Look, tell me the truth. Did you really see Lady Trieu?"

"I swear, it's true. Everything. I could never make all this up."

"Okay."

"So you believe me?"

"It doesn't matter what I believe. It matters what I see. Take me to her."

"I can't take you to her."

"Why not?"

"I don't know where she is."

"I thought she was in the lake."

"She was, but who knows where she is now. I mean she was just …" He pointed back in the direction they had come from.

"Then what do you want to do?"

"I want to go back to the facility. I want to get Cuong out. I want to find my mother and Tho. Maybe Lady Trieu will meet us there, and we can confront Sun Quan."

"Boy, are you naive. How are we going to get into the facility?"

"I got out, didn't I? Isn't escaping prison more difficult than entering?"

She shook her head. "What a foolish boy."

"I'm not a boy. I'm almost the same age as you."

"I'm three years older."

"Two and a half."

"Sorry, I didn't recognize your maturity."

"If you want to see Lady Trieu, our best bet is heading to the facility."

"All right." Nhan walked over to her motorbike and sat on the front edge of the seat. "Leave yours here and get on the back of mine."

Minh balked. "No, I'm not riding with you anymore."

She jumped off and punched him in the arm. "This is not a negotiation. I'll get us into Hanoi, you dumb boy. You get us to Lady Trieu. Now get on."

She was pretty. That's the moment he noticed, with her hand wagging in his face and the insults rolling off her lips. The youngness of her countenance shown through, and for a still moment in time, Minh felt like the boy going through puberty.

"All right." He gulped and obeyed, thinking only about whether he would be able to put his arms around her—not that he liked her, she obviously annoyed him—but putting his arms around her to hold on would certainly be better than holding the hand grips off the back end of the motorbike's seat. And safer, he thought. Because suddenly safety was something to be treasured as they embarked on their impossible and foolhardy journey back to the facility.

"Well?" Her impatience fluttered like a flag in the wind.

"All right."

He climbed on behind her. The hands? Where to put them? And he remembered that he had already hung his arms around her midsection on the previous ride, when her being a girl had meant nothing to him, so he tested it, slowly grabbing both sides of her torso, and she didn't yell. He would enjoy this ride into the belly of hell, for the last ride of one's life should be cherished, should it not?

Nhan guided them through a maze of serene rice paddies which tempered the death and war hanging over Hanoi. One could plant himself knee-deep in a paddy beside a gray-haired water buffalo and believe nothing mattered more than the growth of those young shoots of grain. But then a military helicopter would zoom overhead to remind all of the present realities. The two on the motorbike zipped through tiny villages, crossed streams on dangerous one-way suspension bridges, and eventually had to navigate the suburbs north of the Red River. She came to a stop along the edge of the river with the backdrop of Hanoi proper spilling over the bank on the other side. They hid behind a row of newly built, unoccupied houses.

"Quick, open the back gate of that house."

"Why?"

"Just do it, Minh." He reached through the gate and unlatched a swing-open walking door. "Now go inside the front room, and sit on the floor away from the window."

"Why? What is this place?"

"Do it! I'll be back within an hour. It should be dark by then."

"Where are you going?"

"Just stay out of sight."

Minh walked into the vacant house. It had no furniture, but looked newly painted. He obeyed her last command and sat against the wall away from the window. He waited two minutes. His stomach growled. He couldn't remember the last time he had eaten or drunk anything. He stood up and walked out of the back room and into the kitchen. There was no refrigerator. He turned on the faucet, but water had yet to be hooked up. He sat on the kitchen counter and swung his feet back and forth, hitting the underneath cabinet in a steady cadence.

"I'm so hungry," he spoke out loud. He wondered if there were any shops nearby. He didn't remember seeing one as they streaked to the edge of the river. She told me to stay out of sight, he thought. Wait. She's not my boss. I know more about the rebellion than she does. He stood up and peeked into the front room. I'm hungry. He walked into room and unlocked the wooden door. She's not the boss of me. I have to keep up my strength. He opened the door to a vacant street of empty houses. He turned right down the street. I'll just peek around the corner. I won't go far. He walked down one alley and finally heard some traffic, or at least some semblance of life. He turned onto a side street and ran directly into a bread seller with a small glass display stand on the side of the road.

"Ma'am, could I please have a loaf of bread."

"You see the price."

"I don't have any money."

"Nobody does these days. That's why I'm selling bread."

"Please, just one."

"I can't feed all of Hanoi. Now run along."

Minh came closer to the woman. He paused as he glanced down at his pocket, then he pulled out the marble tablet like a Brooklyn street watch seller. "Look, ma'am. I have the marble tablet." He reached into his pocket and displayed the strange item to the woman looking at him queerly.

"What do I want with a marble tablet?"

"You don't understand. I'm that one you probably heard about. I have it."

"What are you babbling about?"

"The tablet. It's magic."

"Then why don't you make some money appear, so you can buy your bread."

Minh slid the tablet back into his pocket. "Please, ma'am. You don't understand."

"I understand your likes very well."

"I'm with the rebellion."

"Don't be bringing politics into it. I just need a little money. And I don't mean that Chinese money. I only use the real stuff with Uncle Ho's picture on it."

"But ma'am …"

"Run along. I get enough harassment with that blasted patrol. I don't need a whining boy —"

"Patrols come through here?"

"What are you, stupid? All these houses behind here were built by the Hans. They're swarming this place like the mosquitoes at my ankles." She glanced at him with a harsh look. "Don't think about grabbing one and running, either. I'm watching you."

Minh couldn't take his eyes off the bread, but he backed away, hoping that the marble tablet would indeed turn into a crisp bill. That's when he realized two soldiers on foot patrol stared at him from a short distance. They had turned the corner and conversed with each other, pointing over at the boy negotiating his meal. Minh's eyes froze when his glance squared with theirs. He backed up slowly not moving his gaze, wondering which of his limited options would most likely keep him from being captured or killed.

I'm just a boy to them, he said to himself as he continued a slow-motion backpedal.

"See, they're here already," said the woman. "They're looking at you. Whatever you do, don't run."

Minh bolted. He heard a yell behind him, followed by a bullet that ricocheted over a house above his shoulder. He sprinted down the side street with his loose sandals flopping methodically on the pavement. He didn't look back but kept patting his pocket to make sure the marble tablet continued the journey with him. He heard yelling as he ducked down the corner alley off the back end of the row of houses.

"Lady Trieu, please."

He made it to the house and flipped up the metal latch on the walk-in door. He dashed inside and slid against the wall.

I left the gate open, he remembered. He glanced out the window and the two soldiers entered holding their rifles at alert. Think, think. Lady Trieu. Can you hear my thoughts? All he could think of was that flawless face from the water, stern and calm, confident and fierce. He heard talking.

"We found it," said one in Chinese into his device. Minh didn't understand them. "The boy went in there. The one that escaped. Yes. We'll bring him."

Minh had his ear to the wall, listening to the shuffling and muffled voices on the other side. They tried the handle of the door. He had locked it. A thud against the door rattled him, but they couldn't break through. A rifle butt crashed through the glass of the window, and Minh screamed and jolted backwards. The window had bars preventing the soldiers' entrance. One poked a rifle barrel in and fired two rounds. The other soldier yelled at him and a second thud banged against the door. Then another shot exploded through the lock mechanism and they kicked open the door. Minh screamed and ran across the room but froze solid against the far wall after another shot pierced the wall behind him. He turned around, shaking, arms at his side. He slipped his hand into his right pocket to touch the marble tablet, hoping to ignite a little magic.

"No," he said, as the soldiers inched towards him without a word. They could have killed him already, so he figured they wanted him alive. Run was the word he heard in his mind, but his feet felt attached to the floor with concrete. Run, he told himself again. His cement-block feet broke free and he skirted around the corner of the door and into the kitchen. He heard the soldiers yelling as they came toward him. He called for the lady of the lake once more as he huddled in a ball, arms over his face, and pretended he hid in an impenetrable cocoon. They would be upon him in seconds and only fate could save him now. A vision of his mother slipped into his mind and tears formed their overt deeds in the corners of his eyes. He had no escape. He could only welcome whatever fate had willed. As his muddled mind ground out his final thoughts, he jerked violently and lifted his head as two gunshots reverberated in the other room, followed by tandem thuds to the floor. Minh didn't move. Not an inch. He heard footsteps. Then a voice.

"What happened? I told you to stay in the house."

Nhan stood to his left.

"It's clear," said a voice behind her. "But this location is blown. We've gotta go, now!"

She looked back at the hidden voice before turning towards Minh.

"Well?"

He still had not moved.

"I was trying to buy bread."

"You stupid, stupid boy. This was our safe house. Now it's blown. Come on. Now."

His feet obeyed but his being wished it could remain behind. He walked into the back room and both Chinese soldiers lay face down in a pool of blood. A rebel soldier stood behind them with a pistol.

"You know where to go?" he asked.

"Yes," she replied. "What about the bodies?"

"I'll drag them down the bank and toss them in river after dark."

"And this place?"

The man looked at Minh with tense lips but didn't say anything. They all knew what it meant.

"Minh, let's go."

"They'll be on your trail," said the man.

"I know. Don't worry. I got the boy with me." She emphasized "boy" using her best sardonic expression. "What could go wrong? Minh. Let's go."

They exited the house, into the courtyard, across the narrow path on the bank's edge, and slipped over it down to the edge of the river.

"Where are we going?"

"We have to get to another crossing. We got about thirty minutes till it's dark. Keep your head down and stay hidden as much as possible. You think you can do that?"

"Stop treating me like a baby."

"You are a baby. You had to go get food?"

"I was hungry."

"Sorry that this rebellion has gotten in the way of your dinner, you baby!"

"Shut up."

"You shut up!"

"You shut up!"

She turned around with a flailing fist and shoved it next to his mouth. "How about we both shut up before we each get a bullet to the head?"

Minh agreed to such a common-sense compromise.

Chapter 18

The Temptation

The larger-than-life figure sauntered alone at dusk in the hidden recesses of Hanoi. A new curfew had been announced by the Chinese man earlier in the day. The residents hunkered down and fled into the dark corners of their houses whenever the wanderer approached. He brooded and ignored the citizens other than an occasional kick to a desolate hawker stall. His beard had grown longer, now forming a pointed goatee off his chin. He had a sword strapped to his back, and he plodded along like a beast on the prowl. A boy, hidden behind a dumpster, couldn't contain his fright, and a panicked utterance slipped out of him. He stood, straight-backed, like an alert animal and fled. Sun Quan kicked the dumpster off the edge of the street, and it smashed into the metal bars of a store front, shattering its glass. The beast moved on. The pace quickened as he turned the corner onto the street next to St. Joseph's Cathedral—a block away from Hoan Kiem Lake. He looked down at his hands, then pressed them together until his skin turned clear and swirled in circles. His body gave way to a formless ghost. He flew into the sky and hovered over the spire of the church. Sun Quan in human form reappeared, perched on the top, like a solemn gargoyle gazing off towards the lake.

"What are you waiting for? I understand what you're trying to do. I see you're willing to unleash the past. You've joined me in this. Come. Come now. Let's settle this. Let's talk. Let's relive the secrets of the deep. Don't deny the yearning of your soul. I can feel it."

The deep of the lake didn't reply.

"I'm prepared to do this. If you are. If you feel trapped by me. I thought you would be more forthright. What have I hidden? I've shown you everything, but you have chosen the ways of the shadows and the folly of the underground. Is that the way you want it?"

He pleaded to the layers of the sky and the depths of the lake, which had watched the history of this volatile region unfold. The struggle for identity, the pursuit of independence, the fierce tenacity of a people wanting to live outside the clutches of the northern invaders. But Sun Quan wanted something more than just a moment of glory on a battlefield, so he asked her again to consider his plea.

"Why don't you come now and settle this?"

He morphed back to his formless self until the massive warrior reappeared on the banks of Hoan Kiem Lake.

"I could come to you, you know? If I wanted. But I will wait. Be assured. I will not act mercifully toward you, as I will not be merciful to this city. If you do not offer yourself to me, then I will strangle everything you hold precious. That is my promise."

He waited a moment and dipped his toe into the water. It was accepted, but he didn't press further.

"You have chosen."

In that moment, the giant bird landed on top of St. Joseph's spire. Sun Quan watched from below and shifted his appearance until he stood opposite her, face to face and alone with Lady Trieu for the first time.

"I knew you couldn't ignore me forever."

He moved in close to her. She didn't flinch. He was six feet away in the midst of the heavy tension balancing on the edge of the cathedral. They rivaled each other in stature and swagger. Both tall and unmoving. The bird had recoiled its head behind her. Neither engaged their weapons.

"You are beautiful," he said.

"Which is why you want me. Some things never change."

"We were meant to be."

"Stop the useless platitudes."

"You don't understand." He moved closer still. A lover on the move. She froze every muscle. He brushed up against her. Her face remained motionless and straight ahead. His breath touched her ear.

"How did you return?" she asked.

"Always the pragmatist."

"It's our survival. We are a practical people. We must be pragmatic. How much poetry survives at the edge of a sword."

He grinned. "My lady, if you could raise your gaze beyond the mundane of the rice paddy for one moment, what grandeur on the horizon you would see—a reckoning, a revival, a long overdue payment rendered by the gods of the universe. And together ..."

"You've just killed an untold number of my people, and you dare to use the term 'together.' You're wasting your breath."

Sun Quan stepped around Lady Trieu and confronted her straight on. "Damn your petty politics. Don't you realize what we have here? A chance. Only one. To redo this human mess once and for all. We each know the history all too well. The lust for more spilled blood ... for what? For a negotiated peace which endures no longer than the conflict itself. The cycle repeats. We were cogs in the same wheel. I advanced, you countered. And I acknowledge your skill in defeating me."

Lady Trieu glared towards him. "Is that what's happening? You can't defeat me so you want me to join you?"

"No," snapped Sun Quan. "Your strength intrigues me. There's an unspoken beauty in it. In the midst of so much pain and grief, you stand firm. You bond together. You believe there's something worth holding on to. Even if it kills you." He reached out and touched her cheek. "Beautiful."

His face was inches from hers. The bird's head cocked in alert like a cobra ready to strike, but it displayed restraint. Lady Trieu remained unmoved as she felt his breath all over her. Power dripped from him, and she felt the connection in their eyes. A dangerous thrill. An unexplained phenomenon. The world at that moment belonged to them. And maybe he was right. The endless cycle could end if … She closed her eyes, and he leaned in to whisper in her ear.

"Together, what human could stop us. I'm not opposed to bloodshed on both sides, as long as we believe that—together—we can do this."

"Do what?"

"Put it all under our feet. They brought this upon themselves. They unleashed us, but we don't take orders from them. Not anymore. Don't you understand? We're no longer bound by petty politics or geographical boundaries. Look at us. It's marvelous. We're not like them. Could it be more obvious? We are vastly superior to the quagmire they insist upon wallowing in. They grovel at the mundane and beg and plead for one more day of sunlight, when we can shape ourselves at will. We can rise above, you and I. Let's put an end to the bickering and bring a lasting peace, which no human would be able to perceive."

They both breathed heavily in their human bodies. Trieu had turned her head and looked off in the direction of the lake.

"And this lasting peace… what will it cost?"

"Who cares about the cost? Either way, blood will flow. Why not end the shedding of lives with an alliance which will last far beyond the next invasion."

She felt every word. After all, she wasn't human any more. Duty is a human trait. One of self-obligation and order. Duty commands an unwavering world view. It's obligated to stand when ordered, to move when commanded, to sacrifice when needed. But duty had not awakened her. Magic had, by an old man taken with the ancient ways, unable to see any other way forward. Duty had driven him into the lake to find her. But what had awakened her? Certainly not duty. What allegiance did she owe him? She had accomplished her part. She had sacrificed herself for the ideal, for the grand experiment, for the glory. What had it benefited her? A statue? A shrine? A street sign with her name on it? What did all of that mean to her now? Why did she need to preserve them? She had done her part; now it was their turn, but in the hour of need, they fell into the grip of the past and exposed themselves to their own destruction. What did she owe them? She had been summoned from the deep by the fatal whims of a desperate old man to confront an unparalleled evil. But evil is only one part of power. And the thrill of being alive once more allowed her to push the evil to the side for a moment to admire the force attracting her.

As the two warriors from the underbelly of humanity negotiated their allegiances on top of the St. Joseph Cathedral spire, a small group of young boys noticed their silhouettes in the waning dusk. They gawked and pointed, yelling to friends and family to look at the strange exchange on the top of the church. The crowd grew, many of them fearful to leave their homes with the threat of another lockdown being announced. But it was too fantastic to ignore. A giant long-tailed bird next to a massive heroine confronting the demon warrior of Hanoi. The swarming crowd finally commanded the attention of Lady Trieu. As Sun Quan whispered his intentions in her ear, she turned her head to witness either their arms stretched out pointing her way or their hands over their mouths in disbelief. Her countrymen begged to her—not personally, since they couldn't understand her identity—but the linked ties of the past and their existential struggle to survive the endless assaults couldn't escape her. Not at this moment. Not when the sheltered masses had defied orders and dared to fill the square in front of the church to see the stand-off with the demon warrior.

One boy started it first as a monotone chant. But it was quickly picked up by others until the entire square filled with women and children and old men chanted it in unison, and it rose above the cathedral and swirled around the two transcendent interlocutors on the spire above.

"There's nothing more important than independence and freedom."

The saying reverberated above the crowd, and hovered in the air as Lady Trieu absorbed its meaning. Sun Quan pulled away and glanced over the edge of the cathedral. He let out a roar like that of an animal, and the crowd scattered. Some screamed. Some ran for cover. Others still stood defiantly, believing they had nothing left to lose.

"Sun Quan, let me make something very clear to you," Trieu stated. "I am of the Viet tribe of the south. I am and will always be Vietnamese."

She back-stepped and flung a sidekick into Sun Quan's chest, careening him off the edge of the cathedral. His body hit the pavement in a massive thud, nearly killing two people who barely had enough time to get out of the way. The crowd, with horror-filled eyes, circled around and watched him writhe in pain. They pressed in close and spit vindictive expletives his way. A few even dared to touch the demon warrior. One middle-aged woman kicked him in the side, but Sun Quan rose in their midst like a born-again preacher ready to set the record straight. He tore into a few of them, spewing their blood in the square and causing a panicked retreat amongst the Vietnamese faithful. The chaos spread into the adjacent avenues. Sun Quan ripped through the crowd causing as much damage as possible until Lady Trieu bounded off the spire and landed in front of the Chinese warrior. She unsheathed the sword. Sun Quan's sword met hers in a flurry of sparks and sounds reverberating above the chaos. They moved in a frantic fashion with each warrior gaining the upper hand one moment only to lose it the next. The people of the square fell over top of each other to avoid contact with the dueling warriors from the underworld.

Sun Quan sliced Lady Trieu twice in the left arm, forcing her to retreat into a side alley. Unrelenting, he followed her. Trieu countered with a quick move off a side wall and hit a solid blow on him, sending him to the ground. She attacked with her sword, but he repelled and forced her into the open area around Hoan Kiem Lake. The giant bird now circled overhead, and the crowds swarmed the lake to see the epic battle. No words were spoken. Just intense grunts and hits and massive swaths with the swords. Each one landed successful blows, but none were fatal, and they teetered on the edge of the lake, each with their righteous cause on the tip of their swords.

The chorus of words rose above the fray—the words of Uncle Ho—the only ones they knew—and they became bolder as Lady Trieu fought with all the resolve she had against the worthy opponent.

And then it happened. Sun Quan reflected one of her blows and shifted his weight to the side, thrusting his sword under her rib cage. She winced in pain and fell backward, splashing into the edge of the lake and disappearing beneath the surface. Sun Quan yelled into the sky a great cry from a warrior clearly at the edge of his capacity. He panted once and poked his sword into the water before yelling into the air once more. She had disappeared, and the massive crowd which had gathered on all sides of the lake collectively backed away as Sun Quan raised the sword over his head and walked to the edge of the bank.

The water near the edge seemed to explode and Lady Trieu rose out of the depths with both hands on her sword. She thrust it forward and pierced it through Sun Quan's right side. The long-tailed bird circled overhead as the harsh, dark night settled into the city without electricity. Some onlookers held candles as if they attended a vigil, as their fate hung in the balance. Their worn faces urged on Lady Trieu, most still not knowing who she was except that she fought for them against the demon warrior, and she had not yet seen defeat.

The bird swooped earthward. The dueling pair felt the air shift as its long tail curled around Sun Quan's right wrist and jerked him skyward several feet off the ground. The move prevented a sure blow against Lady Trieu, who had recoiled after her strike into Sun Quan's side. She was unsure why she hesitated on a death blow. She watched the bird entangled around him, and within seconds, no one watching could decipher if the bird held Sun Quan or if Sun Quan had captured the bird. The warrior had morphed out of his body and the formless shape encircled like a boa constrictor, wrapping its prey in a death grip. Lady Trieu pulsed upward like the fired light from an explosion, and the three of them wrestled in the air for a few seconds before the two took human form again and crashed to the earth—the long-tailed bird still in Sun Quan's clutches. The bird let out a loud call, and it wriggled free and ascended into the air, seemingly unharmed. Sun Quan turned over, and without looking, pierced Lady Trieu in the torso with his sword. She dropped her weapon, and stood dazed for a moment. All the people on the perimeter of the darkness still peered in wonder and hoped for a miracle. They still believed what they saw was a miracle—one that would surely save them. For what other purpose could there be?

She heard the chant once more—a final reminder of the substance of the fight—a people desiring freedom from the entanglements of a foreign power, especially one with Sun Quan's dark vision of the future. As she juggled these thoughts, she fell backward, limp, unresponsive and slid into the water like a fallen tree, disappearing under the surface. Overhead, the bird let out a terrifying cry, but it didn't try to attack.

Sun Quan backed away a few steps, sword still gripped in his tense right hand. And then Lady Trieu surfaced, not as the vibrant warrior, but as a crumpled corpse. The water moved away from her. She lay on the back of a giant turtle's shell. The bird let out one more violent cry and swooped down towards the turtle, scooping Lady Trieu into its mouth and taking off into the sky.

Sun Quan watched but didn't attempt to stop the bird. Instead, he turned around and sauntered across the street, now barren, toward the church once more.

"You have chosen, and so then have I."

He flipped open his polished steel device and the Chinese man appeared on the screen.

"Sun Quan. Have you made your decision?"

"Yes."

"What is it?"

"Proceed."

The Chinese man smiled. "Finally, we'll put an end to this."

The screen went blank, and Sun Quan shifted his appearance until he stood at the top of St. Joseph's spire once again. This time alone. Even the bird had flown out of sight.

Chapter 19

Hanoi at Night

Minh and Nhan had managed to escape the bullets trying to pock their heads with death blows. They had slipped along the northern bank of the Red River and hid in the shadows until a small boat arrived and ferried them across. All of this was much easier than expected, thanks to the power outage in Hanoi, which dimmed the river to a black void. One person manually rowed them across without a word or any sort of exchange occurring. They exited the boat, climbed the bank, and crept into the back alleys on the northern part of the city touching the southern bank of the Red River. Minh could see the Thang Long Bridge off to his right a few hundred yards away. They ran into their first patrol when they tried to cross a major street. A spotlight exposed them for a second, but they sprinted away as a Chinese soldier, using almost indecipherable Vietnamese, commanded them to halt. They declined, climbed a fence, and slipped into the alleyway of another back street. They didn't stop running, unless to hide for a moment from a passing car or if something else had spooked them. Eventually, Minh asked, "Where are we going?"

"There."

She bolted into a narrow alley in pitch darkness with Minh following. He tripped over something he couldn't identify in the darkness. Nhan had somehow made it through unscathed. They ran dead into the end of the alley, and Nhan knocked on a wooden door. It was not a normal knock; it followed a patterned sequence. The door opened, but no light could be seen. Minh felt someone grab his shoulders and pull him inside. When the door shut behind him, a flashlight beamed like a headlamp in Minh's eyes, sending him cowering backwards and covering his face with his arms. Nhan slapped her hand over his mouth to prevent him from speaking.

146 Mark W Sasse

"Shhhh—"

The flashlight turned off, and three lighters lit simultaneously in different parts of the room, igniting the wicks on three candles. The light slowly allowed Minh's eyes to adjust to his surroundings. Three young men and two young women sat in a spartan room without windows. They had placed a towel across the bottom of the door frame. They all looked anxious, especially at the sight of Nhan.

"Nhan, what are you doing in the city?"

"Does your father know you're here?" asked another.

"Did he send you?"

"No," she replied. "We're covert from everyone, and you have to promise to keep it this way."

"What is this place?" asked Minh.

"Who's this?" questioned one, poking his finger into Minh's side. "He's just a boy."

"I'm a young man."

"Minh, shut up," said Nhan. "I can't tell you what we're doing, but I need a little intel on—"

"Nhan," one of the women cut her off. "Has anyone on the outside heard what has happened?"

"What do you mean?"

"Just a couple hours ago."

"We haven't been in contact with anyone," Nhan answered.

"It's buzzing all over. The demon warrior, he—"

"You mean Sun Quan," stated Minh emphatically.

"Who?"

"Sun Quan. That's the demon warrior's name."

The storyteller looked over at Nhan. "Who is this kid?"

Before she could answer, Minh inserted himself. "I'm part of the rebellion. Probably a bigger part than you are. I could tell you a thing or two about what's going on."

"Nhan, would you tell this boy to shut up?"

"I won't shut up if I don't want to."

"Sorry," said Nhan. "I think he's going through puberty."

Minh snapped and said something a little too loudly. "I'm sick of being treated like a kid. I rode on the turtle's back into the lake. I know more than any of you."

The puzzled looks spread. Nhan raised her hand to slap him, but one of the young men stepped forward. "What did you say about a turtle?"

Minh recoiled a bit. "Nothing."

"The demon warrior got into a battle with an unknown woman warrior at Hoan Kiem Lake," said the man. "And the woman was injured and fell into the lake. Her body resurfaced on the shell of a turtle, only to be snatched away by the jaws of a giant long-tailed bird."

Nhan had a blank stare on her face, but Minh couldn't hide the gut-punch he felt inside. Lady Trieu had fought Sun Quan. Had she lost? Was she still alive? A bird? What did it mean?

"What happened to her?" Minh asked. "What happened?"

"To who?"

"The lady warrior."

"It's just a rumor—"

"It's no rumor. It's Lady Trieu, back to fight for our independence once again."

"Ba Trieu? What?"

"Sun Quan," pleaded Minh. "Don't you understand? Sun Quan was the Chinese king whom Ba Trieu defeated. He's returned, and we summoned her back to help. So what happened to her?"

The room remained in stunned silence. Minh not only believed the absurd rumor, he added to it. He spun a tale of fantastical fiction with such clarity and truth that they all had to wonder if he indeed played a larger role than his thirteen-year-old adolescence presented. Should they have called him a boy? Should Nhan have told him to shut up? Should the rebel base have taken him seriously?

"I already told you about her," Minh said to Nhan.

"Yeah, but did you think I actually believed you?"

"Well how could I make up something like that?" Minh turned to the others. "What happened to Lady Trieu?"

Still silence. Minh poked his head forward to signal he waited for an answer.

"All we heard was that a giant bird came and took her body away."

"Where did the giant bird come from?"

"I don't know."

"And this happened around Hoan Kiem Lake?"

"Yes, seen by thousands of people. No one has seen any video of it, but of course there's been no power."

"And Sun Quan. What happened?"

"They say he was injured but walked off and ended up on the top of St. Joseph's Church."

"St. Joseph's?" Minh slumped down onto the floor, back against the wall. Tears reasserted themselves in the corners of his eyes. He would use every means possible within him to hold them back. But what of his mother? Would he ever see her again? If Lady Trieu had indeed failed when confronting Sun Quan, what was the point of any of this? He certainly didn't know.

One of the young women squatted down in front of him. "Minh. Tell us what happened. All of it."

"What's the point? We did it all for Lady Trieu, and if she's gone—"

"Come on, tell us. You didn't make it this far without a reason."

He sighed and told the story to a rapt audience gasping in silence at every unbelievable word.

Old man Tho felt body aches all over—from the steps to the temple, from the garbage truck, from the ninety-five years of being a Vietnamese. He had found a comfortable enough patch of ground and fell asleep within minutes, even before night approached. The locked-up and vacant Co Loa historical site became their home—an inviting one compared to the black-walled prison or the garbage truck. Lien laid down beside him and soon also fell asleep. A few hours into her slumber, she woke to a strange sound, the biting cry of a bird relentlessly calling into the dark night. Lien walked a few feet toward the sound. She could see something's bobbing head twenty yards away. She approached with caution until she saw the tail of the bird flap up and down against the matted black sky. Then she recognized it. The bird encircled a large body which was difficult to distinguish. Lien leaned over and touched the leg of the person when it finally dawned on her. She turned and ran toward the old man.

"Tho! Tho!"

He didn't stir. She shook him awake, and he growled in pain. "What? What? This is why I never wanted a wife."

"Ong Tho. The bird is back, and Lady Trieu is hurt. Come. Quickly."

She helped him to his feet, and he staggered as a sober zombie toward the screeching bird.

"What is that infernal noise?"

"It's the bird. It's telling us what happened."

"Well, I can't speak lost bird-ese. Especially in the dark."

"Tho, look." She pointed to the immobile figure. "Lady Trieu. She's hurt. She's not moving."

Lien helped the old man down to inspect the scene. "It's too dark. I can't do anything."

"Well, what can we do? I don't have any light."

Tho reached into his pocket for a marble tablet. "Whenever I'm at a dead end, I go back to the tablets. For good or bad."

"Usually for good," said Lien.

"Not always."

He placed the tablet on Lady Trieu's leg, and it immediately lit up.

"Oh my ... the other ones. The other ones."

Tho removed the other two and placed one on her stomach and the other above her chest. All three of the tablets glowed a vibrant light covering her entire body. Her eyes were closed and arms limp at her sides. Her stomach revealed the fatal wound—a bloodless mark several inches across, allowing them to see into her a few inches.

"Look, Lien. Her breasts aren't that big."

"Tho. Stop that. We have to do something."

"But what? Maybe this is the end."

"It can't be? What could have caused this?"

"There could only have been one thing. Or one person."

"Sun Quan."

He nodded in confirmation.

"What does this mean?" asked Lien.

"We are lost once more."

"Isn't there anything we can do?"

"I can't resurrect the dead."

"You did it before."

"When?"

"When you went into the heart of Hoan Kiem Lake on the back of a turtle and brought the ancient female warrior back to life. That's when."

"Oh. Yes. I see."

"So do something."

"Like what?"

"Use the tablets."

"There's only three."

"Maybe there's only supposed to be three."

"Why?"

"I don't know. Try something. Anything."

He lifted the marble tablet from her stomach, and it stopped glowing immediately. He touched it back on her and it lit again. "Does this mean the forces are still awake in her?"

"How should I know?" asked Lien.

"How could anyone know?" He mumbled something.

"What did you say?"

"Even I don't know."

"What are you going to do?"

"Lien—"

"Are you going to try something?"

"Maybe. Give me space."

"No maybe, Mr. Tho. Do something. Use your experience. There's no one like you."

With that, he inserted the tip of the marble tablet into her open wound. The tablet glowed, but nothing happened.

"Hand me the other two."

Lien grabbed both of the others and handed them to him.

"No, you keep them."

"Why?"

"I don't know, but we've done this together. If it ends, it ends together."

"All right, Mr. Tho. What should I do with them?"

"I'm not going to tell you. I'm going to let you decide."

Lien grunted. "Because you have no idea what to do, right?"

"Precisely."

She held one of the tablets in each of her hands. She held them horizontally and put them perpendicular to the tablet Tho held in Lady Trieu's wound. The other two lit, forming a glowing 'T' above the wound. "Lady Trieu, we need you. Please."

At that moment, a chorus of toads sounded all around. They approached, hundreds of them, calling to the voices of the past. The long-tailed bird joined the chorus, and the encroaching knot of toads jumped right onto the body of Lady Trieu. They basked in the glowing 'T' and croaked without ceasing into the night. The bird took flight and swirled around the knot as close as it could without hitting the two humans, who kept the tablets lit against her body.

"Tho, what's going on?"

"Don't you see?"

"No, I don't."

"Toads bring rain."

"But, I don't see any—"

A massive thunderclap gob-smacked them to such a degree that all three of the tablets fell off her body. The darkness encompassed them, but it was now different. The first drop hit Lady Trieu, and then the deluge came. Each drop illuminated fluorescent green on her skin. The toads called to the sky, and the sky answered it deepest remembrance of history, unleashing a flood of water, which washed over the body of the limp warrior. The green, glowing water seeped into the wound. The toads jumped off her body, and Lady Trieu shuttered once, then sat up with a groggy look about her. She took a moment to compose herself. She noticed the toads and the bird flying above her, its tail touching her head at every pass. She winced once at the old man and Lien, sitting in awe once again.

"Thank you."

They didn't reply. The toads hopped off and disappeared into the blackened grass. The green glow of the water had vanished, and the warrior stood up and put her hand on her head.

"This is bad," said Trieu.

"What?" asked Lien.

"I was foolish."

"Can ancient warriors be foolish?" asked Tho.

"What happened?"

"I fought Sun Quan, and I lost. I have underestimated him. He is not just an ancient king. There is something deeper about him. Something more sinister."

"What do you mean?"

"It won't be like the last time I defeated him."

"Is there a way? Can he be defeated?"

"I don't know. But it will take more than one warrior."

"What do you need?" asked Tho.

"An army."

"What about the rebel forces? If we—" Lady Trieu waved off Lien and her enthusiasm.

"Yes, we will need every person who is able to fight, but it still won't be enough."

The woman warrior stumbled a little and glanced into the night sky. The rain had stopped, and the clouds parted directly above—the first star now visible.

"We will need to look deeper for the right path. This place, this ancient citadel might provide the answer."

Lien came alongside Lady Trieu, who towered over her. "Are you alright?"

"I'm afraid my time here isn't long. We need to act fast. I also fear what Sun Quan will do next. We do not have the liberty to wait."

She whistled to the long-tailed bird, which pranced over to her.

"Where are you going?" asked Tho.

"I need to survey the city."

"What do you want us to do?" asked Lien.

"At dawn, go to the Pearl Well, and find a way."

The bird leaped skyward with a weary Lady Trieu clutching the feathers around its neck. It disappeared into the black, leaving Tho and Lien alone once again.

"Tho, what do you want to do?"

"I'm wet and I'm tired. I want to sleep till morning. Why did they have to include such an old man in this?"

"Who is 'they'?"

Tho had already lain down in the wet grass, not seeming to mind the sticky dampness of the night. He snored with ease, allowing Lien a moment of reflection, wondering the whereabouts of her son.

Chapter 20

The Red Switch

The rest of the world knew little of what had transpired in northern Vietnam over the previous two years. A Chinese-backed puppet broadcast released new information daily discussing the unprecedented coup attempt within the Vietnamese government, and how the Chinese had come to help stabilize the democracy. Vietnamese dissidents abroad painted a uniquely different picture of a brutal Chinese takeover—an assertion Beijing categorically denied. Beijing officials even released video of the supposed coup attempt, which the dissidents called a deep fake. Either way, the information flow out of northern Vietnam had been tight-lipped since the Chinese invasion. They had jammed signals, cut off power, destroyed cell networks, severed every Internet cable coming into the country, and constructed their own proprietary communication system. Even so, black market images and video of the truth still surfaced overseas, though no one on the outside could confirm that reality. One Vietnamese dissident set up a demon warrior website which highlighted all sightings, encounters, and video which existed outside Hanoi of Sun Quan. Of course, no one knew his name, nor could they verify the veracity of the website. The dissident went missing one day from his California home. Authorities found his body a week later floating the surf off one of the beaches in Southern Cal. His website had been hacked and destroyed from within. The LA County police had no suspects in the suspected homicide.

The mysterious Chinese man had been in Hanoi since the beginning of the invasion and had become the face of the occupation. No one knew his name or understood his connection to Beijing. But Sun Quan always stood at his side, and the generals and subordinates followed his every command.

One of those subordinates stood next to a bright red switch on the top floor of the facility. The Chinese man signaled to him from a short distance away.

"Sir, are you ready?" The general had placed his hand on the switch. The Chinese man looked blankly. "It's strange, you know," said the Chinese man. "When I was young, my mother used a red switch made from a Chinese red-bark birch tree. She had a small shoot from a branch she kept in the house, and when I did something wrong, she would hit me with it."

Sun Quan had entered the room as the Chinese man reminisced.

"Sir?" asked the general for clarification.

"I learned to hold in my tears after a while."

"You're quite the fictional storyteller," said the warrior.

"My dear, Sun Quan. All life is fiction. But we keep flipping the next page to see what will happen. We can't help it. So, you've come to see the red switch? I think I shall have a picture of a Chinese birch drawn on this wall. Does anyone know if those would grow in this climate?"

"Whatever we want to grow, will grow."

"That is exactly the answer I wanted to hear, Sun Quan."

"Sir?" the general kept his hand on the switch.

"Sun Quan, tell me about the fight."

"She's done."

"So easily? You truly think so?"

"Yes."

"Just pass a sword through her and that's that."

"It's done." Sun Quan walked to the glass wall. The very top of Ho Chi Minh's mausoleum could be seen in the distance.

"Well then," said the Chinese man. "There's no reason to hold back any longer."

Sun Quan looked back at the Chinese man. "Did you ever think that perhaps they will learn to hold in their tears also, like you did when you were young?"

The Chinese man walked up beside him, his head coming only to the tip of Sun Quan's shoulder. "No one has ever seen a red switch like this. General, now."

The commotion inside the windowless rebel hideout came to an immediate pause when a strange noise pulsed through the air from all directions, like someone searching for a frequency on a cosmic radio. Suddenly, the station came in clear, and an ethereal female voice speaking in perfect Vietnamese wooed the most ardent of unbelievers with her Tokyo Rose insistence and honey sweet tone. But the words were not to be trifled with. Their intent was clear and threatening like the line of tanks which swarmed the border of Vietnam two years ago. The words were bullets, and every single person inside the city of the Red River were the targets. Each person felt the wound from every monosyllabic word.

"Residents of Hanoi. Some of you have been resisting us. There is no resistance of democracy. It is the future. It is now. You have fifteen minutes. The rats of the rebellion must be exposed. Point out their nests within the next fifteen minutes, or you too shall be resisting. You have fifteen minutes to expose the traitors. Open their nests. Turn them in. You have fifteen minutes. And the fifteen minutes start now."

All the lights in the city switched on. The great blackout gone, a cry of frenzy and confusion rose up into the streets. People, hidden in the shadows, found themselves yelling at their neighbors on the street's end, but they didn't know the purpose of the yelling. Women accused men of being with the resistance and threatening the lives of their children. Others feared a ticking time bomb and blurted out the seconds one at a time. Others still looked up into the night sky and worshiped the voice, praying to it and asking it for mercy. There were some who saw the battle of Hoan Kiem Lake and said the voice was that of Lady Trieu. A group of vandals started ravaging the shops in the old town leading to brawls around the edge of the lake. The chaos ripped the city apart long before the fifteen minutes expired.

Minh, Nhan, and the small group of infiltrators from the windowless room, wandered into the middle of the chaotic scene, not sure what to do. Three middle-aged women approached two of the young men standing on the edge of the street at the entrance of the dead-end alleyway.

"You two. We've seen you coming and going at all hours of the night. You're part of the rebellion. You're putting our families in danger."

"We'll all Vietnamese," replied one of the rebels standing next to Minh. "We have to stick together."

"Here they are!" yelled the other woman.

"Quiet."

Nhan whispered in Minh's ear. "We need to get out of here."

"And go where?"

She didn't reply, but the two women became more aggressive toward the group. "Last week we had the lights on and food in the market. Things were starting to feel normal, but now—"

One of the female rebels stepped forward. "Normal? They've taken over our city. How can you just accept everything? What's wrong with you?"

"My child goes to sleep hungry every night. I want this to end."

"It will only end when we kick the Chinese out of here and—"

Someone from behind hit the rebel with a wooden plank, and she fell to the group. Two of the rebel men pounced on the man who had swung the piece of wood, but he turned and ran away screaming. Nhan helped the woozy-headed rebel back on her feet as the women pressed further, bringing more unwanted attention from the rest of the gathering mob. Minh found himself cowering behind Nhan, who took an aggressive stance against the mob. He felt very much thirteen-years-old as they pressed in, and he thought of his mother. He also thought about the day, not even a week ago, when he brought Mr. Tho into their apartment to watch the TV broadcast. It felt like a year had passed. That day seemed normal, compared to this. He caught himself longing for that normality, but then he remembered something. His father had been gone for nearly two years, and he hadn't heard a word from him. Also, he remembered the times before the war when he was just a boy and would walk to school with his friends. That's normal, he reminded himself. He closed his eyes and tried to tell himself what he was now. A rebel on the right side. He remembered the stories of his grandmother dragging pieces of artillery up the muddy slopes outside Dien Bien Phu in 1954. This was his Dien Bien Phu, and age had nothing to do with it.

"Nhan, let's go. We need to get to the facility."

She nodded. "It won't be easy through this mess."

"When is anything important ever easy?"

She gripped his hand. "Hold on to me. Let's head south."

One of the rebels made it around the squawking ladies. "Nhan, this way. We're going to leave the city."

"No, Minh and I are continuing on."

"You can't. This is madness."

"We have to stop the madness. Go, get word back to my father. And if he—"

She couldn't finish her sentence. Fifteen minutes had expired. Sirens pierced the night. They belted out three loud pulses and the power was cut, leaving the frenzied chaos in the pit of its own darkness. For the first few seconds, a hush fell over the city. Everyone stopped as their eyes tried to adjust to the new reality. But darkness never invites you in; it surrounds you on all sides and whispers terrible fantasies in your ear. It emboldens the fear in your chest, and the fear allows the irrational thoughts to completely overtake what little rational cognition still exists. The silence gave way to panicked fear and senseless screaming. People flailing their arms and running into each other and defending themselves from the demons they held within their own chests. The edge of sanity gave way to the bitter pill of transcendent fear. The organic destruction pitting Hanoi residents against each other paled in comparison to the real assault which commenced.

Simultaneously, on hundreds of Hanoi streets, metal clicking and swooshing sounds could be heard in all directions. Hundreds of four-foot-tall round robotic devices seemed to pop out of nowhere on the streets, all of them broadcasting a steady stream of messages. "Traitors will die." "Only traitors hide." "Democracy thrives when we work together." "First we pluck the weeds, then society will grow." "Traitors will die."

The relentless messages soaked the atmosphere, and the robots cycled through the streets. They had wheels for moving quickly and probe arms to maneuver effortlessly around obstacles in the street. Sharp lights beamed off the front of them, and they ran over anyone in their way. The night terror had begun. The robots rolled up to closed doors, then stood on robotic legs and fired through the solid structure, smashing metal bars, and wiping out whoever was in the room, whether a rebel or not.

The machines moved quickly and methodically. They even interacted with people, cornering an old lady against a wall, asking the woman where the rebels were. She told them, even if she had no knowledge of actual rebels. The machines ravaged the streets, and the terror and screams of the voices rose up like a whole civilization questioning the sky if they indeed had the will to survive.

Of the five rebels who had been with Nhan and Minh just moments before, four of them were gunned down by the machines. Only one escaped to the edge of the Red River and swam across to the other side, not even waiting for a rebel raft. She doubted they even existed anymore.

Minh and Nhan found themselves caught in the middle of two machines, each approaching from opposite directions. They came upon them so quickly, they had no time to even conjecture what they witnessed. The darkness of the city still encapsulated everything except for the bright erratic lights from the machines. With the lights shining from both directions, it allowed Minh and Nhan to get a glimpse of what they were facing. The machines had large wheels on each side but also legs which allowed two wheels to be off the ground when not in use. The body of the machine was not solid, but a crisscross of polished metal parts and rods. Its arms were types of weapons, but they didn't look like rifles. The machine had no head, though it had an engraved image of a head on the top of its chest. Three camera eyes moved around off the top of the chest as well, and though it looked like some sort of steam-punk device, it had an electronic brain with small flashing lights across its top.

The two machines cornered the teens head-on. "Identify yourselves."

Neither teen responded. They clung to each other.

Both machines extended a tripod into the air with a camera lens on it. They flashed and scanned the entire bodies of the teens.

"Ly Thi Nhan and Nguyen Van Minh. You are to come with us immediately."

Nhan grabbed the robotic tripod arm of the machine in front of her and climbed up over top of it. "Minh, run." She jumped off, and Minh slid out from under the other as the machines repositioned to aim at the girl. They ran down the street with the machines barking out further instructions. "You are to come with us immediately."

Shots fired, and a layer of bullets peppered the ground around their feet. They jumped into an alleyway and ran as hard as they could with the machines giving chase. They sprinted out across a major street. The commotion had spread, and they saw several bodies lying unresponsive in the middle of the street, but they kept moving. They approached the gate of the ancient citadel. The doors had been blown off their hinges. They ran inside and up the steps to the top of the wall. They climbed to the peak of the flag tower and were alone above this old section of the city. They panted as they looked out over the surroundings. Weapons fired. Flashes of light spread out in all directions.

"What's happening?" said Minh.

"I don't know."

"How did we get away from the machines?"

"They let us go. They could have killed us at any time, but they want us alive. They knew our names."

"Why did they let us go?"

"I don't know."

"Nhan, what do you think happened to the rebel cell?" She didn't respond. "The facility is right over there. It's not far."

"Yes."

"We should go."

"Into the lair? Minh, this all seems so foolish."

"I know. But what else can we do?"

"Think. Think. Think. Okay, Minh, what do we know? They know who we are. They don't want to kill us."

"Yes, and we know that Lady Trieu once successfully attacked the facility."

"Yes, but we also heard that she might be dead."

"Nhan, we don't know that. It's all rumors."

The night terrors continued. The metallic swooshing of the machines sounded from all directions. Desperate screams filled the air, and the two in the watchtower had to remind themselves where they were and what they were experiencing.

"This is war, Minh. We're on the battlefield. Do you really want to do this?"

"Yes, for my grandmother. For my mother. And for my father."

"Then let's go."

They descended the tower and crept along the inside wall of the citadel. On the western side, they squeezed through the bars of a metal gate and crawled along the shrubbery of a small park. The facility lay across the street about fifty yards in front of them. Soldiers and robotic machines and vehicles hurried to and fro in all directions. The facility was lit up fully. They realized there was no way to approach it without being seen. Minh pulled the marble table out of his pocket and held it up.

"What are you doing?" Nhan asked.

"I don't know."

"You're expecting some magic to help us now? After all the craziness going on?"

"I don't know."

"And what are we going to do when we get in there?"

"I don't know that either."

"This isn't a plan. It's a suicide mission."

"All I know is I was rescued from the facility, and I promised Cuong I would come back for him. That's where Sun Quan is. He's the one we want to defeat, right?"

"This is the stupidest thing I've ever heard. How can we defeat him? Even Lady Trieu couldn't. Listen to me. I'm talking as if I believe she's real."

Minh clung onto the tablet and said a few words. Like a chant or even a prayer. Nhan looked at him like he was insane. Perhaps he was. But Tho had always taught him to believe in your own just cause and allow the universe to show you its inevitability. He knew the cause was just. He had trouble believing in the outcome, but he would make his mother proud, and if he had to go down, he would go down fighting for justice.

"Follow me."

"Minh, wait!"

Before he stepped out of the bushes, four robotic machines surrounded them and two vehicles of soldiers skidded to a halt in front of the shrubs and ambushed them. The machines blurted out their identities in unison, and the guards had them in custody before Minh even had a chance to see the shocked look on Nhan's face. He thought only of the tablet in his pocket, wondering if he would have to shove it up inside him again, a thought he did not relish. But he would go to great lengths to secure it. The guards paraded them into the ground floor of the facility. No sign of Sun Quan or the Chinese man. The facility walls opened automatically as they mazed through successive rooms before being instructed to sit against the far wall. They obeyed. The glossy black stone wall closed in front of them, securing the two young rebels. Minh's breath labored, but he still managed to tell Nhan to relax and wait for Lady Trieu's sign. Nhan gripped Minh's hand firmly.

"I'm not afraid of them. None of them."

"Me either," replied Minh through a few voice fluctuations which told a different story.

They heard a rumble. The wall in front of them slid upwards into the ceiling. A man stood in the center of the doorway. Minh looked, but shook his head in disbelief. He even unclasped his hand with Nhan and smacked himself on the cheek before looking again. The man took one step into the cell.

"Hello, Minh."

The man wore a Vietnamese army uniform with a small Sino-Vietnam harmony patch on his left chest. Minh's entire body shook and his stomach churned.

"Welcome," the man spoke again.

Nhan looked at the teen and shook Minh from his trance. "Minh, Minh!" She glanced back at the man. "Minh, do you know him?"

"Yes." He wiped the sweat dripping from his chin. "He's my father."

Chapter 21

The Pearl Well

Tho and Lien awakened somewhat refreshed from their sleep on the grass in Co Loa Citadel, twenty miles outside of Hanoi, oblivious to the night of terror in the capital. They also hadn't heard anything further from Lady Trieu.

"Lien, you happen to have anything to eat?"

"I wish I had, Tho."

"No matter. I would give away myself as weak if I wanted food. I'm sure the heroes of the past couldn't afford such luxuries."

"We could look in the buildings over there. Perhaps we could find something."

"No, no. Perhaps the hunger will take me from this life sooner."

"Tho, don't say that. We need you. Without you—"

"We wouldn't be in this mess." He laughed and coughed and felt every aching muscle his body still could feel as he stood up to relieve himself. "Sorry, Lien. You might need to look away. I want to conserve my steps."

She laughed and walked off around the edge of the closest building to do the same. When she returned, Tho had made his way to the edge of the pond outside the gate of the citadel. The center of the pond had a perfect circle made of cement, forming a massive round formation known as the pearl well. The present structure of the well had been reformed many times over the years, but excavations of the region hadn't yielded its origins. Lien walked in beside him.

"Lady Trieu said to wait until dawn and go to the pearl well and find a way."

"Why did she have to be so cryptic? Find a way to what?"

"Come on, Tho. That's sounds exactly like something you would say."

"Well, yes. The old mystic is allowed to be cryptic. I like to give, not receive."

"You don't think a two-thousand-year-old warrior from a lake has a little mysticism in her?"

"Fair point. So what do we do? Go to the pearl well. How do we get there?" asked Tho.

"We need a boat."

Tho cringed at the thought. "That's what I was afraid of. Remember the last time we were on a boat? The whole universe turned itself on its head."

"It did so in an effort to save us. Would you do it again, if you had to?"

"I'm too old for such ruminations. So why not. If our ancestors feel inclined to provide us with a boat, so be it. Otherwise, I'm going to take a nap under that tree over there."

Two elderly men dragged a *thung chai* basket boat to the edge of the pond. They stopped when they noticed the pair looking longingly out over the morning water.

"Did you eat yet?" asked one of the men.

"No food around here," replied Tho.

"Here, I have some banh cuon. Would you each like some?"

The man carried over two plastic bags filled with piping hot steamed rice pancakes stuffed with minced pork and onions.

"Where did you get these?" asked Lien, eyes exploding with excitement.

"The old lady makes them every morning. Just beyond the walls."

"Thank you very much," said Tho, not waiting for any other

niceties before reaching in and placing the divine concoction in his mouth.

"What are you doing with the basket boat?" asked Lien.

"Pulling weeds from the pond. The old lady likes to cook with them."

"When are you taking the boat out?"

"We'll be back in a few moments for it. The old lady made us some noodles. We like to eat them in the boat."

"And you do all of this every day with a war going on around you?"

"Can't fight the Hans on an empty stomach, I always say," said one of the old men.

"I suppose," said Lien. "You ever see patrols around here?"

"No, no. What would they want with this place?"

The two elderly men—still much younger than Tho— disappeared around the edge of the citadel.

"Tho," urged Lien. He had another handful of the rice pancake ready to enjoy. "Now's our chance. Let's get the boat and go to the pearl well."

"We can't steal their boat. They gave me banh cuon."

"Tho, you said if your ancestors gave you a boat, you'd take it."

"Those aren't my ancestors. I'm older than they are."

"Tho, we're taking this boat. Lady Trieu said at dawn."

"But you heard what they said. The old lady made noodles. Maybe they'll bring us back some of that too."

"Now, Tho. We're going in the basket boat!"

She grabbed him by the arm and pulled him towards the boat resting on the edge of the pond.

"Get in."

"This is a bad idea."

"The other boat was your idea."

"I've reconsidered my life choices."

"Too late." She pushed the old man head first over the rough edge of the perfectly round woven boat, that indeed was more of a massive basket than an actual boat. She pushed it into the edge of the water and climbed in, using the single oar to try and get them moving toward the circular well at the center of the pond. Tho continued eating his breakfast, though he complained that Lien had smashed it when she pushed him in.

It took Lien several minutes to get the hang of the oar, but soon the basket had floated out from the edge of the pond towards the circular cement ring in the middle. By the time they had reached the halfway point to the well, the two old men returned to the edge of the water and yelled with an inflamed intensity.

"Come back here! That's our boat."

"Sorry," yelled Lien. "We need to borrow it."

"Bring back the boat. We brought noodles for everyone."

Tho turned toward Lien and complained. "They brought noodles."

"I doubt they would share at this point."

"It's all your fault."

"Tho, focus. I need you in this."

"I'm in it. Can you not see me in the boat?"

"But your head. Focus. I need your wisdom."

"Wisdom stays on shore for noodles."

"Tho, the rebellion."

He breathed in deeply. "All right. The rebellion."

The old men on the bank of the pond continued shouting at the boat thieves. Lien tried to make them understand that they absconded with it for official rebellion business, but the men didn't take kindly to the explanation. One of them stripped down to his underwear and jumped in the frigid morning water. He swam toward them at a steady pace as the basket boat approached the circular embankment at the center of the pond.

Lien used the oar to hold the boat from moving away from the center ring. "Tho, shift your body to this side." He complained that his body just does what it wants. But Lien insisted. The old man tumbled toward her. "Hold the oar. I'm going to try and climb onto the embankment." Lien held the edge of the basket boat as she stepped out onto the circular ring, built up as a perfect concentric circle forming the appearance of a well in the middle of the pond. "I have the boat, Tho. Try and climb out." He tried, as the other old man continued his swim toward them. Tho sat on the edge of the cement, feet dangling in the pearl well. Lien balanced herself on the ring while pulling the boat over the edge and into the pearl well. It now sat right in front of them. "Get back in." He did. They sat in the basket boat in the middle of the pearl well, in the middle of the Co Loa citadel pond, waiting for whatever it was.

"What did she say?" asked Lien.

"I believe her words were 'find a way.'"

"Yes. Find a way. Tho I got us here, now it's your job to find a way."

"How am I supposed to do that?"

"Use your mysticism. I don't know. How did you get us to the great turtle?"

Tho uttered an unintelligible cynical guffaw.

"The old man is here," stated Lien, watching the swimmer put his hands on the embankment just a few feet away from them.

"I don't consider him a threat," said Tho with another laugh. "I can take him."

The man climbed out of the water. "Give me back our boat. What are you doing with it in the pearl well?"

Lien pushed the boat further from the circular cement walkway.

"Give me my boat back."

"Find a way, Tho," she said. "Find a way."

Tho closed his eyes and allowed his mind to focus. He spoke out in stream-of-consciousness as he tried to flesh out her meaning. "Co Loa ... we were brought to the ancient citadel. The first one. The oldest one. 3rd century BC ... build by King An Duong Vuong ... hundreds of years before Lady Trieu defeated the Hans ... and the turtle ... and the lake ... and ..." He paused for a moment as Lien's eyes lit with excitement.

"Do you know what to do?"

Tho let loose his breath. "No. I have nothing."

"Give me my boat back," yelled the old man from the cement circle. "Thieves!"

"The Chinese are the thieves," Tho replied. "This is official business of the rebellion."

"Tho, she said find a way. But find a way to do what?"

Tho perked up. "Maybe it's not find a way to do something. Maybe it's find a way to go somewhere."

"Where?"

"Down."

"Down?"

Tho looked over the edge of the boat and a toad lifted its head out of the water. "Lien, look." She glanced over the rim of the basket. "A toad." It dunked itself under the water once more only to resurface a second later with a mollusk sitting on its head.

"What is that?" Lien reached down and grabbed the shelled creature from the toad's head.

"I would assume it's a gift."

"For what?"

"Let's find out."

"Hey! Hey!" yelled the old man still on the cement ring. "What did you find?"

"A mollusk."

"Open it."

"How?"

"Something sharp."

Tho looked at Lien. "Do you have anything sharp?"

"How about the corner of your marble tablets?"

He handed one to her. "Try it."

She pressed the sharpened corner into the muscle of the mollusk and it popped open as if it had a spring in it. Inside the mollusk lay a perfectly round, white pearl. Lien picked it up and held it between her thumb and index finger.

"What did you find?" shouted the old man.

"A pearl."

"Throw it back. It belongs here."

Tho grabbed the pearl from Lien's fingers, but it slipped from his fingertips into his palm. He curled his fingers to catch the stone, but it rolled off his middle finger onto the edge of the basket boat and plopped back into the pearl well. Both Lien and Tho shifted their heads forward to watch it descend out of sight. A loud popping sound came from the center of the well, and a bubble. Tho's first thought was that they would be encapsulated by the bubble once again. But no. It popped. And after a short gurgling sound, a large swoosh came, as if a clogged drain had been unplugged. The water twirled clockwise, faster and faster, dragging the boat in a circular descending motion. Lien and Tho clutched their hands on the sides of the boat as best they could. The old man on the cement ring stood speechless. And with one great force of suction, the boat sank downwards with great speed and was quickly out of sight from the man gawking from the cement rim. The water closed back in on itself and within seconds turned back into the serene surface of the well once again. From the edge of the pond, the other man yelled to his friend, "What happened?" The man in his soggy, sagging underwear, which matched the dripping, saggy skin of his chest, simply replied, "The well swallowed them." Then he glanced once more at the center of the water. "You can keep the boat."

Tho and Lien clung for dear life as they fell bottom-of-the-basket-boat-first into a tunnel. Air surrounded them, leaving the water as a shimmering ceiling over their heads. They landed at the bedrock bottom of a cave, a solid granite wall to their backs and a dark invisible passageway ahead of them. Their eyes still focused on the iridescent light from the pearl well above them, until the rock ceiling closed and left them in pitch darkness. They couldn't even make out the outline of each other. Lien screamed and reached for Tho, who screamed when he felt her.

"Where are we?" she asked. "I know. You don't know either. We need light."

"We need more than that."

"Well, for now, I'll take light."

"For those who seek light, they shall find it."

"Thank you, Tho. Thank you! I feel like you're getting back to yourself. You've been acting like a big baby."

"A ninety-five-year-old and a baby share the same traits that a mother hates."

She laughed and reached over to slap him gently, because she had no idea where she would be hitting him. Tho pulled one of the tablets from his pocket.

"I shall try one of these."

"I don't know what you're referring to, but fine. Try anything."

He reached out from the edge of the boat holding the tablet forward, edging it slowly toward the rock wall to make sure he didn't damage it. He felt it touch the rock, but it didn't feel hard. It felt like the tablet made an indentation into the stone.

"Strange."

"What?"

"I'm going to try it again."

"Try what?"

He poked slowly until he felt the wall push back a little, then pushed the tablet in further as if it was being inserted into a gelatin mold.

"Tho, what are you doing?"

The walls of the cave lit like a dimmer switch slowly turned on. The cave's walls were not rock. It glowed like a soft fluorescent putty.

"This doesn't look like a cave."

The marble tablet stuck an inch out of the side of the wall. Tho wondered and started to pull it out. The walls remained lit. As soon as he put the tablet back in his pocket, the basket boat took off like an amusement park ride, a logjam, or a giant slide. The boat accelerated through the tunnel like warp speed. They had no controls, but the acceleration didn't make them fall over. They seemed to hover in the boat. Neither made a sound until they approached the end of the tunnel, and they were on a direct collision course to a transparent glassy wall. They screamed. Loud. Frantic. They would have covered their faces to prevent the bloodbath that was sure to occur if they could have managed to move their arms, but at once they stopped, without momentum, taking them forward. In stasis they hung in the air, not even touching the bottom of the boat, and looked through the glass which wasn't glass at all. It was water. They could see fish swimming and a large turtle. It looked at them and suddenly poked its head out of the wall of water. Its head hung over the boat and dripped large wet droplets on them.

It spoke. The turtle spoke. A deep voice which echoed off the glowing walls. "Now, go and tell them about the portal. There isn't much time."

Lien, still looking up at the turtle, shifted her head toward the wall of water and looked upward. She could see it. The small island. "Tho, this is Hoan Kiem Lake. This tunnel goes from Co Loa to Hoan Kiem Lake."

"Yes, said the turtle. "Now go. Tell them."

Its head retracted into the water, but before it swam away, it said in its underwater gargled voice, "Find the one worthy of the magic crossbow."

The amusement ride wasn't over. The basket boat backtracked without warning like a capsule being sucked through a vacuum-sealed pipe. When it reached the end after only a few seconds, the lights of the tunnel went out, and they ascended through the open ceiling and popped back up to the top of the pearl well. The old man was still standing on the edge of the cement ring. The ascension of the boat scared him backwards, and he tripped into the water. He kicked his legs and resurfaced with one clear message: "You can keep the boat." He turned and swam towards his friend on the bank of the pond.

Lien and Tho rested without words in the middle of the pearl well for a few moments until Lien asked the obvious.

"Who do we tell? What did the turtle mean?"

"I think I see it now, Lien. We have one more journey to go on."

"Where to?"

"We have to find the rebel base."

Chapter 22

The Man in the Doorway

Hanoi awakened—dazed—from a sleepless night of terror, different from any other since the start of the invasion. The strange machines roamed the streets, identifying suspects and eliminating anyone thought to have given material support to the rebellion. Countless bodies lay strewn across Hanoi from the brutality and the remnants of Hanoi's population huddled in fear in the back corners of their houses, praying the machines didn't knock down their doors and accuse them of something they didn't do. Chinese officials forced Vietnamese clean-up crews to gather the bodies on trucks to deliver to various incinerators around town. The burning couldn't keep pace with the deliveries of the corpses.

The machines had also rounded up dozens of individuals they thought to be holding relevant intel for operations against the rebel forces outside the city. Sun Quan had led two pre-dawn attacks on rebel nests not far from the city limits. But of all the captives, none intrigued Sun Quan or the Chinese man more than the pair of teens, who had been foolish enough to stage an infiltration of the facility and ended up in a black-walled cell.

They had been in the cell for several hours when the wall opened and in walked Minh's father. Minh's mind churned methodically as it attempted to understand the image standing in the cell's doorway. The familiar face invited him to step forward and run towards it, but his gut wouldn't allow his feet to move. His father had been in the Vietnamese army for more than a decade. He had become a decorated officer. Minh remembered the party the family held in his father's honor when he had been promoted. Minh was only six at the time. After the Chinese invasion nearly two years prior, the family had only heard from his father one time. A benign note telling everyone he was safe and fighting for the freedom of the nation. They had heard second and third-hand rumors from time to time of others running into his father as part of the rebel cause. But they were never sure of his location or what he was doing at any given moment. Minh had a sense of pride and duty knowing his father sacrificed everything for his country. His mother spoke of her husband in glowing terms, another honored member of the Vietnamese army — a family legacy dating back generations. Now as the memories and assumptions lay stirring in a stew of uncertainty, Minh lacked the will, or even perhaps the courage, to step out and acknowledge the man claiming to be the most revered person in his life.

"Minh, I'm not surprised to see you here. You've always had the same love for country our family has had for generations." He walked into the cell further. The door remained open, but no one else was visible. "And your name is Nhan, isn't it?" She didn't respond. Minh remained frozen, staring at the man. "I know your father. Well, everyone knows the commander. But you have no reason to be afraid here. No one will hurt you. I'll see to it."

He walked closer to Minh, who had stood up with his back flat against the wall.

"Minh, you've gotten so much bigger. You must be thirteen now."

"I'll be fourteen next month."

"Yes, on the twenty-seventh. I couldn't forget your birthday."

"Dad, what are you doing here?" The question finally emerged. Minh had been studying his father, not able to comprehend the situation, especially the unification symbol on his father's left chest.

"Are you surprised?"

"You're wearing a unification symbol."

"Of course."

"How could you?"

"Minh, I don't expect you to understand yet, especially when your mind has been poisoned by all the propaganda."

"Poisoned?"

"Yes. They've said many damaging lies about what has happened these past two years. Minh, you do know that your grandmother was Chinese, right? But did you know what happened to her? Forced to leave Hanoi in 1979. Not recognized as a true

Vietnamese compatriot by the traitors who set up this government. Another thing you didn't know, there was a group of ravenous vultures disrupting the Vietnamese government and threatening the peace and stability of the region, so a group of Vietnamese patriots sought help from the Chinese government to allow the region to be free and independent. We are always better and stronger when we are working together. Don't you see?"

"That's a lie," accused Nhan. "All of it."

Minh's father laughed. "I would expect that from you, the commander's daughter. But what about you, Minh. You believe your father, don't you?"

Minh placed his hands on his neck and rubbed his palms nervously over his face. "You look like my father, but you don't talk like him."

"How is your mother? Do you know where she is?"

"No, and I wouldn't tell you if I did."

"Minh, why are you getting hostile toward your own father, whom you haven't seen in two years?"

"Because you're not acting like my father."

"You've forgotten everything about me. Your mother has been listening to that fool Tho for so many years, she'll believe anything he says."

"Mr. Tho is not a fool. He showed me the magic and—"

"What magic? What has he shown you?"

Minh turned away, but Nhan stepped forward towards the man. "I don't know who you are. We've come to destroy this place from the inside out, and there's nothing you can do to stop us."

The man laughed. "I do love your enthusiasm. Would the commander sacrifice his allegiance to his cause over his daughter's well-being? Again, I'm not threatening you. You are safe here, but he doesn't know that. Not yet. Come with me." He turned around and walked toward the open door. Nhan didn't follow. "Please." He stopped, back still facing them, when two machines rolled into view. "Nhan, we'll just have a talk. Minh will be fine, as will you."

She looked at Minh, who nodded for her to go. She walked out of the room and the wall closed behind her. Minh was alone in the cell. At first, he paced back and forth with myriad thoughts bounding off him on all sides. A boy lost his father. Not only to the ideological shift, but to the coldness he showed his son. His fondest memories brought back images of a man who laughed, who teased a young boy, who played ball in the crowded park, and fished at the river, though they caught nothing. He had long been worried that his father had died, but now he wondered if death would have been preferable to a Chinese puppet wearing the unification branding as an honor. He missed his mother and Tho. He even missed Nhan. Would he ever see her again? Would he ever make it out of the facility again?

"Minh." A low ethereal voice filled the room.

He didn't notice at first, still lost in his thoughts, which had translated to tears from the corner of his eyes.

"Minh."

He pivoted but saw no one.

"Minh."

"Who's there?"

A light shimmered across his eyes, and if he looked closely, he could see a faint shape completely see-through, but an image that moved in ceaseless motion.

"Minh." He knew who it was. "Don't talk. Their sensors will hear you. Listen with your heart to understand. Nod if you can hear me."

He nodded. Eyes wide. Brain on edge.

"When the moment comes, use the tablet to open the doors. Don't ask me how, just do. Don't ask when. You will know."

A smile came across his face. The type of smile he had been saving for his father's return. The smile reinforced the hope within. It forced him to speak, even though she told him not to. "I thought you were—"

"Don't speak. I know. Your mother and Tho saved me. We will never give up. Remember what I told you. At the right moment, use the tablet. You will know when. You will know how."

The spirit left him, but he didn't feel alone anymore.

176 Mark W Sasse

Nhan followed Minh's father from a distance into an open courtyard. Minh's father exited and the two machines followed him, leaving her alone for a moment, or at least she thought so. She scouted in each direction and wondered if she should try to escape, but she couldn't leave Minh. They came for a reason, a long shot, perhaps. A way to tempt fate into forcing Lady Trieu into action, if she indeed still lived after the hellish reports of the previous evening. Nhan realized, however, that she wasn't alone. A presence hovered over her until it morphed into the towering warrior.

"The commander's rat," Sun Quan said.

She had never seen him in real life, and everything about him terrified her, especially the eyes.

"Let's see what she knows."

She had in her mind what she intended to say. But the words stopped as Sun Quan grabbed her by the sides of her head and lifted her off the ground. She screamed, which seemed to delight him all the more. "What do you know?" He looked inside her, not concerned with any audible gasp from her mouth. He forced her into his sphere, without her even knowing it. She succumbed to the grasp of history and space which pulsed through her head from hand to hand. He could see it all. The base. The numbers. The movement. They were on the move already. He would act decisively. It would end it. After Lady Trieu's defeat. After the night of terror. The base would be annihilated, and the plan would be complete. He dropped her, her energy sapped. She lay in the courtyard near a bench and fountain, like a dog napping on a hot summer's afternoon. She no longer had any worries and rested on the cement walk.

The Chinese man appeared from the rear.

"I know where the base is," said Sun Quan.

"Tell me. I'll dispatch the machines to take care of them."

"No, I'll do this myself."

"Sun Quan, you should be reminded who's in charge here."

Sun Quan whipped around and pushed the Chinese man to his knees without even touching him. "You should mind that yourself."

"You wouldn't be here without me."

"But now I am. And I said I'll handle it myself.

The giant warrior released his physical form and the spirit

ascended through the facility into the open air. The image from Nhan's mind transported him to the cave's entrance. A long line of rebels moved quickly with supplies toward the opening. An officer barked commands until Sun Quan appeared behind him and impaled him on his sword. The officer's body dropped forward onto two soldiers carrying sacks right below him. Fear ripped through their hearts—the type of fear one gets from an undefeated demon hunting its prey with its eyes. Sun Quan acted without warning, slicing several soldiers with one swath of his foreboding cutlass. He entered the cave and slaughtered the next line of soldiers tripping over themselves in panic. Chaos exploded, yells and screams, instructions drowned out by the fear, as the ruthless demon devoured everyone in his path. Several, who had exited the cave, ran toward the commotion, weapons drawn, as any worthy soldier would. They fired off several rounds into the beast, but the bullets merely disappeared into the flesh of the warrior, each piece of metal making him stronger, each desperate scream displayed on the chest of Sun Quan as a badge of honor.

The chaos in the cave had a rippling effect. The units which had previously descended the hill scattered—small groups without direction, without commands, with only the desire to see another day. Some escaped Sun Quan's wrath, but he hunted all within his reach. He searched the cave for anything relevant, especially the body of Commander Lieu, which eluded him. When the warrior reemerged into the sunlight, the main rebel base had been destroyed.

Lady Trieu watched Sun Quan from the mountain's peak above the cave's opening. She had arrived too late. A quick strike from the back could disable him, perhaps. Though she had underestimated him before, and she couldn't allow the bloodshed to affect any plan, no matter how thin. But she had to let him see her. He had to know she survived; only then could the doubts do their work.

"You have left your fortress."

A quick turn and stare at the lady on top of the mountain, a hundred yards above him.

"You've returned."

"I can't tell if your disappointed or happy."

"I am always happy to be in your presence." He didn't move

toward her. "You see now how weak they've become. A small chat with the girl and the base revealed itself. It will again, if they are foolish enough to regroup."

"Oh, they are foolish enough. You should know that."

"Why won't you see that we are one, you and I?"

"Some claims can never be renounced. Claims that demand a fight till the death. Claims that live on despite that death. It's in our blood."

"Blood that flows freely on the ground today."

"I won't fall for your trap again."

"Then why did you return too late to stop me?"

"Costs are never fixed. But the outcome is assured. I had to face you once more before we meet each other for the final time."

"You think it will be the final time?"

"I suppose it will."

"And I cannot persuade you."

"No."

"Then you know the ending."

"Yes. But do you?"

Sun Quan morphed himself into a spirit and reappeared on top of the mountain, but Lady Trieu had already mounted the long-tailed bird and taken flight.

"You won't follow me?" she asked.

"Not this time."

The bird flew south toward Hanoi. Sun Quan watched it disappear before morphing to the other realm and arriving back at the facility. Nhan continued sleeping on the paved walk. The Chinese man entered.

"Did you find the base?"

"She's alive."

"Yes, I know the girl's alive," answered the perturbed Chinese man.

"No. Lady Trieu."

"You said—"

"I was wrong."

"Is there going to be a problem?"

"No, the base is decimated. Some had left previously, but all who remained behind will never walk this earth again. Now, with the girl and the boy?"

The Chinese man stood over top of Nhan. "Once she awakes, I'll have the machines put her back in the cell. She's still useful to us."

They both walked away, leaving the girl immobile on the floor, but she had heard parts of the conversation. The weary girl struggled to her feet. Her energy sapped, she staggered in two different directions before she heard the machines surrounding her. They corralled her like a pack of dogs surrounding a lost sheep, and she obeyed them. Her body could do nothing different. The wall to her cell opened into the ceiling and she fell inside to her knees. Minh ran to her and knelt in front of her. They hugged. A moment they never would have willingly given, but it felt natural. Minh pulled away.

"Are you all right? Did they hurt you?"

"I'm not sure what happened. Sun Quan grabbed me on both sides of the head with his hands, and I felt weak and collapsed. But I woke up when they were still talking. I heard what they said."

"What?"

"Sun Quan destroyed the rebel base."

"The cave? It's destroyed? Did you hear anything about your father?

"No."

"Are you worried about him?"

"There's nothing to worry about in a rebellion, except the next step forward. That's what my father always said. There is no family in rebellion. Just country."

"That's not true, that's—"

"Minh, that's not all. I also heard that Lady Trieu—"

"Shhhh." He placed his hand over her mouth to stop her from saying it. He nodded with a knowing smile written across his face. "Yes, I know."

"You know? How?"

"I'm afraid the walls can talk. I'll tell you later."

"All right." She stood to her feet. "But if that's true, it also means …" Nhan hesitated. "Lady Trieu is real."

"Yes. I know that too."

Chapter 23

Lady Trieu

The scattered remnants of the rebels dispersed themselves throughout various safe houses and hiding spots throughout northern Vietnam. Sun Quan's attack on their base disrupted communication and few knew what had happened in Hanoi or the next plan of action.

Commander Lieu sped in an open-air jeep through a remote valley, balancing on the delicate dirt road through rice fields and tight-fisted turns around steep peaks to a final outpost on the edge of Thai Nguyen province, sixty miles north of Hanoi.

Without warning, the driver pounded the brakes, and the jeep skidded to a halt, veering sharply to the left so the vehicle slid sideways on all fours and nearly overturned. Lady Trieu blocked the road. Taller than before, leather chest piece hanging low off her chest. Sword sheathed on her back. Dagger at her side. Her arms earthward with clenched fists. Her hair tied back, face sullen, dark sunken eyes peering at her prey in the back seat. Both the driver and passenger in the front aimed pistols at the warrior, telling her to identify herself, yelling commands to lie on the ground, warning her not to take a step forward. But she moved anyways, forcing several rounds at her. She twisted out of their way and jumped once on top of the jeep's hood. She lifted the driver by the collar and threw him into the ragged grass on the side of the dirt road. The soldier in the passenger seat lifted his pistol once more, but his arm shook. He fired anyway. The bullet pierced her torso without making her flinch. She snatched the pistol from his hand and bent the barrel in her palm before throwing it off to the side. The soldier dove out of the jeep and scampered over the ridge of a rice paddy.

The commander watched it all without fleeing, but also without calmness. His arms tense at his sides, palms flat against the seat, neck stretched upwards at the warrior. She stepped over the windshield and straddled the front bucket seats.

"A boy came to you and warned you."

"Boy? What boy?"

"And you didn't listen to him."

"What boy? What …?"

"Yes, the boy your daughter chased after."

"I didn't know. I didn't—"

"Save your excuses. You're coming with me."

The long-tailed bird swooped down out of nowhere. Its cry forced a frightened yelp out of the commander, and he pressed his back against the seat cushion. Lady Trieu grabbed the feathers around the neck of the bird with her right hand and fastened her left hand onto the shirt and collar of the commander. The bird ascended straight upwards, Lady Trieu dangling down off its side with the commander like a kite's tail, flopping in the wind.

"Help!"

With one firm tug of her right hand, she swung her right leg over the great bird while tossing the commander upward into a seated position behind her. He clenched onto her stomach, barely able to reach around her. She glanced back with disgust.

"You can let go."

He didn't listen.

"Let go of me."

She crushed his right hand until he cringed and flinched his arms. As he did, the feathers of the bird strapped him in without comment, and he sat paralyzed over the Vietnamese terrain he knew so well, just not from this altitude.

He didn't speak. He dared not. Lady Trieu also remained silent. The bird soared through the air at a speed unlike any other, and within minutes, it nose-dived towards the ground, and when a few feet from impact, it flattened out and released its strap on the commander, sending him tumbling off the back of the tail and onto the ground with a painful thud. Tho and Lien stood over him in considerable surprise. The bird landed safely several yards away, and Lady Trieu dismounted.

"All of us need to talk."

The commander sat up at attention. The other two waited for Lady Trieu to speak first.

"This is Commander Lieu."

Lien and Tho glanced down in astonishment.

"Yes, the commander and I go way back," said Tho.

Lieu glanced up. "Mr. Tho?"

"Yes."

"Mr. Tho, it's been a long time."

"Everything has been a long time if it's related to me."

Everyone knew Commander Lieu. He became the face of the rebellion after the Chinese had liquidated the upper echelon of the Vietnamese government in the early days of the invasion. He was a lieutenant in the Vietnamese army, who had defied orders, and called upon every Vietnamese to support the resistance with whatever means they were capable. He had eluded the Chinese on multiple occasions and had even led brazen attacks against the invasion force inside the city. Lieu had become a folk hero. The resistance even began identifying themselves by using their right hand in the shape of an 'L'.

"Mr. Tho, I—"

Lady Trieu cut off the commander.

"A boy came to you, and you ignored him. He told you about the true nature of the fight, but you brushed him aside. The powerful always become ignorant."

"But the boy—"

"Quiet. This is the boy's mother."

Lien dropped to her knees and grabbed the right shoulder of the commander, still sitting on the ground.

"You saw Minh? How is he? What happened to him?" He turned his head away from her. "Tell me. Is he alright?"

"Commander Lieu," said Trieu. "Tell her what happened."

He sighed once. "He came to our headquarters, and he said things which were too unbelievable for me to take seriously, and—"

"Are they so unbelievable now?" asked Lady Trieu.

"How was I supposed to know?"

"You saw the broadcast of Sun Quan being shot. You heard the stories."

"Rumors."

Tho kicked the commander gently in the back with his foot. "Not rumors."

"What happened to Minh?" asked Lien, hunched over in his face.

"I told my staff to send him away. But minutes later, we received word of the strange attack in Hanoi, with the vehicles split in two by some strange force." He glanced up at Trieu, now making the connection. "I called him back, but he had already left."

"Where did he go?"

"I don't know. My daughter went after him, but I haven't heard from her either."

"They're in the facility," said Lady Trieu. "I've seen them."

Lien stood up. "You saw him? Is he alright?"

"I could not be there in human form. But when I saw him, he was strong. Focused."

Lien backed away and placed her arms over her heart. Her breath fell into a soft cry. Tho placed his arm around her.

The commander pushed himself up. "Lien, are you the wife of Nguyen Van Toan? From Haiphong?"

"Yes." She stepped forward, refocused on the moment. "What do you know of him?"

"He has become a traitor. He is working for the Chinese."

Lien pounced on him and smacked him once across the cheek. "You liar! Why would you say that? Why would you lie like that?" She hit him again, but he grabbed her wrists and tightened his grasp.

"We had video intel from within the facility, and …"

He let her go and pulled out a device. Lien staggered backwards. Tho came alongside her and grasped her arm. The commander held up the device and pressed play. The video showed a man walking into one of the cells of the facility. His face was that of Lien's husband. He punched one of the rebel soldiers. Then a closeup of the encounter revealed that he wore the Sino-Vietnamese unification symbol on his shirt. Lien collapsed to the ground and sobbed. Tho knelt and patted her head as the commander put the device away.

"I'm sorry. This doesn't provide me with any joy. He was an excellent soldier. The Chinese captured him inside the city about six months ago. They must have broken him. He must have turned."

"No," she screamed. "It's impossible. He would never do that."

"We're facing unprecedented circumstances in this battle. And we're losing on every front." He looked at Lady Trieu. "Now, I'm beginning to see how your presence, Lady Trieu, is making more and more sense."

Lien moaned. "He could have seen him. If he's in the facility. He could have seen him?"

"Who?" asked Tho.

"Minh. If they used his father against him, it could be devastating. Oh …" She fell further onto the ground of Co Loa Citadel and wailed. Tho continued to offer comfort, yet had very little to give.

"I brought the commander here, so the most important members of the resistance can work together to fight this evil in front of us."

Lien, Tho, and the commander all pondered the phrase "the most important members of the resistance." Lien quietly composed herself and returned to her feet. The phrase had refocused her on the daunting task ahead. Tho chuckled to himself at the thought, and the commander asked once more what he needed to do.

"Mr. Tho identified Sun Quan and summoned the past in an attempt to defeat him. He is clever and has the knowledge of history to support him. I have the scars to prove it. We will need everyone working together if there will be an opportunity to defeat Sun Quan. And make no mistake. We are not fighting against the Chinese. We are fighting against Sun Quan, and perhaps one more."

"The Chinese man?" asked the commander.

"Yes, the Chinese man."

"Who is the Chinese man?" asked Tho.

"We aren't sure," said Lieu. "We have little intel on him, but he has been working closely with the demon … Sun Quan from the beginning."

"Who's calling the shots?" asked Lien.

"It's not clear."

"And now the machines are here," said Lady Trieu.

"Machines?" asked Tho.

"So it's true?" asked the commander to Lady Trieu. "We've had sketchy reports about what happened in Hanoi last night."

"What? What happened?" Lien and Tho both inquired.

"A thousand strange machines were unleashed on Hanoi last evening. A night of terror. We have to act quickly before all support within Hanoi has been decimated, if it hasn't been already."

The commander looked perturbed. He threw his hands into the air and looked back at the three with a doubting glance. "Why did you bring me here? What can we do together? I have to reestablish communication between the units, and we need to take stock of—"

Lady Trieu cut him off. "Tho, did you retrieve the crossbow?"

"Crossbow? Well. The turtle instructed us to find the one worthy of the magic crossbow. But ... I don't know what that means."

"The turtle?" asked Lieu, eyes wide like an exclamation point.

"To find one worthy?" asked Trieu. "Yes. You must go again, and take the commander with you."

The commander waved his arms. He'd had enough. "Turtle? What are you talking about?"

"We need the magic crossbow, and we will receive it if you're the one."

"I'm the one? For what?" asked the commander, confusion embedded in his face.

Tho stepped forward, waving his arms. "I'm not ready for another trip down the pearl well."

"Do you want another night of terror in Hanoi? Or will you do whatever it takes to stop it?" Lady Trieu towered over all of them in an aggressive manner. "Take him." She pointed at the commander. "Lien and I will stay here. Whatever it takes. Get the magic crossbow."

Tho walked a few steps towards the pond, turned around, and used his right index finger to inform the commander to follow him.

"Where are we going?"

"It is better you don't ask questions to answers you definitely do not want to know."

"What?"

"Follow me to the pond, and prepare your mind for ... oh never mind. No preparation will be enough."

"I was just flown here on a massive extinct long-tailed lost bird with Lady Trieu as my riding companion. I think I can handle it."

"You have most assuredly underestimated the depths that the rebellion must go to."

"What do you mean?"

"Just follow me to the pond."

"I don't want to—"

His complaint stopped as Lady Trieu pushed him in Tho's direction. He turned around and held up his hands to say enough.

"I'll go. It's the least I can do for Mr. Tho."

Tho laughed. "Let the past be in the past, Lieu."

Lien walked over to Lady Trieu. "I can go with them."

"No. Let them do this alone. I want to talk with you about your husband."

Lien backed up and turned away from the warrior. "I can't believe he could ever turn."

"I came to Minh, not in human form, but I came to him in the facility. The commander's daughter was there too. I don't believe they were captured. They wanted to infiltrate the facility."

"That's foolish. Why would they do that?"

"The why is not important. But I need to know your son, and only you know what he will do. If what the commander said is true, and your husband tried to persuade Minh to give up the rebels, would he? Knowing what you know of your son. Would he?"

"No, never. He was with us. He went into Hoan Kiem Lake with us. On the turtle. He saw you. He knows Mr. Tho like a grandfather. He understands his heritage. No. Never. Nothing could turn him."

"And your husband?"

Lien covered her eyes with her hands. "I thought I knew him … I thought. I don't understand. I—"

"Don't worry. There's much about this conflict we don't yet understand. I told Minh to be ready."

"For what?"

"When the time is right, they are on the inside. It may prove crucial for us. If we can depend on him—"

"You can," snapped Lien. "You can. One hundred percent. You can."

"That's what I needed to know."

"So do we have a plan?" asked Lien, looking into the distance to see Tho and the commander stepping into the basket boat on the pond.

"Yes. A partial one. More is to come."

Lien slumped onto the steps of the citadel. The image from the video replayed in her mind, though not a solitary explanation could satisfy her shattered soul.

Chapter 24

The Magic Crossbow

The absurdity of the toad didn't disappoint. Another mollusk. Another pearl. The bottom of the well opening its sinkhole on Commander Lieu and Tho to welcome them into the pit of fear—the tablet inserted into the soft belly of the magical tunnel and the dead-end stop at the water wall under Hoan Kiem Lake—the commander's face drained white of blood.

Tho chuckled and nudged the underworld rookie. "I thought in your line of work you'd have seen it all by now."

The commander's eyes lit round yet static as a shadow moved in the wall of water. The jaw-locked silence ended, however, as the turtle lifted its head and penetrated through the wall.

"You've returned. Who is this?"

"This is Commander Lieu. He is leading the rebel attack against the Chinese."

"Leading poorly, from what I hear."

"I'm not one to say," said Tho, looking over at the commander, mesmerized at the giant turtle's neck above him.

"Well what do you, Commander Lieu, say then?"

He didn't speak. He couldn't. He tried moving his mouth but the muscles jammed, and a gasp of air escaped like a toddler's coo after awaking in the morning.

"Why did you bring him here?"

"Lady Trieu told me to bring him."

"What do you want?"

"We ask for the magic crossbow."

"Only someone worthy can receive the crossbow. Is he ready to prove his worth?"

Tho glanced at the commander once again. "Yes, he is."

"Are you sure?"

"He is a decorated officer. He's had unwavering resolve against the Chinese when others merely wilted, when the leaders of the government absconded their responsibility, allowing themselves to be eliminated. But this man—"

"I want to hear from him."

The turtle retracted its head a few feet and lowered his massive jaw until its nostrils breathed directly on the commander. The turtle's head was half the size of the boat, and the commander reeled backwards as if one quick snap could chop off his head.

"I see weakness," said the turtle.

"Please, give him a moment. He's been on a disturbing ride through the tunnel."

"And … and on the wings of a long-tailed bird," added the commander, still panting.

"He speaks." The turtle lifted its head and dipped back behind the wall of water once again. It emerged holding a sword and dropped it in the bow of the boat at their feet.

"What's the sword for?" asked Lieu.

"Pick it up and prepare yourself."

"I've never fought with a sword before."

"You better learn."

Three enormous warriors shattered the wall of water and pounced on the commander and Tho in the basket boat. Tho dropped flat into the bottom of the boat. The commander did likewise, but not without first screaming and lunging for the sword, which he couldn't reach. They were Terracotta warriors in animated form and in full attack mode. The first two swung their swords over the head of the commander. The third would have sliced him in two if Lieu hadn't back-flipped out of the boat by placing his palms on the boat's edge and springing in reverse with his feet like a gymnast. He landed on the soft glowing floor of the tunnel, still lit in bright iridescence. Tho remained flat in the boat. He didn't feel particularly afraid since he felt he had a certain rapport with the turtle. Plus, Lady Trieu had sent him. And most importantly, he never had a beef with a terracotta warrior in his ninety-five years on earth.

The commander, on the other hand, found himself, through no desire of his own, fighting three illogical beings set up by a talking turtle in a nonsensical tunnel. The rebellion above ground fell apart by the moment, and here he was, trying to remember his *Vovinam* martial arts moves from his teen years. He reached into the boat and grabbed the sword's handle with both hands. Two of the warriors circled around him while the other stood in the boat taking blind precision steps to avoid the cowering Tho curled in a ball. The warriors were each slightly over six-feet-tall, giving them a half-foot advantage over the short-statured commander. Lieu brought the sword to his chest and breathed slowly, tip straight up in front of his face. The warriors each took another step toward him, but Lieu went left in a frontal assault toward the first one. The terracotta raised its sword over its head and chopped downward. The commander jerked backwards and the sword stuck into the soft floor of the tunnel. Lieu stepped up onto the cross guard of the sword and swung his in a lateral motion, slicing off the warrior's head and vaporizing it. The warrior in the center of the boat lunged toward him, but he jumped back to the floor of the tunnel and ran a circular route to the opposite terracotta soldier. It reversed itself and sparred with the commander a few times. He pinned the soldier's sword against the side of the boat and dove at the soldier's legs in an attempt to remember one of the twenty-one leg grappling techniques he had once learned. The attack confused the soldier, and both swords fell to the ground. Lieu twisted the soldier's leg until the clumsy fellow lost balance and collapsed to the floor of the tunnel. Lieu lunged for the sword and stabbed him in the chest and turned him into a puff of vapor.

The final soldier had climbed out of the back of the boat and now faced the commander. This one was slightly bigger and more agile. It sliced hard twice against the commander's sword. The second strike twisted Lieu's wrist in pain until the sword fell out of his hand. Another swift slice almost ended Lieu in the chest. He turned and ran toward the wall of water. Tho had finally peeked his head over the edge of the boat.

"Don't hit the wall of water," he warned. "It will hurt."

Too late. Lieu stretched out his arms and in a semi-horizontal dive pierced the surface of the water.

"He made it!"

Lieu swam at the edge of the water wall and dared the final warrior to join him by poking his hand into the tunnel and waving him on. The terracotta soldier obliged. It charged into the water, but its sword became unwieldy. Commander Lieu swam over to the warrior and placed his palms flat against its chest. The soldier tried to remove them but the water blows did nothing to Lieu. He pushed gently, releasing his fingers all at once in an upward motion, and the terracotta soldier returned to history, disintegrating into a thousand floating pieces of dust, which dispersed in the deep waters of Hoan Kiem Lake, and sunk back into history.

Commander Lieu walked out of the water, shoulders back, unimpressed by his surroundings. Tho gawked at the man, who had been a mumbling idiot when the drain of the pearl well sucked them into the tunnel. He put his hands on the edge of the basket boat and swung himself inside next to Tho.

"What happened?"

"I remembered my lessons from *Vovinam* fighting. Fighting is not only the aggressiveness of the *ying*; it also embraces the *yang*—the patience, the unexpected. The moments where there can be an understanding between two foes."

Tho scratched his head. "You came to an understanding with a terracotta warrior ghost?"

"We did. He realized he no longer meant to exist."

The turtle reappeared, holding an object in its hand. It dropped it in a similar spot as the sword, but this time Commander Lieu caught it. The crossbow—the mythical, magical crossbow.

"Commander, you have shown your worth. Use it judiciously. Not without pause. Use it humbly to humble the most ardent foes, when the time is right. When the well opens for the last time. Now go."

Tho gripped the sides of the boat. The ride started, knocking Lieu to the hull, as they hurled at great speed through the tunnel and popped up in the pearl well, in the center of Co Loa Citadel pond. They remained silent. Lieu dragged the boat over the cement barrier of the well and into the pond. He used the oar to return them to shore.

They found Lien and Lady Trieu on the steps of the citadel all alone. The long-tailed bird rested in the grass nearby. Commander Lieu, without saying a word, approached Lady Trieu. He knelt in front of her and presented the crossbow with outstretched arms as an emissary presenting tribute to an empress. She received it into her hands and weighed its stature.

"The magical crossbow."

"What is it?" asked Lien.

"The great turtle would not have released this crossbow without cause." Trieu looked up at the three assembled in front of her. "There are secrets. Deep magical secrets of history which the guardians of the past hold on to at all cost. But when they are willing to relinquish an item as precious as this, it can only mean the work ahead of us is far graver than even we know."

Lieu rose to his feet, eyes still fixed upon the crossbow.

"Lady Trieu, I understand now. We aren't merely fighting the Chinese. We are fighting against thousands of years. This is not about me or about my men or even those who have already lost their lives. It's about preserving the future so items such as the magic crossbow and the pearl well and the legend of Hoan Kiem Lake will live in revered perpetuity. I'm ready to embrace any and all tactics necessary to complete this mission. Failure would mean an end to our people."

She glanced at the bow once more, and handed it over to Mr. Tho, who unexpectedly took it into his hands. She nodded at him, and he understood.

"Commander Lieu, leader of the resistance, on a noble fight to preserve our way of life and all its venerable history, I present you with the magic crossbow. Use it as the turtle instructed, and guard it with your life until we use the well a final time."

Lieu took the crossbow in his hands and strapped it over his right shoulder. "I will use it as you say. When will be the final time we use the well?"

"Patience," said Trieu. "We need to gather as many fighters as possible. Commander, after Sun Quan's attack, your troops scattered. Is there any way to contact them?"

"Yes, I just need to return to our auxiliary base. I was headed there when you snatched me."

"The bird will take you there. And you know your orders after that?"

"Yes, I know exactly what must be done. We'll return to the well one final time."

"Yes," she repeated. "Three days time. Now go."

The bird called to the commander to mount its back once again. He walked toward it.

"Commander," Lien called. "I'm sorry I doubted you, Commander. I just …"

He reached for her hands and clasp them in a firm grip. "This war has torn many families apart, in many different ways. Let's not give up hope. One day we will understand."

Lieu mounted the bird, and they disappeared into the sky. Lady Trieu walked toward the pond.

"Where are you going?" asked Lien.

"I have something to prepare."

"What should we do?"

"Rest. You will need it."

"That is the best thing I've heard in days," said Tho.

"Stay out of sight." Lady Trieu changed from bodily form into the translucent ghost appearance and submerged herself into the depths of the pearl well.

Tho walked toward the gate of the citadel.

"Tho, where are you going?"

"I know where those two old men live. Perhaps their wives will cook me some food."

Chapter 25

The Aftermath

Minh and Nhan fell asleep in their respective corners of the black-walled cell. Minh woke up in the middle of the night, stretching his numb shoulder, which had cramped from the hard tiled floor. Nhan rested curled up in a ball opposite him. Tufts of her hair covered half her face, but Minh imagined the other half. She looked peaceful and happy, especially for being imprisoned in the middle of a rebellion. But he knew well-enough the harsh attitude lying in wait right underneath, just out of sight. His eyes felt drawn to her, but he snapped his neck the other way. Stop it, he told himself. She's three years older. Two and a half. Stop. Just stop. We're in a war zone. His eyes continued his gaze until he re-entered the dream world a few moments later.

The room had brightened at 6 AM, and Nhan kicked Minh in the side.

"What?" he jolted awake. "Am I late for school?" He glanced up. Nhan's legs were forced inward in an awkward position.

"How do we go to the bathroom in here?"

"What?"

"The bathroom. They know we're human, right? I'm not a machine. I need to pee."

"Oh." Minh sat up. "Try asking them."

"Who?"

"The walls. They know everything anyhow."

"Speak to the walls?"

"Yes."

She looked upward and spoke to the ceiling. "I need to pee."

"I said walls, not ceiling."

"Doesn't the ceiling hear also?"

The main door opened on command and two machines filled the

doorway.

"Apparently so," said Minh.

He went with her down the hall to relieve themselves. He didn't think of running, not with the machines as escorts. But he also didn't return to the facility just to escape again. Why did he come back? He thought of that question the entire time until they returned to the cell. To their surprise, a hot bowl of rice and broth had been placed inside. They both devoured it without a word to each other.

Nhan placed the empty bowl down first. "So these machines. What are they?"

"I don't know. In some ways they don't even look like machines. Did you notice the engraving on the front?"

"Yes. Some sort of Chinese face. But it looks weird."

"I've seen that before. I remember Mr. Tho teaching me about the terracotta warriors they found buried by the first Chinese emperor. It looks like that."

"Why would that be engraved into the machines?"

Minh plopped his empty bowl on top of hers. "I have no idea."

"What a mess."

"What?" asked Minh.

"This. What we've gotten ourselves into. Sitting here doing nothing inside this prison. My father is missing or dead, and yours is …" She didn't finish the sentence.

"Mine is what?"

"You know."

"What do you mean to say? Traitor?"

"I'm just saying…"

"You're just saying what?"

"Forget it."

"How can I forget it? My father *is* a traitor, but that is not my father. That's not the man who raised me. I don't know what's going on, but he would never turn from the rebellion."

"But that is your father, right?" Minh didn't reply. "The way he walks, talks … the way he looks. He is your father."

Minh turned away. He didn't need to say anything else.

"I'm sorry," said Nhan.

Minh slapped the floor with the palm of his hand. "It just doesn't make any sense."

A long, drawn-out pause passed between them. It was a mess, Minh admitted to himself. He thought of his mother, the last time he had seen her, as the wall of the facility slammed shut, cutting them off—fear written on her face. That's the last thing he remembered about his mother. Fear. A look he wasn't used to.

"You know," Nhan broke the silence. "If you hadn't have come to the rebel base, I would have been there when it was attacked. I could be dead right now."

"But you're not. You're alive in the most secure Chinese prison in history."

"I'd rather be here with you than dead. Besides, you've already escaped from the most secure Chinese prison in history. So, yeah."

Minh smiled and accepted the bizarre compliment. He was preferable to death, a thought he cherished a little too much. He liked the way she looked. Maybe she likes me. Stop. He screamed internally for the little voice to shut up. It did, but his actual mouth had something to say.

"I'm glad you're here too, rather than being dead."

They almost smiled at each other, eye to eye, when the wall slid into the ceiling once more. Minh's father returned.

"Minh?"

The boy turned his head away.

"There's no need for you to be in here. How could you sleep on this dreaded floor?"

That's all his father had to say? He worried about his son's sleeping habits? Minh refused to turn his eyes in his father's direction.

"Come, Minh. I want to show you something."

"No."

"Come. Trust me."

"I don't trust you. Not anymore."

"If you come with me, I think you'll understand. And don't worry about your friend. She'll be fine here."

"Just like the rebel base is fine? I know what happened."

"You know, huh?"

"Yes, I know a lot of things." Minh sprang to his feet, chest out, confident and secure in the knowledge of the past, he looked his father in the eye. "I know you're a traitor."

His father half-laughed. "You're so sure of yourself, aren't you? I'm sure you got that from me. But my eyes have been opened, Minh. I want to show you something more. Come with me."

"Do I have a choice?"

"If you want a choice, I'll give you one."

"What do you want me to see?"

"I want to show you how one night can change a city."

Nhan walked over to Minh and placed her hand on his. "Go. Do it for … You know."

He gazed down at the hand and noticed how it felt next to his. He looked up at her and nodded. Their hands pulled apart, and he walked toward his father, who invited him through the opening using his hand to point the way. Minh looked back. Nhan nudged him on. The confidence in her eyes encouraged him to walk out with his father and leave her alone.

Several corridors down, they entered the large hall where Lady Trieu had destroyed the batch of the armored vehicles with her sword. Now the hall sat empty, a shell without vehicles or people, except for a handful of soldiers milling around the two remaining armored cars. One soldier saluted Minh's father, the traitor, the man who could shake off a lifetime of loyalty without a hint of regret. A man who could climb the ranks of the occupation army and accept salutes from the filthy Chinese soldiers within a year. This fact alone made Minh wonder how deep the treachery of his father went, and the salute made Minh hate him even more.

The soldier opened the door to the topless vehicle, and Minh's father motioned him into the back seat. His father sat beside him, and the soldier climbed into the driver's seat.

"Minh, before we go, I want to prepare you for what you're about to see. It's not pleasant, but it's necessary. The sacrifice for peace must never be underestimated. You will see."

Minh never looked at his father even as he spoke. All he could think about was if he should try to escape, if the opportunity arose. But if he did, would he ever see Nhan again? And, as his reasoning came back around, didn't he want to be in the facility, to find Lady

Trieu?

The vehicle pulled out of the massive hall and into the sunlight of a hot Hanoi morning. The wall around the facility had been removed. There was no longer a guard post or anything resembling security. The vehicle merged onto the wide avenue lined with old French villas. Everything looked in order to Minh, but the streets were empty except for a select few pedestrians, who kept their heads down and gazed straight ahead. He noticed a truck pass with its bed covered in a blue tarp. A Chinese soldier drove it, and he saluted Minh's vehicle. Minh's father spoke something to the driver in Chinese. The driver veered to the right and passed Lenin Square toward the Old Quarter.

"You speak Chinese?" Minh asked his father in a confused tone.

"Yes."

"I never heard you speak Chinese."

"Remember, your grandmother was Chinese, and I learned it in school."

Minh studied his father, but didn't say anything more. His father gave the driver a command, and the car turned down the street where Minh had been just the night before, where he and Nhan had met with the rebel cell before they were accosted on the street by their own people.

The vehicle stopped at the entrance to the street. Minh stood up in shock at the scene. Bodies lay scattered and face down. Pools of blood had gathered at the edges of a clogged street drain. Debris from the houses, felled walls, shattered glass, garbage, trees, and branches made the street unnavigable. The machines stood guard every hundred feet, watching over the Vietnamese residents who cleared the debris and gathered the bodies. Another of the trucks they had passed with the blue tarp was parked halfway down the street—the cleared part—and older men swung bodies onto the truck's bed, while two others stacked them. The blue tarp lay over the cab readied to be pulled back to cover the deeds.

Minh noticed an old woman standing thirty feet in front of him. She knelt down at the side of one of the corpses, leaned over and kissed it on the cheek. She wiped her face and picked up a small branch and placed it in a larger pile of debris next to her.

Minh chocked on his words, though there was nothing to say. He wiped his face of the tears. These were not tears of a boy, not tears of fear for what might happen to him. These were tears of understanding and realizing how foolish he was to feel excitement for wanting to help Tho and his mother in the rebellion. The reality of war had settled upon him. How could any of the rebels he met with last night have escaped from this street? Perhaps their bodies laid still in the truck he had passed. Zeal results in death, as does everything. Now he understood.

"I wanted you to see this, Minh. I know it's difficult. But you must realize that you and your friend Nhan would be two of those bodies you see right now if we didn't allow you to escape."

Minh turned his head toward his father in anger.

"Allowed us?"

"Oh, you don't think the machines couldn't have finished you last night like the rest if they had wanted to? They knew who you were. They called you by name, and they led you right to me."

He reached over and put his hand on Minh's shoulder. Minh jerked away from him, and his father smiled.

"I know you're upset. Perhaps you're too young to understand all of this. It's rather complicated, I know. But you're my son, and I want you on the side of peace. On the side of progress. You have your whole life ahead of you, and it may not feel like it now, but it's a promising life. A fulfilling one."

"And what of mother?"

"Oh, she will understand."

"She will never understand this. She will never understand you."

"Minh, it will take time, but—"

"Not in a thousand years would she bow down to this. Killing our own people."

"The passion is deep in you, son. That's a good thing. You're not so different from me."

"You're wrong. We're nothing alike."

"We shall see." Minh's father spoke to the driver, and the vehicle backed out of the street and turned in the opposite direction.

Minh noticed similar scenes on other streets. Some had been

scrubbed and cleaned while others were in the throes of making the inhabitants pay for the price for someone else's crime. Minh's stomach churned. He wanted to bolt, to jump out of the vehicle and disappear into a small alleyway.

They rounded the tip of Hoan Kiem Lake, a sight that made Minh's heart leap. He couldn't remove his eyes from the center of the lake and hoped Lady Trieu saw him. But he also questioned her. How could she have let this happen? If she really was still alive, why didn't she intervene in the attack on the rebel base and on the unprecedented night of terror? His unanswered questions would have to wait because they turned down Hang Bac Street—his home. The street was neat and clean, with no blood-stained drains and no pocked marked walls signifying a gun fight. Several of his neighbors walked out onto the street at the same time to greet the vehicle. Minh's father stepped out and greeted people by name. He asked Auntie Linh if she was still selling pho in the morning market. He talked with Mr. Thao, a former policeman, and they chatted about the last time they had seen each other. Everyone greeted Minh's father with kindness and respect. They smiled and laughed and … the most shocking one of all … old Mrs. Gia even thanked the man for his sacrifice to the cause. She thanked him. The Sino-Vietnamese Unification insignia on Minh's father's shirt was as plain as day. He had arrived in a Chinese vehicle driven by a Chinese soldier. They all knew what side he had chosen, and here they were, all of Minh's neighbors, the ones who saw him grow up, the ones who interacted with Mr. Tho and his mother on a daily basis. Here they were, praising the traitor for his sacrifice.

Minh stood from the back of the vehicle and jumped over the edge onto the street. His neighbors swarmed him in kindness, praising the boy for following in his father's footsteps, and saying how wonderful it will be to turn the page of this horrific chapter and write a new story of peace for the future. Minh couldn't speak. He was passed from person to person like an overwhelmed puppy in the midst of familiar strangers.

Former policeman Thao spoke, "You must be so proud of your father."

Minh's tongue felt like it swelled up in his mouth, like it choked him, like he was being cascaded with so many lies they began to feel normal, like he should feel happy to see people joyful and appreciative.

Minh's father thanked them all and stated that his family hoped to be back in their house soon. Then he instructed Minh back into the vehicle. Minh obeyed on command, having not said a word to his fake neighbors. They had to be fake, he thought, or all hope was now lost. Minh couldn't decide which was more shocking: the streets with dead bodies or the street with his neighbors espousing dastardly lies as if speaking basic truths of nature.

"I have one more thing to show you, Minh."

They backtracked the route, past the street from the previous night, and past the facility. They pulled into the southern end of Ba Dinh Square, the massive central square which housed the Ho Chi Minh mausoleum and other important government buildings. But Minh barely recognized it. He had been there a hundred times. He had ridden his bicycle on countless occasions around the square, but now he wondered how it could look so different. A massive wall had been constructed on the west side, completely blocking the view of the mausoleum. But even that paled to what had happened in the middle of the square. Thousands of machines—those same machines—had constructed a massive complex, which towered over every building in the square. The side of the building had an elaborate piece of art showing the Vietnamese-Chinese unification symbol.

"How is this possible," he asked.

"Impressive, isn't it? One night. This is what we can do in once night."

Minh made a mental note of the word 'we.' His father had been completely corrupted by the Chinese.

"There's no stopping us. We will rebuild this city, this country, into something we can all be proud of, and I want you to be by my side. Now, I don't expect you to say yes right away. I know what I've shown you has been a shock. But once you have time to reflect upon all that you've witnessed, you'll understand why I chose to join the winning side. We will be on the forefront of the future, not relying on the past anymore. Look at these magical machines. Is there anything they cannot do?"

"What are they?"

"All will be revealed at the right time. All I need from you, Minh, is your help in locating your mother and Mr. Tho."

Minh's spine straightened into the back of the seat.

"I need to talk with your mother. And, Minh, Mr. Tho needs to return the tablets that do not rightfully belong to him."

On the word 'tablet,' Minh instinctively patted his pocket with his right hand. He knew immediately that he had given it away.

"Why did you do that?"'

"No reason."

"Show me what's in your pocket."

"It's nothing."

"Show me." Minh's father reached over and put his hand on the outside of Minh's pocket. Then he laughed. "It's empty, silly boy. Now, will you help me find your mother?"

"I don't know where she is."

"But you have ways to find out, I'm sure."

"No, I don't. And even if I did, I would never help you."

"Minh, I'm your father."

"I will never help you. Take me back to the facility."

"There's no need for any of that. You can stay here with me in the new building."

"No." The answer came quick. "Take me back to the facility."

"Very well. I suppose you need time to ruminate about all that you've witnessed today, Minh. Then you'll know what to do."

The vehicle turned around, and Minh glanced at the indistinguishable Ba Dinh Square one last time. When the vehicle pulled into the open lot of the facility, Minh saw the row of hedges which had helped him escape once. He jumped from the vehicle and ran toward them. Within seconds, machines surrounded him on all sides.

His father walked over. "Minh, there's no escape. The city is wired through the machines. They know every move you make. So make your next move carefully. I'll be back tomorrow to see if you have changed your mind."

He nodded at the machines, and they pushed Minh into the

facility, down the corridor, and into the same cell, but as he entered, he noticed that Nhan wasn't there.

Chapter 26

Something about the Red River

Nhan had been running for ten minutes straight. She had out-maneuvered several machines and had bypassed two horrific street scenes with enough scarlet hues to shame the Red River. But she couldn't dwell on the cost of the previous night. Not yet. She rested against a tree within view of the southern bank of the Red River, attempting to reach a rebel crossing still five minutes away, if it even existed. She had no way to confirm, but it remained her only way out of the city, unless she attempted to swim.

Two Chinese soldiers had attempted to halt her escape at the end of the last alleyway. She had dipped into an old woman's house. The startled woman had a hot porcelain pot of green tea just steeped. When the soldier followed her, Nhan threw the pot at him, scalding his face as he collapsed to the floor screaming. The old woman said nothing—merely an observer to the chaos, slightly glad to have a glimpse of reality for herself. A second soldier entered and chased Nhan through the back end of the house. She managed to climb out the metal bars over a rear window. She was slim, after all. That allowed her to slip out from the row of houses and rest behind the tree, just minutes away from getting out of the city.

Nhan smiled at her cleverness, how a sixteen-year-old had outwitted the facility and how … She paused. … Everything replayed in her mind. … She re-thought through the circumstances … Minh's father had arrived and Minh left with him. But as they left, the opening never closed. She wandered out of the room through a series of corridors. All empty. She had walked slowly, staying alert to any movement, but a massive shadow had followed her. Sun Quan. She recalled their conversation.

"The boy will never return. He will join his father. As you wish to rejoin yours."

"I'm not afraid of you."

"Foolish people may think and feel as they wish."

"You want me alive, or I wouldn't be here."

"Of course. It was you who betrayed your father."

"I would never betray him."

"Your thoughts did. You led me right to them."

"I didn't …" She remembered how Sun Quan had clasped his hands onto both sides of her head when she was still in the facility. She had fallen to the ground, zapped of all energy. "You read my thoughts?"

"And I can read them now. Escape. It's what you desire. What's stopping you?"

She didn't know how to reply, nor did she understand what Sun Quan wanted. "If she wants me to escape, she will help me."

"She? So you too are a believer." Sun Quan had moved closer. "How do you even know if she's alive? Did you not hear? I defeated her, and her limp soul sank into Hoan Kiem Lake like a sack of rice."

"But she lived."

"Did she?"

"I heard you say it."

"As you wish to believe."

At that moment, a whisk of light had flashed in the corridor, and a dark figure, not fully formed, rammed into Sun Quan from behind. He fell forward, almost on top of Nhan, who moved out of his way just in time. Sun Quan turned and morphed out of his body, and the two semi-formless beings interchanged positions several times until one vanished down the corridor and the other followed. A second later, the giant figure of Sun Quan crashed into one of the black walls back-first, as if he had been hurled at a great speed. The force had smashed the wall into pieces, setting off alarms and flashing lights. She heard the voice only once. "Run." Like someone had injected an audible word into her mind. She obeyed. She turned and sprinted down the corridor. More walls opened. Several machines passed right by her as if they were called away on more urgent business. The alarms buzzed, lights pulsed, but she continued running, thoughts bobbing in her head faster than her brain could understand. The adrenaline pushed her. Through the massive hall and out into the street, diving into a back alley, avoiding a machine at a dead end when she had climbed a trash receptacle and jumped headfirst into the unknown of the other side of the wall. She landed in a three-wheeled *xich lo* parked at the back of an alley. She tumbled off, onto the pavement, not feeling a thing, not noticing the bruising, not stopping to assess what had happened. She had followed the voice inside: run!

Her movement never paused, even when the soldiers spotted her and she dove into the old woman's house and out through the grate on the back window, until she found herself panting loudly, leaning against the tree just a stone's throw away from the Red River. And …

Her thoughts returned to the present. She stood up straight and walked out from the tree, no longer hiding. She faced the city. A small dirt street followed the edge of the river. She stood on the other side of it. Myriad small cement houses scattered themselves between weaving alleyways. A hodgepodge of electrical wires on poles crisscrossed each other like balled up yarn a cat had hopelessly entangled. The wires spanned in all directions and connected each house to the other, no matter how small or meager the dwelling. Everything was connected.

The past, the present, the future.

What if … she wondered. She had a terrible sense that she hadn't escaped. What if … She glared in all directions. Her body itched, like ants crawled on her skin, like she was covered with something she couldn't shake off. What if …

What if they wanted me to escape … what if they're watching me right now?

A sense of futility ripped through her chest. It was a game. They wanted her to run. They willed it. Did they? She knew it. She thought it. She played their game and nearly led them to … what? Whatever remained unknown to them yet known to her. She stood near the edge of the river, being no more free than when locked behind the black walls of the facility. One thing she understood clearly, she would not betray anyone, no matter the cost.

"I know what you're doing. I will never help you."

She called out to them. Nothing happened. However, the feeling in her chest grew stronger.

"I know you're there. I know you're watching me."

She glanced to the rear, toward the river. What? What are my options? I won't let them catch me. I won't betray anyone.

Something about the Red River caught her eye. Perhaps the sun glittered its intentions on the turbid water in a way that beckoned hope. Perhaps she noticed how the river gripped the city in a tight noose—Hanoi: the city inside the Red River— holding it like a child in its palm. Perhaps the rebels owed their existence to the river for allowing them to survive for this long under the harsh Chinese regime. The river called to her as a friend. Inviting her to escape on her own terms. Lady Trieu came to mind. What does it mean if she is real? Is Sun Quan really who Minh says he is? Grains of faith percolate in the mind but can grow exponentially when all other explanations pale in comparison. If she wouldn't allow herself to be caught, what were her options? The river and only the river. She learned the stories from history and folklore of Lady Trieu, but who else? What of the two Trung sisters? They also fought against the invading Han army. They fought valiantly, but in the end, what happened to them? They drowned themselves in a river. The Red River. The very river behind Nhan's back. Was that the answer? The river. The Trung sisters ended it that way, but in doing so, lived on for millenniums. Would she be brave enough to do the same? How would the river treat her? And what of Lady Trieu? Would she hear her cry?

The river taunted her with its lore, and at that moment, nothing could have tempted her more than the slow methodical ripples on the water. She blocked out thoughts of her father and of Minh and even of the rebellion. She thought only of the water and what it offered her. She would discover its glory. She had no other option. It compelled her to action, so she waved her arms at the alleyways. The hidden eyes, whatever they were and wherever they were would know her deed. She would tell them. Everything.

"Sun Quan. I know you allowed me to escape. I reject it. I will not be a traitor, nor will I be your prisoner. You may come after me, just as you attacked the rebel base, but you will not win. We will never surrender to you. As the sunrise peeks over the Gulf of Tonkin, so too the Chinese will desecrate our sacred land. But sunrises necessitate sunsets. And you are much closer to your sunset than you realize." She waited. Her heart pounded. "Show yourself. I know you're there!"

The sureness of her breath couldn't drown out her human traits. Sweat dripped from her forehead. She fidgeted with her hands, and she listened to the rattle of the wheels. The machines rolled out into the open. A dozen of them. She had provoked a response. Now it was her turn. All she had to do was run toward the river.

As a first machine edged towards her, instincts took over. The river called her name, and she obeyed. Step after step.

Hurried. Aching legs. Blurred vision. Ears hearing the vibrating rattle of the machines now in pursuit. A shot fired as she stumbled over the bank and tumbled to the bottom near the edge of the water. The machines lined the river bank like an attack on a cliff ready to swoop in and swarm the enemy at a lower position. They possessed a dramatic advantage, but she had the water. All hers. She would give it everything she had.

She held her breath out of instinct and plummeted underneath as bullets pocked the surface. She swam down in the murky water which blinded any hopes of navigation. If she allowed her body to float to the surface, death awaited her in the name of a hundred bullets from a dozen machines. So she asked the water to take her, to allow her a home like the two Trung sisters of old. May her sacrifice in the deep allow the rebels to fight another day. She opened her mouth to allow the water to consume her when a turtle's head rubbed against hers. The turtle smiled, and she smiled back. The turtle dove down, the wake current sucking her in. Terrible thoughts betrayed her, but she followed the turtle. A vortex swirled her downward into a tunnel only inches wider than her body, and she closed her eyes and wondered if the Trung sisters had received such treatment. Before she had an answer, she emerged sliding on wet, matted grass in the midst of jagged limestone peaks. She caught herself on all fours, and twirled in each direction, recognizing her surroundings. She had been here before. Hoa Lu. The ancient capital of Vietnam a couple hundred miles south of Hanoi. She looked up, and a long-tailed bird approached at great speed. After two dramatic, hairpin circles overhead, it landed in front of her with Lady Trieu on its back. She dismounted and walked toward the girl.

"Nhan."

Her lip quivered. "Yes."

"You have been very brave, and so you've been granted a task. One I think you are ready for."

Nhan nodded but studied every inch of the woman.

"You will lead the southern attack."

"What?"

"In two days time, you will lead an army northward to confront Sun Quan."

"I, I, I …?"

"An army like no other."

"I've never led an army."

"No matter. I have chosen you. Do you believe you are ready?"

She was real. She lorded over Nhan like a fairytale, a page from a book she had read coming to life—chosen for a purpose by the greatest of heroines. She had no special skills or training to boast of. She had lingered in her father's shadow for the last two years, willing to help the cause, but mainly ruffling the feathers of whomever she crossed. But now the hero figure of folklore tasked her to do her part—the part she had always wanted to play, an important one, one her father never trusted her with, one her age prevented her from achieving, but now… The warrior asked once more. "Are you ready?"

"Yes, but I don't know of any rebel bases near here?"

"Your army will not be made of rebels."

"I don't understand. Who are they?"

"They will begin arriving tomorrow evening. Be ready for instructions."

Nhan nodded as Lady Trieu walked back toward the bird.

"But who are they?"

Lady Trieu smiled at Nhan, mounted the lost bird, and took off into the sunset. Nhan sat in the grass near the stream splitting the granite cliffs into sides, like two mammoth monolithic giants facing off against each other. She had chosen. She would be on one of the sides, ready to do her part.

A Chinese soldier interrupted Sun Quan and the Chinese man as they looked over Hanoi from the top of their newly constructed building in Ba Dinh Square.

"Excuse me, sir. The girl ..."

"Lieu's daughter?"

"Yes."

"Did she lead us to anything fruitful?" asked the Chinese man.

"No, she drowned in the river."

"We drowned her?"

"No, sir. She jumped in and never resurfaced."

Sun Quan winced at the Chinese man before ordering the soldier to leave them.

"I take it you don't think it's a normal drowning?" asked the Chinese man.

"She playing with us?"

"The girl? I doubt it. She's just a child."

"No, Trieu. She's going to use her. Just like Trieu did. Threw herself in the river. Just like the Trung sisters did. Drowned themselves in the river. No, we haven't seen the last of the girl."

"Oh, Sun Quan. You are so caught up in the illustrious past. I care more about the present. What are we going to do about Trieu?"

Sun Quan didn't respond, but they both knew the answer.

Chapter 27

The Secret of the Machines

L ady Trieu drifted over Hanoi without physical form and risked contact with Sun Quan. But it allowed her to remain anonymous to the crowds of people below, still reeling from the brutal night. She slipped unannounced into the small living room of a house in the Old Quarter on Hang Bac Street. It belonged to Mr. Thao, a neighbor of Mr. Tho and Lien, and a former policeman. Other neighbors huddled around, too. Ms. Linh, the pho seller, old Mrs. Gia, and several more. They spoke in hushed tones as if they spoke salacious gossip. But the quietness of the room ended when Lady Trieu appeared in full human form in their midst—a warrior from an ancient time, commanded full attention. They hollered, cried, and cowered to whatever corner of the small room would accept them. When the gasps had dissipated but their gazes hadn't, she asked them the question.

"Do you know who I am?"

Everyone shook their dumbfounded heads until Thao asked, "A ghost?"

"I am Ba Trieu."

Mrs. Gia's head swooned once before she fainted from her stool. Two other women overcame their shock to attend to her. Mr. Thao turned away mumbling. Tears streamed down his face, and he repeatedly asked the idle air in the room for forgiveness. Ms. Linh started praying to the spirits of her ancestors.

Lady Trieu moved in front of Ms. Linh. The giantess towered over the woman, who had a small hunchback. "Who do you think sent me?"

Linh looked directly up. "You are … You are …" She couldn't

complete the sentence.

"I am here to resist the Chinese and crush their aggression. But too many people cower in the shadows of their own rooms. This permits the evil to continue."

Thao spoke: "We're afraid. The Chinese and that demon. They visited us yesterday and warned us of destruction if we didn't follow the regime. We're afraid."

"When we allow fear to determine our actions, when we allow fear to make our decisions, when we allow fear to consume the breath of the living, we might as well be dead. And you will be if you comply with the invaders. And what of the boy, Minh?" Trieu pressed the room further. "The boy who grew up in your presence, who played on this street. What have your deeds taught him?"

"You know Minh?" asked Ms. Linh, who had helped Mrs. Gia back to consciousness. "The boy was with his father, who wore the reunification pin."

"The boy is with me," snapped Lady Trieu. "I need to know, are you?"

Thao stepped forward. "Lady Trieu, I had been an honorable policeman for many years before I retired. I'm ashamed of my actions. I have cared more about my safety than for my country, and in doing so, I have shamed my ancestors. But no more. I will do whatever it is you want me to do."

"So will I," spoke old Mrs. Gia in a raspy voice. "I used to go to school on Ba Trieu Street. You are not just a name. Not to me. You are an ideal. You represent our Vietnamese identity. I am honored to be in your presence, and I will never again allow the invaders to stir my emotions with fear. I will speak the truth."

Everyone in attendance concurred.

"When did Sun Quan visit you?" asked Lady Trieu.

"It was an hour or two before Minh and his father showed up."

Trieu nodded and turned from them. "After two more sleeps, you will have your chance to show your true hearts."

"And Mr. Tho and Lien. Are they all right?" asked Linh. "We've heard rumors—"

"They're all true. Mr. Tho is my general. He just doesn't know it."

"And Lien?"

"She is the motor behind the general."

"She's the *ba xa*?" asked Gia, using the colloquial term to describe the local woman in charge.

"Yes. Now tell everyone you can trust in Hanoi. After two more sleeps, look to the south. Our salvation comes from the south. Be prepared. And remember. Look to the south."

Lady Trieu morphed into her shapeless form and slipped out of the house into the evening air. She buzzed over the Old Quarter and past the newly-built structure in Ba Dinh Square, landing in human form on the back side of the wall obstructing the view of the Ho Chi Minh Mausoleum. She unsheathed her sword and with a mighty swing, sliced the brick wall in two. She kicked over large chunks of the wall, using some of the pieces to throw at other sections. Relentless, she toppled the barrier, revealing once again the mausoleum to the rest of the square. In a single bound, she landed at the apex of the granite structure, facing the new building with her sword pointed directly at it in a threatening stance.

"Sun Quan," she hollered. "I demand an immediate retreat across the northern border, or you shall regret the decision to come here."

The machines arrived. Dozens of them. They fired at Lady Trieu, but she deflected most of the shots. The ones that made it past her twirling sword did little damage to her human form.

One machine scaled the granite edifice. It had rolled vertically up its side as if gravity meant nothing. It fired repeatedly at Lady Trieu, but undeterred, she attacked it, thrusting her sword at the center of its metal chest. The ancient forged weapon pierced the outer shell of the machine, and it disintegrated into a mere puff of harmless particles. Lady Trieu moved forward to inspect the pile of dust catching the breeze. She turned quickly and looked out at the top of the opposing building. Sun Quan stood opposite her with the Chinese man at his side. The dust revealed the truth to everyone. The machines stopped their attack. They backed away like frightened dogs, realizing they no longer had the upper hand in a fight even though they outnumbered her one hundred to one. The realization came across her face. She knew. Lady Trieu understood, and her bold stance displayed her new found knowledge. She smiled and pointed her sword at Sun Quan, who glanced down at the Chinese man. She knew. And they knew it.

She went formless and flew off over the city. Sun Quan chased after her, snatching the last edge of her form halfway to Hoan Kiem Lake. They turned and tossed in the air, suffocating each other under thousands of years of history and struggle. She had to break free, one last time. She called for the bird, not audibly, but in her mind, and as the cosmic forces wrestled in the early night sky, the bird made its cry known to nearly everyone in Hanoi. Lady Trieu returned to human form and free fell towards the ground. The bird swooped underneath her and caught the warrior in midair. Sun Quan had turned human at the same time, but he fell unobstructed and landed on top of an evening *pho* station. The shocked hawker, already scared enough to try and earn a meager amount on the day after the attack, fainted while the few patrons able to afford such a luxury as noodle soup scattered. Sun Quan shook off the fall and glanced into the sky. She had disappeared.

The bird flew into the heart of Hoan Kiem Lake and slipped under the surface of the sacred water. Witnesses gawked and spread word of the mythical bird and the lady warrior, previously feared to be dead. The buzz reached the outer portions of Hanoi in under an hour. It even reached Hang Bac Street and the house of Mr. Thao, but he wasn't surprised.

The arduous task given to Tho and Lien challenged their wits as well. Lien instructed Tho to design a pontoon bridge while she rallied support from the community surrounding ancient Co Loa Citadel north of Hanoi. She found the previously-scared-off two old men playing Chinese chess on the first road past the gate of the citadel. One of the men whacked all the chess pieces from the board with the back of his hand and stated that, while the game may have originated in China, she could count on their complete loyalty to the rebellion. The other man simply cowered in respect and informed Lien she could keep the basket boat.

"I am keeping it," she confirmed. "But I need your help. I need many more of these boats." They jumped into action without question. They had seen the bird—all of the local community had— and they had heard the rumors of the strange happenings at the pearl well; rumors they had spread.

"We'll get them. How many do you need?"

"As many as you can find. And rope. Lots of it. And long pieces of timber. Many of them."

They received the orders from Captain Lien. One even saluted her before he grabbed his bicycle and began hollering down both sides of the street like a bread seller. But he sold nothing. He searched for an army and any and all able-bodied persons, and even some who weren't.

Lien returned to the edge of the pond where Tho stood like an orator with his arms spread out wide over the water.

"Tho!"

"I don't know how to design a pontoon bridge." His arms smacked down at both sides.

"Never mind. I took care of it."

"Then why did you ask me to do it?"

"Because I wanted you to rest."

"Why didn't you just tell me to rest? I was stressing."

"It doesn't matter." She pointed to the rear. "Look."

The two old men led a parade of townsfolk, a ragtag corps of army engineers, dragging behind them basket boats with knotted rolls of rope hanging off the sides. Men and women, of different ages and abilities, pulled long pieces of wood, some of which had been ripped off the roofs of sheds and houses. Children as young as five meandered along with cloth or rope or strands of twine.

Lien barked out orders, which no one questioned. No one wondered who put her in charge. She just was. She waded chest-deep into the pond. Others joined her. Boat after boat plopped into the water, and they bound them together with any type of string or twine or rope they had scrounged. They tied together a pair of basket boats, which would be connected to long planks reaching to the next pair of basket boats ten feet or so away. They repeated the procedure until the final planks reached the cement ring around pearl well. The plank ends laid flat upon the edge of the cement, and Lien instructed the men and women to bring several sacks of sand to stabilize the base of the planks.

Within two hours, they had constructed a pontoon foot bridge sturdy enough for even ninety-five-year-old Tho to wobble across.

Every remaining soul in the village gathered at the foot of the bridge with Tho and Lien standing over them. The rowdy crowd shouted questions, previously unvoiced during the construction phase. "What is the bird? ... What is going to happen here? ... What is the purpose of the bridge? ... Is it true that Lady Trieu has appeared from the dead? ... What do we need to do?"

Lien waved her arms in the air to focus everyone's attention.

"Listen. We can't answer all of your questions now. But we can say that your work here today will play a big part of the resistance. Thank you."

"What now?" yelled one of the old men.

Tho wobbled to the stage with Lien reaching out with her hand to help stabilize him. "Listen, friends. The best we can do is pray for rain and a strong cover of clouds which might hide our deeds here for one more day. In the morning, all of you need to be ready."

"Ready for what?"

"The day we've been waiting for. Now go. Disperse. We mustn't draw attention. Not today. Tomorrow we'll make ourselves known. Be ready."

The cryptic words did little to lessen the worry on their faces. The townsfolk dispersed from the citadel, asking more questions than they would ever get answers to. They especially wondered about a silly pontoon bridge, which connected the shore of the pond with the ring of cement in the middle. The purpose would elude them for one more day.

Chapter 28

A Traitor

The Chinese man brooded. Sun Quan masked emotion with the thin glass shield over his eyes as he surveyed the destruction left in the wake of Lady Trieu's daring attack.

"She's playing you," he said to the warrior. "She visited Hang Bac Street. I've seen the footage." Sun Quan still didn't respond. "The boy's father needs to pay them one more visit."

"Then make it happen."

"Why does it feel like we have everything securely in the palm of our hands, and yet it continues to seep right through our fingers? You should have finished her when you had a chance."

Sun Quan grabbed the Chinese man and pushed him backwards and lorded over the man who was still not intimidated. "Maybe your plan to unleash the machines will unleash something much bigger. You have no idea what you're doing."

The Chinese man poked a finger into Sun Quan's chest. "Be careful what your careless attitude produces. Don't forget what you owe me. Don't forget Beijing."

"We are far beyond Beijing at this point," said Sun Quan. "When was the last time we followed an order from them?"

"Oh, Sun Quan, you have it so backwards."

"What do you mean?"

"I'm not here for Beijing. I'm here for all humanity. This is just the beginning."

Sun Quan snapped. "You can't even control a small patch of earth wrapped around a river."

"Me? Almighty Sun Quan was brought here for one purpose, and you just wallow in your soft spot for her."

"I have done my duty. And I'll do it again."

The Chinese man smirked. "I have no doubt. In the meantime, I'll have the boy's father discover what he can."

The Chinese man tapped the warrior on the chest and chuckled. The man removed a cigarette from his pocket and lit. "I do like these … these cigarettes." He blew smoke on Sun Quan and exited into an elevator. Sun Quan approached the edge of the building and jumped off, flying through the air and landing at the edge of Ba Dinh Square, beside the shredded wall in front of the mausoleum. He studied the sharp-edged, precision-sliced cuts committed with great force.

"How do you think this will end?" He gazed skyward. "Can you hear me?" He sensed she could. In a single bound, he jumped to the top of the mausoleum. Through the trees to the north, the south-facing facade of the Presidential Palace poked out of the leaves. Her form moved around it and rested on its colonial facade. She morphed human and raised her sword till it glistened between the tree tops.

"It will only end one way."

"Desolation," he whispered.

"But whose?"

"He's playing both of us, you know."

"Who?"

Sun Quan glanced back at the newly constructed building in front of them. "You know who."

Lady Trieu pondered his meaning. "He was the one who brought the machines to life, but you couldn't hide their reality from me." Sun Quan didn't respond. "You still think you can turn me?"

"Trieu, do you like the living? Or is your soul content to languish in the depths of history? Ha. You're still the foolish young woman who convinced herself that she could defeat the entire northern army."

"And she did."

"But at what cost? You could have been much more."

She lowered her sword. They talked almost without audible words at this point. Their thoughts rose as whispers through the twisted air of converging times. "That I am here. That I was able to distinguish the cries for help once more, and offer myself for my people is enough."

"I could destroy you right now."

"You haven't been able to yet. Maybe you didn't want to. Maybe you wished that when I fell beneath the surface of Hoan Kiem Lake, I would arise again. Stronger." She paused. "I have."

Sun Quan shook his head. "So if the sides are set, the end is imminent."

"I know you will show no mercy, Sun Quan, as I ask for none."

He watched as she became a vapor and lifted into the wind before disappearing into the other side. He could have chased her. He could have forced her to kill him now if she wanted to survive, but he wanted to see it. He wanted her to show him her plan. Was it an act of mercy to allow her to flee without a fight? He wasn't sure. Nor did he care what the Chinese man thought.

Minh languished for the last day and a half in isolation inside the black, glossy walls of the facility. He had exhausted his energy wondering about Nhan, his mother, Tho, and especially the appearance of his father. Nothing made sense, especially the marble tablet, which seemed visible only to him. He often fondled it in his hands in plain sight of the all-seeing walls, but nothing ever happened. This fact alone gave him hope.

The wall opened and his father entered, prompting Minh to stand at attention.

"Minh, I hope you've had time to think about everything."

"Where's Nhan?"

His father pulled a device from his pocket and glanced at it.

"Where's Nhan?" Minh asked.

"Minh, she's dead."

The stunned Minh staggered towards him a step, mouth open. He readied himself to call his father a liar, or a number of other treacherous words in his mind, but his father preempted them by holding up the device and showing him the scene—Nhan running down the bank of the Red River, wading in chest deep, and slipping under the current. Two machines skipped across the water and dipped their probes beneath the surface. After a few seconds, they returned to the bank, and the video ended.

"She refused to be caught, so she drowned herself."

"No, no ..." Minh backed away.

"Minh, the rebellion is powerless. Commander Lieu is corrupt. Did he help you when you went to him in the cave? We know the answer to that. It's all unraveling. You can still save your mother and Tho from making grave mistakes. I need your help, Minh. Please."

The confused boy backed himself against the wall. The man he loved and wanted to emulate strung him along with convoluted thoughts. His head swirled. Confused. Angry. Disillusioned. Hurt. His father enticed him to go, one more time, "... just come with me again. You will see."

Minh did. His blank mind followed his blank stare as they trudged through the corridors of the facility and into the same open-air vehicle previously used. They navigated the peaceful streets of Hanoi. The population seemed dazed, unwilling to engage in their surroundings, unwilling to acknowledge the man in the unification shirt, sitting beside his son, who once was at the forefront of the resistance. Now Minh didn't know where he sat.

The vehicle came to a stop on Hang Bac Street. Minh glanced at all the familiar sights, the houses, the shops, but they all seemed distant, like he was in a simulation, and his father held the controller. He stepped out of the vehicle. He followed the man he once knew into the familiar house—that of Mr. Thao, the former policeman.

Mr. Thao bowed to them with excitement. His wife poured scalding hot water from a tumbler into a small pot to steep the green tea. Small talk simmered in their midst, as if a war never existed, as if they had a casual visit with Thao to discuss the latest neighborhood gossip. Minh's father reached in his pocket and handed Thao a reunification pin. Thao snatched it with a smile and attached it to his left lapel.

"Thao, word has it you were visited here recently?"

"Yes, yes. A woman. She was dressed like a warrior, carrying a sword. She said she was Lady Trieu." Minh's eyes locked on Thao's after the admission. "But we know that is impossible."

"Indeed," confirmed Minh's father. "So what did this impostor want?"

"She wanted us to be ready. She said the rebels will attack tomorrow morning."

"She did? Any other details."

"Yes, they are amassing an army in the south and …"

Minh reached for the pot of tea, picked it up with his bare hands—ignoring the searing heat on his palms—and tossed it at Thao. The water splashed all over him, and he screamed.

"You traitor!" yelled Minh. "We trusted you our whole lives, and you betrayed your own people."

"Minh," his father scolded, grabbing the boy by the arm. But Minh broke free and jumped over top of the coffee table onto the former police officer. He flailed his arms and punched the old man, repeating refrains like "traitors must die" and "you betrayed your own people."

Thao's wife tried to pull him off her husband, but the tenacious boy wouldn't relent. His father punched a few keys on his device and two machines entered the room, each using their probes to lock down Minh's two wrists and pulling him off the old man who had burns down the front of his body.

"Take him back to the facility," instructed Minh's father without looking at his son.

The machines dragged Minh out of the house—the fuming boy yelling curses at the old man and his father, while thinking mainly of Nhan. A vehicle with a Chinese driver pulled up. The machines escorted Minh into the back seat, keeping his wrists clamped, and they drove him back to the facility. He screamed the entire way, not caring who saw him or what strange looks the weakened souls of Hanoi cast his way. The machines tossed him into the same cell. His sprawling body lay flat against the cold floor, and he cried the tears he could no longer hold back. When he finally allowed the moment to settle in, he opened his eyes to notice the marble tablet had fallen out of his pocket, just out of his reach. He crawled over to it and clasp it in his hands.

"Lady Trieu. Lady Trieu."

He felt movement up his spine and a whisk of air in his ear.

"Don't move," said the voice. "I know where you've been. Be ready to act in the morning. You will know when."

Minh shifted to his side and readied a reply.

"No, don't say a word. They will hear you. They will see you, but they can't see me. I know where you were this morning. I know. Just wait for the dawn."

Her presence left him alone. He caressed the marble tablet in his hands. But all the machines saw from the walls were two empty palms rubbing against each other.

Nhan rested against a large rock in the middle of an open field surrounded by the jagged mountain peaks of Hoa Lu, the ancient capital of Vietnam until emperor Ly Thai To spotted the dragon ascending out of the Red River and established the new capital of Thang Long, Ascending Dragon—now called Hanoi. Hanoi had been battered for the past two years, and now waited for the answer from the warrior in the lake. Nhan waited for answers, too. She had been isolated for the past two days, awaiting the return of Lady Trieu and the army she had been promised.

A strong wind grabbed her attention. She glanced northward but only saw a single bird, without a long tail. She froze against the rock and listened to the whirling of the wind as if she expected it to speak to her. It had a message. One she couldn't decipher. But she listened anyway, without moving, feeling a tingling on her back and a shadow forming around her, spreading out in all directions until the light of the fading western sun was blocked completely by the dark movement. She would turn and look and not be afraid, she told herself. But still she hesitated. After everything she had seen, she wondered if her eyes could be trusted to believe in something using senses beyond only sight.

She turned. A blob of floating bodies hovered behind her. Their dark faces eluded her as the final sparks of sun slid through the cracks between the bodies, which drifted left and right in small increments. She stared at them, mammoth figures each ten to twelve feet high, not touching the ground, like giant blown-up balloons, but she could tell they had substance. Gravity did not limit them, however, and the forces gathered, more and more, until the sun no longer shone on Nhan's face and the menacing army waited in formation like a mountain cliff.

"Who are you?" she demanded.

They didn't reply. Not one of them. As if they had no ears. Their dark gazes continued straight ahead.

"Are you whom Lady Trieu spoke of?"

What a silly question. Non-human entities hovered over her. Who else could have sent them?

"What shall we do?"

No response. As she moved closer, she noticed their bodies were not solid, but shifting shades of light pulsing through the translucent beings. Their faces only resembled the face of a human, but there was a deformity about them, with noses slightly off, and mouths that revealed toothless cavities inside their heads.

They don't look like warriors, she said to herself, examining their goblin bodies.

"Nhan." A voice beckoned her to pivot. "Your army."

Nhan glanced at Lady Trieu then quickly back toward the massive group behind her. "They don't look like an army."

"They aren't."

"I don't understand."

"Before dawn, ride on the wind and assemble at the western edge of the Yen Lenh Bridge."

"Yen Lenh? That's right outside the limits of the Hanoi District."

"Yes."

"Why there?"

"Ride off on the wind and assemble just before dawn."

"How can I ride off on the wind?"

"My bird will lead you."

She looked behind the warrior at the long-tailed bird grazing harmlessly in the faint shadows of the background.

"The bird? I don't understand—"

"Nhan, do as I command. Lead them into position. When the Chinese attack, you will know what to do."

"I will?"

"I have faith in you."

"But who are these—" She looked back at the lifeless ghosts. "What are these …? Lady Trieu, they don't look like warriors."

"Oh, they are, Nhan. They are. We are counting on you. May the spirit of our ancestors go before you tomorrow. May you succeed, so we all may succeed."

"I thought you said they weren't warriors?"

"They once were farmers, peasants, and common folk—just like your family."

Nhan looked at them again. She would lead them. She would follow the commands, worthy of a leader blindly putting one's actions into one's faith. She would ride on the wind, and she would lead this silent group into position. Then she would wait to see what it all meant.

Chapter 29

The Assembly

Nhan waited in silence as the night arrived and mirrored the darkness she had felt when she had plunged into the river. It heightened her senses, and she peered into the sky as if she could see into the heart of Hanoi itself. She would be there in the morning. The goblin, faceless, non-emotive warriors hung behind her like a thousand tethered balloons. The long-tailed bird rested its neck in the grass next to the meandering water flowing between the granite cliffs. Her mind vacillated between the morning's attack and the boy she left behind—Minh. She hadn't seen the strength in the scrawny boy when he barged into the rebel headquarters commanding attention. Everyone sneered at him, especially her father. She did likewise. But now? They were bound by foolishness, because only a fool would have barged her way back into the facility just to desire escape once more. She had left him alone. She had taken the bait and run, but now she was here, like Lady Trieu had planned it. She looked around at the sullen shadows behind her and remembered submerging herself into the water. What happened next? A turtle. A dark passageway. A—the blurriness of it tired her mind. But she knew one thing. At dawn, she would ride the strange bird at the behest of a long dead heroine. She would do it for two reasons: to cut through the Chinese and rescue her friend, Minh.

"I won't leave you behind. Believe, Minh. Believe."

Hundreds of miles to the north, in the small community surrounding the pond with the makeshift pontoon bridge, Nhan's father and commander of the resistance walked down the main street toward the ancient citadel with a small contingent of camouflaged commandos surrounding him. The peering eyes of the villagers followed every step. They knew him. Everyone did. He had been the one sending messages of hope and exhortations of fierce resistance through the airwaves and through clandestine printed messages for the past two years. Here he was, without an army, walking toward Co Loa Citadel.

Lien and Tho had been sitting in the edge of the grass near the newly constructed bridge as the contingent arrived. Lien rose but Tho couldn't yet be bothered to make use of his legs.

"Commander Lieu."

Lieu glanced beyond Lien to the bridge behind her. "The bridge looks unstable."

"It was the best we could do with our time and resources."

"How can a great resistance army cross such a flimsy span?"

Lien bit her lip, but only for a moment. She had no reason to hold back. "Where's this great resistance army?" Her condescending eyes scattered around at the few true soldiers at the commander's side. The ragtag villagers formed the remaining bulk of this supposed great army.

"Pray they will come," he said.

"What do you mean?"

"We sent out word to the scattered cells. Now we can only wait."

Lieu walked past Lien and shook the first pontoon with his hand. Lien followed and edged right up into his face. "What if they don't come? It's tomorrow. At dawn. Do you understand? We have no backup plan. This is it."

"I know." Lieu had a shortness in his voice. "Do you think I need to be reminded of the gravity of the situation?"

"My son's life may be on the line."

"All of our lives are," said Lieu, in a low, growling voice.

Tho grunted and pushed himself up the best he could. "Help me." Lien reached down and stabilized his arm. "Everyone has short fuses at the end of a war. It's a wonder we have any fuses at all remaining. This is, perhaps," he laughed, pointing at the bridge, "...not the prettiest of pontoon bridges. And if your guerrilla warriors want to strengthen the span overnight, they are welcome to fiddle all they like. But sleep might be a better idea, or we might find ourselves in a deep permanent sleep by tomorrow evening. But someone of my age never minds the thought too much." He chuckled again. "One way or the other, my young man. One way or the other." He looked at the other old man from the village standing behind Lieu. "Does your wife have any more of those noodles? Anything at all will do."

He nodded and motioned Tho forward, but Lieu stopped the old man by grabbing the edge of Tho's loose cotton sleeve.

"What will happen tomorrow? What have you seen? What do you know?"

The sage squared himself with the troops. They all peered through the myriad heads and shoulders to see his pointy white beard that looked like an upended snow-capped mountain peak.

"All we have is history, and it's come alive, as we know. It is our only guide as we try one more time to hold tight to this sacred land entrusted to us by our ancestors. If we trust our determination and our resolve, perhaps, just perhaps, it will again be enough and our ancestors will look favorably upon us once more."

Silence. The solemn faces showed hope and confusion in equal measure. No one spoke until one of the commandos stepped forward. "That's all you have? Platitudes?"

Tho leaned over to Lieu's ear. "Not much faith from your troops, I see. Have you lost it, as well?"

The commando continued. "We're exposed here. If they were to hit us now..."

Tho raised his arm to stop him. "They'd hit a bunch of old men and women and a few soldiers like yourself. How would that change anything?"

Lieu took the reins of the conversation from his subordinate. "What are you trying to say, Mr. Tho?"

"It's a blessing our numbers are small tonight. Now come morning, if our numbers remain small, then it surely will be a curse." Tho chuckled and gazed back at the old man. "Do you think she has made soup? Your wife."

"I see the boy came back on his own," said Sun Quan as the Chinese man entered the private headquarters of the newly constructed building in the middle of Hanoi's Ba Dinh Square.

"He has grit, that's for sure. More than his father."

"So the south?" asked Sun Quan. It was less a question and more to let the Chinese man know that the information had preceded him. "And the reports, do they confirm the south?"

"Nothing firm," said the Chinese man. "There's been little movement in any direction. The night of terror did its trick."

"We shall see."

"The south will meet our army, and the majority of the conventional troops will remain in the center of Hanoi."

"Sir!" A Chinese soldier barged in the room.

"What is it?"

"Heat sensing radar picked up a group of people in Dong Anh District."

"Dong Anh. That's north east of the city. How big?"

"No more than a hundred."

"What's in Dong Anh district?"

"Co Loa Citadel."

"Probably a bunch of geriatric incense burners. Send a drone to check it out."

"Yes, sir."

"I'll go do it," said Sun Quan.

"No," snapped the Chinese man. "We have planning to do."

"We already know what to do."

"No. I need you here." He pointed back to the soldier. "Send the drone."

Sun Quan obeyed and took his position on the right side of the

Chinese man. In front of them, a wall of monitors blared, each one tuned in to the machines and other means of espionage at their disposal. Sun Quan's eyes zoomed in on one boy, all alone rubbing his hands over an invisible item. The small screen turned large until it displayed on the entire wall.

"You worry about this one?" asked the Chinese man.

Sun Quan zoomed in closer on his hand. "Why does he do that? That motion with an empty hand?"

"Oh, Sun Quan, you are always looking for reasons to be suspicious."

"What will he do to us?" asked Sun Quan in a rhetorical pose.

"Nothing we couldn't predict with his father. Maybe one day they will be together."

"On whose side?"

"Oh, it will be ours."

"Don't be so sure. Your time here may not be as long as you think," threatened Sun Quan.

The Chinese man laughed. "Tall foreboding warriors from the past have such a mystique about them. Don't overstep your bounds, Sun Quan."

"I'm sure that would frighten you if I ever do. You'd be looking up from the bottom of my heel."

"So dramatic." The Chinese man laughed as Minh, the boy on the screen, stood up and looked toward the wall camera. He stared at both of them still holding the invisible marble tablet. He mouthed something.

"What did he say?" asked the Chinese man.

"I hate you."

"Apropos. Apropos." The Chinese man motioned with his hand and a thousand screens, each one with a machine awaiting orders stared back. "Secure the south. Look to the dawn."

Lien had led Lieu and his commandos to the cement ring around the pearl well. The soldiers complained about the unstable nature of the pontoon bridge, but Lien insisted it would hold. When his commandos doubted the veracity of the pond and its nature, Lieu didn't speak. He knew full well what had happened to him, but he wasn't about to relive it. Not on the eve of the attack.

"What is the point of all this? Why did you build a bridge to nowhere?"

Lien glanced back at Lieu. "You mean you didn't tell them?"

Lieu looked away.

A commando spoke up. "What haven't you told us?"

"Lieu, tell your men what happened. Tell them why we're here."

He ignored her and dipped his hand into the water. Nothing magical occurred. Single droplets fell off his hand and pattered the surface.

"Lieu. Tell them."

"I hate leaving anything to chance."

"This is nothing to do with chance." Lien clenched her fist and poked her face right close to his cheek. "You know the story. Tell them."

"We're ill-prepared, ill-equipped. We have no assurance that they will come and if they do …" He stopped.

"What happens if they do arrive?" asked one of the soldiers. "Why did you build a pontoon bridge to this?" He pointed at the cement ring they stood upon around the well. "How will we get to Hanoi? We could have three-thousand men here by morning. What are you not telling us?"

"It won't be enough," said Lieu.

Lien grabbed the commander by the neck. "Stand up. Be a man. Tell them about the turtle!"

All the commandos shifted their heads in a queer manner toward Lien, until one of them jerked upward and pointed into the sky. "There. A drone, sir. Hide!" He jumped in front of Lieu, almost knocking him into the water.

"Did it spot us?" asked Lien, looking back to the shore. Many of the villagers milled around the entrance to the citadel.

"It's coming closer."

"We have to disable it before it starts transmitting our images back to Hanoi. It might have already grabbed us."

"Here it …"

Before any other words of panic could spread, the drone exploded just beyond the pond's perimeter and debris scattered into the edge of the water. The shock of the blast sent everyone to their knees, except Lieu. He held a crossbow in his hand and rubbed his leg nervously.

"You used it. The magic crossbow," said Lien.

"Magic crossbow?" asked one of the commandos.

"You mean you didn't even tell your men about that? They have no idea what's going on, do they? How do they think they're going to defeat the Chinese and Sun Quan if all they think they have is a group of geriatric villagers? When are you going to clue them in? They don't even know how they're getting to Hanoi." Lien slapped Lieu across the back of the neck. He turned as if he was going to hit her but didn't.

"You're as intense as your husband was," said Lieu.

"Let me see it in you, too!" Her veins popped out of her neck. "Tell them."

The commandos encircled Lieu. "What's she talking about? What's the magic crossbow?"

Lieu lowered his eyes to the simple wooden weapon. He gripped it with determination and held it up in front of him. "Let me tell you how we will get to Hanoi tomorrow."

A Chinese soldier barged back into the meeting room of the Chinese man and the brooding warrior. "Sir, the drone we had dispatched to Dong Anh exploded."

"Was it shot down?"

"It's unclear. It sensed no military presence and none of its sensors transmitted any ballistic residue before it went off line."

"Could it have been a malfunction?"

"Seems unlikely, sir."

"Now, I'll go check it out," said Sun Quan.

Before he could move, another soldier tripped into the room in a great rush. "I'm sorry, sir. But we're under attack. To the south."

"What? There's been no reports of an army."

Sun Quan nudged the Chinese man's side and pointed toward the monitors. It showed Lady Trieu slicing her sword through machine after machine, all of them disintegrating to dust.

"She's preparing the way." Sun Quan smashed the screen with his fist and shattered the image of his female nemesis. "She knows they can't touch her. It was foolish of you to awaken them. Dressing them in a modern sheer. Who knows what else this will awaken? I could have done it alone."

The Chinese man snickered. "You are capable, yes. But slow."

Sun Quan grabbed the Chinese man by the throat and shoved him against the broken wall of screens.

"Oh, Sun Quan. You know you have no power over me. Remember who made you. And I can end you at any time. But I do admire your bravado. You still display so many human emotions. It's fascinating, really. Now remove your hands from me."

Sun Quan backed away. The Chinese soldiers who had delivered the messages had scattered. "I'll go meet her. That's what she wants."

"Not only her, Sun Quan. It's what you want, too."

Sun Quan glared back at him. His smile told it all. He somehow knew what Sun Quan had told her. He knew it all, and yet he allowed the warrior to continue. "I've been watching you the entire time. I don't mind the betrayal, so much. It's to be expected. Power does that. It's a gut level I can understand. But you are straying dangerously close to walking away from the Middle Kingdom, and that I can't abide."

Sun Quan roared like a ferocious animal and jumped forward, slamming his massive fist into the center of the Chinese man's chest, but his fist went right through him, like slicing the air with a knife. The Chinese man disappeared, only to show himself again on the other side of the room.

"Like I said, Sun Quan, I love the bravado. Now go take care of her."

Lady Trieu stood at the edge of the water of the Red River southeast of the city. She anticipated his arrival. For the past thirty minutes she had attacked the machines which had set up roadblocks on all the major arteries out of the city. She had destroyed dozens of them while mostly leaving the regular Chinese troops alone. She closed her eyes in deep concentration. "Nhan." She held her arm out and pointed southward. "Nhan. Allow yourself to feel it. Nhan."

Nhan felt a whisper in her ear, and she sensed the tongue-tied, brain-dead warriors behind her had nothing to do with it. The darkness of the night settled in, and she waded into the stream but didn't feel the wetness. It moved around her but didn't penetrate her clothing. She reached down with her hand and felt the water, but the droplets rolled off her dry palm like she was standing in the summer sun. She paused and listened. "Nhan." The voice whirled around her.

Lady Trieu remained in a trance facing southward. "Listen. Nhan. All is prepared. Ride at dawn. Focus on the machines."

Nhan heard it. The machines. Focus on the machines.

"Nhan, don't worry about the losses. They will be great. Focus on the machines."

Nhan spoke into the breeze. "I will sacrifice everything. Even my own life."

Lady Trieu awakened and felt his presence. She morphed formless and floated over the river. They collided and tossed each other in a spiraling ball the breadth of the water. Lady Trieu donned her human form once more and dove downward until she plunged beneath the surface of the water. Sun Quan followed, but the water repelled him once again the same way the history of Hoan Kiem Lake refused his entrance.

He stood on the banks of the river. "Face me."

She would. But not yet.

Miles to the north, Commander Lieu, Tho, and Lien hid themselves in the citadel. They instructed the villagers to stay out of sight and await dawn in their houses. They all waited for reinforcements. They waited for the resistance to poke their heads outside their caves and clandestine protected structures one last time. They waited for them to show themselves, for a final push toward the unknown. At midnight, the first dazed and unsure-of-themselves troops stumbled into the darkened citadel, wondering if they had heard the correct instructions.

"Hello?" Tho, who had been sleeping in the grass, awakened to the sound. Two of the commandos nearby shined flashlights on the unknown arrivals.

"Tuan?" Tho spoke. Lien had awakened also.

"Tuan?"

The young comrade of Cuong, who had helped them into the Ho Chi Minh historical site, stood in front of a group of out of breath soldiers.

"Who is it?" Tuan asked, shielding his eyes from the bright lights.

"It's Tho and Lien," she said.

Tuan smiled and moved towards them. The commandos lowered the lights to the ground to allow them all to adjust back to the darkness.

"Tuan, it's so good to see you," she said, holding out her hands to him.

"I wouldn't be here, none of us would, without you and Mr. Tho."

"Oh, don't be so quick to flatter," said Tho with a wry smile.

"It's true. I was angry at you all for what happened to Cuong and …" He didn't need to mention the soldier who lost his life that night.

"I know," Lien reassured him.

"But you were right. All of it. And now I'm proud to fight alongside you."

Commander Lieu came around the side of Tho. "I hope you brought more than these, soldier."

"Yes, sir. The word is out. They are coming. You can count on it.

Nothing will stop them, and nothing will stop us."

"I like your enthusiasm, Tuan," said Lieu. "And I hope you're right."

Before Tuan could reply, the next contingent walked through the outer gates of the citadel, with another group behind them. The assembly had begun.

Chapter 30

At Dawn

Nhan paced and pondered all night at the edge of the stream with a robust energy which mocked sleep. At the darkest moment before dawn, the long-tailed bird called for her, as if it knew the timing. The teen mounted, her body contained in its wide span, and she clutched the long plumes of feathers like she had ridden a thousand times before. The bird ascended, and as it rose, Nhan released her grip from the feathers and balanced herself in the rush of air around her, feeling adrenaline and feeling alive. Her body remained upright regardless of the dip, turn, or swirl the bird performed. They swooped over the area of Hoa Lu, and she called out to the deadened troops in a rousing voice.

"It's time! We ride to Yen Lenh Bridge."

Her voice commanded authority, like its echoes bounded off the early morning cloud cover. She didn't recognize her own voice, but the bizarre troops did. The zombies awakened and lifted into the air like flying ghosts, eyes glowing, sparkling metal swords in their hands. They hadn't had swords before, but she dared not ask about them. The massive contingent flew north at high speed, and as the first streak of light painted the eastern sky a pale rouge, Nhan spotted the bridge below. Lady Trieu had instructed her to amass and wait for a signal, but Nhan pushed onward, feeling there was no time to waste. She exhorted the beings into attack formation, and they swarmed downward onto the bridge, a band of rabid locusts seeking to devour the enemy. Machines let loose a torrent of fire. Bullets ripped through the first wave of warrior ghosts and disintegrated them to nothingness. The battle had begun.

Nhan's massive force suffered extensive losses, but she pushed them onward. As the light finally illuminated the battlefield, a garrison of Chinese army regulars had holed up a quarter mile behind the bridge. She motioned for the bird to land, and she grabbed a sword which had been strapped to the side of the bird. She assumed it had been Lady Trieu's, but it was now the only weapon she had, and she sprinted toward the garrison hidden behind staggered jeeps and heavily armored vehicles. Voices shouted, then the automatic weapons fired. Pock. Pock. Pock. The first bullet ripped through Nhan's chest. She staggered backwards for a moment and looked down. No blood and no pain. Another bullet caught her shoulder. But again, it disappeared into her body without causing any effect. She raised her sword and two bullets ricocheted off the blade like harmless flies. She maneuvered the weapon back and forth, stopping numerous oncoming bullets with ease. In the rear, the machines continued the destruction of the ghost ranks, but there were also fewer machines. She remained unharmed against human troops firing at her at point blank range. She remembered Lady Trieu's words: "You'll know what to do." She jumped forward, a massive leap atop one of the armored vehicles. She sliced through one of the soldiers and then another. She flicked away their bullets with her sword, and she advanced on a group of panicking Chinese, who withdrew from their positions. She persisted and decimated a slew of soldiers with her precision sword strikes. The air couldn't contain her force. The modern weapons couldn't contain her destruction. A smile crossed her face. The power she had always wanted, now in her grasp. Had Lady Trieu given it to her? The turtle? The Red River? If only her father could see her now. The exhilaration consumed her, and she terrorized and hunted every soldier from the roadblock, showing no mercy and flattening them all to the ground in silence.

But joy turned, as it does. She felt a burning in her leg. A bullet had lodged there and remained when no other one had. She writhed in pain and twirled around to face off with a rogue machine. It fired again and grazed the side of her stomach. She lunged forward and pierced it in two with her sword. It disintegrated into dust. She leaned against the back of an armored vehicle and witnessed the destruction. Her ghost army sacrificed themselves one at a time to take out additional machines. Numbers on each side dwindled in the relentless fight. Thick dust coated the air with the stench of staleness, like history had been unleashed from the books and its smell soaked the environment. "You'll know what to do." She had witnessed what the machines could do and what the humans couldn't. Had the attack been successful? She had no way to know. Lady Trieu had said the losses would be great, and she decided to let the battle of her strange warriors play out on its own. She had one person in mind: Minh. She whistled once for the bird. It swooped down toward her. She climbed onto the hood of the vehicle and jumped headfirst onto the back of the long-tailed bird, soaring into the sky.

"The facility."

The bird let out a mighty call and charted a path toward the heart of Hanoi. Nhan had a bird's eye view of the battlefield. Thousands of Chinese troops mobilized into position along the myriad roads leading out of south Hanoi. They barricaded the streets and waited for word from the battlefield between the dead-headed force and the machines. She had been the decoy, but no longer because she had survived. She would spearhead the attack against the heart of the beast.

They did indeed come. From all over. Small bands of resistance forces overwhelmed the Co Loa Citadel in the dead of the night. Lieu instructed his commandos to divide into battalions, each one commanding one of the groups. The villagers formed their own ragtag crew with the two old men—who typically played Chinese chess—now vying with the other to instruct the group to kill the Han at all cost.

As dawn approached, they amassed on the shore of the pond, spilling over into the courtyard of the citadel. No one used light of any kind, lest they be discovered. Lieu, Tho, and Lien were the first ones to make their way over the pontoon bridge and onto the cement ring of the pearl well. Tho crawled on all fours and twice nearly slipped into the water, but Lien held him steady. Some of the first battalion followed. Those who could took their places on the cement ring as well, while others balanced on the unstable basket boats as the rest waited their turn on the shore. Most had no idea why they were there or what they waited for, and the long wait in the dark took its toll on the psyche of some of the resistance soldiers. One started a rumor that Commander Lieu had lost his mind. Others called old man Tho a sorcerer, some even questioning if he was actually Chinese.

The disgruntled rumblings of the masses slithered to a still stop, however, as a bright light—a glowing angel—descended over them and landed in the midst of the group on the cement ring. The crowd all goose-necked to see the wonder. A mighty warrior, sword in hand, towering over everyone else, with long flowing black hair and a thick leather chest plate. Lady Trieu.

"Listen," she commanded. "The southern attack has begun. We will take grave losses there, but it will allow us a brief moment of surprise, and we must not disappoint."

"We have no one attacking from the south," said Lieu.

"Yes, we do. Led by your daughter."

"Nhan? But—how?"

"I appointed her to run the diversion. It has begun, now we must move quickly."

"But we have no troops there?"

"I have raised an army."

A murmur spread through the ranks until one of the voices rose above the rest. "But we're still far from Hanoi. How will be get there?"

Lady Trieu looked over at Lieu, who nodded. He removed the magic crossbow from his pouch, inserted an arrow into the release point, and, without warning, shot the arrow at the center of the pearl well. The water parted and a fluorescent tunnel formed with a great gust of wind whipping out of it and over the heads of the onlookers.

"Follow me," said Lieu. He jumped into the tunnel. The first battalion roared at once and followed their leader blindly into the center of the pond. Dozens upon dozens of men jumped in and the pontoon bridge held its weight as the soldiers moved from the shore to the jumping off point. Lien, Tho, and Lady Trieu watched from the edge as wave after wave of men were sucked into the past, whirling through the magic tunnel until the final group of villagers joined them. Men and women. Young and old. No one warned them of their fate to come. No one said they were too old or too young. Everyone was welcome. In fact, everyone was expected. It was the only way the Vietnamese knew. Everyone, in concert, facing the daunting challenge and the mysterious unknown using whatever meager resources were available to them.

As the last old man belly-flopped into the tunnel, Lady Trieu took Lien and Tho by the hands. "Come. I have a special task for you. You both are our final hope. I will show you your guide. You've met before."

She smiled slightly, an odd thing perhaps, on the edge of a day of great destruction. But the smile calmed Lien and Tho, and they gladly followed her into the colorful, pulsing tunnel which sucked them in. As Tho passed the threshold of the top of the well, the water crashed in behind him, and the well returned to normal. The quietness of the citadel permeated the area—vacant of people, and completely still except for the haunting calls of history which buoyed them onward toward Hoan Kiem Lake.

Mr. Thao, the former policeman who had informed Minh's father of the planned attack from the south, awakened to a dark shadow standing over his slatted bed covered with a reed mat. Sunrise was still hours away.

"L ... Lady Trieu." He bonked his head on the wall behind him as the startled look stared back at the intruder.

"I was right about you."

"I'm at your service, Lady Trieu. I'll do anything."

"True. You'll do anything for anyone. You've already completed your part. I thank you for it."

He scrambled to sit up more properly. His head bobbed in a perpetual nod and his rotten teeth shone from his fake smile. "Yes, of course. Anything to help."

"Thank you for telling the Chinese about our attack to the south. They diverted their troops, so we have a chance."

"What?"

"And now your reward."

She raised her sword until it hit the tip of his chin. He squirmed backwards against the wall. "No, Lady Trieu. I was afraid. I thought they were going to kill me."

"No, your betrayal did that." She slid the sword through him and removed it in a quick retreat. He fell into a ball on top of the reed mat, slumped over, dead.

The Old Quarter of Hanoi awoke without Mr. Thao to the early morning sounds of heavy fighting to the south. The first light illuminated plumes of smoke hanging lazily in the distance. The weary Hanoi population gathered in the center of the city to await the unknown. Word had been spread, but no one was sure how to react until further information reached them.

The eighty-seven-year-old Mrs. Tuyet had been coming daily to Ngoc Son Temple in the middle of Hoan Kiem Lake for the past thirty years. She had started the routine after her husband died suddenly of a heart attack. At dawn each day, she walked the red curved bridge from the shore to the islet and lit incense in the inner hall to remember her family, and especially her husband. She prayed for many things: health, a blessed afterlife for her long dead relatives, and she always ended her prayer with a request for the miraculous. She wanted to see a miracle, whether a sighting of the great turtle of the lake or an unspoken blessing for her family. On this particular day, she didn't alter her routine one bit. She ignored the sound of fighting to the south. She had heard that before. In fact, her husband had been on the front line of resistance against the Chinese invasion of the north in 1979, as they ferociously fought to keep the northern invaders out. And they barely did. She lit her incense and prayed as usual. As she ended her prayer, she asked for the miraculous.

A vibration shook the Ngoc Son Temple, and the center of Hoan Kiem Lake opened, like a giant sink hole had swallowed the water by trapping gravity inside it. Light pierced out of the center of the lake, like a massive searchlight shooting into the sky to announce to the world a special promotion. The hole expanded until it reached the edge of the western shore of the lake—the same place that Sun Quan had tossed Lady Trieu into the water, not far from St. Joseph's Cathedral. Mrs. Tuyet moved to the back edge of the temple to watch. The resistance troops, led by Commander Lieu, touched dry ground, and marched out of the center of the lake like General MacArthur returning to the Philippines. Tears streamed down Mrs. Tuyet's face, and she stretched her arms upwards towards the heavens and asked to be reunited with her husband. The time had come. She fell over on the wooden floor, and joined her husband in the afterlife, her prayer finally answered.

The army continued emerging from the opening onto dry land. Lieu stood on the edge of the lake and barked out instructions. They had not met any resistance, but he knew it wouldn't last. Small platoons of rebels spread out street by street until they created a perimeter around the Old Quarter. They awaited instructions on how to proceed. They were to coordinate all intel back to Lieu at Hoan Kiem Lake so he could piece together the whereabouts of the occupying forces.

The citizens of Hanoi stretched along the perimeter of the lake and looked on in disbelief. Lieu tried to send out word for the mobs to dispense and stay quiet, but nothing worked. After two years of anguish, they stood at the edge of a miracle. All the legends, all the lore, all the history exposed itself in the blatant way the resistance marched onto shore from the soul of the nation of Vietnam. They believed it all. No story too outlandish. No prayer unanswerable. No outcome unthinkable. They banded together and pushed in against the commander, who pushed back with his frantic words for the population to be patient, but it was no use. The people had been loosened. The mental chains which bound them had fallen frayed and worn onto the ground, so Commander Lieu relented to the moment, understanding the thirst in their eyes—the hunger for justice—the love of country. He would use it in that moment, and he said, and his commandos enforced, "Go. Take back Hanoi."

Nhan soared across Hanoi on the back of the lost bird and landed on top of the facility without any resistance. She had passed over Hoan Kiem Lake moments before Mrs. Tuyet had prayed for her miracle. Solitude didn't faze the teen as she prepared herself for a fight to the death, if need be, to rescue Minh from the facility—if he was still there. The sound of the battle still echoed from the south, but as she prepared to move, a massive light shone into the air from the center of town, accompanied by a rumble. She watched from a distance, not knowing the rebels hit the ground using a magical tunnel. Sirens blared around the facility and Ba Dinh Square. Troops mobilized, machines sounded, and a buzz of activity surrounded her at ground level. She watched alone for a long time, trying to discern its meaning. As she pondered her options, she caught a quick glimpse of a shifting shape behind her.

"Nhan."

"Lady Trieu, I—"

"Get the boy. I'll go after the source of this occupation."

"You're going to fight Sun Quan?"

"No. Get the boy."

"I will. On my life."

Lady Trieu nodded and jumped off the edge of the building. Nhan shifted to the edge and looked over, but Lady Trieu was already out of sight. Nhan ran to the roof access door and swung it open, sheering off the lock with ease. She descended one flight and ran along the corridor of the top floor. A Chinese guard yelled for her to stop and fired three errant shots. She turned and attacked him without mercy, piercing him twice through the midsection before she descended further into the boughs of the maze. An internal alarm sounded, and she heard the clanking of walls locking down the sections of the facility. As she approached the first wall, she held her breath and pushed on it, only to fall through it unencumbered, like she was a sound wave passing through a solid wall.

"What?" she questioned. Her heart pounded; she felt like electricity pulsed through her veins. She sensed something. She stared at her feet and the floor seemed to flicker, like a glitchy TV screen, which flashed to allow her a view straight through the solid floor. Minh rested below her, curled up in a ball with his head dipped between his knees. He could have been sleeping, or contemplating the nature of his life. She noticed one other item—he gripped the marble tablet firmly in his right hand. She held her breath once more and closed her eyes. She jumped off the floor and floated downward in ethereal bliss through the solid structure to a spot in front of the boy.

"Minh."

He looked up. "Lady Trieu?"

"No, it's me."

"Nhan?" He jumped to his feet and shifted his head in for a closer look. "Nhan?"

"I'm here to rescue you."

He sprang toward her and gave her a hug, but he backed away quickly with a strange look.

"Nhan? You look different."

"Minh, I would never leave you behind. We have to go."

"But ... how? How did you ...?"

"I'll explain later. Come."

"But I'm locked in. I'm—"

"No matter. I'll help you."

She floated through the wall and looked back to see Minh pounding his fists on the black granite, yelling for her to return. "Minh, wait there. I'm going to open the walls."

"Where else am I going to wait? I'm locked in here. Hey. Hey, come back. Nhan! How did you do that? Nhan?"

She backtracked through the hallway—lights blaring, alarms

sounding—and dispensed three machines with two sword thrusts and one ricocheted shot off its blade. She passed through walls unimpeded on command but didn't think it strange. She jammed her sword into a control panel, and all the walls of the facility disappeared into the ceiling. The openness of the massive hall spread out in front of her, and the prisoners all stood in unison. Weary men with long, gray beards sulking over their crouched shoulders, sat dazed at the freedom ahead of them, no longer in their solitary confines. Scores of men and women stood watching her. And one boy. A thirteen-year-old. Minh. Rubbing the marble tablet in his hand. No one moved, for where would they go? Most couldn't move, decrepit and wounded from abuse, vagrants of the war, pawns of the Chinese.

"Release them. Use the boy and release them," a voice called from behind. Nhan knew its authority, and she didn't look back. She ran toward Minh, but he pointed at something beyond her. Nhan paused her approach and looked back.

A dozen machines attacked Lady Trieu. They climbed on her from all sides, ripping their bladed weapons into her side.

"Nhan, we have to help her."

Lady Trieu threw off several of them and sliced them to dust, but more came in unrelenting waves. They swarmed her like a mountain of ants turning on its queen. They tore and ripped, but she shrugged them off like the wounds only made her stronger.

"Nhan!"

"Minh, she told us to release them."

"Who?"

Nhan turned Minh's head toward the rear. "Them. All of them."

"Who are they?"

"Minh!"

"Why don't they run?"

"They can't. They're too old."

"What can we do?"

"Minh, they're not meant to be old."

Minh noticed an old man in front of them, just ten feet away, maneuvering himself up on his knees with great concentration. He held out his hand and spoke in a soft tone. "Minh."

Minh walked toward him, eyes locked on to the strangely familiar face.

"Minh."

"Cuong? Is that you? Cuong?"

The old man reached out for the boy, and Minh placed the tablet into Cuong's hand. The old man fell to the floor, unresponsive for a moment, until he turned around, still at Minh's feet, and spoke, "I'm back." Cuong, the rebel soldier who had helped them discover the truth on Hang Ngang Street, stood to his feet, exhausted, yet free. "The others, Minh. Release the others."

It finally dawned on the boy. All the old men and women moaned for him. One by one, Minh approached each person, Nhan by his side, and placed the tablet into their hands to release the generational spell. Each freed prisoner thanked Minh then quietly approached the fight on the other side of the massive hall. Shattered metal parts littered the area like a random explosion had occurred. Wisps of dust fluttered in the air. One figure walked through the center of the chaos and stood alone amidst the damage: Lady Trieu. Nhan and Minh and the rest of the rejuvenated rebels joined in the circle of spectators. One man approached Lady Trieu from behind. He walked slowly and methodically without angst or worry. It wasn't Sun Quan. This man was of normal height, yet he too had a sword in his hand. He didn't attack her but worked his way through the carnage and dust until he stood opposite her.

"At last we meet," he said.

"Why do you wear such foolishness on your face?" she asked.

"I like the game. It amuses me."

"It will end here," she said.

"Yes."

Minh approached, still a hundred feet away, but he knew him. He knew both of them. It made no sense. Why was he holding a sword? Why was he not afraid of her? As they both raised their weapons to start the fight, Minh called out. "Dad!"

Chapter 31

The Beast

The rebels spread through the streets of Hanoi with little resistance and much fanfare from the beaten population. Shouts of "onward" and "resist" echoed through the chaotic alleyways of the Old Quarter. Commander Lieu stood across the street from the giant portal still visible in the lake behind him. He had a communication device in his hand with a black bag strapped to his back.

"Commander. The streets are empty. Do we push forward?"

"What's your perimeter?"

"At the flag tower. Just a quarter mile from the Facility."

"Hold there. Wait for incoming."

"I think we can reach it."

"No. We can't spread ourselves too thin. We have to hold the ground we have. Wait for the counteroffensive."

"But Commander, there's no one in sight."

"Wait for it."

A rumble approached. Vehicles sped through the streets, firing indiscriminately, and hitting anything in their path, including innocent bystanders. The clattering of the machines could be heard as well, and all the diverted resources miles to the south had now turned northward. Lieu had no aerial support. Lady Trieu had not arrived and the lost bird wasn't in sight. They had no artillery, just the rifles they clutched in their hands. He didn't have the belief in the materials he possessed at the moment, because they weren't enough.

He knew that. They would be met with an overwhelming response from the Chinese. The diversion allowed the rebels to slip into the city and fortify their positions behind cement walls and sturdy structures, but that's all it did. It didn't give them an advantage on the battlefield. Victory looked elusive in the eyes of the man who hadn't slept in days. But as long as the miracle tunnel under the ground showed itself proudly at the rear, he clung to the hope that the material needn't be everything. Options existed, even if they made little sense.

Conventional fighting first erupted on the outskirts of the Old Quarter. Armored vehicles blasted holes the size of small cars into the sides of buildings, scurrying the rebels to one hiding place after the other. Rifles poked over walls, off of roofs, and through splintered glass half-shattered in windows of abandoned houses. Grenades in coming. Rebels shifted. The steady stream of soldiers, backs to the walls, slithered at the scattered souls trying to kill them. Each fox hole. Each measured piece of ground, protected by a rebel soldier, fell one at a time. The Chinese crept forward, blowing holes in roofs, knocking over walls, dispersing the remaining glass in windows to powder white dust on the abandoned floors, now occupied by dead rebel soldiers. The blood made its own red river, and they were in it, all of them, like the city of Hanoi sat strangled by the crooked turn in the real river. Trapped. All of them. Word trickled back to Lieu. "Bloodbath in the Old Quarter."

And then the machines. They started against a rebel group near the old train station. The machines shot up the outside until the walls—or what remained of them—looked like craters on the moon. The swarming machines overwhelmed the rebel forces, impaling them with long, sharp metal rods protruding from their mechanics. The rebels fired back, but the shells bounced off without harm. The machines killed every rebel at the train station who wasn't smart enough to run at first sight. Their high-pitched metal wheels rolled along past the station and toward the lake. Several brave rebel martyrs attacked them. Some even with their bare hands. They scraped the metal with their nails and yelled at volumes not often heard from human vocal cords, yet they were discarded to the afterlife by the machines. The methods were many, but all irrelevant to the outcome.

Lieu witnessed the arrival of all three of them—the retreating rebels running with their backs to their attackers and hoping the portal of escape in the middle of the lake still existed. The Chinese conventional troops emerged from the shell-shook buildings of the Old Quarter north of Hoan Kiem Lake, roping in the rebels along the lake's edge. The machines arrived from the south and west, barreling toward the frozen commander, who had retreated across the lake road and stood at the edge of the still open and glowing tunnel in the lake.

"Commander." It was Lien. She emerged with Tho from the tunnel. "Lieu. What's the status?"

"We're trapped. Chinese regulars have retaken the Old Quarter. The machines are swarming from the south and west."

"Lady Trieu?"

"Nowhere to be seen. I thought she was with you."

"No, we parted ways," said Lien. "What word of the attack from the south?"

"No reports." The stoic commander watched as the machines approached in a methodical step-by-step action as if to foreshadow the outcome. It would be slow. It would be purposeful. It would be definite.

"And Sun Quan?"

"Nothing. You both need to leave." Lieu motioned into the heart of the lake. "Go back through the tunnel. As I said before. It ends today, one way or the other."

Tho ignored the warning and shuffled up beside Lieu. He held the three marble tablets in his palms, face-out. "Such a curious thing, having only three."

"Old man. Leave!" Lieu commanded.

"Listen to him," Lien insisted.

"I need to get to Van Mieu."

"Van Mieu? That's impossible. It's a mile that way," pointed Lieu, over the heads of the oncoming machines. "And what good will it do?"

Tho insisted Lieu make a pathway through the machines so he could get to Van Mieu, the ancient university and formal imperial academy, which honored Confucian thought.

"Do whatever it takes to get me there."

"It's impossible. I—"

A great groan sounded from the rear, and the still water on the side of the open tunnel swelled up and arose a great sight, a turtle with a massive shell, emerging from the water. "Make a way," it said in a gravely low voice. "Didn't I teach you anything?"

Lieu froze. No matter how many times he witnessed the proof of history, he still lacked belief to trust his eyes. The chaos of the city seemed calm for a moment as the commander slipped the backpack from his arms and unzipped. He pulled out the crossbow and held it up in front of the turtle.

The turtle nodded.

"But—"

"Use it," said the turtle, stepping onto shore.

"The machines are made of metal. What am I—?"

The turtle flung its head forward until it smashed into Lieu's jaw, sending him flying to the grassy bank on the edge of the lake.

Lieu was furious. He picked up the crossbow and pointed it at the turtle.

"Are you nuts?" asked Lien. "Shoot the damn Chinese!"

"But they're machines."

"It's called a magic crossbow! Shoot!"

Lieu swallowed the rage in his throat and focused it on the machines. He raised it in his hands and fired the only arrow he had. In mid-air, it split into four and spread out in different trajectories, each of them piercing the metal of four different machines. The machines sputtered for a moment and exploded into a flume of dust.

The entire scene froze. All looked surprised, whether machine or bystander, rebel soldier or Chinese regular. No one was more surprised than Lieu himself. "Did you see that?" Tho and Lien confirmed with a silent nod. "I wish I had more arrows."

Lien nudged him and pointed down. Another arrow sat in the quiver, ready to be released. He let it fly. This arrow split five ways and disintegrated five more of the machines into a pile of dust.

The turtle motioned at Tho and Lien with its head. Lien helped Tho onto its back, and it made its way toward the southern end of the lake. Lieu marched in front of them, firing arrow after arrow, each one felling multiple machines like they were constructed of parchment paper.

Lieu concentrated only on arrows. More. Faster. Pull and release. The machines didn't relent. They moved forward in lines toward the commander leading the turtle. Each row of machines cut down by precision strikes of autonomous splitting arrows, which kept the rows of machines at bay. The turtle, with Tho and Lien on its back, moved as swiftly as it could—at a slightly faster pace than if Tho had been walking on his own. They cleared the edge of the machines and headed straight down Ba Trieu Street at the end of the lake. Lien read the street sign aloud. "Ba Trieu. Where are you, Lady Trieu?" The turtle turned right on Tran Hung Dao Street, another reminder of a past hero who had repelled the Chinese. Commander Lieu continued his assault on the machines from the southern tip of the lake. Any machine which tried to follow the turtle entered the eternal dustbin of history.

"Tho, why are we going to Van Mieu?" asked Lien. "What did Lady Trieu say to you before she disappeared?"

"The turtle knows."

Indeed. The turtle moaned as an assurance of its intention. Prying eyes, hidden from the brutal fight, couldn't help poke themselves into the light. It was a giant turtle, after all, carrying two people on its shell in the middle of a battlefield. Perhaps if there had been a circus nearby or a magic show it would have made sense. But no one seemed shocked. Everyone seemed content to see the turtle. It was *that* turtle. *The* turtle. The one from lore. The one from history. The one that tilt-headed lovers yearn to view from their paradise bench at the edge of the lake. Sense didn't matter. The eyes made sense of it, and through the stares, slowly the words came. The accolades. The exhortation. It buoyed them on to wherever they went. There was now hope sitting on the back of a turtle shell, walking down Tran Hung Dao Street.

At the edge of the facility, the elderly, recently returned to their true ages, gathered around Nhan and Minh to watch the match—their capture being the admission price to the fight of the century, and now they would see if the fight was worth it—the outcome determining everyone's fate.

Lady Trieu towered over the man Minh called father, and they slashed their swords back in forth in a medieval way without either giving ground.

Minh's tense arms clutched both sides of his face. "Dad!" he called several times. He couldn't think of anything else to say. His patriotic father fought willingly against an ancient Vietnamese heroine. As a small boy, Minh's father had regaled him with the stories of the past—the heroes and heroines, Lady Trieu, the two Trung Sisters, Tran Hung Dao. His father would stand in their small living room and act out the ancient stories—always about repelling the Hans. Victory. Vietnamese victory. Lessons he learned about loyalty, family, nation, society. He grew up in this great man's shadow, alongside his mother who also joined in the stories and the playacting. But here he was, doing the opposite. Holding a tip of a sword at the throat of the heroine, like he played a role on a stage, under the lights—a role he had never auditioned for.

Even the machines that had survived Lady Trieu's onslaught monitored the fight from the opposite perimeter, awaiting their fate.

"How's he doing that?" asked Nhan, as Minh's father nicked the edge of Lady Trieu's side. "How's a human holding up against her?"

"He's the strongest man I know. Dad!"

His father rushed forward and sideswiped the sword out of Lady Trieu's hand. The force of his thrust sent the female warrior to the floor, and he lorded over her weaponless body.

"You're a fool. And you're weak. Sun Quan could have crushed you many times, but he has a soft spot for you. Me? I'll just chop your head off and watch your rebellion tear itself apart. It's who you really are, anyway. Uncivilized outcasts, mooching off the Middle Kingdom when it's convenient then spitting in its face when you fail to recognize your true station." His sword lightly touched the edge of her neck. "Look how weak you are. Even a mere human like me can overpower you."

"No," said Lady Trieu. "I know who you are."

"I'm Minh's father." He glanced over at his boy. "Right, Minh? Everyone knows me." He locked eyes again with Lady Trieu. "You're a relic of the past. We're in a new era of Sino-Vietnamese relations. It's time we see our similarities, not our differences, and relics like you dwell in history. Now you'll live there permanently."

He thrust his sword downward, but she had turned formless into a shadowed vapor and the sword slid through like a cloud. He screamed at her to return, but she said two words as the shadow floated upward. "Join me."

He turned toward Minh and yelled. He threw the sword at the boy, but it passed right through him before nicking Nhan in the side. She fell injured to the ground. Minh felt his body. All in intact. He held his breath, and glanced back and forth between the injured Nhan and his seething father, foam coming out of the sides of his mouth.

"Nhan." Minh reached down to help her, keeping his eyes on his father. "You're not bleeding," he said when he finally looked back at Nhan.

"Minh, look."

The man he had known and admired his entire life had vaporized into his own shadow, and wrestled in spirit form with the great female Vietnamese warrior.

"Dad! What's going on? I don't understand."

No one did. But Nhan was beginning to.

Commander Lieu had continued decimating the machines with the magic crossbow. He worked his way farther north along the edge of the lake after Tho and Lien escaped on the turtle. The Chinese conventional troops pushed southward against the rebels and had swarmed the northern end of the lake. As the first Chinese troops approached, Lieu shot an arrow in their direction, but it missed. He reached for the next arrow on the crossbow, but none appeared. Did he drop one? He looked frantically at the path he took. Nothing.

There were no more arrows. The remaining machines continued their creep northward, and now he had no way of stopping them.

But that wasn't all. The battle paused—everyone and everything—for a moment as the mysterious figure strolled down the side street from the cathedral—Sun Quan. He had been absent from the battle to this point, but the ancient warrior walked methodically toward Commander Lieu. "Fire," the rebel commander instructed. The pocket of rebel soldiers which had followed every one of Lieu's moves all opened fire on the imposing force. The bullets jolted him back a few feet, but he emerged through the smoke unfazed.

"Fall back!"

En masse, they fled toward the opening of the florescent tunnel still glowing at the edge of the lake. The rebels, who had made it to the lake's bank, slid headfirst into the tunnel, tumbling head over heels into what they hoped to be safety. The machines cut down many of them before they made it. The Chinese troops did the same from the northern end of the lake. Sun Quan eyed one person and pounced on him with a great leap. Lieu fell hard onto the ground at edge of the lake. His back had been shattered in two places. He wriggled in pain, and in defiance looked up at the warrior. "Kill me now, Sun Quan. But it won't be the ending. Another will come, and then another." Sun Quan pushed his boot into Lieu's chest and the commander screamed in pain.

"Like rats, you mean?" asked Sun Quan. "Bred in filthy hovels. You have to bring them into the light and end their miserable existence. You wish I do you that favor, don't you?"

The rebel soldiers still alive huddled at the edge of the tunnel. It hadn't taken them. It hadn't sucked them back to the citadel. It exposed them, and their only hope was that the ancient magic would protect them from attack. But in that moment, they had no assurances.

The machines and troops assembled around Sun Quan. The fighting had stopped. It was pointless to continue. All they had remaining was to wonder if they would live or die.

Sun Quan pointed at the injured commander. He had one question. "I will. I will do you the favor and extinguish your miserable life. But before I do, where's the old man?"

The two formless beings moved freely around the facility. Human heads shifted back and forth to follow their paths. They wrestled in a formless circle, but Trieu saw his true self. It slipped from him, uncontrollable, glimpses of an animal underneath, a force she had only heard about but now confronted in the non-physical realm. But she knew she had to get him back to human form one more time.

"You're afraid of Sun Quan, aren't you?" The humans below couldn't hear or understand this conversation from the other realm. She held him in her clutches. "I know who you are. You think of Sun Quan as being too loyal. Too loyal to the past. Too loyal to Beijing. You want to destroy him."

"I will," he snapped and broke free from her grasp. "You have no idea what you're dealing with. You think I care about this pathetic little country."

"Then why don't you show yourself. Your true self. Show the boy. Then you can devour me."

He attacked her again, but the forces swirled around them interchangeably with neither gaining the upper hand.

"You think I care about the boy?"

"No, but you tried to sway him."

"I nearly did."

"Try again. But show him who you are."

Lady Trieu morphed into human form and landed in the same spot in front of the gawking eyes of the murmuring crowd. The form of Minh's father flew around them in a swirl and careened onto the floor. His back turned from the Vietnamese onlookers. He was on his knees for a moment.

"Dad!" Minh moved toward him, but Nhan held him back. "Let me go."

"No, Minh. Look."

His father stood and turned, but the man's face had changed. They had seen that face countless times in the past two years. Everyone recognized it. The entire group of onlookers stepped back with fear in their eyes. They cowered their heads in the presence of the Chinese man.

Minh, speechless, clung onto Nhan's arm. The machines pulsed forward a few feet.

"What I hate more than anything," the Chinese man said, "is loyalty. Especially from a boy, standing on your ideals, thinking you will make a difference, thinking your father was some kind of hero." The Chinese man walked toward Minh. Lady Trieu watched carefully, sword now in her hand. "I'll suck your loyal bones dry." Then the Chinese man shifted his attention to Nhan. "And you. Thinking you can escape into the water, like a fallen heroine, like you can resurrect the past stories. You see, she—" he pointed back at Lady Trieu— "is just your imagination. The oral storyteller did a wonderful job with her, and the depths decided to try and bring her back, so you all could have illusion of destiny. But you have no idea what you're dealing with. You never did. And now your so-called rebel army has been pushed back to the brink."

The marble black walls of the facility flashed on, displaying the image of Sun Quan towering over the writhing figure of Nhan's father. Behind them the remaining rebels huddled in the opening of the tunnel at the center of Hoan Kiem Lake.

"The diversion was clever. I love a good diversion. It invigorates my soul, and you, dear Nhan, were the face of that diversion. A minor short-lived success."

The Chinese man poked his head in close to Minh's face.

"It was you," said Minh. "It was never my father."

"Such a smart lad you are."

"I knew it. I knew my father could never betray his country. Where is he? What happened to him?"

The Chinese man laughed. "Nothing is at it seems."

"Including you," yelled Lady Trieu. "You're still wearing a mask. Why don't you show us your true self?"

The Chinese man turned with anger in his eyes. "Because I would devour all of you." He said with contempt.

Lady Trieu stepped towards him. "I know who you are."

"You know nothing." The Chinese man walked toward her, unafraid of the sword she wielded. "Strike me if you think you know."

"Not until you show your true self."

"Because you know you can't strike me."

"Show me your true self."

"I will drag you to the pits of hell if I do."

"Show yourself, Qiong Qi."

He stopped. His head shifted slowly to the right and his eyes trained on her as if he watched a bird in flight. "What did you call me?"

"Qiong Qi. Show yourself."

The Chinese man roared. He looked at Minh, "I'll devour you and your father. All the faithful ones will die." Two large wings pierced through the skin on his back. Fur grew from his neck outward. The wings expanded until they perched over him like massive arches. He roared again, this time less human. His jaw protruded, the colors of his face morphed to stripes of black and dark burnt orange. His teeth enlarged, and his head turned into that of an adult tiger. The wings lifted the beast off the ground and it leaped towards Minh. Jaw open, claws on its feet extended, the beast lurched forward to snap off Minh's head, but Nhan pushed the teen out of the way and the beast careened through the group of gawking rebels standing behind him. The tiger didn't turn and try again. It took off across the great open hall toward a single walled-in structure in the far corner. Lady Trieu chased after him. Nhan and Minh followed. The tiger pounced through the wall and slid past a nearly comatose man lying flat on the floor inside the single black walled cell. Lady Trieu arrived at the wall and pierced it through with her sword. The wall vibrated and opened into the ceiling, allowing the warrior into the cell. The tiger had grabbed the head of the man with his mouth, his teeth resting on the man's neck like razor sharp knifes ready to sever it. The man's head was completely hidden inside the mouth of the tiger.

"Let him go," shouted Trieu.

The tiger growled and slowly shook its head back and forth, not yet putting enough pressure on the man's head to kill him.

"It's me you want. Come after me." She showed the tiger her sword and slowly placed it on the floor. Then she kicked it away from her. "Let the man down and take me, instead. Who's more loyal than me? For eighteen hundred years, Qiong Qi. Who's more loyal than me? Take me."

The beast's eyes stared with desire. It opened its jaw and the limp head and shoulders plopped to the ground. With one great leap, the mighty beast sprang on Lady Trieu and threw her on her back, landing on top of her. She used her arms to hold back the ferociousness, but its teeth tore into Trieu's skin. She threw her legs around the back end of the beast and tightened her grip. She poked her thumb into the beast's eye, and it jerked back for a second. As it raised its head and roared, Nhan slid headfirst on the ground with her sword outright.

"Lady Trieu!"

The sword slid across the smooth floor—edges tinged with orange-flamed sparks. Lady Trieu reached back and grabbed the handle with her palm, and shifted the blade upward—point blank at the center of the beast. The tiger pulsed forward and the sword impaled it through the chest. The beast roared and stretched out its claw to swipe across Lady Trieu's neck. Trieu kicked upward with both feet and the attacker careened to its side, no longer on top of Trieu. Its wings flapped as it tried to reset itself, but her sword cut off the top of the closest wing.

"Go back to where you came from," ordered Trieu. She sprang to her feet and swung the sword once more as the tiger pulsed forward in a seething jump. With a final grunt of determination, the sword sliced through the tiger's outstretched claw and severed its head. The beast's head fell to the floor, and the entire beast disappeared—all traces of it gone. Lady Trieu fell backwards on the hard granite floor. She caught her breath as Nhan and Minh ran over to her. They braced themselves under her arms and helped her to her feet, whether needed or not.

"Where'd it go?" asked Minh.

Lady Trieu staggered about. Nhan picked up the sword. Strands of orange and black fur hung onto the blade's edge, but there was no blood. "It can't hurt us now," said Lady Trieu. "Go. Attend to the man. See if he's alive."

"Who is it?" asked Nhan, running over to the lifeless body left on the floor by the beast.

"Minh," said Lady Trieu. "Go."

"But …"

Nhan had leaned over and felt for a pulse. Her face went flush. "Minh!" she yelled. "Minh!"

Minh approached as Nhan lifted the man's head toward them. "Dad!" It was his father. He knelt down beside him, but the beaten man lay unresponsive, face battered, limbs mangled. Nhan continued checking for a pulse.

"He's alive, but it's very faint."

Red indentations from the tiger's teeth remained on his neck.

"Dad!" He pulled out the marble tablet and placed it in his father's hand. He bowed his head in reverence, not only to his father, but to his line of ancestors. To his great grandmother who fought at Dien Bien Phu. To the unknown soldier of the 18th century, who had fought alongside Quang Trung. They had been loyal, all of them, and Minh now knew the lies he had been tricked into believing about his father. He had been betrayed, and if his father would have breathed his last breath in that moment, Minh would still have been at peace, because he now knew the truth.

But it worked, as it did with the others, and the spell broke. His father's eyes opened and Minh placed his hand on his cheek, still displaying remnants of his wounds.

"You're free, Dad."

His father smiled and slowly pushed himself up to a seated position on the black granite floor. His puzzled look at Lady Trieu drew his attention away for a moment, but not for long, because he focused back on his son with another smile.

"What happened?"

"We don't have time to explain," interrupted Lady Trieu. "Lieutenant, are you capable of leading a group of soldiers?"

He stood without help with an air of confidence. "Yes, anything for the cause."

Minh smiled. He knew it all along.

"Lieutenant, take this group, find all the weapons you can in the facility, and make your way to the southern tip of Hoan Kiem Lake. Don't go through the Old Quarter. We will assemble there."

"Yes."

"Dad, can I go with you?"

"Minh," interrupted Lady Trieu. "I need you to go with Nhan. It's time to get you to your mother and Mr. Tho."

Minh's father patted him on the back. "Now it is your time, son."

"Dad, I ..."

"Go. No words need to be spoken now. We all need to do our job. And you've done yours very well," said his father, hand firmly on the boy's shoulder. "We must go now."

"What about the machines?" asked Nhan.

"Fire at them," said Lady Trieu. "They are vulnerable now that the Chinese man is gone?"

Minh's father looked at her strangely. "Dad, there's a lot you don't know."

"But we don't have time now," insisted Lady Trieu. "We must go."

The screens embedded on all four sides of the massive facility walls flashed to the scene at Hoan Kiem Lake. Sun Quan stood over the unresponsive commander Lieu. Then he turned back as if staring into a lens of a camera. His deep eyes penetrated the consciousness of all of them, especially Lady Trieu. He waited for her as time slipped away.

Chapter 32

What Awakens

The giant turtle used its head to bust through the shuttered gate of Van Mieu, the Confucian university-cum-temple founded in 1070 AD. A trailing crowd entered behind the strange spectacle, curious as to what the hallowed grounds could mean in such a desperate hour. In the central courtyard, outlining the main temple hall, sat eighty-two stone stelae, sitting on the shells of eighty-two stone tortoises. Each stelae honored a famed Confucian scholar from the past who had completed a Doctorate in Confucian studies. These scholars had understood the way of wisdom and reason and had embedded their indelible mark on the foundation of modern-day Vietnam.

The giant turtle stopped in the center of the courtyard and moaned for the passengers to dismount. Lien slid off first and helped Tho to the ground.

"Tho, what are we doing here? Why doesn't the turtle tell us?"

"It seems to have made up its mind to keep us in the dark."

"But why? It talked to us in the lake?"

"I don't know. Maybe it's the water that allows him to speak because I'm not understanding any of his turtle grunts."

"Tho, is there something here that we can do which will help the rebels? If so, we can't delay."

"It's only a delay if you know what to do and decide not to do it in haste."

"Tho!"

"Well, it seems the turtle brought us to eighty-two other turtles."

"Why?"

Tho walked a few feet towards one row of stone turtles but stopped. Befuddled, he turned and tried the other way only to pause again and scratch his head. The turtle continued to moan.

"That is not helping, my great reptile friend. You could just tell us!" He stumbled about some more as he mumbled how if he had all four of the marble tablets, perhaps he could ask the universe for an answer.

The crowd encroached around the three in a full circle, and Lien yelled at them to back away. No one listened. One of them wanted to pet the turtle. Another kept asking who Tho and Lien were. Another one wept while describing the brutal fighting around the lake they had all been privy to.

A loud call echoed overhead. The long-tailed bird swooped down past the curved ends of the temple roof.

"Mom!" Minh clung to its back and waved to his mother with Nhan riding behind him. The crowd scattered as the bird circled. Lien ran after it, holding her hands to the sky, as the bird came to a soft landing in front of the turtle in the middle of the courtyard. Minh slid off the bird's wings and into his mother's arms. They allowed the tears to speak for the moment as they squeezed each other. Tho came alongside both of them and he rubbed the boy's hair. Minh tucked his head under Tho's shoulder and hugged him. The three stood as one for a moment as Nhan dismounted the bird and waited in the rear.

"Mom, I—"

"Shhh— I know. We can talk later."

"Cuong is alive. He's free now." Minh reached into his pocket and held out the marble tablet. "They were old. All of them. And I used the tablet and now they're back to their old selves. And … oh … Mom, the Chinese man became dad and tried to trick me, but—"

"The Chinese man?" asked Tho.

"But he's dead. Lady Trieu killed him. But he was actually a winged tiger named Qiong Qi."

"Qiong Qi?" The name struck Tho hard, and he grabbed the tablet from Minh's hand as Minh continued to explain all the strange encounters.

"Your father? You've seen him?"

"Mom, Dad's alive. He's leading a group of rebels."

"What?" Lien began crying softly. Tears fell from her cheeks, and she allowed them to flow uninterrupted. She finally noticed Nhan standing in the background. "Who's this?"

"Oh, Mom. This is Nhan. Commander Lieu's daughter. She rescued me."

Lien looked at her strangely. "Thank you, Nhan. Your father fought valiantly, and it allowed us to escape and come here. Are you all right, Nhan?"

"Why do you ask?"

"Your skin. It's glowing."

Nhan looked down at herself in surprise. "Yes. I don't know why."

"And she walked through walls," added Minh.

Lien looked at him queerly, "Minh, where is Lady Trieu?"

Both the turtle and the long-tailed bird let out a loud cry.

Nhan spoke up. "She went after Sun Quan."

"By herself?"

"That's all we have left," said Minh. "Sun Quan overpowered Commander Lieu and has the rebels trapped at the edge of the lake."

"No," said Lien. "As we left, the commander was using the magic crossbow and …"

"It's true," confirmed Nhan. "We saw it all at the facility. They're all trapped."

"Oh my," Lien sank into her thoughts. "And Minh, what's this about your father?"

"He's leading an attack from the south with all those who were prisoners in the facility. But it won't be enough."

"No," said Tho, standing in front of one of the stone turtles. He had all four marble tablets in his hand raised over his head. "What we see is never enough, but we are not alone in this endeavor. We have the past to guide us. The faithful, faithful past which has brought us here. They're showing the way once again. It's why Qiong Qi appeared."

"Who's Qiong Qi?" asked Nhan.

"Tho, what are you doing?" Lien had made her way through the crowd to Tho's side.

"We must see what awakens. Help us. May the wise words on these stelae return to life as action one more time."

A crack formed on the top of the stone stelae and ran downward through its length and across the stone tortoise's shell. The stone fell off like the tortoise was shedding an outer layer. Its eyes opened, and it stared at Tho for a moment before announcing its return with a giant shriek. Now there were two turtles.

Lady Trieu returned to the spire of St. Joseph's Cathedral, a short distance from the lake's shoreline. She watched for him and spoke. She knew he would understand.

Sun Quan, the troops, and the machines had secured the entire perimeter of the lake. The remaining rebels still huddled at the entrance of the water tunnel, protected for the time being from even Sun Quan. Commander Lieu laid on the ground at Sun Quan's feet, half-unconscious. All that remained were Lien, Tho, and Lady Trieu.

"I am here," she said.

He lifted his head and glanced toward the cathedral peeking out over the treetops across the street.

"Let us finish this," she said.

Sun Quan motioned to his commander to stay put. He walked through the troops, and they backed up, including the machines. He continued into the edge of the cathedral's courtyard and waited. She appeared on the street in front of the church alone, sword strapped to her back, and she walked toward him.

"He's dead, you know," she said. "The Chinese man. Or as dead as he'll ever be." Sun Quan didn't respond. "You don't believe me?"

"I'm surprised, but I believe you."

"He didn't come here to conquer Hanoi."

"No."

"But you had your own plan, to wait for me. Isn't that right?" Trieu stopped in front of him just out of reach. Both remained calm. Neither reached for a weapon.

"Yes. Correct," replied Sun Quan. "I don't think as small as some. Thank you."

She took a step closer. "For what?"

"For killing Qiong Qi. Now I'm free."

She paused for a moment. "You wanted me to kill him because you couldn't. Because ... he brought you here."

"We can be free together." He reached his right hand out towards her.

"After everything you've done? After the destruction of my people?" Lady Trieu fumed.

"That's where your thinking is wrong. These aren't your people. Your people died centuries ago, and they were foolish to bring us back, so let's paint them the fools they are. They mean nothing to beings like us, but they could afford us the world if we only stop battling each other."

"You think I will turn so easily?"

"No," replied Sun Quan. "That's why you were able to defeat him. But if you choose to go against me, I will see to it that you never rise from the depths again."

Lady Trieu unsheathed her sword and held it with one hand across her front. "I will bet on history."

At that moment, the eighty-two turtles from Van Mieu revealed themselves between the streets and shops and trees of the western side of Hoan Kiem Lake. The citizens of Hanoi gathered around them, impervious to the bizarreness. They invited the turtles into their consciousness as they would a spring breeze. It seemed right and good that they were there. When all of history peers into the present and decides to coalesce around a moment, who stands to question it? All of Hanoi's fabric had woven itself together for a final attempt to throw off the shackles one more time.

The giant turtle of the lake sauntered in behind Lady Trieu. Tho, Lien, Minh and Nhan all riding on its back. It stopped beside the lady from the lake. Nhan dismounted first, unsheathed her sword and stood next to Trieu. Minh joined her side. Lien instructed Tho to stay on the turtle's shell as she slid off to stand at Trieu's left. The four of them stood opposite Sun Quan. At the southern tip of the lake, a contingent of rebels, led by Minh's father, waited further instruction. The great long-tailed bird swooped down and perched on top of Turtle Tower in the middle of Hoan Kiem Lake. Behind Sun Quan, protected at the edge of the tunnel, massed the other rebel troops, uncertain of their role. Their commander lay wounded in their sight.

"We will give you everything we have," said Trieu.

Sun Quan nodded. "So be it." Without warning, he threw himself forward like a missile, barreling over Lady Trieu onto her back. The force of impact had scattered Lien, Nhan, and Minh—now each watching from the ground themselves. Lady Trieu threw off Sun Quan with her legs and twisted around back onto her feet as the Chinese demon gathered himself and turned back toward her.

"Lien, look!" said Tho, still sitting on top of the turtle. "Her breasts have grown."

Sure enough, Lady Trieu's breasts had doubled in size. "Yes, Tho. Yes." Lien stood to her feet and yelled at the top of her lungs, "Onward!" Minh and Nhan echoed the sentiment. The crowd of citizens joined in and a chorus of hopeful voices repeated the phrase. "Onward!"

The eighty-two turtles led the charge. They were not bound by typical methodical turtle movements. They moved freely, barely touching the ground, half-spirit, half-physical body, and they targeted the remaining machines around the edge of the lake. Each one shot a venom of fire from their mouths and devoured the machines one by one into piles of ash.

The rebel soldiers once again stormed out of the edge of the tunnel and ran along the western rim of the lake to clash with the Chinese conventional troops at the southern tip of the Old Quarter.

Nhan moved into position beside Lady Trieu. "I'll fight Sun Quan with you."

"I will too," said Minh.

"No, this is my fight. And mine alone." She pointed with her head to the long-tailed bird swooping down. Nhan leaped onto its back with ease and took off into the air. The turtle moved forward,

Tho rubbing the tablets in his hands, as Lien and Minh escorted it on both sides as they made their way to the lake.

Chaos reigned. Blood from both sides poured into the streets. The first two turtle casualties appeared—floating, shell upside-down along the edge of the water. Dust from the machines filled the air like fog. Minh's father and the contingent from the facility fought through the line of machines. Human bullets now decimated what they earlier couldn't touch. This group quickly moved up the eastern shore of the lake and flanked the Chinese soldiers on the other side of the Old Quarter. Sirens sounded, every last Chinese soldier, every last machine, every last citizen of Hanoi squared off in the heart of their sacred land.

The giant turtle had made it across the street, but an armored vehicle cut it off from reaching the lake. Several shots ricocheted off the turtle's shell, almost hitting Mr. Tho. Lien and Minh both had weapons now, and they hunkered down on each side of the turtle and fired toward the armored car.

"Do you need some help?" asked a voice from behind. It was Cuong, now once again the young warrior.

"Cuong?" asked Lien, looking back at the rebel holding a shoulder-mounted RPG. "Where did you come from?"

"Your husband sent me over here as backup. But I wouldn't be here at all without your son."

Cuong aimed the rocket propelled grenade resting on his shoulder and fired. The force of the blast knocked him backward a few feet. Lien had covered her ears as the whizzing sound of the projectile hit its target, and the armored vehicle exploded in pieces. All in the vicinity shielded themselves from the blast, except the turtle which continued walking directly toward the lake, down the slope and into the water's edge. As soon as its legs had touched the water, the massive glowing tunnel fifty feet north crashed in. The water shook itself and the wave shifted the turtle up and down in a violent manner which made Tho lose his grip and fall into the water. The old man went under.

Minh yelled from the shore. "Mr. Tho!" He slid down the bank and jumped in headfirst. Lien and Cuong joined him. Minh surfaced with Tho's arm flopped over his shoulder. Lien and Cuong helped pull the old man and his savior back to shore. Tho gasped once and looked out over the lake.

"The tablets. I lost them in the water."

"I'll go look for them," said an eager Minh.

"No." Everyone stopped and looked at the old man. "Leave them. It's where they belong."

"But Tho, you've had them all your life."

"Yes. But maybe my time is up."

The turtle made a great noise and submerged itself into the lake, causing one more great wave to sweep up over the shore and drench the four a final time. They helped Tho to his feet and surveyed the battlefield. The eighty-two turtles had neutralized the contingent of machines at the southern tip of the lake. The rebels, now led by Minh's father, had blocked off the Chinese troops at the edge of the Old Quarter. Nhan rode on the back of the long-tailed bird and terrorized the troops with her death-defying attacks. She dive-bombed down on the trapped troops time and again. She wielded her sword and sliced through vehicles, ripped through arms and legs, and left a bloody trail after every swoop.

Minh, Tho, and Lien made their way to Commander Lieu. He still lay unconscious and Lien checked his pulse and looked around for anyway to treat him. "What can we do for him?" The tablets were gone, and the other beings didn't seem to possess the magic to do anything to help him.

"Win the battle," said Tho.

Trieu and Sun Quan floated over the city. They tumbled and wrestled without rigid form—two microcosms of thought, two destinies wrapped around each other. Sun Quan gripped her firmly and Trieu couldn't wriggle away. Did she want to anyway? It seemed a silly question to her with all of history blaring in her face. The countless times the Hans had been repelled. This was more of the same. She had led the charge once herself when she was young and human—standing in the gap when no man of courage could muster the attack. She completed the task, sending Sun Quan's lackeys limping into the mountains—away from their luscious fertile fields. She wasn't the only one. There were many. The Trung sisters. Tran Hung Dao, the great hero who had repelled the Chinese more than once. Then the great warrior from the south, Quang Trung, who trudged north in the 18th century to repel them again. There were others, of course, under different circumstances. The ardent fighters who threw off the French, who confounded the Americans. All for what? A chance to live in peace and work the land and be a Vietnamese nation united. There was 1979—when the last generation witnessed the invaders once again. But now, today, it all seemed different. This battle didn't rest in the hands of the humans; not really. It rested in the past and on the whims of magic which allowed it all to come to life—through no will of its own. This rough and tumble spiritual battle in the sky between Lady Trieu and Sun Quan had human origins. But did it need to have a human ending?

All of these thoughts and memories flowed through Trieu's mind. Sun Quan had wanted her to join him. In what? For what purpose? Was she ready to just fall once more into the pit of the lake when she felt so alive in this moment? If he asked her again, how would she respond?

Her mind, distracted, allowed a moment of vulnerability. Sun Quan thrust his arm, still in semi-fluid form, through her. The walls of her sides collapsed and the pull of gravity weighed on her skin— her human skin. She fell from the sky looking upward at the floating ancient king above her, watching her descent. She landed back-first in the lake and plunged beneath the depths. She gasped for air but couldn't breathe under the water this time. She felt her body hit a hard object, moving in the opposite direction, upward, toward the brightness of daylight above the surface. She emerged, her stomach half torn, but still alive in this realm. The turtle held her on its shell beside the curved red bridge leading to Ngoc Son Temple on a small islet in the lake. Sun Quan had descended and lorded over her from the red wooden bridge. She panted, still on her back, sprawled out across the shell, still unsure if she could move on her own.

"Your armies did well. They defeated Qiong Qi's machines as I knew they would. They had no heart in this fight. Mindless worker ants from history was all they were. Cheap modern terracotta soldiers. And your rebel commanders have finally trapped the rest of the troops. But look at you. Was it worth it? You gave yourself to this cause for what? So I could disembowel your passion? So you could witness with your own eyes that they can't defeat me? Once you're gone, I will only be getting started."

The turtle turned and gazed upon the broken warrior. Time bled her dry. She rested her head against the turtle's shell.

"It didn't have to be like this, you know. I asked you once and you rejected me. We were always meant for each other, but the thought frightened you. You think of loyalty and lineage as something to be treasured. Qiong Qi was right on that regard. You failed to see the possibilities, and you were too frightened to admit to yourself how similar we are. We have the same struggles. The same passions. The same foolish desires, but it's always freedom you want. You will pay the price for your desire of freedom. It will suffocate you until you are free eternally, but not in this world."

Trieu attempted to lift her head, but she laid it back flat and closed her eyes. They didn't remain closed. She heard the bird. It soared at Sun Quan, Nhan still on its back, and she raised the sword over the wing of the lost bird and roared once. A battle cry. She sliced through the air at the head of the giant, but Sun Quan raised his mighty arm and deflected her attack with a great force. Nhan careened off the bird and rolled into a defeated ball at the edge of the shoreline. The bird, too, had fallen off course and pierced its side on a lamp post near the walk on the water's edge. It whimpered alone in the sight of Nhan, who barely moved.

The fighting around the lake had all but stopped. The ultimate outcome would rest on the two warriors in the middle of the lake. Chinese troops watched on with the Vietnamese rebels in the same vicinity, weapons at their sides, gazing over the lake. The eighty-two turtles, now a few turtles short, huddled around Nhan. A few of them licked her wounds. Tho remained with the broken commander while Lien and Minh had moved northward a bit for a better view of the struggle unfolding at the center of the lake.

Lady Trieu rubbed her hand along the scutes of the great turtle's shell. She felt its ruggedness, how it had survived in lore for centuries. Each layered groove in the scutes marked the time in its own way, and she wondered if it also marked the end of her time, of a new epic, one she couldn't understand; one she didn't want to understand. She turned her head and looked upon Sun Quan holding onto the railing of the curved bridge.

"Kill me if you must." She struggled to regain her strength and propped herself up with her arms behind her. "Or should I say, you must kill me. If you don't, I will fall into this lake only to rise again. And again. And again." She now sat up fully, arms at her side. Her neck was partially ripped out from the Chinese man's last effort to kill her. Her stomach sat hollow from Sun Quan's wound. But she ignored the eternal yearnings within her, the history she couldn't control. Her only thoughts gravitated toward the boy Minh, who had fought his way back into and out of the Facility, and the girl Nhan, who had thrown herself willingly into the river. Each generation brands its own heroes and fights its own battles for freedom to persist. If she would fail, she would do so facing her foe and throwing a final punch. "I say it again, Sun Quan. You will have to kill me."

"Very well," he nodded. He raised his sword over his head, and with one giant leap, landed on the front of the turtle, towering over the seated Lady Trieu. The force of the landing shook the entire reptile. Trieu lost her grip and her hands slid down the side of the turtle's shell, when she felt something smooth, unlike the texture of the other scutes. She glanced over the curved body of the shell and saw them. All four. Each of the smooth black marble tablets had embedded themselves into the turtle's shell. She rubbed her hand across all four and felt a rush of energy through her. Sun Quan's sword descended at her. Lady Trieu shifted to the right and the tip of the sword pierced the outer portion of the turtle's shell, but as soon as it did so, the turtle turned spirit and descended formless into the black void of the water. Trieu and Sun Quan likewise crashed through the surface. Trieu grabbed his arms and tried to pin him down, but his strength tore himself from her, and he reached for the sword he had lost. Lady Trieu turned toward the bridge and shot out of the water with great force. She clung onto the side of the bridge and flipped herself over the railing. One of the Van Mieu turtles approached her from the shore with Nhan's sword on its back. "This is from the girl," it stated. She clasped it in her hands and twirled to face Sun Quan, who had repositioned himself, armed and dangerous, on the islet side of the bridge.

"Ba Trieu," he said. "I had hoped you wouldn't make it too easy."

You have many supporters, who have helped you. But no matter. None of it will be of consequence in a moment."

"And what of your supporters? You also didn't arrive here by yourself, and it would not have been possible for Qiong Qi to bring you back without human help."

Sun Quan shook his head. "Indeed."

"Where is your master?" she asked.

"Maybe we'll meet him in the pit of hell."

He rushed her, and the tip of his sword whizzed by her ear. She clanked it away with a side swipe of her own. The ancient chimes of history sounded with every clambering hit of ancient forged metal against metal.

Attack. Repel. Lady Trieu backed Sun Quan onto the small island holding the famed Ngoc Son Temple. The place where Mrs. Tuyet had prayed for a miracle and fallen down dead just twelve hours earlier after placing her incense sticks on the alter. Now they battled for the outcome of the incense whisking into the air through the tips of both of their swords.

Sun Quan tripped over the step into the temple, and she caught him once in the throat with the tip of her sword. But his long arms held off the final thrust, and pushed her aside. He stormed into the temple and swiped all the statues off the altar. A Buddha fell onto the floor, hitting the corpse of Mrs. Tuyet, which still laid undisturbed. Sun Quan continued ransacking the place. A Confucian king landed on top of a burning candle. The tapestry, depicting a colorful long-tailed lost bird, fell to the ground and caught on fire. The flames erupted through the wooden structure as the duel intensified around it. Smoke rose off the small island, but no one from shore moved to help as the trees shielded their prying eyes from what happened. They had nothing to watch but the lazy smoke wafting into the evening air.

Toss. Jab. Thrust. Tear. They grunted through the smoke and singed their wills on the edge of the flames. Each one staggered under their own wounds.

Lady Trieu had struck him twice with her sword. He retaliated in kind, but neither gave ground. Sun Quan came at her shoulder first and threw her against a Confucian altar, defacing it with her entire body. She picked up the statuette of Prosperity and hurled it at his head. It slammed him backwards as he grabbed his face with his left hand, still clutching the sword in the right. The flames had reached the roof and threatened to release their fury on both of their heads.

"I'll leave nothing behind," shouted Sun Quan, finishing the destruction of the temple with a series of vicious spin moves which even split a round pillar holding the structure in place. The roof shook and collapsed. Lady Trieu surged forward and pushed Sun Quan into the side vestibule. Walls on both sides of them were torched with fire. Trieu laid on top of him. Her overgrown breasts pushed against his chest and their eyes locked.

"You're stronger than I thought," he said.

"But I can't defeat you. Not on my own."

"Will we let the temple finish the deed?" he replied.

A part of the charred wall broke off and crashed behind them. Sun Quan grabbed her sides, and she his. He pushed her into the fire and the flames lit the back of her garment. She rose in great pain and ran down the corridor out of the back of the temple, at the same place Tho, Lien, and Minh had once taken a boat out to meet the great turtle. Sun Quan followed her and tackled her to the ground. The fire engulfed them both, but they wrestled. Arms interlocked. Grips fierce. Pain in their eyes. In a ball of fire, they rolled off the edge of the bank. This was the same bank which once heard the prayer of Mrs. Tuyet asking for a miracle. As they plunged into the water, eyes closed, the lingering prayer of decades swirled in their midst.

The water counteracted the fire, but Sun Quan had the favored position on top with Trieu underneath. Only her face, breasts, and toes stuck out of the water.

"Release us," she said.

"It's impossible for me to be submerged in the water," said Sun Quan. "But you'll drown for eternity here, never to be released again."

"I wasn't talking to you," snapped Lady Trieu, as she repeated, "Release us!"

The water formed into a glowing hole beneath her body with only a thin layer of water keeping them afloat.

"Take us both," she said.

"No!" yelled Sun Quan.

The water parted and the hole opened up beneath them. The force pulled them in like a wind tunnel, and above the surface of the water, a great spout whirled into the air as the two warriors were sucked into the belly of the lake.

Chapter 33

Underneath

They disappeared into the void. The water crashed in above them, and they let go of each other and floated freely in opposite directions. Sun Quan looked around, disturbed. He had entered the realm previously denied to him. Lady Trieu had whispered "release us," and the water obeyed, accepting them both. The wrestling match no longer mattered because a reckoning awaited them. They would not be alone for long.

Something swam past Sun Quan, and he jerked back to identify it. He couldn't see it clearly and moved his head back and forth as if spooked.

"You wanted to meet me here. But we aren't alone. We never will be," she said, releasing her sword and allowing it float away. A ripple of water tingled Sun Quan's back, and he rotated quickly again in a frantic search.

"You're being hunted," she said. "But yet, so am I."

She relinquished her freedom to the history of the water. Massive arms reached around and clasped onto her wrists and bound them behind her back. She didn't fight it. Something bit Sun Quan on his side, and he tried to slice his sword at it through the water, but it slipped from his arms and floated away into the black. The giant turtle fastened its jaw onto Sun Quan's wrist, immobilizing him. He attempted to fend off the turtle with his other arm, but the weight of the water pushed him down, like his whole body was setting in a frame of concrete.

A gargantuan face appeared behind Lady Trieu. It was several times larger than her and its arms clasped the lady warrior in its grip. Behind the face stood an army of terracotta warriors with animated expressions and weapons on alert. To the rear of the tortoise encroached a bale of turtles, which had escaped from Van Mieu but had been lost in the battle above. The two sides stared down each other and waited for a signal. The giant head, that of a man with a long beard and massive eyebrows seemingly weighing down his face, pointed at Sun Quan.

"She brought him here, not me."

"Yes, but he invaded our sacred land, and now the sacred water," replied the turtle.

"Give him back to me."

"A trade. One for one."

"No," said the giant face. "The battle cannot remain unchanged. Not after this round. The counterbalance has not yet come. It must sway one way or the other."

The giant turtle still held Sun Quan's wrist. The warrior centered his gaze on Lady Trieu, and she did likewise. They were pawns at the mercy of history. But also more. Things they couldn't yet conceive. They awaited their fate with stoic stares and patience.

Lady Trieu remembered lying flat in the water with Sun Quan on top of her. The towering fire of Ngoc Son Temple burned to her right. The eyes from the shore waited for an answer, but now underneath, the answer still was not clear. Her body had been badly deformed by Sun Quan's many blows. His body didn't look as ruinous. He was bigger. He claimed longevity over her. He had had technology and weapons and innovations at his disposal. She had had struggle, and fight, and determination. Sometimes foolish. Sometimes courageous. But all the time just on the brink of survival. She had asked the historical water to allow them both in, knowing that they may never return, or that maybe only one would. But she wasn't sure which one, because there were no safe waters. No safe havens. Even the most sacred of places holds an element of fear. It holds the seeds of destruction, whether one wants to admit it or not. The great turtle may be the caretaker, but he could not preserve at will without risking his own destruction. They played the gentle dance, all of them, in the epochal current of the region, and none of them could be assured of anything.

Trieu nodded at Sun Quan, and he seemed to understand. He nodded back in kind. Trieu, still bound at the arms raised her chin high and spoke.

"Honorable forefathers. May I offer a compromise." The large head squinted towards the turtle as if peering far off into time.

"Proceed," stated the turtle, like a judge in a courtroom.

"Loosen the one, and let him decide."

The head leaned back and released Lady Trieu's arms. She didn't try to fight but continued to stand in its shadow. It looked at the turtle, which let go of Sun Quan's arm. He too remained docile, perhaps even immobile.

"Will that be a fair fight?" asked the turtle. "I could not guarantee impartiality."

"When has the fight ever been impartial for us Vietnamese?" replied Trieu.

The turtle nodded and the giant head spoke for both of them. "Then we will entrust it into Sun Quan's hands. If he agrees, we will loosen the one—a judgment neither of us can reverse. Is this what you want?"

"Yes," said Lady Trieu.

All eyes looked upon the ancient emperor. It had come to this. A binary choice distanced from both of their hands. It would mean a separation, unless there was a way to defeat the one. But he had never lost before. Trieu and Sun Quan came to an agreement with the eyes. They exchanged almost friendly glances and even smirked. A smile for the ages. Sun Quan nodded his head.

"I agree."

The turtle turned to its side. Four other turtles converged and each grabbed one of the marble tablets from the scutes of its shell. Two of them were handed to Sun Quan and the other two were delivered to Lady Trieu by the Van Mieu reptiles. Sun Quan and Trieu held one of the tablets in each of their hands. They raised them vertically at the same horizontal height. The two warriors stared at each other and without saying a word, they dropped all four of the tablets simultaneously into the water. Each tablet formed a corner of a chute, which opened deep into the depths of the lake. It didn't glow of iridescence. It was black. Dark. A lonely road to hell, or an envious way of escape. The bubbles burst forth from the deep. Small first, then growing, then large, then a bubble so big that it grew into a massive balloon between the parties with its opening still attached to the sides of the dark chute. Into the middle of bubble rose wings flapping frantically, and then rose a ferocious body of burnt orange and black with a massive Tiger head. Qiong Qi glanced to his right and saw Lady Trieu, unarmed, backed by a contingent of her enemies. It almost pounced but shifted its gaze to the turtles and the Chinese warrior also in enemy territory. Qiong Qi roared and the bubble burst. The sinking of the water commenced, and each side held back the other's protagonist. The arms of the giant head held onto a leather strap on Lady's Trieu's back. The current whipped past her as if she stood on the precipice of a great cliff with just a feather's weight holding her in place. The turtles, too, held onto Sun Quan, as the tiger roared again and pounced onto the Chinese warrior. It ripped opened the warrior's chest as the turtles released him. His limp body floated downward as Qiong Qi attempted to devour him.

Lady Trieu yelled. "Fight!"

Sun Quan heard her plea and reached out for the beast, which had already shredded his sides. But the warrior revived, clasped onto the tiger's body, and squeezed. Qiong Qi screeched and tried to lift itself upward in the water, but the weight of Sun Quan was too great. Sun Quan squeezed with all his might and they descended like a fallen rock pushed off a cliff, through the four corners of the chute held together by the four marble tablets. They careened downward into the abyss. The tiger roared, but Sun Quan made no sound. They disappeared into the black and the four tablets were released from the spell and floated innocently in the water. Four of the Van Mieu turtles pounced on the tablets and returned them to the great turtle. The massive head, without saying a word, turned around and disappeared into the water with the contingent of terracotta warriors following it. Lady Trieu rested alone and looked down where the portal would have been. She glanced up at the turtle.

"Come," it said.

She went to them and the bale of turtles surrounded her, attended to her, and used their mouth to touch her many wounds. The great turtle held the four marble tablets in its mouth and reached its neck out to her.

"No," she said.

It nodded and reached towards her again. She took the four into her hands.

"Take them back to where they belong." Trieu nodded. "And you know what to do with the girl?"

"Yes. I will do it."

Trieu looked upward through the surface of the water. The fight above ground continued.

Chapter 34

Above Ground

A moment passed before anyone viewing the spectacle from the edge of the lake dared to move. The temple burned over the tops of the trees. The water spout had dispersed into the heavens. Many witnessed the dueling warriors plunge into the water and disappear into the depths of the lake. But amidst the silence, Minh's father raised a rifle over his head at the northern tip of the lake and ordered a full-scale attack. All of the machines had already vanished when Sun Quan passed the threshold of the lake's surface. The remaining Chinese soldiers retreated for their lives or threw down their weapons in defeat and surrender.

Lien and Minh returned to Tho beside the dying Commander Lieu—his body contorted and broken.

The remaining turtles, without fanfare or comment, swam one by one to Turtle Tower on the small islet at the center of the lake. They marched over the land, through the center of the tower, and submerged themselves in the lake's long-forgotten history to join those who had previously left. Nhan, riding on the back of the long-tailed bird, landed on the edge of the shore. She slid off the bird and approached her father. She leaned over him. Minh placed his hand on her shoulder but moved it away quickly with a strange look. Nhan's skin glowed, and the light from her face radiated into her father's eyes.

"Father?"

He didn't stir.

"I'm sorry, Nhan," said Lien.

"Me too," said Tho.

The great turtle emerged from the surface of the lake behind them and let out a loud, discordant call.

"Mr. Tho! The turtle," exclaimed Minh.

"Great turtle," said Tho. "Did you find the tablets?"

The turtle glanced skyward.

"What?"

"Heal the land." A voice rose in their midst. They staggered and looked into the sky like waves of sound passed over them from an unknown source, yet the voice was familiar. Commanding. Her form descended and she appeared at the turtle's side, once again in human form.

"Lady Trieu!" Exclamations came from all sides.

"What happened in the lake? How were you able to return?" asked Lien.

"Ask the one who dropped the tablets into the lake."

Everyone looked at Tho. "I didn't do it on purpose."

"Or did you?" questioned Trieu. "Mr. Tho, these are for you."

She stepped forward and handed him the four marble tablets. In haste he turned and placed the four on the commander's chest with Nhan, Lien, and Minh all gathered around.

"Once more, dear ancestors. Allow a good man to live for such a time as this."

The commander jolted awake. His body restored. He looked up into his daughter's eyes. "Nhan."

"Father!"

She reached for him, but she wasn't able to feel him. She backed away and looked at her hands. The commander sat up, still gazing at her. "Nhan."

She breathed heavily and moved away from the entire group, which slowly retracted from her.

"Nhan," said the commander. "You did it. You ..." He looked closer. "Nhan?"

"Father, what's happening to me?"

Her skin bubbled, and she rubbed her arms but couldn't feel anything.

"Nhan!" yelled Minh. "Mom, what's happening to her?"

No one had an answer, except the turtle, still half-submerged in the water. "She's coming with me."

"I don't understand." Minh moved towards her but stopped.

Her father had stood up and reached out to her. "Nhan?"

"She's not coming with you," demanded Minh. "She's ... she's my friend. I … I was just getting to know her. She saved me."

"But she chose not to save herself," said Trieu, moving alongside Nhan. "This girl …" She reached out and touched the side of Nhan's face. "She drew the machines away, unwilling to give up the rebel secrets, and when she could do no more, she jumped into the river to preserve the fight. To keep the knowledge she had locked forever inside."

Tho looked down at the marble tablets in his hands. "And the tablets won't help her now."

"No."

"You mean?" Tho paused, and Lien gripped his hand.

Trieu continued: "Her faith awakened the path. The great turtle rescued her and allowed her unselfishness to be used in the fight, and we will forever be grateful."

Minh stared at Nhan's solemn face, now mostly unresponsive. He had stepped out from his mother and stood like a weary soldier at the edge of a battlefield, surveying the devastation, and realizing life had changed for good. "She's dead?" he asked, knowing the answer.

"A martyr. Like the Trung Sisters. Like Lady Trieu. She sacrificed herself for the cause of freedom," replied Tho. "Remarkable girl." Tho looked at her father. The commander's eyes swelled with tears but his tight jaw and unflinching eyes dammed the emotion inside.

"What will become of her?" asked Minh, voice softened, hands slid in pockets slightly shaking.

"That is up to you," said Lady Trieu. "How will you remember her? What will you do with that memory?"

Commander Lieu moved next to Minh. They watched Nhan's skin fall off her, like shedding a new body, and her temporal one fell to the ground while its shadow lifted a few feet into the air.

Minh leaned over and touched the hair of her physical body silent on the ground. "They did this. Sun Quan. Qiong Qi. The Chinese. They killed her. She didn't kill herself." His voice was low and tense. "And what will happen to them? Did you destroy them? Did you, Lady Trieu? Will they pay for what they did?" He stood up aggressively toward the lady warrior. "Did you destroy them once and for all?"

Nhan's likeness, unmoving, hung in the air over the back of Trieu's head. "The likes of Qiong Qi or Sun Quan can not be killed as humans understand death. As long as the evil they do lives on in the hearts of men, the possibility exists for them to find a way to return."

"Where did Sun Quan go? I want to face him." Minh clenched his fist. "Give me your sword and I'll slice him down."

Nhan's hollow shadow shifted back and forth as if caught in the breeze. The translucent being resembled Nhan's human features, but the vacant eyes didn't acknowledge her father or Minh. She stared into the meaningless space behind them like the goblin soldiers she earlier commanded.

Minh touched the cheek of her human body and glanced up at the being.

"What's wrong with her? Why isn't she like you?"

"She will find her voice," Lady Trieu said. "As the voices of this world reach her, and show the appreciation of her sacrifice."

"Will she ever return?" Minh's eyes fixed at the ghost of Nhan behind the warrior.

"Minh, don't worry of the future. Focus on rebuilding the present, with the eternal thanks of the past in your heart. Do you understand me?"

He nodded. "I will build her a shrine."

Commander Lieu placed a firm grip on Minh's right shoulder. "I will help you."

"And you, Ba Trieu? What will become of you?"

At that moment, the young soldiers Cuong and Tuan approached. They were followed by Minh's father, and all three of them walked straight toward Lady Trieu and bowed on their knees in her presence.

"Oh Great Warrior of the past, we honor you for this victory."

"Stand," she commanded immediately. "I am not the one to honor." Trieu drew her sword and pointed at the man with the long white beard.

They nodded and turned their attention toward Tho. Knees on the ground. Commander Lieu joined them. Four symbols of the victorious rebels in a row, head bowed, in front of the ninety-five-year-old sage. Lien stared at her husband, who hadn't yet spoken or glanced her way. But she smiled at him.

"Mr. Tho," Minh's father said. "We honor you."

"We honor you," the other three echoed.

Then the commander took charge.

"Most revered wise sage, Mr. Tho. We honor you with this victory. We owe you everything. We couldn't have achieved this outcome without your courage and knowledge."

Then Lady Trieu, the mighty warrior, still scarred from her attacks, bent her right knee into the ground as well, prompting all of the onlookers to join. Tho kept repeating "No, no," but they didn't obey. They lauded him with praise as he stood flanked by Lien and Minh.

"Please, please. I most assuredly didn't do any of the fighting. Please stop."

"Always modest, he is," said Lien with a smile. She glanced down at her husband, who looked up at her for the first time.

"It was teamwork," said Tho. "This woman right here"—he grabbed Lien's hand and raised it in the air, doing likewise to Minh—"and this boy were the ones who wouldn't let it go. I would have been content to nap over a hot cup of tea, but they insisted on rebellion."

The laughter spread through the crowd as everyone returned to their feet. Minh's father quietly walked to Lien's side and grabbed her hand without fanfare or words exchanged. Minh stood between them and leaned his head back against them both. All three of them smiled, but not at each other.

"I am proud of you all," said Commander Lieu, glancing back at his daughter once more, both her body on the ground and the apparition floating at the rear.

The turtle let out a large groan.

"It's time," said Lady Trieu.

"What will you do?" asked Lien.

Lady Trieu looked out over the crowd of people assembled on the shore of the lake. "As the people give, the past will take. And we will always stand as protectors if you believe in the past and what it has to teach."

The giant lost bird with its massive pinpoint beak and long

286 Mark W Sasse

flowing tail took to the sky and nosedived into the heart of Hoan Kiem Lake. The water parted as it disappeared into the open pathway. Lady Trieu reached down and picked up Nhan's sword lying next to her physical body. She reached back and touched the hand of Nhan's ghost, and they both floated to the top of the great turtle's shell at the edge of the water. The turtle let out a final cry and dove into the depths one last time. The waters swallowed them, and the shiny, metal tip of the sword, held straight into the air, glistened in the waning sun as it slipped back into the history beneath the surface.

Cuong and Lieu turned over Nhan's body and laid it flat and proper in the grass. Tuan had found a stretcher in an abandoned Chinese armored vehicle at the edge of the street and placed it alongside the corpse. Minh's father helped them move her body onto the stretcher, and they carried her toward the street when Minh approached and motioned for his father to change places with him. Minh grabbed the stretcher handle from his father, and they proceeded. Lien moved close to her husband. Their arms touched, but nothing else. Minh and the soldiers placed the stretcher on the back of an open-aired vehicle. Lieu stood over the body and placed his right palm over her face. He lowered his head and closed his eyes. After a moment, he turned toward the gathering crowd eager to hear from the de facto leader.

"Let's begin by cleaning the streets. Show the bodies the respect they deserve, even the enemy ones, for this battle wasn't theirs. Not really. Fix the broken windows. Patch the holes in the walls. Help each other on this long road back. Let us not worry of recriminations and revenge. The moment for justice will come. I'm sure of that. But not today. For now, let us show compassion to everyone as we incrementally move forward one day at a time."

The solemnity of the moment sunk in across the worn faces. These were not happy faces. No contentedness shown itself in anyone's eyes. But they were resolute faces, which understood the weight of history sitting on their shoulders. They would rebuild. They would move forward. They were, after all, Vietnamese.

Chapter 35

The World Responds

Two weeks after cleanup commenced, the citizens of Hanoi, through various representative factions, chose Commander Lieu as Interim Administrator of Reconstruction to lead the new government of Vietnam since the vast majority of the old leadership had long been decimated by the Chinese occupation.

Lieu destroyed the facility and the newly erected building inside Ba Dinh Square. They removed the structure surrounding the Ho Chi Minh Mausoleum and cleared the square to its pre-war state.

When the first international communication system had been reestablished, Lieu announced to the world the war crimes and atrocities committed by the Chinese government over the past two years.

The world body censured China at the United Nations after the Russian and Chinese representatives on the U.N. Security Council declared surprising abstentions. The censure was followed quickly by a statement issued by the Chinese government eagerly wanting to explain the irrefutable evidence presented by the new Vietnamese authorities: "We regret to inform the world body that a rogue faction within the Chinese government was responsible for the unsanctioned war in Vietnam. We respect Vietnam's sovereignty and do not condone the actions of a few rogue actors. We are committed to aiding Hanoi in their struggle to rebuild. They can be assured of our commitment and goodwill toward this effort, and we wish nothing more than mutual peace and cooperation moving forward."

Administrator Lieu invited Devin Nichols, an American journalist, to travel to Hanoi in order to document the atrocities of the previous two years of isolation. His report aired just three weeks after the cleanup of Hanoi had begun. Here is an excerpt of his initial broadcast:

NICHOLS: Good evening. This is Devin Nichols. I'm standing here at the ancient temple complex of Van Mieu, the first Confucian university built in Hanoi in 1070. What you see behind me are the remains of sacred turtle statues, which were completely destroyed in the Battle of Hanoi. I'm here with Commander Lieu, former leader of the rebel resistance, and the current lead administrator of the reconstruction efforts. Commander Lieu ...

LIEU: Please call me Administrator Lieu. The war is over.

NICHOLS: Yes, of course. Administrator Lieu, I've toured through Hanoi and I've seen the breathtaking devastation and destruction. What do you have to say to the people of the world watching this broadcast about what you have experienced here?

LIEU: The Vietnamese people are resilient. We had great odds stacked against us, but we bonded together and were willing to sacrifice everything for the country we love. We all did our part, and I am proud of every person who stood up to the aggressors. As our beloved Uncle Ho said, "There's nothing more precious than freedom and independence." We resolutely regret the deaths and the necessary sacrifices, but we know we have achieved our goal. Once again, we are a free and united Vietnam.

NICHOLS: Administrator Lieu, there have been numerous reports of supernatural occurrences, so-called demon warriors, and even turtles coming to life. There was even one report that stated these broken turtle statues behind us actually were not destroyed by the Chinese, but were summoned forth into this world to help defeat the Chinese. Can you comment on that?"

LIEU: War always creates a fog of uncertainty. These turtle statues are symbols of great scholars and heroes from our past. The Chinese destroyed this sacred institution because the ideas threatened their power. That is all that happened here. But we will rebuild every statue to its original state.

NICHOLS: And what of this mysterious Lady Trieu? There have been numerous reports of the emergence of the ancient heroine Ba Trieu. There have even been leaked videos of such events. What can you tell us about that?

LIEU: We have a group of creative people who cleverly used our stories of the past to instill fear into the hearts of the Chinese soldiers. We used holograms and the latest technology to confuse the Chinese. It sounds like these tactics worked.

NICHOLS: And the turtle from the lake? Many have said that the turtle had returned, and even the sword? Can you comment on that?

LIEU: Oh, I don't deny that the turtle lives. You won't find one Vietnamese patriot who will deny such a thing. It's in the heart of every Vietnamese.

NICHOLS: It is known that your daughter was killed in the final battle of Hanoi. What can you tell us about her?

LIEU: My daughter is one of many sons and daughters who sacrificed their lives for the love of their country. I respect the memory of every one of them the same.

NICHOLS: What's next for this country, Administrator Lieu?

LIEU: We don't seek retribution. We will rebuild, and we will reestablish ourselves as a peaceful yet powerful nation among the community of nations.

Tho turned from the TV. "I'm going to bed."

"I thought Commander Lieu did well in the interview," said Lien.

"Why did he say all those things?" asked Minh. "They weren't true. Why can't we talk about Lady Trieu? Everyone knows she's real."

"Oh, my good boy. Why can't the bird describe to us mere humans how to fly? Wouldn't it be nice if we could flap our arms and ascend into the sky?" Tho laughed and raised his arms up and down.

"What? Mr. Tho? What about the bird?"

"I sure hope someone has redrawn the figure on the wall of Hung Temple."

"What?"

"Is your boy always so literal about things?" asked Tho, looking at Lien. "I did tell you I'm going to bed, didn't I?"

"Yes," said Lien.

"And when will the Vice Administrator come home?" asked Tho.

"Dad said he would be back tomorrow," replied Minh. "Mr. Tho?"

Tho stopped at the door. "Yes, Minh?"

"Do you think we'll ever see Lady Trieu again?"

"I wouldn't doubt if she's in the crowd when you dedicate that shrine to Nhan. I'm fairly certain she'll be there."

"I'm going to do it, you know." Minh stated emphatically.

"Oh, I don't doubt that. I might even have a few artifacts for that shrine. My house is too cluttered as it is."

"But Mr. Tho, everything in your house has a purpose and a story," said Lien.

"Yes, but who'd ever believe any of those crazy stories of mine?"

"After this past month, most anyone, I suspect." Lien smiled.

Tho laughed again and glanced back at the TV once more "Isn't that the Vice Administrator speaking?"

Minh turned to see his father giving an interview with journalist Devin Nichols. Lien quickly focused on the screen as well, putting her back to Tho. The old man smiled, then descended the steps one more time. His bed awaited him. He would sleep as long as he could—as long as the turtles and birds and demons would allow him.

The End

Dear reader,

If you enjoyed this story, please consider writing a review online wherever you buy books. Your review will help others find and enjoy this story. Thank you!

Mark W. Sasse

If you liked this story, check out the magical realism novels also from Mark W. Sasse

THE FORGOTTEN CHILD TRILOGY

An old corrupt businessman is visited by a strange being with a preoccupation with pomegranates. But she won't leave him alone, not if he's the unlikely candidate to give her what she wants. Time travel, magical realism, and around the world travel in an adventure unlike any other.

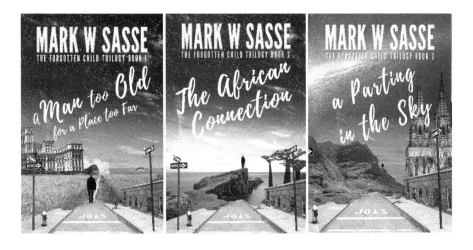

Mark W Sasse is a novelist and award-winning playwright. Originally from Butler, Pennsylvania, he has lived all over the world including Vietnam, Malaysia, and Saudi Arabia. He is a theater enthusiast and loves writing, directing, and producing for the stage. His plays have been featured in such diverse places as New York City, Kuala Lumpur, Penang, Columbus, and Sydney, Australia.

He loves to dabble in different genres and has written novels categorized as historical fiction, young adult, adventure, magical realism, and fantasy.

He loves to cook, and he is a baseball enthusiast. He lives in Western New York, close enough to PNC Park in Pittsburgh for a day trip of bliss.

He'd love to hear from you. Mark@mwsasse.com

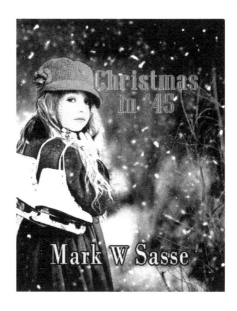

On Christmas Eve 1944, two men in uniforms knock on the door of the Ares' house to inform Mrs. Ares that her husband had been killed in the war. At that moment, nine-year-old Roberta enters an adult world of inconsistencies and inexplicable grief as she tries to make sense of her father never returning. Before he left for war, her father told her he had to cross the water far away to help fight for their country. Roberta becomes convinced that if she can cross the large lake by their house, she will be able to find her father and discover the truth about what happened. Through trial, error, and painful lessons, she embarks on a journey in her mind in search of peace and understanding as Christmas in '45—the year anniversary of her father's death—approaches.

Other Novels by Mark W Sasse

MYTHS & TALES of the WINASOOK IRON HORSES
Book 1 – A Diamond for Her
Book 2 – The Lost Lineup
Baseball, adventure, history, and Greek gods.

THE FORGOTTEN CHILD TRILOGY
Book 1 - A Man Too Old for a Place Too Far
Book 2 - The African Connection
Book 3 - A Parting in the Sky

MOSES THE SINGER - Finalist - YA Novel of the Year 2021 - TheKindleBookReview.com

A LOVE STORY FOR A NATION
THE REACH OF THE BANYAN TREE
WHICH HALF DAVID
THE RECLUSE STORYTELLER
BEAUTY RISING

For information: www.mwsasse.com

Milton Keynes UK
Ingram Content Group UK Ltd.
UKHW011117201123
432909UK00004B/127